Christmas in Duke Street

Copyright

Published in the four-novella compilation, Dancing in the Duke's Arms, by cJewel Books, PO Box 750431, Petaluma, CA 94975-0431.

ISBN: 978-1-937823-43-6

Cover design by Pixiegraphix.

Couple Image Copyright © PeriodImages.com

Table of Contents

Books by Miranda

The Wild Quartet

The Second Seduction of a Lady (novella)
The Importance of Being Wicked
The Ruin of a Rogue
Lady Windermere's Lover
The Duke of Dark Desires

The Burgundy Club

The Wild Marquis
The Dangerous Viscount
The Amorous Education of Celia Seaton
Confessions From an Arranged Marriage

Also

Never Resist Temptation
Christmas In the Duke's Arms
Dancing in the Duke's Arms
At the Duke's Wedding
At the Billionaire's Wedding

Books by Carolyn

Books by Shana Galen

If you enjoyed this story, read more from Shana in her next anthology, A Gentleman for All Seasons.

Or dive into one of Shana's many series...

The Covent Garden Cubs series begins with Earls Just Want to Have Fun.

The Lord and Lady Spy series begins with Lord and Lady Spy.

The Jewels of the Ton series begins with When You Give a Duke a Diamond.

The Sons of the Revolution series begins with The Making of a Duchess.

The Misadventures in Matrimony series begins with No Man's Bride.

The Regency Spies Series begins with While You Were Spying.

The Rake Who Loved Christmas

BY
MIRANDA NEVILLE

In memory of my father and so many happy Christmases.

Chapter One

～

CHRISTMAS WASN'T FASHIONABLE. The languid denizens of the London beau monde cared little for the winter holiday. Oh, the tedium of having to prepare Christmas boxes for the servants and tenants. Such a bore to make merry with one's relations. As for dragging around Yule logs and bringing in greenery, it did terrible things to the perfection of one's garments.

This year Sir Devlyn Stratton didn't have to worry about holly prickles snagging his coat or mud on his boots. His broad shoulders would not be put to the undignified task of hauling half a tree trunk. He was spending Christmas in London.

He dodged out of the emporium in High Holborn, keeping an eye open for anyone who might have strayed out of the more refined parts of town. At Noah's Ark, famous as the best toy shop in London, he'd had his choice of rocking horses for his nephew, who at three was begging for a living pony, but would be satisfied, for now, with the splendid dapple gray on green rockers. He bought a set of carved wooden animals for four-year-old Maria, the cows, pigs, and horses so perfect he wanted to play with them himself. But his oldest sister and her family weren't coming south this winter. Neither would he see seven-year-old Sally arrange the lavish doll's house. His purchases would be packed and sent by carrier to Yorkshire by Mr. Hamley, the proprietor of the store.

Devlyn was doing his shopping early, which had the advantage that no chance acquaintance had seen him in the shop jumping a wooden horse over a fence or pondering miniature drawing room furniture. Next, gifts for his mother, grandmother, and younger sisters. The feminine brigade was to join him soon at his Curzon Street house. He preferred them to remain in Sussex where they would not interfere with the pursuit of pleasures unsuitable for the ears of ladies. They belonged in Sussex, to be visited at his leisure, as was the proper order of things. So it had been since he left university and came to town to sample the array of delights available to a young man of good birth and ample fortune.

Mud from a passing dray, more noisome than country dirt, splashed his breeches. Truth to tell, he would miss the greenery gathering, log dragging, Christmas box giving, etc. For Devlyn had a secret shame he kept well hidden from his fellow sportsmen and men about town.

He loved Christmas.

Worse still, he loved giving gifts. Others pretended to. They sent their wives or secretaries out with a list and did their duty by their dependents. But Devlyn enjoyed hunting down the perfect object for each and every servant, tenant, or aged aunt. He loved the anticipation of their pleasure, surpassed only by his secret satisfaction when their faces told him he'd chosen well.

Usually, the ceremony of exchanging gifts took place in the great hall, the Yule log in the ancient hearth. No room for that in his London house with its small, efficient fireplaces burning coal.

In Oxford Street he ordered a pair of shotguns for his brother Merrick, who would soon be shooting on his own estate. The emporia of Mayfair yielded pearls for the girls, Emma and Susan, and a diamond brooch for his mother. He spent a full hour picking out huge paisley shawls of the finest cashmere for all the ladies. In St. James's he ordered hogsheads of port and sherry at Berry Bros. and hampers of delicacies from Fortnum & Mason for far-flung cousins. Great-Aunt Emma was especially partial to their scotch eggs.

An item in the window of a small curio shop caught his eye—a small gilded cage containing a jewel-studded bird. Drawn like a magpie into the tiny shop, he admired the diamond wings and ruby breast, but the bright emerald eyes attracted him most. That and the melody of an old French love song that played when the proprietor released the hidden mechanism. The work of the celebrated Jaquet-Droz, the shopkeeper's pretty wife assured him, and named an appropriately celebrated price. With no one in mind for the toy, he bought it anyway. It was always handy to have an extra gift. A bird for a ladybird, perhaps. Except the piece didn't seem right for the kind of woman he usually showered with expensive jewelry.

A few yards from Hatchards bookshop in Piccadilly he encountered a familiar figure. A gentleman does not carry parcels, and Devlyn, naturally, had ordered all his purchases delivered to his house. Tarquin Compton managed to look impeccable with a brown package under his arm.

"Book shopping again, Compton?" The dandy's exquisite taste was complemented by his renown as a collector of rare volumes.

"What else? Not that Hatchards has much to offer of a *recherché* nature. Still, I managed to find a nice edition of Pope's Homer while hiding from ghastly old women pretending not to be looking for the latest Byron."

"Where's Iverley? You usually hunt in pairs."

"Sebastian is in Shropshire. He's to be married."

"Good Lord. The girl must be mad."

Compton grinned. "I would have thought him the last man to succumb. Watch out, Stratton. The hounds will be snapping at your feet next."

"Not I. The only thing I'm shopping for is a book."

"I'll let you brave the horde of beldames."

"I think I'll avoid the place." He paused, thwarted by the fear of his mother's gossiping friends spying on his purchases. "Pity there isn't another bookshop nearby."

"There is. On the Shelf is just around the corner in Duke Street."

"Is that really the name of a bookshop? It seems too good to be true."

"It belongs to a man called Merriweather. Its real name is Duke Street Books or some such thing, but the old man's daughter began to stock it with volumes of particular interest to ladies. It became infested with spinsters, and some wag with a bellyful of wine and a pail of red paint embellished the sign."

"The sort of thing that happens when you attract ladies so close to Jermyn Street and all the gentlemen's lodgings."

"Precisely. Looking for Christmas gifts, are you?"

"Just something to read. And I vastly prefer young ladies to old. The ladders in bookshops offer such possibilities for judging a woman's ankles."

On the Shelf proved to be a somewhat shabby place with ranks of shelves up to the high ceiling and a rolling ladder to meet his ankle-gazing requirements. The only man in the place, a dark fellow with a foreign air, appeared to be asleep, leaning against a bookshelf. Dev made a note to avoid that section unless suffering from insomnia.

Being Dev, he appraised three or four young women, none of them, alas, braving the ladder. Another conducted a transaction with a young woman whom he took to be the opinionated daughter of the owner. The arrival of a voluptuous, fair woman with a tiny waist drew a silent whistle. A widow.

The gorgeous creatures of the demimonde who had enthralled his youthful self no longer held the same appeal, the reason why his other house had remained empty for months. A lady of birth with some conversation and secret vices might be just what he needed. But the unrelieved black garb of the blond beauty denoted a recent bereavement. Too soon.

He scanned the shelves for novels, until, in the depths of the shop, four letters on the spines of a three-volume work caught his eye. When he reached for them, his hand collided with that of a browsing female he'd failed to notice in the corner.

"I do beg your pardon..." His words faded away.

Mossy-green eyes set in an oval face looked up from under the brim of her bonnet. A low burr infused his head, and a delicious paralysis seized his limbs. He gaped down at her, vocal cords and brain turned to sponge. He tugged off his glove, his hand aching to touch a smooth cheek. He almost did it before an inner voice of decorum and common sense warned him that caressing the face of an unknown lady in a public place was just not done. It was the kind of behavior likely to lead to hysterics and the summoning of the constable.

Heat tinged his cheeks, and he returned to a normal state of consciousness, unable to take his eyes off her. Who was she? A well-bred lady, surely, but not one he'd ever met. And he knew everyone.

Then she smiled, just a tentative widening of soft lips. He had a momentary sensation of falling. Wrenching his gaze from that face, he realized the bare wooden floor had not turned into a mill race and his boot-clad feet stood firm.

"We are interested in the same book," she said. Her voice was all he could wish, the mundane words a carol of laughter and joy.

Who *was* she? If this was a spinster, every man in England belonged in Bedlam.

"Yes." His powers of address, equal to the charming of dowagers and courtesans, had deserted him.

"Are you fond of novels? Miss Merriweather makes a point of stocking all the new ones."

Right. That's why the place was full of women.

"Do you come here often?"

She lowered her lids, displaying thick, dark lashes. "Annabelle Merriweather is a friend."

"Which is Annabelle?"

"At the counter, speaking to Miss Hooper."

"I hear the shop is popular with the ladies."

"Indeed. We sometimes scare off the gentlemen."

"I am not easily frightened."

"I would imagine not."

"Why is that?"

"You seem a gentleman of unusual size and strength."

She was flirting with him, by God. "You flatter me, madam." He glanced at her left hand, but her glove would hide any wedding ring. She was no dewy-eyed debutante, perhaps twenty-five or -six. Surely his fellow men hadn't let this one get away. Unless... The notion that she might not be a lady of virtue aroused the instinct of the hunter.

"You didn't answer my question about novels." She certainly wasn't shy.

"What would you guess about my tastes?"

"I would take you for a *Waverley* man. Tales of adventures and derring-do. Or perhaps epic poetry with noble verse as an excuse for sensational action."

"Does one need an excuse for sensation?"

Wise woman, she declined to respond, averting her head to offer him a view of her profile. The tiniest bump in her nose marred the line, intriguing him with a hint of imperfection. At the back of his mind he assessed her figure—not overly slender and well proportioned—and her garments: a well-cut redingote of dark green wool topped with a bonnet trimmed with matching ribbons and one small feather that added a certain dash. Fair quality, but neither of the first stare nor the latest fashion. Her gloves were not new. She dressed like a respectable lady, perhaps lately come from the provinces. Yet the gleam in her eye, the coquettish curve of her mouth contradicted him.

She removed a glove, her right unfortunately, took the first volume of *Emma* from the shelf, and opened it. "By the author of *Pride and Prejudice*," she said. "I don't think this is what you are looking for. Not much sensation here."

"I am looking for a gift for my sister who happens to be named Emma. Do you have any suggestions?"

"What does she like?"

"Being sixteen, Emma prefers the sensational. Ghosts, mad monks, and a heroine kidnapped by an evil foreign nobleman."

"I have read *Pride and Prejudice*, and I doubt anything by its author will answer to that description."

"But Emma is not the only one I must satisfy. Our grandmother, who is not backward in expressing her opinions, believes that books for young girls should convey a high moral tone."

"Miss Hannah More, perhaps?"

"Grandmama gave Emma a copy of *Practical Piety* last year, and, I regret to say, my sister left the volume out in the rain."

"Quite by accident, I am sure."

"Certainly."

"So the trick is to find a work that meets the approval of both ladies?"

"A task that may be beyond my powers. I believe it needs a lady's cunning."

She turned a page or two. "This book is dedicated to the Prince Regent. Would your grandmother not be impressed by the connection?"

Dev looked down at the open page and casually brushed against her hand where she pointed at the fulsome words. Her skin was as soft and smooth as it looked. "I highly doubt it." Lady Stratton's opinion of all the king's sons was better not repeated.

"But your sister would surely like to read about a heroine who bears her name, even if she doesn't experience the thrill of being kidnapped."

"If you can promise me the fictional Emma suffers no worse than the occasional scolding and a broken heart, I will take it."

"I cannot promise anything."

"I shall take the chance."

Dev cast about for something else to say, some way to learn about this glorious creature. If only an acquaintance were present who might perform an introduction. He was still not entirely sure that she was of the station that merited such polite formality, but he would not take the risk of insulting her. The door to the premises opened and fulfilled his wish, though not in the way he would have chosen. The Earl of Frogmore was not a man he ever cared to speak to, let alone in the presence of a lady. What the devil was he doing in a respectable bookshop? The dissolute nobleman's reading tastes, if he had any, ran to sensations of a most unrespectable kind.

The lady had also seen the new arrival. "Excuse me, sir," she said. "I see someone I need to speak to. I hope your sister and grandmother both enjoy the book." She nodded her head and joined Frogmore near the door, greeting him with a bright smile. The old rake, whose corsets failed to disguise his fondness for rich dinners, dropped a slobbering kiss on her bare right hand, an attention she seemed to accept with pleasure. Apparently she had been browsing the shelves—and flirting with Dev—while awaiting a tryst. She took the earl's arm and disappeared into the street.

Dev's stomach turned sour. No lady of virtue tolerated Frogmore, who frequented the worst company in town, while his wife, sensible woman, stayed fixed at his country estate. Dev had no use for a lady—woman—of uneasy virtue who consorted with a creature who might provide temporary wealth but at a price: an almost guaranteed dose of the pox.

Chapter Two

O RIEL TOOK FROGMORE'S arm with a repressed shudder and wished it were a younger, stronger arm. Her neck itched to turn for a last look. Why did she never attract the attentions of gentlemen like *him?*

That wasn't altogether true. The unlikely visitor to On the Shelf bookshop *had* been interested, and slightly to her shame, she had reciprocated. Having learned that men spent more money if offered a little feminine sugar, she had allowed herself to empty the butter boat as though selling a portfolio of rare etchings rather than advising him on Annabelle Merriweather's novels. To be honest, she hadn't *allowed* herself to flirt with the unknown gentleman. She couldn't help it. For a few minutes, she'd entertained the fantasy that this glorious specimen of masculinity was someone with whom she might have a future. But such a Corinthian—his figure reeked of wealth and fashion—would have only one use for a shopkeeper such as herself.

A fate she'd avoided even though Lord Frogmore had obvious plans for her. So far she had managed not to tangle her reins in dealing with the lecherous earl.

"My dear Mrs. Sinclair, I've come to take another peep at that collection, and your boy told me you'd be here," he said, patting her hand. Why hadn't she replaced her glove? She'd let the other man touch her. There was a hand, with strong, firm fingers, nails neat and well-trimmed. Frogmore's were soft and pudgy, the nails long and buffed to a high sheen. The thought of them on her skin made her flesh creep. The idea of the other man's caress on *any* part of her at all was something she'd better not think about when she had business to conduct, much-needed money to earn.

She pushed open the door to Markham's Print Gallery, a grandiose name for premises so small they merited only the smallest window. Crowded in with Charlie, the sometime helper and delivery boy she borrowed from the Merriweathers, and Frogmore, the little room seemed stifling.

"You'd better go, Charlie," she said reluctantly. "They've been busy next door and will have deliveries. Will you come back later and see if I have anything for you?" She prayed that a large portfolio of French prints would be making its way to Frogmore's house in Berkeley Square.

Alone with Frogmore, she stepped behind the big square cabinet that occupied the center of the space. She knew from experience that he had a hard time squeezing past it. She opened a shallow drawer and placed the folder of prints on top. Eagerly, and not for the first time, Frogmore pawed through them, eyes bulging. The quality of the engravings was exquisite, but Oriel knew that wasn't the main appeal for this particular collector.

"Such a pretty bosom," he remarked of a young woman reclining in a garden, her hidden swain eyeing the décolletage as avidly as Lord Frogmore.

Most of the prints were unexceptional—too suggestive perhaps for either a grandmother or young sister—but some were distinctly on the bawdy side. A bare breast here and there, a couple clothed but on a bed, a lady clad only in wisps of fabric. Frogmore frowned, even as a fat finger hovered over a lady being undressed by her maid, a gentleman lurking behind a half-closed door.

"Have you anything else?" he asked. "Something more amusing?"

Oriel knew exactly what he meant by *amusing*. "Mr. Markham would never allow it." Her father had sputtered with rage when he'd wandered downstairs and found this group of engravings she'd picked up at auction for a good price. He preferred the religious works of the early days of printing. Unfortunately, they didn't sell well, or not to her clientele. "I am sorry they are not to your taste," she said, endeavoring a mixture of firmness and regret. "Surely the appeal is in the beauty and subtlety of the images."

Frogmore had little use for subtlety. "They are very fine, of course. What did you say was the price?"

Oriel refused to name a lesser sum than she had the day before, or the day before that. The figure she had in mind would clear all her bills and enable her to take her father to the country for a holiday after Christmas, closing the shop until things became busy again with the onset of the season.

Frogmore was not ready to bite, though she sensed that he was near. "Are you sure you have nothing else to show me?"

As a matter of fact, she did. In the same bargain lot at the auction, stuffed into a shabby portfolio, there had been three engravings of an explicitness to make any woman blush. Even a widow like herself, no stranger to the male anatomy, found them hard to look at. She hadn't been able to bring herself to show them to any customer, though she knew she could ask a handsome amount. She needed a gentleman of louche tastes who was satisfied with titillation on paper rather than in the flesh, and such men were thin on the ground. She'd heard rumors of Mr. Tarquin Compton's area of collecting, but the young dandy wasn't nearly infirm enough for her to risk showing them.

She shrugged in answer to Frogmore's beady-eyed request. "Is there anything on the walls you like?"

To her surprise, he selected a comical caricature of blowsy ladies and spindly young men dancing a quadrille. "Will you take it with you, or shall I have Charlie deliver it?"

"Not today," he said. "I shall be out. Bring it yourself tomorrow afternoon. Come to the front door, and we'll celebrate with a glass of wine and conclude our negotiations for the French collection."

"I'm afraid I cannot reduce the price. They are worth much more."

"My dear Mrs. Sinclair—Oriel, if I may be so bold—I have no doubt you can offer something to sweeten the transaction. Things aren't always a matter of lucre."

She could have retorted that to a widow with a small income and an invalid father, lucre was never filthy. But that would give Frogmore too much power. Inured to treating her male customers with just the right blend of flirtation and reserve, she trod a tightrope with this rich pigeon, and there was always the danger she'd tumble off one way or the other.

No, only one way. Things would have to be much worse before she'd give in to his odious advances. As for joining him in his house for a glass of wine and *negotiations*, she'd cross that bridge when she came to it.

Once he'd creaked his way out into the street, she shot the bolt and went upstairs to the small set of rooms over the shop.

"Is that you, Oriel?" The querulous voice told her that Arthur Markham was not in one of his rare good moods. "That girl went out hours ago, and I need my tea."

"Nonsense, Papa. She left just at three, at the same time as I dropped round to see Mr. Merriweather. I'll make it now if you are ready."

She heard a paroxysm of coughing while she poured water over the leaves in the small kitchen. She must get him away from the coal dust and damp of London before an infection went to his lungs. Pooling their inadequate incomes and coming to the city to buy the lease on a small building, where they could both live and open the shop, had seemed a fine idea. She'd had no idea of the effect of the London climate on a man of fragile health.

"It's weak," he said, tasting the brew. She hoarded the expensive leaves since he would complain more if she bought a poorer-quality blend.

"It's warm and wet," she said.

"That girl should be back by now. Wasting her time making eyes at the tradesmen, I'll be bound."

"I doubt it." Mary was a poor little excuse for a maid, but she was willing, patient with her crotchety employer, and the best they could afford. "It's a long walk to Berwick Street."

"Why go all the way there when Fortnum & Mason is but a step away?"

"The prices in St. James's are too high."

"False economy. Always buy the best." Which was one of the reasons they had so little money.

"I'm worried about your cough, Papa. Shall I call Dr. Johnson?"

"He's a quack who will prescribe some rubbish and send a large bill." In this, alas, he was correct. The better physicians in this part of London commanded high fees.

In a sudden change of mood that made Oriel owe him her love as well as her duty, he reached for her hand and stared hard at her face. "You look tired, my dear. You do too much. What were you doing at the Merriweathers'?"

"I told you I hoped they would display some of our more festive prints on their walls before Christmas. They have far more customers."

"And did they agree?"

"Mr. Merriweather was out. I will try again tomorrow."

"Why were you gone so long, then?"

"I waited in case he returned."

"Did you see anyone there?"

Only the best-looking, most charming man she'd ever encountered. "Lord Frogmore came looking for me."

Her father's frown deepened the wrinkles in his pallid brow. Age and illness had reduced the once-handsome face to a gaunt mask. "I cannot like the man."

"Liking has nothing to do with it. He's a good customer and bought a Rowland-son." She didn't mention the engravings because they would certainly send Papa into a rage.

"When we opened the shop, we intended only to sell the finest etchings by the great masters."

"Let's not revisit this. We cannot afford the stock, and we don't have the cus-tomers. The popular works feed us." When buyers could be lured away from the sumptuous Bond Street premises and breadth of choice offered by Ackermann's. All Markham's had to offer were the taste and knowledge of its owners and her own beauty, an attraction that would one day fade.

A fishy smell heralded the return of Mary, her basket laden. "I got a bargain on a nice piece of cod," she said proudly.

Judging by the aroma, the bargain was the fishmonger's. Oriel hoped their din-ner would be edible.

"I told you she should have gone to Fortnum's," Mr. Markham said.

Of all the habits that had caused Arthur Markham to quarrel with his wealthy family and Oxford colleagues, to the point that he was no longer on speaking terms with any of them, his insistence on having the last word was the one his daughter found most annoying.

"I'll get this cooking," Mary said. "That young man with the fancy waistcoats is hanging around the pavement waiting for you. I said you'd come right down."

Glad to escape parental ill temper and the smell of fish, Oriel sped downstairs. Merrick Stratton was one of her favorite customers. Not her most lucrative. He rarely bought anything, and then spent only a shilling or two. He liked to sit in the shop and listen to her talk about prints, and auctions, and the less objectionable foibles of her customers. His youthful cheerfulness reminded her of happier days, when she went to assemblies and expeditions in Oxford and fell in love with Lieutenant James Sinclair. In the four years since her husband died at Waterloo, life had held precious little in the way of jollity.

Today his chatter failed to raise her spirits. Life seemed drearier, her problems greater even than usual. Her father's health and the specter of Lord Frogmore hung over her. The few delightful minutes with *her gentleman*, as she had slipped into thinking of him, had contributed to her despondency. She wasn't in the mood to be bright and amusing.

At least Mr. Stratton was shopping. He selected a copy of "First Steps," a sentimental print of a toddling infant that was one of Oriel's best sellers. "For my grandmother," he said. "The old girl will love it."

Oriel thought of the other grandmother she'd heard about that afternoon and wished she had one, even one with high morals or a taste for chubby babies.

He couldn't just pay for his purchase and leave, however much she hinted that she had books to keep, columns of numbers that wouldn't add themselves up to their depressing totals. He followed her to the back room, plunked himself down at the table, and proceeded to regale her with *his* troubles.

"Hope and the Hendersons are coming to London in a few days," he said. "I'm supposed to offer for her."

"I thought you were happy about the engagement."

"I'm very fond of her, of course. I've known her all my life. But she's so young— only eighteen."

"And you are, what? A hoary twenty-three? Think how she will look up to your superior wisdom and experience."

He was too intent on his own thoughts to recognize the hint of sarcasm. "That's just it. She's a child. I find ladies more interesting when they have some knowledge of life. More conversation."

"There may be some truth in what you say, but Miss Henderson will grow older. It's something we ladies can't seem to avoid."

Mr. Stratton shook his head, brushed a floppy lock of fair hair from his forehead, and smiled dreamily. "You're not old."

"I hope not, yet."

"I don't want to marry Hope. It's my brother's idea because she's the heiress to the Henderson estate, and he wants the land in the family." Mr. Stratton's elder brother was a baronet and a leader of society whose name often appeared in the columns of the newspapers as a guest at Lady Such-and-Such's assembly.

"He can't make you marry against your will. He could marry her himself, unless he's already married or betrothed." Oriel felt a little impatient with the sorrows of the rich.

"Not Dev. I don't know when he'll find someone good enough for him." He pouted a little and looked much closer to the despised eighteen than a mature twenty-three. "It's unfair that he's making me get married and not even letting me choose my own bride."

"You are of age, you know. No one can make you do anything." She had a sudden thought. "Unless you have no money of your own."

"I've a competence. Nothing compared to Dev, of course, but enough to support a wife."

"You could find a profession too."

"I'm to manage the Hendersons' estate. Mr. Henderson's a Member of Parliament and a magistrate and needs help now he's getting on."

"And how old is he?"

"Fifty, maybe? Dashed old, anyway. And running to fat, so he can hardly find a horse to bear him. Think of not being able to ride and hunt. Terrible thing to happen to a man."

"Knowing your preference for country life, it seems an ideal arrangement."

"But it means I have to marry Hope. Besides, lately I've been enjoying London."

"I hope you aren't gaming." Situated in St. James's, Oriel knew the temptations and ruin that threatened foolish young, and not so young, men in fashionable London.

"Lord, no. I think I'd like to keep a shop like you. Seems a very jolly life."

"Very jolly." Oriel barely restrained herself from throwing the inkpot at the deluded youth. "But hardly an occupation for a gentleman."

"You're a lady."

"Hanging on to gentility by my fingernails. Take my advice. Marry your heiress."

He appeared struck by a brilliant idea. "I could marry you instead."

She should have seen it coming. "This is so sudden!" she said, trying to laugh it off. "When did you get this extraordinary idea?"

"Just now, but it's been coming on for a while. Ever since a few weeks ago when I thought I'd like to kiss you. You're a dashed pretty girl."

"Thank you. Am I the first 'girl' you've ever wanted to kiss? Do you always want to marry them?"

He flushed and looked younger than ever. "Of course not. It's not just that. I think we'd be happy together. We get on so well, and I could take care of you and your father." He stood up and came to stand beside her chair, regarding her with an earnest dignity. "I'm not a boy, you know."

Oriel tried to adjust her vision of him to that of a potential romantic partner. He was a handsome lad, tall, slender, well-made. And he was correct that he was not a boy. He reminded her a little of her husband when they had met and fallen in love. But she was a different person now. Had he lived, James and she would have gained maturity together. In her mind, he was still the dashing young soldier in red, and she could not see the Oriel she had become with him now. With a pang, she realized she had almost forgotten him, recalling him with affection as part of a distant past that had little relevance to her difficult present.

Merrick Stratton was a nice young fellow but very far from her ideal of manhood. Yet for a moment she was tempted. She could do it. She could draw him in and turn his whimsical admiration into a real love—real enough to get them past the wedding. As a man of honor he would, as promised, take care of her family. It would be lovely to have another pair of shoulders to share her burden. Then she looked at Merrick's lithe figure and repressed a laugh. Not broad enough.

Besides, she couldn't do it to the young man. He didn't deserve to have his future ruined by a momentary infatuation.

"Listen, Mr. Stratton," she began.

"I wish you will call me Merrick."

"Certainly not. I am touched and honored by your offer." She must let him down in the least hurtful way. "But your family would never approve, and I know how much they mean to you."

It was apparently the wrong thing to say.

"I make my own decisions," he said. Then rushed into speech. "Besides, they will love you once they know you. Don't say no yet. Meet them first. Come to the theater on Friday. Dev has taken a box to celebrate my mother and sisters' arrival in town."

"I couldn't do that. It wouldn't be suitable."

"There is nothing improper about inviting a friend to a theater party. Do say yes! It will be fun."

Fun. An evening out to see a play with nothing to think about but actors on the stage, a respite from harsh reality. No bills, no Frogmore, no impossibly attractive gentlemen she'd never meet again. Mary could stay with her father. And truly, the more time Merrick Stratton spent with her, the sooner he would get over this mad idea and return to Miss Hope, or another lady of the right age and background.

Chapter Three

ONLY ONE MORE day before the ladies descended. Devlyn and Merrick breakfasted in manly silence, glancing through the morning newspapers. Dev needed the soothing ritual. At Brooks's the previous evening, enjoying a quiet rubber of whist with friends, his vision had been assailed by the sight of Lord Frogmore lowering his bulk into a chair at the next table. Not that this was an unusual occurrence. What differed from the norm was Dev's unprecedented urge to haul the unpleasant peer up by his neckcloth and smash his rouged face.

Judged objectively, the man had done nothing to deserve the assault. It was the principle of the thing: Frogmore needed hitting, just for existing. Just for meeting charming women in bookshops. Dev had calmed his emotions by drinking too much brandy, and this morning he was not in the best of moods.

Leafing through a pile of mail delivered by his butler, most of which he cast aside, he broke the seal on a missive in his mother's handwriting. Susan had a slight cold, she wrote. Nothing to worry about, but she'd prefer to keep her at home before exposing her to the London air. Susan, in Dev's estimation, had the constitution of a cavalry charger and would be furious to have her visit to town postponed by such a trifle. He accepted the respite with gratitude.

About to share the news with Merrick, he realized what he'd been vaguely aware of before and ignored: The boy had something on his mind. Dev hoped it wasn't a gaming debt. A tailor's bill he could handle, but a passion for dice and cards was hard to cure. His father would have known what to do. Damn it, why did Sir George Stratton have to die and leave him with all the responsibility?

"The Hendersons arrive soon," his brother said.

"Yes."

Merrick chased a morsel of ham around his plate with a fork. "I don't want to marry Hope," he blurted.

What foolery had got into his head? Dev swallowed his impatience.

"You seemed happy when we agreed to spend Christmas in London so that Hope would have a few weeks to enjoy town before the betrothal. Have you heard something from her to make you change your mind?"

"Nothing. It's just that I want to marry someone else."

Dev couldn't say he was surprised. It was more shocking that Merrick had never had a female entanglement until now. At his age Dev had fallen for any number of "ladies." He had not, however, felt the urge to wed any of them.

"This is a sudden decision," he said, treading as carefully as the throbbing in his brain allowed. "In my opinion, you are bound by honor to Hope."

"Oh no. I never offered for her, and she never accepted."

"But it's an understood thing."

"Understood by you and her parents. Oriel says you can't force me to marry against my will."

"I see. Is Oriel by any chance the girl you wish to marry?"

"Yes. I love her."

"I expect you think you do to take such a radical step as letting Hope down."

"Hope won't mind. With her estate, she'll have lots of suitors. Or you could marry her."

"I have no taste for the very young." A mistake, a bad mistake.

"And neither do I. I like a woman with experience of life."

Worse and worse.

"And how old is this Miss… Oriel."

"Mrs. Sinclair, for your information, is a highly respectable widow."

"Where did you meet her?"

"In her shop."

"A shopgirl? Really, Merrick, I should think you'd know better." The sooner the boy was married off the better. He was a danger to himself.

But Merrick, normally the most amenable young man, had a streak of stubbornness, and Dev had awakened it. "She is a lady not a shopgirl. She keeps a gallery of prints with her father, a retired Oxford tutor."

"You've met the father?"

"No. He is in poor health and remains upstairs."

Dev highly doubted the existence of this sickly scholar. Also of the woman's respectability and probably even her first marriage. Poor Merrick had fallen into the clutches of an adventuress. She would have to be scared or bought off.

"I don't know if she'll have me," Merrick went on. "She wasn't that keen when I mentioned the idea."

Dev made a mental note to instruct Merrick about the proper way to make an offer of marriage, once he'd got him back in a frame of mind to propose to Hope. *Mentioned the idea* wasn't good enough. Still, it didn't sound as though Merrick had wandered into breach of promise territory, and that was a blessing.

"If she turned you down, there's nothing to be done. Would you like to come with me to Jackson's this morning and put on a pair of gloves?" Merrick was a mediocre pugilist, but no sacrifice was too great.

"She hasn't said no. I've invited her to join us at the theater. You and Mama will be able to see that I am right."

The percussion section of a military band had taken possession of the area behind Dev's forehead. He retained just enough sense not to argue. Since Mama and the girls had postponed their arrival, and, thank God, the Hendersons weren't yet in town, he had a few days to solve the problem.

"Good idea," he said, pleased by Merrick's look of shock at his easy capitulation. "I look forward to meeting her."

Seeing his inamorata among the *ton*, Merrick would realize how ill-bred Miss Oriel was. And if that didn't work, there was always money. Probably what the rapacious harpy wanted. It wasn't as though Merrick was such a great catch.

A POLITE LETTER from a print publisher refusing credit until her account was settled. A less friendly note from the banker reminding her that the quarter's interest on the mortgage was almost due and last quarter's still outstanding. A doctor's bill, a grocer's bill, a stationer's bill. And not a single customer. Such was Oriel's day: bad news punctuated by visits upstairs where Mr. Markham's cough increased and his temper declined in a grim minuet.

In an hour she must make the delivery to Lord Frogmore's house and decide whether she dared venture inside to conclude the negotiations that would make all her troubles vanish. As she rubbed her eyes over her recalcitrant accounts, the sound of the street door came as a harbinger of hope. Would this be the rich customer who would save her from Frogmore?

Stopping short in the doorway, she blinked in disbelief at the figure peering through the window into the gray, chilly street. His fine beaver hat and great coat enhanced a set of shoulders broad enough to take on any burden. Wishful thinking gave the impression that *her gentleman* had found his way to Markham's Print Gallery. Yet surely fortune was not so kind as to put her in the way of two such magnificent males in two days? Just in case, she smoothed her hair and straightened her gown, checking hands and skirts for ink stains.

"It *is* you," she said stupidly when he turned around.

Somehow, in one day, she'd forgotten just how splendid he was. Not only his figure, tall and strong and anything a woman could dream of. Her foggy brain couldn't seem to care that he wasn't strictly handsome, though there was nothing to criticize in his features. The impression she'd carried for twenty-four hours was of appealing good humor, straight dark brows slanted upward over eyes that narrowed when he smiled, leaving attractive crinkles at the edges. His eyes were wide open now. A light golden brown, they bore into her. He was apparently as stunned as she. Her hand fluttered to the doorjamb for support.

"I wasn't expecting to see you here," he said.

So he hadn't sought her out. Never mind. She'd take the coincidence and call herself lucky. Neither did he appear to have noticed her imbecilic opening remark.

"Whom did you expect?" she asked, regaining her aplomb and a note of impertinence.

During a silence in which he removed his hat, revealing well-tended brown hair, thick and wavy, she had the oddest impression that he was about to turn tail and run. Seconds or minutes ticked by before he spoke again. She'd have recognized those sherry tones anywhere.

"A print shop," he said. "I take it you are the owner, Miss..."

"Mrs. Sinclair. My father is Mr. Markham."

"I am looking for a present for my grandmother."

"The one who likes a high moral tone, or a more tolerant one?"

"Do you have prints suitable for each?"

Inevitably, she pointed to the print that hung on the wall among a selection of the most sought-after offerings. "'First Steps' is popular with grandmothers, so I have been told."

He walked around the central cabinet and stood but a few feet from her, his large body exuding an impression of heat that cut through the chill where the small fire in the back room could not. The delicately colored print showed a young mother in the classical dress fashionable a decade ago, on one knee to encourage her infant son to walk into her outstretched arms.

"I can see why," *her gentleman* said with marked disfavor. "Who is responsible for this atrocity?"

She pursed her lips to repress an appreciative grin. "Adam Buck is the name of the artist, and I'll have you know this representation of motherhood appeals to all ladies of taste."

"Bad taste, you mean. The lady is pretty enough, I grant, but I've never seen such a child. He's as solid as a rock and has been walking at least six months, if I know anything about it." She'd often thought the same thing as she praised the quality of the work to sentimental ladies. "And why," he continued, "is he dressed in a sort of toga? Every infant I've encountered wears long skirts."

Her heart plummeted to her feet. "You have children of your own?"

"Sisters, a younger brother, nephews and nieces, and a plethora of prolific cousins."

"And a grandmother," she said, adding her best teasing smile. "Or two."

"Just one, as it happens."

"Is this moral enough for her?"

He tilted his head, but instead of looking at the picture his eyes were on her face with a concentration that sent a mild flush right down to her toes. "What could be more innocuous than a mother and child? Especially since the only one showing much in the way of skin is the infant. I confess it isn't the kind of thing I expected to find here."

Now she flushed in reality, feeling her cheeks turn scarlet. Did he intend to insult? Had she gained a bad reputation without knowing it?

"Is your visit by chance or by recommendation?" She forced her brain to think about practicalities and those expensive French prints. This man, whoever he was, must be able to afford her price. She considered her words carefully. "Have you perhaps heard of some of the more unusual items in my stock? Only a fraction of what Markham's carries is displayed on the walls."

"Indeed?" He raised his brows, and she could imagine him capable of delivering a sharp set-down. "I'm afraid I don't remember where I heard of you. Do you have unusual items? Perhaps those of which my grandmother would disapprove? I'll take the print, by the way. Luckily I shan't have to look at it myself, except when I take tea in her sitting room."

"I'll wrap it, then."

"No need to do so now. My footman will collect it. A gentleman, you know, does not carry parcels. And you may send the account to my man of business. I'll write down the address."

"To whom shall I make out the bill?"

"Just send it to my man. He'll know it's mine."

For some reason, the man who almost certainly wasn't *her* gentleman didn't want to reveal his name. "Is there anything else I can show you?"

"By all means."

For the first time, she found something to dislike in his face. His smile wasn't precisely lascivious, but neither was it pleasant. Gulping down her hesitation, she opened the drawer and removed the portfolio.

He leafed through the prints, strong hands turning over the crisp sheets with gentle respect. She cringed quietly when he passed by the warmer examples and was oddly glad to see that he paid them no greater attention than the more subtly amorous images that she preferred.

"Well?" she said, her pulse racing as he came to the end.

He raised his head and smiled. "Why, madam. These are beautiful."

Her heart calmed to a regular beat with relief and pleasure. They *were* beautiful. She'd come to see them through the eyes of disapproval—her father's—and lust—customers like Frogmore—and forgotten her original feelings when she'd examined the portfolio in a shabby auction room. Yes, the images were a little spicy, but they were also romantic, depicting love and desire with mischief and tenderness.

With all the charm she could muster, she spoke of the history behind the prints, most of which were intended as book illustrations. She praised the artists, detailing their fame. She pointed out the sharp incisions of the ink, indicating that they were early impressions made before the plates became worn. And look at the splendid width of the margins. These examples had never been trimmed.

He listened, asking the occasional question, but he looked at her as much as the merchandise, and not in an admiring way. He appeared skeptical. Her heart sank. Experience told her when a customer was ready to buy, and he was not.

"Don't decide now," she said before he could deliver a definite no. "It is growing late, and I have a delivery to make before it gets dark."

"I would offer to take you in my carriage, but I am on foot today. May I offer you my escort?"

"There's no need. I shall be quite safe between here and Berkeley Square."

"In that case, I insist. Your destination is close to mine."

Whatever his moment of distrust, he was all friendliness now, and she was by no means reluctant to accept. Perhaps she could persuade him en route to buy the prints and save her from Frogmore.

"If you don't mind waiting five minutes, I will fetch my coat and bonnet and speak to my father."

THE BEST-LAID PLANS of men and Strattons are subject to instant reconsideration. Quick thinking on Dev's part, when he'd been knocked into incoherence by the discovery that Mrs. Oriel Sinclair and the lovely lady of the bookshop were one and the same. He'd looked at her prints and heard her persuasive arguments, liberally sweetened with her smiles. His eyes had kept wandering to her face, alternately certain that her charm was genuine and convinced that she was drawing him in. And succeeding. He'd come close to offering a large sum for something he didn't need, simply because it would have made her happy.

Once his brain had regained its function, he changed his mind about his next move.

Not about Merrick. He would not allow his brother to marry her. But he immediately knew that a cold commercial transaction, a nice sum of money in exchange for her withdrawal from the ranks, was not the right strategy.

Mrs. Sinclair was a lady—of sorts—and no naïve but grasping shopgirl. She also appeared to know her business, as a print seller. He knew enough to recognize that she was right about the quality of the French prints. Not quite grandmother material, though his mother's mother, a beauty in her day and long deceased, would have enjoyed them.

Not to Frogmore's debased taste he would have guessed. What had she sold him? Something, for surely he was her customer in Berkeley Square. Curiosity to have that fact confirmed accounted for his offer of escort. Nothing to do with a desire for her company. Not one bit.

On impulse, keeping his ears cocked for the sound of footsteps on the stairs, he opened the lowest drawer in the print cabinet and had an answer: a handful of prints, cruder in execution than those she had shown him. Cruder in subject too. The activities depicted between men and women would make the most tolerant of grandmothers collapse in shock. Mrs. Sinclair was feeding some of Frogmore's desires. How many remained to be determined, but he had a good guess.

What a waste.

He was back at the window when Mrs. Sinclair returned, clad in the same out-door clothes as the previous day and carrying a flat package wrapped in paper and string. He wondered again how she managed to look so stylish without benefit of a top modiste, and insidious attraction wormed its way under his skin. He was supposed to be getting rid of this woman, for Merrick's sake, not pursuing her.

Instinctively he reached for the package.

"A gentleman does not carry parcels," she said with a quizzical smile.

"A gentleman does not allow a lady to carry parcels. That rule trumps the other."

"But I am not, today, going out in the guise of a lady, but of a delivery boy."

"You don't look anything like a delivery boy." This last was almost whispered, close to her ear, as he opened the door for her. She shook her head but didn't shy away, permitting the slight intimacy with a ghost of a smile.

This was a woman who could tie a man in knots. No wonder Merrick was be-witched.

The idea came to him in a flash of brilliance. He was a much better catch than Merrick. Any adventuress worth her salt would prefer rich Sir Devlyn Stratton to his younger brother. He'd have to move carefully, so as not to hurt Merrick by trying to steal his beloved. But if the beloved turned to a better prospect of her own accord, Merrick would see her for what she was.

Better that he, rather than naïve Merrick, tangle with a siren. He could enjoy her soft hands and sly smiles without the least danger of sinking into foolishness.

The chilly walk to Berkeley Square looked much more enjoyable.

IN DECEMBER ANY day that didn't produce rain or snow counted as fine, and shoppers were out in force. A carriage going too fast, too close to the pavement, sent a spray of mud in its wake, splashing her escort's boot and causing a careless young man to leap out of the way and almost knock Oriel over.

Her gentleman seized her arm efficiently and pulled her out of the path of a cou-ple who were, for some reason, eating tarts in the street. "Are you all right?"

"I can never get used to the worst London crowds, even after three years."

"Where did you come from?"

"I spent most of my life in Oxford."

"I'm a Cambridge man myself. Were you named for the college?"

"I was." She tilted her head. How very odd. She hadn't mentioned her unusual Christian name. "How did you know that my given name is Oriel?"

"I must have seen it somewhere in the shop," he said, holding on to her arm. Maybe he had sought her out after all, discovered her name, and come to find her. She would ask Annabelle if he'd inquired at the bookshop. "Your father's college, perhaps?"

"My father was a fellow of Oriel for over twenty years. Then he retired, and we opened the gallery."

"Does he work with you in the shop?"

"He is in poor health and keeps upstairs."

He made no comment beyond a heightened brow. A well-respected fellow of long standing should not need to descend to making a living in trade. She had no intention of telling this attractive stranger how her father had quarreled so badly with the provost of Oriel that he'd stormed from college, university, and city without claiming any of the emoluments to which he was entitled. Arthur Markham was good at burning bridges.

She was more interested in discovering the identity of her escort. "I don't want to take you out of your way," she said when they turned off Piccadilly. "I thank you for coming with me so far. To whom do I owe my gratitude?"

"We're not there yet."

"Where do you live?"

"Not far from here," he said unhelpfully.

"Do you live in London year-round?" She assumed a man of obvious wealth had a country estate, and perhaps she could get a clue to his identity that way.

"Yes."

The deuce with subtle inquiry. "Who are you, sir?"

"I am a man who does not allow a lady to walk the streets alone and a man who is not afraid of parcels."

"I think you are laughing at me."

"Just a little." The blasted man actually had a touch of a dimple in his left cheek when he suppressed mirth. Could he possibly be more attractive?

"Is your name a secret for reasons of state? Are you a long-lost foreign prince?"

"Alas, such creatures exist only in the pages of my sister's novels. I promise that you will find out, but not today."

She shook her head. "I think you are a little mad."

That was a promise to return, and her heart sang. She would see him again—and have the chance to sell him something expensive. She only hoped he wouldn't be shopping under the same terms as Lord Frogmore. Shamefully, she had to admit this man's advances would be a good deal harder to resist. Her destination—Frogmore's house—hove into view.

"This is where we part company," she said on the pavement, her moment of optimism turning to bile. A shiny door painted an ominous black loomed above her. Beyond it lay *negotiations* that terrified her.

Her gentleman handed over her parcel. "Make your delivery. I will wait and find you a hackney. You shouldn't walk home in the dark."

She thought about the money she needed so desperately and balanced it against Frogmore's horrible fingers. Her nerve failed, and she grasped at the unwitting offer of rescue. "I won't be a minute," she said, and hurried up the steps to rap on the knocker.

"His lordship is expecting you," a manservant said.

"Please give this to his lordship and tell him I won't come in. Pray send my apologies, but my father is unwell and needs me. Tell his lordship that I look forward to seeing him at Markham's Print Gallery in the near future."

The servant peered out into the street where her escort had found a hackney. She'd used his existence as an excuse to run away from Frogmore. It wouldn't do for a potential customer like that to see her enter a man's house, by the front door no less. He probably knew who the owner was. Members of the *haut ton* all knew each other.

Frogmore could wait.

Chapter Four

~

ORIEL WAS A little uneasy when Merrick came alone to take her to the theater, and she learned that his mother and sisters' arrival in London had been delayed. He was most apologetic and assured her that there was nothing untoward about a married or widowed lady attending the theater in a box in company with two gentlemen. His brother would meet them at the theater, and he was a damned stickler when it came to manners.

She hoped her father wouldn't find out. Since neither Frogmore nor the unknown gentleman had appeared in her shop for two days, she'd had nothing to do but worry about the bills. She'd taken the likely hopeless step of writing to her father's cousin for help, another thing Mr. Markham mustn't know, or he might well be carried off by an apoplexy. A farce at the Theatre Royal Covent Garden was just what she needed.

"I say, Oriel," Merrick began once they set off in the carriage, "have you thought any more about what we were talking about? You know." Another romantic proposal. At least, that's what she thought it was.

"Mr. Stratton. I told you then that it is quite impossible."

"You're worried about the family, but when I told Dev about it he was quite agreeable."

"I find that hard to believe."

"He made a fuss at first, saying I was pledged to Hope, which I am not. But he came around. He was delighted you'd agreed to come tonight, and he looks forward to meeting you."

"And I look forward to making Sir Devlyn's acquaintance, but—"

"Don't say another word now. You'll see then that everything will be dandy."

The first time she'd visited a London theater was with James, during a short visit to the capital before he left for Belgium and Waterloo. They'd seen Kean in *Hamlet* from the bustle of the pit. Before her father became ill, the two of them had bought cheap seats in the gallery a few times. The experience of attending in a box was very different. The broad staircase and corridor lined with white statues and plush benches, the parade of fashionable patrons, the confident hum of well-bred conversation, all communicated a different world than that of people who'd scraped up a few precious shillings for an evening's entertainment. Merrick settled her in a comfortable chair at the front of the box, and she blinked, adjusting her eyes to the vast auditorium illuminated by the new gas-lighting. She was in a different world from the shadowy confines in which she passed most of her life, a world of gaiety and drama and infinite possibilities. Her burdened heart lightened, and she prepared to enjoy herself.

"It's beautiful, Mr. Stratton," she said. "Thank you for bringing me."

"Merrick," he said. "I wish you will call me Merrick."

Before she could again refuse, she sensed a new arrival in the box.

"Here's Dev."

"Good evening, Merrick."

She jumped up from her chair and spun around, her mind awhirl. He stood in the entrance, revoltingly attractive and confident, and the last person she'd expected to see.

"Mrs. Sinclair," Merrick said, "may I present my brother Sir Devlyn Stratton?"

"Mrs. Sinclair. What a pleasure." He showed no acknowledgment that they'd already met. His only sign of recognition was a smooth smile. No dimple.

"Sir," she said. She waited for him to mention their previous meetings.

"I feel as though I know a great deal about you... thanks to Merrick."

"I told you she was a beauty," Merrick said eagerly. "Wait till you discover how clever she is."

"Sir Devlyn," Oriel began. And stopped.

His gaze went back and forth between his brother and her, belying his relaxed stance. Assessing.

What could be the reason for his odd behavior? It would be natural for a concerned brother to discover what he could of a woman who threatened to spoil an engagement to an heiress. That he didn't wish her to marry his brother was no shock. That, she understood. She could even forgive him for jumping to the conclusion that she was some kind of scheming wretch. But he'd made a game of her. If he'd only asked she'd have set his mind at rest. Did she look like a scheming wretch?

Arrogance, pure arrogance. Why else would he have led her on and teasingly withheld his name when he knew exactly who she was?

The guilty remembrance of their first flirtatious encounter at On the Shelf was thrust aside as blood rushed to her head.

"The pleasure's all mine, sir." She heard herself release a distinct titter. "I've heard so much about you from Merrick, haven't I, my dear? Why didn't you tell me your brother was such a big, handsome fellow?" She considered—and rejected—running her hand down his arm.

Merrick looked shocked, while Sir Devlyn narrowed his eyes.

"I've been nervous about meeting Merrick's family," she said in a vulgar tone of voice. "I couldn't say if I was glad or sorry when I heard the ladies weren't joining us.

I was that pleased, I was, to make the acquaintance of your mama and the girls. I just love the name Emma. Makes me think of a character in a novel. Are you fond of novels, Sir Devlyn? Of course you aren't. Gentlemen don't have to read stories, because they lead such fascinating lives all by themselves. All sorts of naughty things I daresay you get up to without having to get ideas from silly stories." With a quick pause for breath and a coy smile, and before either man could say a word, she hurried on. "But it's a rare treat to spend an evening with two handsome gents. Just little old me. Fancy that."

Offering a rest for her lungs and powers of invention, music arose from the area of the stage.

"The play is starting," Merrick said hastily. "Won't you sit down? Are you quite well?" he whispered as she settled back into her seat at the front of the box.

She hit his arm with her fan, a rarely used souvenir of happier days. "I've never felt better. I'm that excited. What's the play?" She spoke loud enough to make sure that Sir Devlyn, sitting behind her, could hear every word.

Little Red Riding Hat.

As Merrick lowered his voice, she raised hers. "Ooh!" She clapped her hands. "I love that story. I can't wait to see the wolf. Whoops. I don't want to spoil the story for you gentlemen, but there's a *beast* in the theater tonight."

"I've never seen this play, but I am told the music is very fine."

"No one likes a good song better than I. Pinch me if I forget myself and sing along with the actors."

She did not, refusing to spoil the performance for those in the neighboring boxes. Not that they would have noticed. She was hardly the only one talking without cease. By the time the curtain fell, she was exhausted.

"Merrick," his brother said. "Why don't you find a servant and order wine for us all? Unless you'd prefer lemonade, Mrs. Sinclair."

"No thanks," she said. "My throat's as dry as a bone, and I'm in need of a little something to pick me up. I don't suppose they serve gin in a nice place like this."

"Now, Mrs. Sinclair," Sir Devlyn said into her ear once Merrick had left. "You can relax and speak normally. I suppose I can guess the reason for your behavior tonight."

"Can you?" She turned in her seat to half face him. "You have the advantage over me. I can't guess the reason for yours."

"I'm sure you understand why I don't want Merrick to know that I was looking into his so-called beloved behind his back."

"You have an astonishing ability to deliver insults in the most normal tone of voice. Do you find that makes you popular among your acquaintance?"

"I believe I am tolerably well-liked."

Oriel arched her brows.

"Did *you* like me when we first met?" he asked.

She folded her arms and pursed her lips.

"I liked you, you know. Very much. And then I discovered that you were the kind of woman who lures a younger man into an unsuitable marriage. Was your performance tonight designed to make me offer you a handsome sum of money to go away?"

She hugged herself closer to resist the urge to slap him. "Are you going to offer one? I do hope so. I am very fond of handsome sums. I wonder if our notions of handsome are the same."

"You seem like an accommodating woman." He stood and leaned over her, a very angry man with the intent to intimidate. She stiffened her shoulders and stared back. "But if you thought to drive up your price by behaving like a trollop, you may drive down your value. It works that way, you know. In fact, you may drive Merrick away altogether and save me the trouble. He's not a fool, my brother, whatever you may think."

"Neither am I, sir. Whatever you may think."

"Does he know of your... acquaintance... with Lord Frogmore?"

Oriel gripped her fan hard enough to endanger the delicate sticks. "He may have come across him in my shop. His lordship is an enthusiastic collector with excellent taste."

"A taste for what, exactly?"

"I don't discuss my customers' business with others."

"Is that what I am? A customer? If so, we should discuss terms. Be warned that I am a hard bargainer."

"Are you making me an offer?"

He rocked back and blinked, taking his time about the reply. She had the impression he didn't know what to say, was as surprised as she about the turn of events. How far Stratton would go to rescue his brother from a nonexistent threat remained to be discovered.

"Dev, my dear fellow!" An extremely stout gentleman with a red face stood in the doorway to the box.

Sir Devlyn's head whipped around, and he swore under his breath. With visible reluctance, he turned to greet the gentleman, who was followed into the box by two ladies.

"Sir, Mrs. Henderson, Hope," he said with a bow.

Oriel examined Merrick's intended bride with interest. Pretty with soft, curling brown hair in a modest but obviously costly yellow silk gown. And so very young. Oriel recognized the shy excitement flushing her milky complexion. She'd felt the same when first admitted to the sober delights of an Oxford assembly. The girl's eyes darted. Looking for Merrick.

"We arrived in town a few days early and decided to come to the theater tonight." Mrs. Henderson, a handsome, sensible-looking woman, was exactly as Oriel would have expected of the wife of a prosperous country gentleman and Member of Parliament. "We're only three boxes away on the same side. Lady Staunton told us you were here. She said it sounded like quite a merry party you were having in here." She noticed Oriel and looked her up and down, her friendly smile turning cool. She tilted her head questioningly at Sir Devlyn.

"Mrs. Henderson, Miss Henderson, may I present Mrs. Sinclair? Mrs. Sinclair, this is Mr. Henderson."

Restraining the urge to laugh at his discomfort, Oriel curtseyed demurely. She could have resumed her outrageous manner and embarrassed Stratton by confirming Mrs. Henderson's suspicion that she was a woman of dubious virtue, but ruining Merrick's match was no plan of hers. Whatever his dastardly brother assumed. "How pleasant to meet you. I hope Merrick will be back soon with the refreshments. He'll be happy to see you."

"You must be a London acquaintance, Mrs. Sinclair," Mrs. Henderson said. "I know everyone in Sussex."

"What a lot of people. How busy you must be," Oriel replied. "It's so much quieter in London."

Sir Devlyn jumped in. "Mrs. Sinclair is an expert in prints. We are thinking of having her come in to look over some things my father bought long ago and I've never really looked at."

"Indeed?" Mrs. Henderson looked unconvinced. It wasn't a very good story, but it gave Oriel an idea.

"*Indeed,*" she replied. "We had agreed that I would come to Curzon Street in the morning and see what they have." A sideways glance showed Sir Devlyn looking like a juggler whose ball had taken off in an unforeseen direction. "Sir Devlyn was kind enough to invite me to the theater because we were talking about illustrations of the old stories, and I happened to mention that *Little Red Riding Hood* is a favorite. So interesting that they call it a hat in this version. Do you enjoy fairy tales, Miss Henderson?"

"Yes, I do," Hope said. "I was wondering about the hat too. The girl playing Rose is quite large, isn't she? I wonder how the wolf will eat her?"

Mr. Henderson gave Oriel an appreciative, though entirely seemly, smile. "Perhaps Hope would like to stay in the box with you for the second half." Unlike his wife, he had apparently noticed nothing amiss about her presence. And why should he? Oriel might not be a woman of fashion, but there was nothing objectionable about her appearance. Her heart hardened at Sir Devlyn's assumptions about her. He had no right.

"Ah, here's Merrick. My dear boy, look who couldn't wait to see you."

Merrick looked wildly around the box, but said nothing foolish. He managed to greet Hope with apparent pleasure, if not quite the enthusiasm of an imminent fiancé. Hope blushed scarlet and peeped at him through her lashes. If Oriel wasn't mistaken, she adored him. Now to make sure she did nothing to break up Merrick and Hope while keeping the former's appalling brother on the hook. Unlike Sir Devlyn, Oriel was used to juggling under adverse circumstances.

The appalling brother had recovered his poise. "Why don't you sit at the front with Merrick, Hope? You don't mind, do you, Mrs. Sinclair? We can have a few words about my etchings."

Oh no, indeed. She wasn't finished with the arrogant Sir Devlyn.

HE'D BRUSHED THROUGH that pretty well, Dev thought. For a moment, he'd feared Mrs. Henderson would storm off, believing one of the Strattons had brought his mistress to the theater. Better he than Merrick, so he'd made up that nonsense about the prints.

He had no intention of giving the woman a penny. She wore a smile of avaricious triumph, and he now had no doubt a payment had been her plan from the start. And yet, she could have made trouble with the Hendersons in an effort to increase her price. He shook his head hard. Something about Oriel Sinclair robbed him of his ability to think straight. He should never have mentioned money when his plan remained in place: to turn her ambitions toward him. He had a lot of ground to make up since he'd stupidly lost his temper.

Settled in the back of the box, he continued to ignore the stage. From the way she gulped her wine, she wasn't as comfortable as she'd appeared. Her eyes were fixed on Hope and Merrick, who chatted happily about the play.

"Lovely girl, Miss Henderson," he remarked, urbanity restored. "Merrick and she have been devoted to one another for years."

"Yet, she is a few years younger. As children, the age difference must have seemed considerable."

"They became closer as they grew up."

"What an unusual arrangement of time." She had dropped her vulgar posture. The droll note he found so attractive entered her clear, ladylike voice. "If your brother has managed to resist five years of aging, I'd like to know how. Shall I ask him?"

"Not during the play."

"Oh no. It is essential that we, like everyone else here, give our full attention to such a fine dramatic work."

"I'll grant you that the piece is silly. I chose it because it would amuse my sisters."

"Where are your sisters? Did you arrange things so they wouldn't have to meet me?"

"No need. My mother postponed the journey, so I was able to agree without qualm to Merrick's suggestion you join us."

The flash in her eyes made them almost like emeralds. "A deft insult."

"If you don't like it, don't behave as though you deserve it."

"I believe my conduct is exactly what *you* deserve."

"Good, we're taking the gloves off." He leaned in to make sure no one but she could hear. "Give me a straight answer. Are you planning to marry my brother?"

"An engagement would make a lovely Christmas present. But maybe I'll get a better offer." She presented her profile, wearing an enigmatic smile.

His pulse, already heightened by her proximity, sped further.

"Do you have someone in mind?" If he wasn't mistaken, she would prefer him to Merrick, given the chance. Or to Frogmore, for that matter. If there was one thing Dev could recognize, it was flirtation.

"A wise woman is discreet in her affairs."

"By all means, let us talk about our affairs. At what time would suit you to come to the house and look at my collection?"

She turned full face, her mouth forming a surprised oval. "Your offer was an excuse, and mine was made to embarrass you. Do you really have anything for me to see?"

"I don't know, but my father kept all sorts of odds and ends in the library at the London house. I should look them over."

"Is nine o'clock too early, or are you so fashionable that you remain in bed until noon?"

"I take my morning ride at eight."

"I must be back by noon to see customers."

"Frogmore?" No sooner said than he wished he had not.

"Lord Frogmore is a customer," she said flatly.

"I doubt I could rival his value as a *collector*. My arrangement with you would be that of an adviser."

She raised her chin and hit him in the chest with her smile. "My services do not come inexpensively."

"My dear Mrs. Sinclair. Nothing worth having in life ever does."

Chapter Five

A T TWO MINUTES past nine, by the mantelpiece clock, Sir Devlyn Stratton stuck his head around the door of his library. "Have you been waiting long?"

"I was early," Oriel said.

"Give me a quarter of an hour to change out of my riding gear." Hair clung to his forehead, testifying to the sleety mess that had come down during her journey. She was more grateful than ever that he had sent his carriage, a thoughtfulness she hadn't expected.

While she waited, she browsed the shelves of the room, which the master of the house obviously used for business and correspondence. She'd already resisted the temptation to investigate the unopened letters piled high on the desk. The library was smaller than she'd expected, given the lavish proportions of the house, the largest she'd ever entered in London. Sir Devlyn probably had a bigger library at his country place. A scholar's daughter, she approved of the variety of volumes, many richly bound but giving the impression that they were owned for use, not show.

Her mind was only half on the task at hand. Her father's cough had worsened overnight, and she hoped she could charge Stratton enough for her "advice" to afford a better doctor. Meanwhile, the overdue mortgage and any number of other bills preyed on her mind. She worried that she'd been a fool to brush off Frogmore. Surely he wouldn't have actually forced himself on her if she'd entered his house. A dull ache settled in the pit of her stomach, and even the weak tea she'd swallowed for breakfast made her stomach jumpy. Or perhaps it was the imminent return of Sir Devlyn.

He entered, immaculately turned-out as usual. She rather wished he'd remained in his riding clothes, wet with an odor of horse. This morning, he was every inch the wealthy and connected member of the *ton*. Until he smiled and he was *her gentleman* again. The man had her in a perpetual state of confusion.

"What do you think of the library?" he asked.

"A good reading collection. Are these your books?"

"Some. Some I inherited from my father."

"I haven't seen anything special that requires my attention."

"Are you a bibliophile too?"

"We originally opened a bookshop, but my father would buy works he liked and refuse to sell them. I found more demand for things that could be framed and hung. Thus, Markham's Books became Markham's Print Gallery." With a mortgage on the lease to pay for new stock. "What do you have to show me?"

He pointed at a row of cupboard doors underneath the bookshelves. "Let's take a look at those. Unless you would like refreshment first."

"Thank you, no. I can only spare a couple of hours this morning."

"And what is a fair price for two hours of your time?"

"It depends how long it takes for me to assess your collection. I will come back if needed. Does ten guineas seem unreasonable?"

She held her breath, expecting him to argue with such an exorbitant sum. He raised his eyebrows, but nodded and strode over to open one of the cupboards. She came up behind and peered over his stooped shoulders, curious to see if her presence was a pretext she didn't understand, or if he actually had anything worth looking at. The contents were a mess, unexpected in a house furnished and maintained with as much perfection as its owner's person.

"I have no idea what this is." He pulled out a thick pile of papers of varying sizes that seemed to have been thrown in at random. "These are my father's. Like yours, he kept things. Oh well," he said, and she detected a certain reluctance, "we'd better get on with it."

Between them they emptied one shelf and placed the contents at one end of a rectangular table that stood in the center of the room. On top were a number of childish drawings: still lifes, landscapes, and portraits.

"This one is Merrick," Oriel said.

"Just about recognizable," he agreed. "Susan's work. She rather fancies herself an artist. She must have given it to my father. This one is me. I remember sitting for it." Susan had an ability to catch a basic likeness. She'd emphasized her brother's unusual eyebrows and had caught his humorous look. "My mother had a better version framed and hung in her bedchamber where no one can see it." A slight upturning of his mouth, that intriguing hint of dimple, contradicted the dismissive comment.

"It's quite good. How old is Susan?"

"Fourteen." It couldn't have been done more than three or four years ago, unless Susan had been unusually precocious.

He picked up another drawing, a stiff pose of a young woman holding a small child. The mother's arms had given the artist trouble, so they were bent oddly. "This is my sister Margaret and her boy. Note, Mrs. Sinclair, that he is wearing skirts. I come by my knowledge of infant fashions honestly."

"I did not doubt it. I envy you coming from a large family. My father has only me."

"Count yourself lucky. It's a confounded nuisance having four younger than I, always needing to be rescued from some disaster or other."

She winced, recalling the "disaster" he thought Merrick was in. But his mind was elsewhere, smiling fondly at the charming, inexpert family gallery spread before him. She wouldn't have expected sentimentality from this unruffled man of fashion. Yet he'd taken the trouble to find a book his sister would like.

Her eagle eye spotted the corner of something under the litter of paper. A portrait of Admiral Lord Nelson, spoiled by damp spots.

"Have you found a treasure?"

"I have sold a few copies of this print, though in rather better condition. It's quite common since Nelson remains a popular hero. These days, engravings of the Duke of Wellington sell even better. Since you are paying me for expert advice, I recommend you leave this in the cupboard."

"Thank you," he said gravely. "What about these?"

These were quite a collection of Nelson memorabilia. "It's astonishing how many commemorative prints were issued after the Battle of Trafalgar," she remarked.

"My father was a great admirer." He picked up a large, colored engraving of HMS *Victory*. "This is rather splendid. I like ships. As a boy I dreamed of running away to join the navy and seeing the world."

"Why didn't you? Not run away, but enter the service?"

"Oldest sons don't do things like that. I came to London, instead. More comfortable and less dangerous."

"You should have the print framed. It's in good condition, and the hand coloring is excellent."

"I am happy to find it. Why don't you keep searching while I look through these letters and documents?"

They sat side-by-side at the table, helping themselves to items from the heap, occasionally exchanging a letter for an illustration. His father's miscellany held little challenge for her, so she sorted things into neat piles, covertly observing her host, who went through the written matter briskly, occasionally muttering that he couldn't believe this rubbish hadn't been thrown away, sometimes smiling, and sometimes sad. She could imagine having the same reactions looking at her father's papers, and offered a quick silent prayer that she wouldn't be called to the task for many years.

However she had envisioned this morning's work, it hadn't been this amiable, almost domestic, mutual undertaking of a mundane task. The only expected aspect of the visit was Merrick's absence. She guessed he'd been sent on an errand to some distant part of London to keep him away from her.

But why allow her to come here at all? True, she'd talked her way in, but he could have resisted. She couldn't understand the man. Any initial attraction he'd felt for her hadn't survived his belief that she was trying to entrap his brother into marriage.

Sneaking a sideways glance, she found him doing the same. She bent back to the table to avoid his eye. A few minutes later, it happened again, and their gazes held for a few seconds.

"Look at this," she said hastily.

Near the bottom of a pile, she had found a drawing, not the work of any of the young ladies with whose style she was now familiar. A man and a youth were dragging a small tree trunk by a rope.

"Is this you and your father?"

He stared at it. "The Yule log," he said, almost under his breath.

"You didn't say you drew."

"I don't. One of my sisters must have done it."

She didn't believe him. He couldn't be more than twelve in the picture, and his sisters would have been too young. A touch of color on his cheekbones spoke of embarrassment at the idea. He hunched his shoulders as he leaned over the image.

"But the young man is you, with your father?"

"Perhaps. Foolish, those old country customs. But he enjoyed them."

She was seized by envy again, of his family and of knowing the customs. In Oxford, her father and aunt hadn't made much of the celebration. Church on Christmas Day and a good dinner, that was all. She'd rarely received a Christmas gift, though once or twice Arthur Markham had emerged from his self-absorbed haze with one of his surprising bursts of generosity. She had met James in January and lost him in June, with never a chance to enjoy a Yuletide together.

"When did your father die?" she asked.

"Over a year ago." He stood up before she could offer a condolence. "Time for refreshment."

They sat either side of the blazing fire. Oriel poured tea and served a delectable lemon-flavored cake that had been brought in by an impeccable footman.

It was the easiest morning's work she'd ever had. Duke Street seemed far away, and she pushed the ever-present unease to the back of her mind. She was making money, and this afternoon she'd summon the doctor recommended by Mrs. Merriweather. Last night, she'd set aside her troubles with mischief. Today, she did it with warmth and comfort.

"YOU'VE HEARD A tedious amount about my relations this morning," Dev said, accepting a slice of cake. "It's your turn. Did you always live in Oxford? Isn't it unusual for a fellow of a college to be married?"

"My father moved into rooms at Oriel after my mother died giving birth to me. I lived in a small house nearby with my aunt, my mother's sister. Papa," she added hastily, "visited often."

"So I should hope." The morning had brought back memories of his own affectionate father. He wished he'd spent more time with him. He wished he'd been there when a cold took a turn for the worse. He should have done something.

As usual, he thrust aside the thought and considered the life of a little girl without a mother and an absent father. Pity made it hard to envision Oriel Sinclair as an unprincipled adventuress. "Were you lonely?"

"I had lessons with the sons of an acquaintance who kept a tutor. Later, I attended a school for young ladies." She gave her brightest smile, the one she used to sell a print.

"Did you enjoy that?"

"Not much. I was different from the other girls. I'd been given a boy's education, along with what my father taught me. He would bring books when he visited. We looked at them together."

"It doesn't sound like much fun."

"Don't you find pleasure in doing something with someone you are fond of?"

He'd enjoyed sorting paper with her that morning. Still, he had the impression from the way she spoke of her father that the choice of what to do had always been his. Looking at her now, he wondered how she had acquired her innate grace and purely feminine appeal.

"Mrs. Sinclair, I am going to be blunt."

"When are you not?"

"And honest."

"Hm," was her only comment on that, but not in a defiant way. Like him, she seemed to have put their differences aside, for the morning anyway.

"You are a beautiful woman."

Her hands flew to her cheeks. "Oh no!"

"Think of me as a scholar, a seeker of truth, looking for the answer to a mystery. How in the name of Jupiter did a woman of your upbringing become one of the most alluring females I've ever had the pleasure of meeting?"

"I wish you wouldn't say things like that."

"You must be used to all sorts of compliments from the men who patronize your shop." Like Frogmore.

"I find," she said, choosing her words carefully, "that happy gentlemen spend more money. I wish it weren't so, but I have a living to make."

"What does your father think? Does he know about this unusual approach to commerce?"

"My father is too ill to be worried, and it is not uncommon. Have you never been persuaded to open your purse to a pretty woman?"

He thought about the proprietor's wife in the little shop where he'd bought the singing bird, purely on a whim. Had he been influenced by her smiles? Not with any lascivious intent, but she'd seemed so happy that he liked the piece, so eager that he should take it home. "Sometimes," he said, "though I don't believe I ever buy anything I don't want."

"And I don't sell anything my customers don't want. I simply encourage them to make up their minds."

"You were charming to me when you sold me a gift for my grandmother, and showed me those French engravings."

"And did you buy anything you didn't wish to?"

"No," he admitted.

"But let us face it, Sir Devlyn. If there was any deception in that transaction, it was yours. You came with the sole purpose of investigating a lady your brother admires, because it doesn't suit you. You wasted a good deal of my time, and I earned the guinea you paid for that print."

It sounded reasonable. Still, there was Frogmore. More than willing to believe the man was harassing her, he couldn't forget that she'd greeted him with pleasure at the bookshop, left on his arm, and later had gone to the front door of his house. Not the action of an innocent tradeswoman.

He rose and stood close to her chair. "Tell me, what is between you and my brother? You have the right to do anything you wish, but Merrick's future is my concern." He desperately wanted the answer.

He leaned in so they were almost nose to nose and he could hear her heightened breathing. "Tell me."

She glared back. "I will not tolerate interference with my business, from you or anyone else. Stop bullying me."

He sprang back, shocked at himself. He would never intimidate a woman, be she duchess or maidservant. "I meant no threat."

"Didn't you?" Then, continuing more calmly, "I am not engaged to your brother."

A knot in his chest unraveled. "Has he offered for you?" From Merrick's account of his muddled proposal, she might be in doubt.

"Ask Merrick."

"Ask Merrick what?" His brother, damn him, came into the room. He shouldn't have been here for at least another hour.

Mrs. Sinclair proved quick on her feet. "Ask Merrick what he thinks of those drawings we looked at."

"What drawings? And what are you doing here, Oriel?"

"Didn't Sir Devlyn tell you that he asked me to come and look over the library?"

"Why didn't you tell me, Dev? Instead of sending me off on an errand that could have been done any time. Luckily, the ride to Soho took less time than I thought."

"Did you call on the Hendersons with my message?"

"I was too early. The ladies weren't down yet, and Mr. Henderson was out."

Damnation. Dev had intended to have Mrs. Sinclair safely out of the house by the time Merrick returned.

"Show me what you found, Oriel. Any masterpieces?"

She bestowed a dazzling smile on the young man, who looked suitably dazzled. Much more of this, and Hope didn't stand a chance. There was not a thing Dev could do as the pair of them started to look through the family drawings together.

"Look at this one of me," Merrick said. "Susan has no idea how to draw a cravat."

"Perhaps you weren't always so skilled at tying one. Your neckcloth is most elegant now."

Dev ground his teeth. If Merrick's linens looked halfway decent, it was because of hours that he, Devlyn, had spent teaching him. Had Mrs. Sinclair even noticed the intricate Mathematical he wore?

Worse was to come.

"I think this must be my father and Dev bringing in the Yule log, not that you'd know by the likenesses. Good thing Dev gave up drawing."

"Is this Sir Devlyn's work? He did not own up to it."

"Would you?" Merrick said with a distinct snigger. "See that little fly in the corner? He used to sign his things that way. Books and letters and such."

"It's a bee," Dev said through gritted teeth. He preferred to forget his youthful affectations. "It's Egyptian. I went through a period when I was very interested in Egypt."

"The bridge between our life and the underworld," said the scholar's daughter. "Was it a case of the road to hell being paved with good intentions?"

Merrick laughed again, and Dev felt one hundred years old and foolish with it. And jealous. His brother's mirth spoiled the kinship he'd enjoyed with Mrs. Sinclair over the library table.

"Look at this!" Merrick picked up one of Susan's portraits of a girl Dev hadn't been able to identify. "It's Hope."

"Are you sure?"

"Of course. She always wears that locket. By Jove, I'll have to show her. What a laugh."

Dev felt slightly better.

"Miss Henderson is much prettier now," Mrs. Sinclair remarked.

"I suppose. Not as pretty as you."

Dev felt worse.

Thankfully, the ghastly exhibition was brought to a close when she announced she had to leave. He managed to shake off Merrick and see her to his carriage. "Will you return tomorrow?"

"Is there anything else for me to do? Entertaining as it was to explore your family memorabilia—"

"Family rubbish, you mean."

"Never that, but the value is personal. You hardly need advice from me. I'll take five guineas for the morning."

"We agreed on ten, and I will pay you when the task is complete. There's another cupboard to go through."

"Two, actually."

"No need to look in the one on the left. I know what's in it. Please come." He was begging. He wanted more of her company, more of her, and this time he'd send Merrick to Scotland if necessary.

He offered his hand, which she accepted reluctantly. "Very well. Tomorrow."

Christmas had come early.

Chapter Six

~

O RIEL DID NOT return to Curzon Street the next day. She spent the morning with a secondhand-clothes dealer. Word of their woes had spread, and the supposedly superior doctor demanded payment in advance. Daring not wait until the precious ten guineas were collected from Sir Devlyn, she sacrificed her last evening gown. She didn't need it. The visit to the theater had been a rare treat, unlikely to be repeated.

She might as well have saved her blue muslin and the trouble. Arthur Markham took an instant and violent dislike to the new physician and drove him from the flat with a bowl of gruel to the head. The man took his indignant leave with a soiled coat, her money, and the assurance that there couldn't be much wrong with a man who could throw a dish with such accuracy.

Her father spent the rest of the day wheezing and coughing and unable to sleep. Oriel sold a couple of inexpensive prints to customers sent by Annabelle Merriweather and wrote to Lord Frogmore. In a calculated risk, she told Frogmore she had another customer interested in the French prints and he needed to give her an answer at once. She closed her eyes when she sealed the letter.

She had no other customer. Sir Devlyn wasn't a buyer. That was about the only thing about him she was sure. Knowing herself deeply drawn to him, she didn't trust her own judgment.

She suspected her attraction was returned. There had been a warmth about him when they'd worked and talked in the library. When he'd called her beautiful and alluring, he'd sent her heart tumbling.

She hadn't answered his question, hadn't explained that Aunt Sophia had taught her sister's child manners and deportment. When Oriel turned eighteen, Sophia had insisted her brother-in-law spare some money for gowns and taken Oriel to the staid Oxford public assemblies. She'd done it for her sister's sake since, like most others, she could not get on with Arthur Markham. As soon as Oriel married, Sophia had retired to Wales, where she lived with an elderly cousin. Oriel missed her, but would not ask her aunt, whose income was as small as hers, for help. She would not inflict her quarrelsome father on her again. Sometimes, she wondered why she put up with him herself. With his moods and extravagance, taking care of her sire was a duty paved with rough stone.

Instead of speaking more about her background and family, she'd behaved like Papa and picked a quarrel with Stratton. Instead of setting his mind at rest about his brother, she'd told him to mind his own business.

She had done so because, if she didn't keep him at arm's length, he might turn out to be like Frogmore, and she wouldn't be able to bear it. She wanted to believe he was a better man than that. She was also afraid that if Sir Devlyn Stratton set out to seduce her, he might very well succeed.

With a sigh, she ran next door and asked Charlie to deliver her letter to Frogmore.

AFTER A DAY of nursing her father, Oriel returned to Curzon Street. Dreading to see the master of the house, she was perversely put out to learn that he was out. He had left a message that she was to look at the contents of the second cupboard without him.

Which had he told her was the one? She knelt, opened one of the doors, and discovered a treasure trove: jewel boxes, luxurious shawls, and the copy of *Emma*, among other things. These must be Stratton's gifts for his family. If she needed further proof that he loved them dearly, the carefully chosen objects provided it. She was sure that all of them, like the book, had been selected by him personally. He projected an air of worldly carelessness, but when it came to his near relations, the man possessed a molten core.

Guilty at prying into a private side of him, she examined each item, envying the recipients. At the back of the cupboard, she found a small golden cage containing a richly bejeweled bird. Examining the delicate workmanship of the piece, she discovered a key and, with a nervous glance at the closed door, wound the mechanism. With a whirr, the bird flapped its wings and opened and closed its beak in time with music playing in the base of the cage. Her eyes pricked as she recognized the tune, an old French folk song that Aunt Sophia had taught her, saying it was a favorite of her mother's.

Who would receive this enchanting gift? His mother?

Or his mistress? She wondered if he, like many gentlemen, kept a lady in a discreet house. If so, she was a lucky woman.

To be receiving such a lovely gift. Not for any other reason.

Replacing the booty, she turned her attention to the other cupboard and found it stuffed to bursting with a mélange of paper similar to the contents of the first. She took a pile to the table, started to sort it, and hadn't got far when she was interrupted by the arrival of two ladies.

"Who have we here?" asked the younger, a poised middle-aged woman whom Oriel guessed, by her likeness to Merrick, to be his mother.

Oriel rose and curtseyed. "I am Mrs. Sinclair, looking over part of the collection in the library for Sir Devlyn."

The lady appraised her from her hair down to her sensible half boots. After an eon, she nodded with apparent approval. "How surprising. Has my son taken to scholarship? Maybe there's hope for him after all."

The other lady emitted a distinct snort. "I doubt it. In my day, ladybirds didn't come to a man's house under the guise of library work. Gentlemen kept them well out of the way, so we didn't know about them. Or so they thought."

"Margaret! Put on your spectacles. You are putting this poor young woman to the blush."

The old lady raised a gold lorgnette to her nose. "You look respectable enough, I suppose. Who are you?" This must be the grandmother who was about to be presented with two copies of "First Steps." Her family must know her tastes, but she didn't look like the kind who relished sentimentality, in art or literature. Oriel wouldn't be astonished to learn the elderly tartar read racy French novels in secret.

"She said she was Mrs. Sinclair. Are you becoming deaf as well as blind?"

"You know what I meant, Gussie. She must have come from somewhere. Sinclair's a Scottish name. You don't sound like a Scot."

"My late husband was Scottish. My father is a member of a Lincolnshire family."

"Hear that, Margaret? Only charming people come from Lincolnshire. As you may have guessed, I am Lady Stratton. And this is the Dowager Lady Stratton."

"I am honored to meet you, Lady Stratton and Lady Stratton. I understood that your journey to London was postponed."

"My daughter recovered from her cold, so we set off and here we are."

"Those girls never stop talking. I told them to stay in their rooms for at least an hour while Gussie and I came in here for a bit of peace and quiet." Oriel had never heard anyone harrumph, but the Dowager Lady Stratton had mastered the art.

"I can leave and come back another day," Oriel said.

"Oh no!" said the younger woman, Gussie. Augusta? Sir Devlyn's mother. "Here's tea. Splendid! There are three cups. Now let's sit by the fire. I want to hear all about you. Which part of Lincolnshire? What was your name? Do you know my family, the Devlyns?"

Overwhelmed by this energetic pair, who seemed on excellent terms despite their mutual sniping, Oriel gulped at her tea and explained that she'd visited Lincolnshire only once or twice as a child. "My father's name is Markham."

Gussie's family, it turned out, lived only fifteen miles away and knew the Markhams. "Let me see. Your father must be the odd younger brother who went to Oxford. Oh, I do beg your pardon."

"Don't worry, my lady. My father has been called far worse. I prefer to think of him as eccentric. He and his brother were not fond of each other."

"Oh dear! Families can be so difficult."

"I know some Markhams. Dreadful people," the dowager barked. "She was a Hungerford and a connection of mine. My great-niece's husband's cousin. I'm glad to say I don't see them often."

"My cousin William, who now owns the estate, rarely leaves the county."

"Good thing."

"And I," said Gussie, "shall make a point of calling on them next time I am in the county and tell them I met you."

"I'm sure they will be delighted." To be called on by a baronet's widow. Not to hear about Arthur Markham and his daughter. It was too soon to expect a reply to her letter, but Oriel wasn't expecting a welcoming response from a cousin she remembered only as an unpleasant little boy.

After a thorough discussion of various Lincolnshire families, to which Oriel could contribute nothing, Gussie asked about her work in the library. Oriel explained about Markham's Print Gallery and Sir Devlyn's commission. She did not explain how they had met or mention Merrick.

"My late husband, Sir George, never threw anything away. His library here and his book room in Sussex were both festooned with papers and so forth. I suppose after his death all of it was thrust into the cupboards and forgotten. I certainly haven't felt able to look at it."

"Devlyn should have seen to it," the dowager said. "The boy does nothing but racket about town in unsuitable company. Time he saw to his responsibilities."

Gussie leaped to the defense of her son. "He is attentive to the estate and the younger children."

"You spoiled the boy and always did. He'll never be the man his grandfather was. Thrown at a fence during a hunt and never said a word about it until he dropped dead. Walked and talked perfectly normally through dinner. These young men nowadays think of nothing but their mistresses and the cut of their coats."

"Merrick does not."

"Merrick's a good boy. Not too bright in the head, but sensible enough to find himself a nice little heiress. That older son of yours needs to settle down, Gussie."

Sure that they'd forgotten her presence, Oriel listened to the intimate discussion. Nothing would have persuaded her to interrupt the fascinating look at Stratton family life.

Sir Devlyn's mother looked a little worried. "I thought he would after George died. You expect a young man to be a little wild. I'm sure he will settle down now."

"You're talking nonsense as usual. The boy's halfway to becoming a rake, and so I have told him more than once."

"And what does he say to that?"

"Tells me I'm a fussy old stickler and should mind my own business."

Her daughter-in-law laughed. "I do beg your pardon, Mrs. Sinclair. This must be very dull for you. Tell me about your father."

Gussie gave her such a warm smile that Oriel found herself confiding some of her worries, not about money, but about Arthur Markham's health. Sympathetic female company was sorely lacking in her life. She chatted with Annabelle Merriweather about the bookstore's stock and customers, and Mrs. Merriweather was always kind, but busy with her own family and business. The two Lady Strattons, sugar and vinegar, were interested in Mr. Markham's disease. Sir George Stratton had also suffered from weak lungs.

"It's so difficult to find a good doctor," Gussie said.

"They are all quacks," the dowager retorted, and recommended a list of home remedies, a couple of which sounded worth trying. "But country air is what he needs. Only those in the best of health can survive London."

CURSING THE ENDLESS and tedious matter that had taken him to his solicitor's chambers, Dev hurried home and hoped Mrs. Sinclair was still in the house. He was not happy to hear of the arrival of his female relations. He dashed into the library, praying to find it empty. Alas, a footman was removing the remains of tea for three, and Oriel Sinclair sat at the library table, leafing through a new pile of paper. Had she affected the vulgarity she'd used to tease him at the theater? If so, he could expect an earful from the dowager about allowing his mistress to visit the house under the pretext of scholarly inquiry.

Sadly, there was no such relationship.

"You were here when the ladies arrived."

She looked up with the arch smile that had almost slain him at their first meeting. "I had tea with your mother and grandmother. Look at this."

He didn't want to look at anything, except her. He also wanted to know what she'd said in his absence. "Did my grandmother terrify you?"

"I found her most entertaining. And your mother is charming. This is a family tree your father drew. The Strattons seem to produce an enormous number of females."

"We are so blessed."

"You like ladies, don't you?"

He tried not to let his tension show. "What have they been saying to you?"

"I don't think I should tell you."

He wrenched out a smile. "That bad?"

"Don't worry. I behaved myself. Do you want to see what I found today?"

He took a seat beside her, but the last thing on his mind when Oriel was so close was his father's rubbish. He heard her describe an old etching that had some value, but all he heard was the music in her voice. All he saw was her slender fingers caressing the old paper and lines of ink. A warm, indefinable scent bathed his senses.

"Where do you think your father might have acquired this? I'd have to ask my father, but I am fairly sure it's a Dürer."

He didn't care. He didn't want to think about his father, or hers. He didn't want to be in this room, or in this house, infested as it was by female relations who could come in at any moment. He wanted to be alone with Oriel in his house in Park Lane, in the big soft bed, and bury himself in her enchantment. Then he wanted to take her shopping, shower her with jewels and the products of the best modistes. She was much too fine for the grubby life of a shopkeeper. Much too good for a boy like Merrick.

"You're not paying attention." She turned to look at him in quizzical exasperation, her elbow on the table and cheek resting on her hand.

Gazing at her oval face, he saw her eyes grow large and languid and impossibly green. Her mouth parted, but nothing emerged. He touched her flushed cheek, a slow, light brush of the fingers, exploring the texture. Soft. Smooth. Alive.

"Oriel," he whispered. "I've wanted to kiss you since the first moment I saw you."

She shook her head almost imperceptibly.

"Please." Was that a nod? "Yes?"

"Yes." So low he hardly heard it.

He waited, savoring the silken skin, the soft hair beneath his hands. His forefinger traced the slope of her nose and the plump, damask lips. A tenderness he didn't care to examine invaded his heart as she stared at him without guile or reserve. Reverently, he brought his mouth to hers and rejoiced at her instant response.

Thought fled his brain and left only feeling. "So sweet," he murmured during a brief respite from a fervid kiss. Her hands clasped his skull and her body nestled into his chest. He drew her in with questing hands, encircling her shapely waist, wanting to be ever closer, not letting a trace of air divide them. There was a rightness to Oriel in his arms, and he never wanted to let her go.

A firm hand thrust him away.

"No."

He tried to pull her back, but she slid from her chair and stood, rumpled, flushed, panting a little.

"Merrick," she gasped.

One word, and his brain lurched back into use.

"I can offer you more. Much more. Please." He was begging, desperate, not even sure what he said.

"I don't want what you have to offer," she said deliberately.

His jaw hardened. "Marriage, you mean. You still think you can entrap that boy. And what will you do with him after you have ruined his life?"

Her hands fluttered to smooth her hair and her skirts. "I don't wish to discuss the matter. I must leave now. My father expects me," she said, her face pinched and closed off.

"An ever convenient excuse. I beg leave to doubt the existence of the gentleman. What were you doing yesterday when you had promised to come here?"

"I cannot spare any more time here. I have other responsibilities, other customers too."

Frogmore! He embraced the fury kindling in his chest. He'd been weak, exposed himself to her, and been rejected. "I'll call the carriage," he said curtly.

"I prefer to walk. The air will do me good."

Not even angry would he allow her to go alone, but sent one of his footmen to accompany her through the cold streets. Then he returned to the library and stared unseeing at his father's detritus. What the hell was he going to do about Merrick? Short of killing the boy.

Frogmore too.

"My dear Devlyn."

While he contemplated mass homicide, he'd add his mother to the list.

She embraced him affectionately, patted his cheek, and told him he looked tired. He drew back hastily, not in the mood for maternal caresses.

"Did Mrs. Sinclair leave? I suppose she had to get back to her poor father."

Oriel must have filled his mother's ears with the sad tribulations of a man who might very well be a product of the lady's imagination.

"I have reason to believe she is something of an adventuress. Merrick has a mad idea in his head that he'd like to marry her."

"Merrick? Oh no. I can't believe that. They are quite ill-suited. If Merrick has cold feet about proposing to Hope, it's only to be expected. He'll be quite all right by Christmas." She peered sharply at Dev. "Have you done something foolish?"

"Just trying to protect my brother."

"Unnecessary. Mrs. Sinclair's a lovely woman, of course. More to your taste than Merrick's, I would have said."

"Well, you would be wrong."

"Whatever you say, my dear. I like her very much. We had a lovely talk about her family. She's a Markham of Lincolnshire, you know."

"I doubt it. She *claims* she grew up in Oxford."

"Family trouble. What a pity she has to keep a shop, but some things can't be helped. It's delightful to be here, Devlyn. We're going to have such a happy Christmas." And off she went, twittering about greenery and plum pudding when all he wanted to do was sit down and bang his head on the table.

Chapter Seven

~

JUST BECAUSE SHE came from a good family, or the margins of one, didn't mean that Oriel Sinclair wasn't an adventuress. If innocent, why was she still pursuing Merrick?

At least she hadn't claimed to love him. Faugh!

She didn't return to Curzon Street, telling him in a note that she'd done little to earn the unaccountably trivial sum of ten guineas. Merrick, meanwhile, was made to accompany the ladies on expeditions all over town, often in company with Hope Henderson. His mother, thank God, was keeping him away from Oriel and giving him a chance to remember why he'd wanted to marry Hope in the first place.

Paradoxically, Dev was furious at his brother. If Merrick wanted Oriel, he should be a man and go after her. That's what Dev would do in his position.

Except he hadn't, idiot that he was. Feeling better than he had since Oriel had walked out of his house, he set off for Duke Street and found Markham's Print Gallery locked. Rapping hard on the door brought no response. Glancing upward, he saw a figure looking out the upstairs window. Oriel. Avoiding him.

Instead of going home and forgetting the whole matter like a sensible man, he went into the bookshop next door. Refusing an offer of help from Miss Merriweather, he selected a book at random and took it to the window, pretending to examine the first volume of *The Mad Monk of Mongolia* in minute detail and keeping an eye on the street and half an ear on the chatter in the shop.

The sleepy gentleman, now wide awake, flipped through volumes at such speed he couldn't possibly be interested in their contents. More taken by the pretty widow, who had also returned. Since she kept sneaking glances back, it shouldn't be long before those two struck up a conversation. There must be magic in this little shop that encouraged meetings of a romantic nature. Little wonder it was popular with spinsters.

Dev checked the window again—nothing—and heard the man apologize to another customer in a foreign accent. He reminded Dev of the Duchess of Wyndover, who was some kind of princess.

Miss Merriweather and her red-haired friend sat at the counter, writing something and laughing a great deal. "You can't say *passion*," one of them said, provoking giggles and some furious scratching with a pen. Dev looked back outside.

After half an hour of curious looks from the ladies, he felt like a bull in a hen coop and wondered if he was mad to spy on a lady who didn't care for him.

Persistence. He should try again and see if Oriel's attitude had softened.

A lavish private carriage with a gold crest on the door blocked his view of the street. A footman let down the steps, and the loathsome figure of Frogmore lumbered out and went to the door of Markham's. After a few minutes, the coachman must have received a signal from his master and whipped up his horses. Frogmore, unlike Dev, had been admitted.

A bad morning got worse when his sisters, of all people, burst through the door in noisy high spirits, along with Hope Henderson and Merrick.

"Have you become a spinster, Dev?" Susan asked. "We wouldn't dare come in here in case we are doomed to be old maids, but we hear it has the best novels. What are you reading?" She shrieked. "Look, Emma. Dev's reading *The Mad Monk of Mongolia.*"

"Very good it is too," Dev said.

"I haven't read it," Emma said. "But I want to."

Merrick wore a titanic grin and whispered something to Hope, who giggled.

"I have decided to buy it," Dev said with all the dignity he could muster. "I will lend it to you when I've finished. Excuse me. I have an appointment."

He was never going to hear the last of it and had a good mind to leave the damn book out in the rain and foil Emma. He coughed a couple of times to distract Miss Merriweather and her friend from their literary composition at the counter, handed over fifteen shillings for all three blasted volumes of the wretched book, and decamped in a panic, carrying, damn it, a parcel.

Frogmore could have left while he'd suffered sisterly persecution, and Oriel could have gone with him. Thick sleet descended on his shoulders—and the package—as he stared at the front door of Markham's.

ORIEL WAS UPSTAIRS when Devlyn knocked, trying to persuade her father to accept a mustard plaster to his congested chest. Those ten guineas, carelessly thrown away, had never been needed more. Not carelessly. Regretfully, but with agonized consideration. She dared not return to Devlyn's house. When he'd kissed her, she'd almost given in.

I can offer you more. Much more.

How much she wanted to accept frightened her. Gossip had taught her something of the perquisites of a kept mistress: a house, servants, jewelry, money. Frogmore would offer her those, but with Devlyn, there would be more: him. To protect herself from the impulse to accept, she'd brought up the subject of Merrick, who was laughably unimportant to her, and run away to her empty shop, her cold flat, her unpaid bills, and her querulous father. She wasn't sure how long she could last without selling her only remaining asset: herself.

Another knock. Why wouldn't the man leave her alone? She looked out of the window for the indulgence of a glimpse of that splendid figure, and her stomach roiled with excitement and repulsion.

Frogmore had come at last.

She removed her apron and trailed her feet downstairs. His lordship stood in the doorway like a giant poisonous toad, wearing a smug expression that put her instantly on guard.

"My lord."

"Well, let me in. It's cold and wet. And in here too," he said with disfavor. She hadn't paid the coal bill. "Never mind, Oriel. I'll keep my coat on."

The purple wool garment, lavishly frogged with gold braid, had several capes that made him seem larger than ever. He filled the small space, more so than Sir Devlyn had, because his presence came with an air of menace.

"When I didn't hear from you, I assumed you were no longer interested in the prints. Luckily for you, the other party has yet to make up his mind. As you're a favored customer, I'd prefer you to have them." She held her breath, waiting to see if her gamble had won.

Frogmore squeezed himself around the print cabinet. "I am happy to hear that I am favored. I will buy the prints at your price and more. As long as we can come to terms in all our affairs, I shall be very generous."

"I can't imagine what you mean, my lord. It seems a straightforward transaction to me. I have something to sell, you wish to buy." She retreated, and he kept on coming.

"Let us not start our happy partnership on such a harsh note. I don't think I need to spell out what I intend. And my first gift to you will be this." He removed his gloves and set them down, then thrust his meaty hand into his pocket and removed a paper, which he unfolded and, keeping a firm grip on the parchment, held it up to her face.

The mortgage. She'd always had a bad feeling about that banker, but no one else would lend them money against the shop. She didn't ask how Frogmore knew about it. All these days waiting for an answer, and he'd no doubt had her investigated and found her creditor, who would be only too happy to sell off a risky debt for ready money.

Slapping his face would have been her preferred response, but she'd save that until all other paths had been explored. "I'm sure we can come to an agreement. Let me fetch some wine, and we can discuss repayment."

"I won't stay in the cold," he said shortly. "A celebration will certainly be in order, but in a charming house in Covent Garden that is furnished and staffed and ready for you."

Just like Sir Devlyn Stratton, she thought bitterly. Rich men with no morals and money to burn.

It wasn't hard to appear shocked. "I am a lady, sir. I also support my father, who is too sick to look after himself."

Evidently he hadn't considered Mr. Markham, even though he had met him a couple of times. He waved a hand as though swatting a fly. "Your allowance will be ample to keep him in modest rooms with a servant."

"He needs country air. You can have the prints. The value is enough to pay the overdue interest on the mortgage, and more."

"Oriel, my dear. I did hope it wouldn't come to this, but I fear I shall have to speak crudely."

"You haven't so far?"

"I am offering you a home. The alternative is to lose the one you have. You have defaulted on your obligation, and I intend to foreclose."

"Do you want a mistress who hates you?"

"I am confident that any slight resentment will fade as you accommodate my desires. You have no choice." Frogmore neither knew nor cared about anyone else's feelings. Physical repulsion aside, life as his mistress would be more like indentured servitude than "protection."

She should have let Sir Devlyn in earlier. Whether he'd come to berate her about his brother, or to offer his own dastardly arrangement, anything would have been better than this. "I need time to consider," she said.

"You have been playing me like a fish, enticing me with come-hither glances out of those fine green eyes and then retreating. I know you were with Stratton when you came to my house and refused to come in. Don't believe for a minute that you weren't seen in his box at the theater. I know your game. You hope to catch a younger fish, perhaps entice him into marriage, which I cannot offer. Stratton won't either, and since you are still in this shop arguing with me, you haven't coaxed the other kind of offer from him either. You want time to lure him, and I won't give it. Say yes now, or I go to court tomorrow."

Oriel had never been entirely without hope. Always she had a plan, an iron in the fire. She'd plotted and contrived and somehow managed. Now she could see no way forward, other than debtors' prison. Even if she and her father threw themselves on the mercy of Aunt Sophia, or one of the other relations with whom Arthur Markham was no longer on speaking terms, their debts remained. Sneaking out of town and trying to escape her obligations ran contrary to every precept of honesty. Turning her back on Frogmore, she gulped in great breaths and told herself that she would not cry. She disdained to show her desperation. Was there a different card she could play with the monster?

A heavy hand on her shoulder set off a wave of revulsion. "Don't cry, my dear," Frogmore said in tones that were probably meant to be comforting. "Soon this unpleasantness will be over, and we'll never think of it again. Turn around and give me a kiss."

She was turned and grasped in an elephantine embrace. Her gorge rose at his sweet violet scent. Before she could even begin to struggle, a fleshy face came down to hers, and a wet mouth covered her lips.

A guttural protest was all she could voice, and kicks had little effect against Hessian boots. There wasn't room for her to raise her knee and hit him where it would hurt.

She heard the door open and wrenched away, but couldn't escape Frogmore's iron hold, until a male voice spoke.

"Apparently, I have interrupted something."

Free to move, she dodged sideways. Sir Devlyn Stratton stood in the doorway, looking furious. Or merely disgusted.

"Not at all," she said, desperate for him to stay. "Lord Frogmore was just leaving."

"I'll wait while you take care of *business* with Stratton." Frogmore's face had turned a repellent shade of puce veined in red.

Oriel smoothed her skirt with trembling hands. "I'm afraid we may be some time. Sir Devlyn is interested in the prints you decided not to buy." *Please don't leave.*

"Certainly, I am. There are a good many of them, and I wish to examine them in great detail. Let us not keep you, Frogmore."

Confronted by a man who was younger, taller, and clenching his fists, Frogmore surrendered. "My carriage! I cannot stand outside in the snow."

Devlyn smiled and produced a coin from his pocket. "The crossing sweeper at the corner of Jermyn Street will summon your coachman for a small consideration."

Frogmore blustered, and Devlyn flexed his arms.

"I'll return to conclude our discussion tomorrow," the earl said, and shoved his way out, first snatching up the mortgage from the table.

Too humiliated to speak, Oriel busied herself rearranging a perfectly neat pile of prints. She wished Stratton would go away and leave her to her misery. The last thing she needed was another lustful male on her hands.

"Are you quite all right, Mrs. Sinclair?" he said gently. "It seemed to me that you were pleased to be interrupted. Did Frogmore force himself on you?" The kindness threatened her tenuous dignity. "If so"—his voice hardened—"I will take great pleasure in teaching him a lesson in how to treat women."

"Please," she said on a barely suppressed sob. "Leave me alone."

"You are unwell. Come, let me see you upstairs and make you comfortable."

"Impossible," she spat. "You are the last person who can make me at ease."

"This is the way, yes?" He seized her hand, and she followed him, willy-nilly up to the flat.

The small sitting room on the floor above completed her shame. Loose papers and unmended clothes lay scattered, and the few square inches of furniture open to sight were dusty, as were the windows. She'd been too busy nursing her father to tidy up, too frazzled to supervise the maid, Mary, who had no idea what to do without specific instructions.

Her dirty breakfast cup sitting next to the revolting mixture of mustard that her father had disdained was the final straw that broke her composure. Collapsing into a chair, she hid her face in her arms and sobbed. Despair came in noisy, wet gulps. She cried out her misery at everything that was wrong, because she had no idea how to solve anything, and because the man she had stupidly fallen in love with had witnessed her every mortification. If only a lightning bolt would descend and strike her dead.

Lost in anguish, she was vaguely aware of a firm hand rubbing her back. Little by little, the silent comfort soothed her, and she collected herself, at least physically. Blowing her nose hard—could there be anything less elegant?—she sat up and folded her hands in her lap, her throat tight. Not that it mattered. She had nothing to say.

"You need something to drink," he said. "Tea or wine. Do you have a servant?"

"I gave her the day off to visit her family," she said dully.

He found the half empty bottle of Madeira, a remnant of evenings before her father took ill, on the shelf of the corner cupboard. "Drink this," he said.

The wine made her feel a little better. Warmer but still numb.

Devlyn pulled up a chair next to her, just as he had in his library, and almost set off a new bout of weeping, which she suppressed with a sniff. "I think you'd better tell me all about it," he said.

Kindness demolished the last bastion of discretion and reserve. Out it poured, her fears for her father, her money troubles, the scarcity of paying customers apart from Frogmore, even the mortgage. Contrary to pride, not to mention all the rules about sharing information about personal business with relative strangers, she kept nothing back. Except her feelings for the man who listened without interruption to her sad tale.

"So you see," she concluded, "I've made an utter mess of everything. I should never have come to London."

"I am glad you did." He didn't look glad. His grave face surely expressed nothing but a desire to leave such a pathetic, troublesome creature as soon as possible.

"I don't know why. All I've caused you is annoyance."

"Untrue. You uncovered what may be a rare Dürer engraving."

"I'm probably wrong, and it's nothing of the kind."

"Disparaging your own advice, Mrs. Sinclair? That won't do."

Her eyes prickled at his teasing, the hint of that dimple. She blinked hard and managed a broad, false smile. He deserved the truth about Merrick.

"I may as well tell you—"

A loud thump from the chamber upstairs interrupted her. "Oriel!" Arthur Markham's irate voice dissolved into a wild coughing attack.

"I must see to my father. Thank you, Sir Devlyn, for listening to me. I won't keep you." It would be better if he left at once, before she threw herself onto his chest and begged him to take her as his mistress.

"Or-iel!"

"Excuse me. Good-bye, sir."

And drat the man if he didn't follow her up another flight of creaky stairs and into the sickroom where her father lay, wispy gray hair lank and unkempt, coughs racking his desiccated body, specks of spittle staining his nightgown. "Oh heavens, Papa." She snatched up the spittoon and a cloth to wipe his face.

"Who are you?" Arthur Markham could manage belligerence even in the midst of a coughing attack. "Leave my daughter alone, or you'll face me."

His sudden protectiveness and ridiculous threat made her want to laugh and cry at the same time.

"Sir Devlyn Stratton, sir. Your daughter has been helpful to me on some family business, and I happened to be here when you called her."

"Stratton. She says you may have a Dürer. Probably wrong—"

Another bout of coughing cut off his opinion of Oriel's expertise.

"When you are better, you may see it yourself." He turned to Oriel. "He needs a doctor. Whom shall I send for?"

"There's no point. Dr. Johnson does nothing to help, and Papa took the greatest dislike to another doctor."

"I'll see to it. Don't worry about anything."

Her protest died on her lips. Sir Devlyn Stratton would certainly be able to command the best physician in London. As for the bill, what was one more debt if she ended up in prison?

"Anything, you understand? I will take care of you."

"I don't need another quack," her father yelled. "And get that fellow out of here!"

On the way downstairs, she tried to apologize for his behavior. "He can be difficult, but I don't want him to die." Her lips trembled.

"Of course you don't. And I will not let him. I know the very man you need, and I'll send for him now."

His broad shoulders offered a refuge she longed to cling to. She wanted to send Charlie for the miracle-working physician and beg him to stay. But he pulled on his gloves, his eyes distant as though already somewhere else. Who could blame him for being anxious to depart after the scene she'd inflicted on him?

I will take care of you. Was that the same as *I can offer you more*? Had she agreed to accept his protection after refusing Frogmore's? Did he even want her? She was an awful lot of trouble. Utterly forlorn, she let him out into the street and returned to cope with her father.

An hour later, the famous and wonderfully efficient Sir William Knighton arrived, accompanied by a middle-aged woman who bustled around, cleaning and tidying, while the doctor examined Oriel's father. By some miracle of bedside skill—Arthur Markham was unimpressed by titles—the doctor had the patient submitting to his prescriptions with a protest so subdued that, in her father's case, it passed for passive acceptance.

"He should be easier now," the doctor said. "My nurse will see to him. Give him lots of water and another dose of my powders this evening. I'll return tomorrow."

"Sir William, your account—" Oriel wondered how much a knighthood added to a medical bill.

"Sir Devlyn has seen to the matter. His mother asked him to do so since you are related to her."

He'd claimed her as a kinswoman, as an excuse for covering the doctor's bill without raising awkward questions. This thoughtfulness, almost more than anything else he'd done, turned her insides to porridge. Whatever was in Devlyn's mind, whatever he would ask in return, Oriel didn't care. She could refuse him nothing.

AFTER TAKING CARE of some business at Brooks's club, Dev returned home and went straight to the library. He whipped through his neglected correspondence, wrote a long letter to his steward in Sussex, then asked a footman to have his mother join him. Lady Stratton, he was informed, was out with her daughters. Instead, he was blessed with the appearance of his grandmother.

"Doing something useful for a change," she said, eyeing the neat pile of letters ready for the post.

"I decided it was time. I would like your advice, Grandmama."

"Has the world come to an end?"

"I was going to ask Mama if she would mind me clearing out Father's papers and such from the library. Would it upset her? I want to respect her grief."

"Gussie's no wilting violet. Make sure you offer her the chance to see if there's anything she wishes to keep."

"Another thing. I would like to move into his rooms here and in the country."

"Why should she object? I can tell you that when your grandfather died, I expected that George and Gussie would take their places at the head of the family without any nonsense about my grief."

"I didn't like to ask because she was distraught."

His grandmother regarded him through her lorgnette, in the way she had of making him feel ten years old. "Is that the reason? In my opinion, since you ask, it's not Gussie's grief that's kept you in London playing the rake when you should have been attending to your responsibilities."

Dev thought he might choke. "I met a man today, sick in his lungs. Just like Father."

"Will he live?"

"I don't know. I hope so."

"That's all you can do, hope and doctors, and Lord knows they don't know much. And prayer. I'd wager, if I were in the habit of doing anything so immoral, that you never go to church in London. Do you good to listen to a sermon or two."

"I'll bear that in mind, but why do I need a parson when I have you to keep my morals in order?"

"And a very poor job I do of it. What was that young woman doing here? I haven't seen her lately."

"If you imply anything untoward between Mrs. Sinclair and myself, please do not. She is a lady of high respectability."

While Oriel might not always conduct herself as his grandmother would approve, he'd never confess it. As far as he was concerned, her straits excused everything, even her consideration of Merrick's offer. Worse, now that he knew about Frogmore's foul demands, he was ashamed. Though he'd never stoop to extortion to win a woman, the fact was, he wasn't much better. She'd stopped him before he made his offer in detail, but it would have been very similar to Frogmore's. He resolved to do what he could for her and leave her alone.

His blood urged him to rush around to Duke Street and ask after Mr. Markham. And Oriel. Instead, he sent a footman to inquire.

Good behavior might be balm to the soul. It was damn frustrating for the heart.

Chapter Eight

〜

December 23rd

Dear Sir Devlyn,

As you know, since your footman has inquired daily, my father is very much better. Bless you for sending Sir William Knighton to us. I am sure his account is far more than I may have earned in your library, but I accept with gratitude. Also your generous gift of a hamper of food from Fortnum & Mason. My father has always held that we should shop there, and I do believe that the sight of their largesse has capped the improvement wrought by the efforts of the doctor and nurse. His enjoyment of ham and fresh country butter for this morning's breakfast was nothing to mine at seeing him with a good appetite and in good cheer. He was even well enough to dictate a long and, I am afraid, impolite letter to one of his former colleagues at Oriel College, refuting every point in a recent article. Thank you from the bottom of my heart.

What I cannot accept, though do not doubt my gratitude for the offer, is the mortgage. It must have cost you a good deal to acquire it from Lord Frogmore (whom I have not seen since that day and am all the better for his absence). You must and shall be paid, and I ask only that you give me time to get my affairs in order.

My cousin Mr. Markham has offered us a small house on his estate. Once I dispose of our London property and the contents of the Gallery, I shall make all good. With care, we will be able to live on the interest on our investments in the funds.

Sir William says that my father is well enough to travel as long as we make the journey slowly. As soon as the weather improves, we shall set out for Lincolnshire, where clean country air will make my father's recovery complete.

There is no way I can express my feelings for your kindness, so I will not make the attempt. I wish you the greatest happiness, for you deserve it. Also your brother. I must confess that I never took his attentions seriously but pretended, only to annoy you. I am ashamed of my abominable behavior at the theater. You did not deserve it.

Dev stopped reading. Of course he'd deserved it. Against every instinct, he had persisted in believing Oriel an unprincipled adventuress, and he knew why. It had given him an excuse to pursue her himself.

> *As I write, the snow is falling on Duke Street, rendering London clean and new. It reminds me of one Christmas in Oxford with Aunt Sophia when my father surprised us with a drive on Port Meadow in a sleigh drawn by two beautiful white horses.*
>
> *May the season be joyful for you and for all your family.*

Your most respectful servant,
Oriel Sinclair.

P.S. Ask Merrick what he bought your grandmother for Christmas.

Dev had never felt less Christmas spirit, even last year with the family in mourning for his father. The scent of spices wafted up from the kitchen floor, penetrating even to the library. The ladies of the family ran around muttering mysteriously or, in the case of his sisters, giggling. He had a cupboard filled with gifts, and normally he'd be keen with anticipation at their reception. He couldn't even muster an interest in Merrick's present for the dowager. He had little interest in his brother at all. He supposed he should worry that the boy was heartbroken, but he doubted it. The Hendersons were still expected for Christmas dinner, and after his conversation with his mother, he'd left the whole question of Merrick's marriage to her to manage. Lord knows he'd made a hash of it. For the first time in his life he had no interest in the delights London had to offer, even the female ones. Especially those. Only one woman interested him now, and he could not have her.

Oriel was leaving, and life seemed impossibly dreary. Occasionally looking out at the thickly falling snow, he dutifully dealt with his correspondence.

CHRISTMAS EVE, AND not even fresh snow on the ground could lift Oriel's spirits. In the shop she worked on a list of prints to be sent to auction, while her father read in the sitting room. Almost restored to health, he'd resumed his usual solitary pursuits. She wondered what life would be like in Lincolnshire and hoped she would find agreeable company. Country life, she feared, might be dull. Perhaps Lady Stratton would call when visiting her relations. Maybe she'd bring her elder son.

She snapped her mind shut against the fantasy that there could ever be anything between them. His failure to call in person was all she needed to know.

She was glad to be leaving London. Glad. Why, yesterday someone had thrown rocks through the window of On the Shelf. If they weren't safe in St. James's, where would they be? Much better to live in rural fastness where nothing like that would ever occur. Nothing like that and nothing else.

No one would make her an indecent proposal, but that wasn't happening in London either. Since he'd left her to fetch the doctor, she hadn't set eyes on Devlyn. She was indeed far too much trouble.

While taking inventory, she found a brown paper parcel, hastily wrapped. With nothing to indicate its ownership or contents, she opened it and found three volumes bound in plain boards. How on earth had *The Mad Monk of Mongolia* arrived in her shop? She could only conclude that Devlyn had brought it when he interrupted her with Frogmore. Another gift for Emma to be presented in the absence of the dowager? She smiled for the first time in days. The book must be returned to him.

Cataloging the French prints gave her an idea. Most of them must be sold to clear their debts, but she could spare one or two. He'd thought them beautiful. He had said she was beautiful, but he didn't want her. If she couldn't have him, at least she could make him a farewell gift.

Tickling her nose with the quill of her pen, she leafed through them, remembering that afternoon with Devlyn and guessing which he had liked best. Not the one of the woman in bed, though doubtless he'd enjoy it. The gift was to mark her gratitude, not issue an invitation. She had more pride than that.

The Stratton footman arrived with his daily inquiry after Mr. Markham's health, but this time he delivered a note and said he would wait. Her composure all to pieces, she tore off the seal.

The coach is waiting for you. Please come. I have a surprise. DS

"I'm going out," she told her father, who barely looked up from his book.

The coach slithered through the streets to Hyde Park, stopping at the Chesterfield Gate. Why here? Descending from the carriage, she beheld a dark green sleigh harnessed to a pair of horses and, best of all, Devlyn wearing a devastating smile. Lord, she'd missed the sight of him.

"Your sleigh awaits, my lady," he said.

She shook her head in wonder. "How did you find it?"

"Not without difficulty. I'm sorry it isn't painted gold and festooned with ribbons and bells, but beggars can't be choosers. I also apologize for the dull chestnut of this pair, but there were no white horses to be had at short notice."

She almost jumped up and down with glee. "I don't care if they are donkeys. This is the most wonderful Christmas gift ever."

He helped her onto the leather bench and climbed in next to her, covering their knees with a fur blanket. It was a snug fit, his body against hers ensuring that she wouldn't feel the cold. The sun sat low in the icy blue sky, catching the pristine snow of the great park in a million sparkles. She laughed in sheer delight.

A few children were throwing snowballs, but the sleigh soon left them behind. They glided over the snow, the horses at an easy canter. She took in great breaths as the wind whipped her cheeks. The snow seemed to have blown away the pervasive coal dust of the capital. As they gathered speed, she clutched his arm with both hers and shrieked like the girl she had once been, more carefree than she'd been in years.

At the far end of the Serpentine, Devlyn drew the horses to a stand. "Nothing like a sleigh, is there?" His broad smile reflected her glee. Her fingers itched to trace his slanting brows, touch his generous mouth.

"We could be in the country."

"I wanted to leave you with a good memory of London. And of me."

That was that, then. She had his kindness, but not his love. He was leaving her. No, she was the one leaving, but he hadn't asked her to stay. Joy seeped out of her like water from a cracked bucket. A hot tear rolled down her cold cheek.

"What is it?" He wiped away the moisture with his thumb. "What has distressed you?"

"Nothing. I am crying because I am happy."

She looked at him through wet eyes and met his brown ones, warm and concerned, then gathering heat. She might never breathe again. In the middle of the vast city, they were alone on a white ocean, just she and Devlyn. She did not know if he initiated the kiss, or she did, or if they had the same idea at the same instant. His lips were cold and his mouth hot, taking her deep and long and so sweetly. She pulled him closer and met him more than halfway in a tangle of breath and tongue. She put all her love into this union of mouths, and passion arose, and thought fell away, leaving only a burning need she had never known.

She would have spent all day, all year, thus, but the horses wouldn't allow it. The sleigh lurched, and he let her go to quiet them. She leaned back on the bench, bereft, her breast heaving. Was this all there was to be?

Having settled the horses, he turned to her. Laughter and desire turned to dismay. "I beg your pardon, Oriel. I didn't mean that to happen. All I wanted was to give you an hour of joy."

As though she had not found joy in his embrace. "Don't you think I wanted to kiss you?"

He shook his head, intent on his own train of thought. "I have done nothing but insult you since we met, leaping to conclusions and treating you without respect. I am little better than Frogmore."

"That is too absurd to answer, after all you have done for me."

"I don't want your gratitude."

"Nonetheless, you have it. I do wonder how you persuaded him to sell you my mortgage."

"I won it at cards."

"He wagered it? Well, really! I suppose that shows my value to him."

The dimple appeared. "I had a devil of a time maneuvering him into the stake."

"Tell me."

"It's a little embarrassing to admit that I made him think my plan was the same as his. That your virtue was so impregnable I needed the mortgage to lure you to my bed. The notion tickled him. I'd have rather taken him by the throat and made him eat the document, but we were in our club, and it would have caused difficulties."

She chuckled. "So I can imagine."

"So instead—and believe me, I didn't enjoy it—we shared a bottle of brandy. When he was drunk enough, I proposed we settle our contest with a pack of cards. The man's self-esteem is monumental. My only satisfaction was his expression of chagrin when I won. The mortgage cost me nothing, so there is nothing to repay. Burn the thing."

Because she could, she put her arms around him and leaned against his chest. "I wish I had seen his face."

"Vengeful girl."

"I can never thank you enough."

"Regard it as a small token of my repentance for wishing to seduce you."

What was the matter with the man? Here she was, hugging him without so much as a squeeze in return. Clearly a hint wasn't enough.

"Did you wish to seduce me?"

"Remove that wicked smile. You know I did."

"I wasn't entirely sure. Were you going to set me up in a nice house in Covent Garden?"

"Certainly not. Do you take me for a nipcheese? Park Lane was where I planned to take you. Only the best for my mistresses, and very convenient for Curzon Street."

Thankfully, he had stopped talking about repentance and respect and gratitude, not to mention impregnable virtue. Her virtue was distinctly pregnable, if there was such a word. "Do you own such a house?"

"We shouldn't be talking about these arrangements."

"The house must be very near. May we go there now?"

"Good God, Oriel!"

She almost kissed him again. "I would like to see what I will be missing."

He looked stern, but the dimple had reappeared. "No."

"Please," she wheedled.

"If I took you to that house, do you understand what it would mean?"

"I'm a grown-up woman, Devlyn. I have been married. Of course I understand." And because she wanted him to know that he was under no obligation to her beyond his own desires, and hers, she said something that would have broken her heart if she'd thought too much about it. "In a few days, I shall be far away, and we will never meet again. Today I want to see your mistresses' house." She kissed him again, nibbling at his lower lip, probing the stubborn mouth until, thank Providence, he gave in and kissed her back.

"Are you sure you won't regret this?" he said hoarsely as he took up the reins again.

"You're the one with maidenly coyness. I fear I shall have to seduce you."

"You're wrong about that."

Judging by the way he took the return journey at a gallop, she'd overcome his qualms. She had none. Desire, long dormant and kindled by Devlyn, writhed in her belly. Holding on to her bonnet, she drank in his beloved face, intent on his driving and wearing an anticipatory grin. He might not feel as she did in every way, but he shared her desire. At the back of her mind, she nurtured a hope that there would be more.

At the gate he turned the sleigh over to his waiting coachman and groom, and they slithered their way along Park Lane to one of a row of small terrace houses she had never even noticed. A desperate quality tinged their laughter: urgency, longing, no time to waste. A cold wind buffeted them while Dev fumbled with the key.

"Brr." Oriel hugged herself. "It's not much warmer in here."

"The house has been empty for some time."

"No servants? No wine and sweetmeats? I am disappointed." She was thrilled that the house was unused. "I hope the place is furnished in scarlet silk with mirrors everywhere." His eyebrows slanted in comical despair. "It is! Show me at once."

"Uh, only the bedchamber."

"Does it have blankets, or do your mistresses loll around naked?"

"I'll keep you warm."

"What are we waiting for?"

A minute later, they were upstairs on a red satin bed, wrestling off their clothes. "Hurry, hurry," she said. "It's freezing."

She hardly had a moment to inspect her prize before they were under covers, face to face. She lay still, examining her sensations: a hard chest against her nipples, which were stiff with cold and desire; a rough leg tickling her calf; a ridged stomach beneath her questing hand; his hands conducting their own exploration. Every part of him was strong and hot, including *that*, the thing she never named in her head, although suddenly she could think of nothing else except having it inside her, assuaging the ache that had become a delicious pain.

"You don't seem to be shy, Mrs. Sinclair."

"Should I be, Sir Devlyn? I'm afraid I forgot all about maidenly coyness after my wedding night."

He stilled. "Your marriage was happy?"

"Very happy, very brief, and a long time ago. Let's not talk about it now. Kiss me and show me what you can do."

So he did, and he was very good at it. He made love like a man, not an ardent boy, taking his time so she, already eager, was aroused to an impossible pitch. When he laid her on her back and entered her, at long, long last, hard and smooth, she cried out with blessed relief and forgot everything except their two bodies. She reached fulfillment twice before he threw back his head and shouted her name, then collapsed, murmuring incoherent praise into her neck.

Now that it was over, he felt different, relaxed and very big, and it filled her with tenderness. Her throat thickened with laughter and tears, because she was happy and had a terrible feeling she never would be again.

When he came to, they kissed some more and cuddled, nestling beneath the blankets. Burrowing into his neck, she inhaled clean, masculine sweat.

"Thank you, Oriel." His breath hovered in the chill air.

"No thanks needed. Or I should thank you."

A long leg laid a happy weight on hers. A hand played with her breast. Oh, to remain here forever, a pair of animals warming each other in the frozen winter.

But gradually, intimate satisfaction gave way to awkward silence. Reality and the world outside could not be forgotten, or the practical and social truths that divided them.

"What will you and your family do tomorrow?" she asked, deliberately making conversation. At the foot of the bed, one of the promised mirrors reflected their heads, dark against white linen pillows, a false picture of the closeness that she felt slipping away.

"What?" He seemed to emerge from a trance. "I had forgotten it is Christmas. It isn't fashionable, but we have always made a fuss of the celebration. The late Christmas Eve service, then decorating the house in the morning. Mistletoe and holly, wassail and carols, gifts for all, down to the youngest kitchen maid and bootblack."

"And a Yule log."

"Of course."

"Can you do all this in London?"

"I suppose not. I've never spent the holiday here." His voice grew tight. "Last year my father was lately dead, and we had a quiet time with gifts only for the servants."

"I'm sorry. How sad for you all."

He sniffed as though threatened by tears, which she found touching in this large, confident man. "It won't be the same now that he is gone." Despite his dispassionate tone, she sensed that he had confided something he felt deeply, and she loved him even more.

"Oriel," he began, and changed his mind. Had he been about to invite her to join him at Curzon Street? But of course he wouldn't. She was a stranger to his family, and she had her own duty. "What will you and your father do?"

"The goose from your hamper will be roasted at the cookhouse, but we will be quiet, as befits his state of health. He's much better, thanks to you."

"At least I could do something for *your* father. Mine died of a pneumonia quite suddenly. I hadn't seen him for weeks." He kissed her temple softly. "It sounds foolish, but helping yours made me feel better about mine, and for that I owe you my gratitude. So you see, we are even."

Even. All debts paid. Good-bye.

She shivered, and at once he was all concern. "Much as I would like to spend all day and night with you, it grows cold. I had better take you home."

As they dressed, she set her mind on practicalities. Speaking to the manager of the auction house, packing their possessions for the carrier, hiring an inexpensive carriage for the journey to Lincolnshire. She would not think about leaving Dev until she was alone and could weep in private.

They walked back to Duke Street in silence, through streets where white snow was turning to filthy wet mush. "This is good-bye, then," she said at the door.

"Good-bye? Surely you aren't leaving yet."

"Any day now."

He kissed her hand. "Then we *shall* meet again. Count on it. Our afternoon may have consequences."

She watched him stride away. Naturally, he would take responsibility for a child. Her mind reeled at the potential complication, and she fervently prayed it wouldn't be necessary.

Chapter Nine

〜

LADY STRATTON, THE younger, had arranged for a cartload of greenery to be delivered from Sussex, and the ladies of the house rushed around amid a chaos of leaves, berries, and ribbon. Instead of enjoying the ritual, Dev barely paid attention to his assigned tasks. When he snapped at Susan, who had demanded he move the nail for the kissing bough for the third time, his mother called him out of the drawing room.

"You are in the most dreadful mood, Devlyn, and spoiling our enjoyment. I won't have it."

"I beg your pardon, Mama." Dev widened his mouth and hoped he looked happy and filled with Yuletide spirit.

Obviously he failed.

"What on earth is the matter with you? Have you bad news of Mr. Markham? I thought he was getting better." She and his grandmother had been following the progress of her fellow Lincolnshire native with avid interest.

"He is. He and Mrs. Sinclair are leaving town any day now."

"I am glad to hear it." She gave him one of those searching looks that he suspected she'd copied from his grandmother. "I want you to go for a long walk, and don't come back until you've recovered your temper, or it's time for dinner, whichever comes later. Take Merrick with you. The boy is quite useless when it comes to decorating."

Was Merrick in the house? Dev hadn't even noticed.

"Don't even think of disturbing Mrs. Sinclair on Christmas Day," was her parting order.

Feeling like a pair of chastised schoolboys, which was certainly his mother's aim, the two men set out in the direction of the park.

At the corner of Park Lane, Dev stopped, overcome by the melancholy that had overwhelmed him since last night. Oriel had given no hint that she wanted to remain in London. She had said good-bye.

"Dev! Dev!"

"What?"

"Did you hear me?" Merrick asked.

"Did you say anything worth hearing?"

"I'm not going to the park, and I want your advice."

"Don't even think of going to visit Oriel."

"Oriel?" Merrick might as well have said, *Who is Oriel?* "I'm going to the Hendersons. I was going to make my offer to Hope before dinner, but I think I'd like to get it over now. I'm terrified."

How his brother could have so quickly forgotten lovely Oriel in favor of silly little Hope, Dev couldn't imagine. "What do you want to know?"

"What shall I say?"

"Going down on one knee is *de rigueur*. Are your breeches too tight? Wouldn't do for them to split."

"Dev! This is serious."

"Be straightforward. Ask her to marry you. *Will you do me the inestimable honor of being my wife?* Or some such thing. And tell her you love her. Do you?"

"Yes. I had this idea about Oriel, but as soon as I saw Hope again, I knew. We were apart for so long I rather forgot. But it's all right if we are married, because we will be together all the time."

"I strongly recommend that you do not mention that to her. The best of luck, brother. I look forward to raising a toast to you and Hope at dinner."

He slogged on through the melted snow and decided to avoid Hyde Park in favor of the smaller Green Park. He'd never visit the former again without thinking of their sleigh ride. His mother had ordered him not to call on the Markhams today, and he supposed she was right. He wondered if Mr. Markham would be in one of his good moods. He hated to think of Oriel not having a happy Christmas. He walked three times around the slushy park, reliving the previous, miraculous day and working out how many hours and minutes there were until ten o'clock the next morning, the first moment he could justify calling. The walk and the arithmetic cleared his head. In the New Year, he decided, he'd make a visit to his relations in Lincolnshire. Among other reasons, he must make sure Oriel wasn't with child. If she were *enceinte*, he would make her marry him.

His feet stopped of their own accord.

Not once had he ever thought about being married. Merrick was going to take care of an heir to the Stratton baronetcy and estates, enlarged by the Henderson land, while Dev continued his merry bachelor way, a man about town and a charming uncle to many nephews and nieces, present and to come. But with the right woman, matrimony seemed like an excellent idea and a child or two of his own a good thing. Perhaps even more. There was nothing wrong with a large family.

He was close to Piccadilly. In one direction, his house was but a step away. In the other, Markham's Print Gallery wasn't much farther. Should he spring a shopkeeper, albeit a lady with Lincolnshire connections, on his family? He had responsibilities that he was finally trying to take seriously. But he was also in love.

ORIEL ATTENDED THE morning service at St. James's Church. It was melancholy to be alone among so many smiling families dressed in their best and lustily singing the Noel hymns. Her shoes leaked in the dirty melting snow, and she turned off Jermyn Street, utterly depressed at the prospect of roast goose alone with her father. Even Mary had gone home to her family in Islington.

All at once, summer arrived when she saw the carriage outside the gallery. She'd ridden in it to the theater, and to Curzon Street. Ready to hurl herself into Devlyn's arms and beg him to keep her as long he wanted, to the devil with Lincolnshire, her father, and propriety, instead she found his footman with a note.

Not from Devlyn.

Dear Mrs. Sinclair,

I am sorry to trouble you on Christmas morning. Devlyn tells me you found a print or engraving (I don't know the right word) that may be a Dürer. I would like to give it to my mother-in-law. I should have thought of it earlier, but with so much to do, the idea struck me only this morning. I am aware that this is a terrible imposition, but I wonder if you would come to Curzon Street for a few minutes and have another look at it. I would be so very grateful.

Yours etc.
Augusta Stratton

P.S. Both my sons are out this morning, so neither of them will bother you.

"It's the oddest thing, Papa. Lady Stratton has written and asked me to look at the possible Dürer I mentioned. This morning. I won't be long." She decided she owed the lady a debt of gratitude for protecting her name with the doctor, even if she didn't know it. And she'd like to see the house once more. Just possibly she'd catch a glimpse of the owner on his return home.

"Why would she ask *you*? You know nothing about the early masters."

"That is what I told Sir Devlyn."

"The woman's a fool. I'll come with you. Help me tie my cravat."

Assured that he was well enough—though he complained quite a lot about the nuisance, the attention he gave to his dress told her he was pleased to have an outing—she tidied her hair and put on her best bonnet, glad she'd worn her most attractive morning gown for church. While the footman handed her father into the carriage, she asked him to wait a moment. The prints she'd selected for Devlyn were packed and ready for delivery. She might as well take them instead of asking Charlie the next day. On impulse she pulled a few more out of the bottom drawer and wrapped them, and at the last minute, she remembered *The Mad Monk of Mongolia*. In the street she summoned Jemmy, the crossing boy who must be having very poor trade that morning.

"There's a roast goose at the cook shop. If I'm not home in two hours, give them this shilling and take the bird home to your family. Otherwise, you keep the shilling."

"Cor, Happy Christmas, miss."

"Happy Christmas to you, Jemmy."

They might be coming home to cold ham, or she might be happy. If the former, she wouldn't be in the mood for goose.

DEV KNOCKED ON the door in Duke Street. Sounds of jollity came from an upstairs window at the bookshop, but at Markham's Print Gallery, all was quiet. How would Oriel react when he asked her to come to his house to join them for Christmas dinner? With jitters in his stomach—he spared a moment's sympathy for Merrick and hoped his quest had met with success—he had decided to bring the two families together. If the current Lady Strattons didn't approve his choice of the next holder of the name, they'd have to lump it. He was ready to exercise his best Head of the Family authority, just as his father would have.

How could they not love Oriel once they came to know her?

After five minutes of continuous knocking, he had to face the fact that she either wasn't there or was avoiding him. Several upward glances revealed no lurking figure.

A small crossing sweeper lingered at the top of the street, looking chilly. "I say, lad, do you know if the lady who lives here, Mrs. Sinclair, has gone out?"

"Went in a carriage a while ago."

"Alone?"

"Nah. The old cully was with 'er. 'Adn't seen 'im in months."

"Do you know where they went?"

The boy looked bewildered. His life, Dev guessed, was confined to his pitch on Jermyn Street and whatever hovel he called home. Dev thanked him and gave him a gold sovereign. Someone might as well have a happy Christmas.

Flown the coop without a word. Mr. Markham wouldn't have gone out, unless they'd decided to start their journey north early. Dev dragged his way home and considered claiming illness and taking to his rooms. Christmas dinner with Merrick and Hope cooing like happy lovers was more than he could stand.

"Her ladyship—" the butler began when Dev handed over his coat and hat.

"Not a word," he said, and went straight to his library.

"—said you should go to the library," he heard as he slammed the door.

On the table his gifts lay, wrapped in cloth or silver tissue or brown paper, depending on the contents. An inexpert packer, he'd prepared them without enthusiasm after dinner the previous evening. Parts of their contents emerged from some of them. He didn't care. What he needed was a drink.

He made for the brandy that stood on the console table by the window.

"Are you going to offer me some?"

The heavy glass decanter landed with a thud.

Oriel sat on his favorite leather chair by the fire, and he'd never seen anything so beautiful in his life.

"My God! I thought you'd left for the country. The boy said you went off in a carriage, you and Mr. Markham."

"And so we did. To come here."

She explained about the Dürer, which her father, never a man to shilly-shally, had proclaimed the work of a lesser master. She laughed as she told the story, and he drank in the sight of her, his heart ablaze that she was here, sitting in his chair in his house on the best, most beautiful day ever. It was Midsummer's Day in the library, filled with sunlight despite the leaden skies outside.

"Besides, I had to come," she said with the wicked smile that set flesh and blood on fire. "You left a book in my shop." She picked up a volume and leafed through it without taking her eyes from his face. "I wouldn't wish you to be deprived of *The Mad Monk of Mongolia*. It looks like a sensational story, which I am sure you will enjoy immensely."

"I shall read it aloud to you." Dev knelt at her feet, set aside the book, and took both her hands in his. "When I found you gone, I almost set off for Lincolnshire on foot."

She seemed pleased and stroked his face. He leaned in, dizzy from eyes warm and green as the sea, and turned her hand to kiss the palm. "It's a miracle that you are here. What is my mother about? Never mind. You are staying for dinner."

"Am I invited?"

"You are invited to stay forever. No, wait, I'm not doing this right. I am supposed to be down on one knee."

"Uh, Devlyn, you are down on two."

"Splendid. I needn't fear for the safety of my breeches."

"What?"

"I'll explain later if you are very good. Now for the next bit."

Her expression would have been the epitome of maidenly coyness were it not for the glint in her eye. "Lud, sir. What can you mean?"

"Mrs. Sinclair. Will you do me the inestimable honor of being my wife?"

"This is so sudden."

"Only because I am a fool. I realized this morning what should have been obvious for weeks. I love you madly. Please marry me, Oriel."

"I need to think." Since she ran a finger along the line of his ridiculous eyebrows, he wasn't too worried, but leaned shamelessly into her touch. He couldn't wait for her to be his, in word as well as deed.

"Think fast."

"I've thought. Yes. Yes, I will marry you," she said in a rush.

A minute later, he was in the chair with Oriel on his lap, kissing between exchanges of nonsense. He discovered a new appreciation of sentimental cliché. He didn't mind in the least telling her she was the sweetest, cleverest, most beautiful woman who ever lived, or hearing how much she adored him.

"When did you fall in love with me?" he wanted to know.

"In the bookshop, over *Emma*."

"I did too."

"Of course, love at first sight is common and usually followed by deep disillusionment when the object turns out to be an arrogant swine."

"But that's not what happened."

"It is exactly what happened. Then you turned out to be not so bad after all, and I decided to stay in love."

Discussing every one of their meetings, punctuated by frequent kisses, was as delightful as sentimental nonsense. Things were getting a little out of hand when his mother walked into the room. Oriel slid to the floor, rumpled and embarrassed.

"Mama, Oriel and I are to be married."

"Dearest boy, I am so glad. I wish you every joy." Embracing them both, she insisted they come upstairs to join the rest of the party in the drawing room. "What a Christmas this is! Both my sons betrothed on the same day."

"Why did you tell me not to call on Oriel this morning?"

"I had to get you out of the house while I sent for her. I suppose you went anyway."

"Of course."

"I do hope, Oriel, that Devlyn treats your wishes with more respect than he does his mother's. What fun it's going to be to have three Lady Strattons."

EATING ROAST GOOSE while one's betrothed insisted on holding hands under the table was a challenge. Everything else about the dinner was splendid. Mr. Markham and Lady Stratton discovered a Lincolnshire acquaintance they both detested. A thorough dissection of his character was followed by the mutual certainty that they had met as children. Emma and Susan, excited about having two new sisters, pelted Oriel with questions. Hope, who had nothing new to tell them, smiled sweetly and mostly talked to Merrick. The dowager managed to look benign and disapproving at the same time.

After dinner the family exchanged gifts around the drawing room fire, which even contained a Yule log. Rather a small one, but quite adequate to the dimensions of the hearth.

"Where did that come from?" Devlyn asked.

Hope giggled, and Merrick laughed. "Since you failed to provide, Dev, Hope and I went to Hyde Park this morning with a hatchet."

"I hope no one saw you," the dowager said. "I believe you have committed petty treason."

"Good work, brother," Devlyn said. "It's only a minnow, but next Christmas, in the country, we shall have a whale. The biggest ever."

Everyone was happy with their gifts except the dowager, who loathed both copies of "First Steps," proclaiming it sentimental pap. Oriel offered to take them back and exchange them for something more to her taste. She would have to hide half the stock from the old lady.

She gave Devlyn the French prints, and he gave her the musical birdcage.

"I have never seen anything like it in my life," she said. Just a little lie so as not to spoil his pleasure in her surprise—or admit to snooping. "I love it."

"I bought it just before I first met you," he said. "I didn't know who it was for, but I am prescient. I think I have the gift of foresight."

While thanking him, she whispered in his ear that she had another gift for him, something she couldn't show him in public but would give him all sorts of ideas. The prospect of reenacting the poses in those shocking prints made her warm all over.

"Whatever can you mean? I can't wait to find out." He wore such an exaggerated air of innocence that she wondered if *he* had been poking around in her print cabinet and found the bottom drawer. Sir Devlyn Stratton had some explaining to do. To be followed by a demonstration.

A Seduction in Winter

BY
CAROLYN JEWEL

Acknowledgment

Many thanks to my colleagues in this project, Grace Burrowes, Miranda Neville, and Shana Galen. Thanks also go out to my sister Marguerite for her unwavering support of my writing and to my son Nathaniel.

Chapter One

HE WAS HERE. Honora reread the list again to be sure she'd not conjured his name from hopes and wishes. She hadn't. The *Monarch*, with Lieutenant Lord Leoline Marrable on board, had arrived from Bombay one week ago today. After seven years in the Navy and three years employed with the East India Company, he was in England again. In London. Not that their paths would cross, but London!

The door behind her opened and then closed. Honora slid the paper under the collection of pages that took up most of the desk where she sat. When she was not working on one of the pages or creating a new one, she kept the lot of them in a wooden box, at present set away on the top section of her desk.

"Papa." Her father removed his hat and coat. "A good morning's work?"

"Indeed yes." He unwound his scarf and draped that over the back of a chair. "I'll warrant there will be snow tomorrow."

Thanks to the increase in commissioned work and in other paintings sold over the last two years, they had better quarters at the Morin Hotel than for their previous stays in London. Two bedchambers, naturally, but a larger parlor and a dining room for meals if they brought them upstairs. They were on the fourth floor this year, a savings of two flights.

"Yes, Papa." In addition to the record keeping and accounts, she did much of the detail work for his commissioned projects. "Shall I send Gilman to fetch our luncheon, or did you eat downstairs?" The tavern attached to the hotel made an excellent roast beef and an even better duck. Both were favorites of her father's.

"I've eaten thank you." He came into the parlor where she spent most of her day when she was not at the studio with him. He wandered to the table where she'd left the newspapers she'd read front to back. She took care not to turn her face too much toward him. He picked up the morning *Times* she had carefully refolded earlier in the day and brought it to a chair by the fire. "I shall dine out tonight."

"Noted." She slid her secreted page from underneath the others. He kept a mistress at another hotel on Manchester Square. Papa supposed her to be unaware of this fact. "You are at home until then?"

He snapped open the paper. "Yes, I think so."

She picked up her scissors and cut the notice from the paper, to be added to her album of clippings about Lord Leoline. She'd kept track of and recorded the ships to which he'd been assigned and the actions and battles he'd seen while he was in the Navy. She'd gathered all the descriptions of engagements involving those ships she could locate and transferred the information to her project. Over the years, she had amassed a thick stack of neatly clipped articles and hand transcriptions of his naval battles, interspersed with illustrations of her own in pen and ink or watercolor. Some of her drawings were inventions of her imagination, others came to life on the page from facts gleaned of his battles and the ships he'd sailed on.

The project, born of idle hands and no particular goal, had become absurdly elaborate. She would be the first to admit that. Illustrating or decorating the pages had become a way of passing the time. She ought to put away the pages for good now that he was back in England. There was little reason for him to remember her, if he remembered her at all, but she would never forget the day he'd come to her rescue. To him, she could only be a child who had briefly intersected with his life. She, however, had grown attached to her private homage to his bravery.

She pasted the section containing the notice of the *Monarch*'s arrival onto a fresh sheet of paper and beneath that wrote the words, "The Hon. Lieutenant Lord Leoline Marrable, Lord Wrathell."

She drew a border and curlicues around his name. He was a marquess by courtesy. The new *Debrett's* was published and contained the recent amendments to the line of succession for the dukedom of Quenhaith. She did not dare clip pages from their copy of the peerage, but she'd copied the text pertaining to the Marrables onto pages of her own, suitably decorated with the family motto and coat of arms.

Pages of the *Times* rattled, and she sent her father a questioning glance. He coughed once and said, "I'll need you at the studio tomorrow to finish off Mrs. Rosen."

"Of course." Some years ago, after he'd been accepted into the Royal Academy, he'd made arrangements for the use of a fellow artist's studio in the other Duke Street, which arrangement had brought them to London every winter since, for the stated purpose of exhibiting his work and obtaining and finishing commissions. While they stayed in Town, he found it convenient to have his mistress across the street instead of the other side of Bury St. Edmunds.

She evened out the curlicues around Lord Leoline's name. They had been born on the same day five years apart, on December the twenty-fourth, a fact she had discovered from Debrett's. He had been born in Lincolnshire at Marrable Gate, his family's country seat, whilst her birth had occurred in Elderford, the village attached to the ducal estate.

"Papa," she said when he put down the paper. "Did you know Lord Leoline is in London?" She amended that quickly. "I mean, Lord Wrathell."

"No." He nodded with approval. Lord Leoline had always been a favorite of his.

Since he was sitting to her right, a fortuitous arrangement of the parlor, it was easy to prop her left elbow atop the desk and lean her cheek against her forearm.

"I suppose it's to be expected given the tragedy of his brother," her father said.

"Yes." She recognized his restlessness. He would stay an hour or so longer before he made an excuse that would take him to the other side of Manchester Square. She wished she'd left more work on Lord Wrathell's papers, for she would have an evening alone to do exactly as she liked.

"There's a young man who's made a good account of himself." His gaze lingered on her, and she made sure not to move. His pity made her heart ache. The disgust she sometimes saw in his face when he caught a glimpse of her face pierced her heart through. "When did he arrive, do you know? I ought to pay my respects."

"From the notice, a week ago Tuesday." Because she rarely went out except for solitary walks, she filled the hours of her day with reading, sewing, and writing letters to the editor that she tore up as soon as she had fashioned a suitably scathing reply. If she wasn't at her father's studio, she was here reading every newspaper, magazine, or book to be found. Gilman collected broadsheets and pamphlets for her enjoyment. She had an excellent collection of them. There was little she did not know about London, or politics, or much of anything to appear in the papers.

"A week, you say. Well." He fiddled with his watch. "I wish him well. I truly do."

From necessity she was expert at keeping herself at angles that did not disturb him. When they dined together, she often ended those meals having eaten nearly nothing. "He's in residence in Queen Anne Street, not Marrable House."

He tapped a finger on the table beside him. "No reconciliation between him and his father?"

"I do not know."

"Pity if not."

She shrugged one shoulder. Lord Leoline—Lord Wrathell, she must remember that—had joined the Navy against his father's wishes. Their estrangement was the stuff of legend and, in a strange twist of fate, she was likely the only person besides Wrathell himself who knew the reason for the altercation between Lord Leoline's elder brother and him that had caused the rift with his father.

"They must reconcile now he's the heir."

"I suppose they must." The duke did not know the true reason for the disagreement between the brothers. Lord Leoline would never have betrayed his brother. Nor her. He would never have mentioned her to his father.

She wondered if he was still handsome. Perhaps the beauty of his youth had not survived maturity. His elder brother had not retained his good looks. He'd gone to fat and lost a great deal of his hair. Lord Leoline had been fair to his brother's striking dark hair, though both possessed the same piercing gray eyes. Whatever Lord Leoline looked like now, she would always remember him as tall and handsome, forever eighteen years old, and the bravest man who ever lived.

Chapter Two

❦

O N HIS WAY home after luncheon in St. James's, Wrathell took a wrong turn, went too far in the wrong direction and ended up on Duke Street. Not, alas, the Duke Street he wanted. He stopped to get his bearings, obtained them and saw he'd stopped in front of a book shop. The name of the establishment was The Duke Street Bookshop, which stood to reason. What did not stand up to scrutiny was why some wag had painted the words "On the Shelf" above the lintel and no one had troubled to remove the defacement.

Through the windows, he could see a woman behind the counter wrapping up a customer's purchase. The wind whipped along the street again. He shivered because his coat was not warm enough. He could be wearing ten coats, and he'd not be warm enough. Bloody London in winter was an abomination. While he stood on the street thinking fond thoughts of warmer climes, a customer exited the shop, package under his arm. The gentleman tipped his hat as a waft of warm air blew in Wrathell's direction.

Without thinking, he grabbed the door before it closed. *Warm air* was all that registered on his frozen brain. In he went to books and welcoming warmth. The proprietor, God love whoever it was, had not stinted on the coal in the stove in the opposite corner. He removed his hat and nodded to the pretty woman behind the counter. "Good day, ma'am."

Three young ladies in a corner of the shop began to whisper. One of them used a gloved hand to pin a sheet of paper to the table where the charming cabal sat. He smiled and bowed to them too. What gentleman would not smile at three pretty young ladies? They giggled. One of them blushed.

"Good day to you, sir," the woman behind the counter said. "Do let me know if I may assist you in any way."

"I shall, thank you." He went farther in. He'd not intended to come inside at all until that blast of air, but now he was here and it was warmer inside than out and there was no wind to cut mercilessly through his greatcoat, coat, waistcoat, shirt, and unmentionables.

Since he was here he might as well buy a book or two to read until he got his library straightened out. He stayed in the vicinity of the stove and rubbed his hands until the feeling in his fingers came back. There was a quite good selection of magazines offering a range of perspectives and sentiments for gentlemen and ladies alike. He did like the looks of the place. It wasn't large, but there was an impressive selection of new books and a decent-sized area of used ones, and that so charming bevy of young ladies in the corner who continued to glance his way and giggle among themselves.

Ahead was a shelf marked "poetry." There was nothing worse than bad poetry and nothing more sublime in all the world than a poem in the hands of an artist. He would bring home a history, he decided, a selection of magazines, and a volume or two of poetry and have a pleasant way to pass time and continue his personal education.

Before he was close enough to see what the shop had on the shelves he found he was not the only customer who hoped to find something worth reading. In the aisle formed by two shelves, a woman in green perused the titles. He knew just enough about fashion to know she was dressed acceptably. The three young women in the corner were dressed more fashionably than she.

He suspected she might be a beauty. Dark hair peeked from beneath a bonnet trimmed with tiny yellow flowers, and her figure was excellent. Her cheek was pale and smooth, her mouth utterly delicious. A black net veil covered her hair and, one supposed, would be lowered to protect her face from the bitter cold of the streets.

He stayed where he was, wondering how he could manage to be introduced to her without breaking all rules of propriety. She tipped her head to one side in a motion of intense alertness that cast him back a dozen years. Awash with memories of his boyhood, he gave himself a mental shake. How odd that a stranger encountered in a bookshop would so strongly remind him of Honora Baynard.

The young woman, for she was young, he could see that, looked at another book with a scrutiny so familiar he wondered if it could be her. No. Surely, no. This would be too great a coincidence.

He was twenty-eight, which would put Miss Baynard, wherever she was, in her early twenties. This young lady was at least approximately that old. The contrast between her inky hair and her moonlight-pale complexion reminded him of her. Though he had her right side in profile to him, the curve of her cheek and the point of her chin were hauntingly familiar.

She progressed along the shelf, walking away from where he stood. She examined each of the titles, as yet unaware of his presence. If she were to turn to her right, he would know if it was her. The woman wasn't short, but she wasn't tall either, which proved nothing since he'd grown several inches since he'd left Marrable Gate, and Frederick Baynard's daughter had been all of thirteen at the time.

Her gloved fingertips brushed the lower spine of a book on a shelf above her head. Everything about her seemed maddeningly familiar with just enough different to give a measure of doubt. She stuck her tongue into the corner of her mouth, and even without seeing more of her face, he was beyond certain.

He moved in and plucked the volume off the shelf for her. "Allow me."

She craned her neck to look at him, her far arm still stretched upward.

His heart gave a lurch. "It is you," he said.

She froze.

"Honora," he said.

Her cheeks flushed bright red except where she was scarred. She yanked down her veil, but the reflexive reaction failed in its goal. He had seen all he needed. One did not forget a scar like that. Nor was his memory so faulty as to forget those dark blue eyes, pools fathoms deep with thick, absurdly thick lashes, not even when their possessor was a girl years from womanhood. As had been true of the girl, inky eyebrows made the contrast between her complexion and the darkness of her hair the more stark.

Her hand slowly returned to her side. She backed away, but there was a wall behind her and shelves of books on either side. He stepped back to allow her to move past him if she so desired. She did not bolt as he'd feared. Instead, she took the volume from him without comment and said in a quizzical voice, "Do I know you, sir?"

"Good Lord, of course." He brushed a hand over the top of his head. "You've not seen me since I was eighteen. Forgive me." He bowed to her. "It's Lord Leoline."

This time he got a sense of quiet from her, and this too was familiar. She'd been a peculiar girl, but then what child would not be, living isolated as she had?

"Lord Leoline?" She looked him up and down, understandable under the circumstances, and ended by searching his face. "Yes." She spoke crisply. She was grown up now, wasn't she? "Those are your eyes."

"They are." He grinned and tapped the top of his head. "I may've grown some since last you saw me."

"Some. Some?" Her mature voice was full and rich and edged with smoke. What an absurd description, but he could think of no better words for her shockingly seductive voice. She extended her hand, the one with the book, to a level below her waist as a demonstration of his supposed height last she saw him. "You are a giant now."

He stared at her hand and the book, unable to separate his pleasure at seeing her from the change that maturity had made in her. She wasn't a girl any longer. "I was never that small, Miss Baynard. But no." He shook his head. "You cannot be Miss Baynard any longer. You must have married by now."

"I have not." The grave child she'd been had become, not surprisingly, a grave young woman. Had she smiled yet? With the veil now hiding her face she could have any expression at all. "You seem a giant to me."

"Six feet and two inches is all." Taller than his father, but he refused to say that. Taller than his brother had been.

"I should not be so astonished to encounter you as I am, but I confess I am beyond shocked to see you. You have been in London ten days now, and there is less than a mile between our lodgings and yours. That's if you've remained in Queen Anne Street. I have not heard that you removed to Marrable House. Have you?"

How did she know any of that? "I am at Queen Anne Street."

She continued in the same tones of warm silk. "Your solicitors and bankers were more ferocious in their protection of your credit deposits and properties than they were the contents of your brother's home."

She was correct again. "How do you know any of that?" His father had taken everything that wasn't nailed down, including the contents of the library.

"There was extensive discussion in the court journals. The *Gazette* published an inventory of the late Lord Wrathell's library. Nearly three thousand titles."

Her manner was so solemn that without the ability to assess her expression he was not certain what she wished to acknowledge between them. Most of their shared past must be exceedingly unpleasant to her. His father had insisted that Baynard not allow his daughter to be seen at church without her face covered, and his brother—His brother had been beyond cruel to her. The second of his altercations with Wrathell on the subject of his unkindness and cruelty had led to an irreparable split between him and his father.

"They published an inventory?"

"I have a copy, if you think your solicitor would be interested to see the titles. I presume it would assist you in suggesting a figure in settlement if the contents cannot be returned to you."

"It would be. I would be much obliged." He did not think matters would come down to lawyers in court. His father had meant to make a point.

She hesitated, then pushed back her veil, slowly. Testing him for revulsion? The scar had thinned and stretched with the natural growth of a child into an adult and consequently covered more of her cheek. The thicker scarring that disappeared into her hair just at her temple remained more or less as he recalled. She blinked several times. Distracted by her spectacular eyes, he did not immediately understand that she expected some expression of disgust from him.

"Does it bother you?" she asked.

"I've seen sailors with worse." Blunt. That had been too blunt.

"That is not at all a charming lie." She smiled when she said it, but Wrathell found her reply too frank by half. "Thank you."

"You are welcome." Still a peculiar little thing. Grown to an adult, yes, but still peculiar.

She smiled, and her scar reshaped with the movement of her cheek. "Forgive me. I've been calling you Lord Leoline when you are Wrathell now." She put a hand on his arm and gently squeezed. She kept her head turned so he could see little to nothing of her scarred cheek. "Papa and I were sorry to hear of your brother's passing."

"Thank you." Under the circumstances, this was better than his brother deserved from her.

"He wrote to me." She held the book he'd fetched for her close to her stomach, so earnest, it pained him. She, of anyone, had the right to see the world as a bleak and terrible place, yet she appeared not to. After all that she had endured, why did she not seethe with resentment? "Did he tell you he had?"

"Yes."

She cocked her head. "I thought so. He swore you had not put him up to it."

"I didn't. I promise you."

"His words were very pretty." Her reply was neatly delivered. Efficient and cool. "Naturally, I suspected your hand in it."

He grinned. "On my honor, my hand is innocent."

There was the merest hesitation before she replied. "He apologized for his unkindness to me."

"Did you accept?"

She nodded. "I did. He did not ask for my forgiveness. I thought that well done of him."

"Did you?"

"Yes." She nodded gravely. "I wrote you and your father letters of condolence when I heard what happened, but I think since you are here in London now, there is a very good chance my letter to you arrived in Bombay too late."

"It must have. I would have remembered hearing from you. But how would you have known where to write?"

"It was quite simple."

He'd never spoken to a woman so painfully innocent yet mannish in her speech. "Was it?"

"Yes."

Her breezy manner set him back on his heels. What sort of woman was this? A beauty tragically scarred or a woman too bold in her speech? At Elderford, her father had kept her inside and away from the public eye as much as possible. Even on those occasions when he'd been at the Baynard house, he'd rarely seen her. He did recall she had been precociously verbal, and he'd wondered each time if Baynard had been behind a curtain somewhere putting those words in a child's mouth.

"I made inquiries of the East India Company. They replied with the direction of their offices in Bombay. It would have taken more time to obtain the direction for your residence, and I feared my letter would have no hope at all of finding you if I did not write immediately."

"I see."

She gave him a smile devoid of flattery or deference. "Now I may tell you in person that I am very sorry about Lord Wrathell's passing. If his letter to me is any proof, and I daresay it was, he had made great strides in improving his character."

Considering his brother had gone out of his way to be unkind to her in every possible way, this was something. Whenever his brother had believed he would not be caught out, he'd pestered her without mercy. He'd lain in wait for her and taunted her, and when she'd lagged behind her father one Sunday, his brother had pelted her with sticks, rocks, and clods of dirt. She had met every insult with a searing dignity that had enraged his brother. He'd not given up his persecution of her until Wrathell had broken his nose.

"Mr. Frederick Carstairs gave a very moving eulogy," she said. "You would have liked his speech."

"You attended his funeral?"

"Certainly not. It was printed in the paper." She curtseyed. "My lord."

He did not know how to behave with her. Not as a stranger, for they were not strangers. Not as a friend. They scarcely knew one another. Yet their connection had the power, even all these years later, to evoke strong emotion in him. "That is not necessary."

"I cannot continue calling you Lord Leoline." He had the unsettling notion that she saw past his polite expression and into his heart. "You are Wrathell now."

She spoke those words as if they were the same as saying he was still in Bombay. There might as well be ten thousand miles of separation between them, given the distance between the heir to a duke and the daughter of an artist. Though, come to think of it, Baynard was a member of the Royal Academy now, and that did not happen to just any man with the ability to take a likeness.

"Miss Baynard." He bowed and gave up trying to decide how to behave except as he would behave with any young lady. "What a happy coincidence to have met you. A true and real pleasure to see you again."

She bent a knee. "Likewise. Papa said he would call on you. Has he?"

"No." In truth, he had no idea. An astonishing number of cards awaited him at home. He'd yet to look at a single one. "Is he here in London?" But of course Baynard must be in town. Honora was not married. "May I inquire where you and your father are staying? I should like to pay my respects. Is he still instructing rascals of meager talent?"

She laughed, and there was silk and smoke in that beguiling sound. How had peculiar Honora Baynard become this ravishing, ruined creature?

"He no longer tutors young gentlemen." She tugged on one of her gloves. "You and your brother were the last."

Twenty-three. She was twenty-three and ought to be breaking hearts across London but for the damage to her face. What might a painter do with a woman like her as his model? Not him, with his middling talent, but an artist.

"To me, your father will always be waiting at Marrable Gate to remind me his daughter is my superior in every way."

"He never said any such thing." Her eyes were wide open and hopeful.

"Indeed he did." His heart folded over. Was she starving for such crumbs of praise?

"Honora?" The speaker's voice was indisputably male and as familiar to him as anyone's.

She looked past him, and Wrathell glanced over his shoulder.

"Papa." Honora went to her father, and he breathed in the scent of lilacs when she passed. She hooked her arm around her father's and leaned against his side. Baynard flicked his daughter's veil over her face. Wrathell found himself offended by that quick reaction. She went still, but spoke in a cheerful voice. "Look who I found lurking among the poetry. Is it not remarkable?"

Baynard examined him, and the light of recognition came quickly. "Lord Leoline." His smile was slight, barely there. This, Wrathell could forgive. What father would not be wary to find that someone had accosted his daughter in a public place? "Forgive me, my lord, I did not expect we would encounter anyone we knew." He took Wrathell's hand between his and pressed briefly. "It is a pleasure to see you after so long." He bowed. "My most gifted pupil."

"The pleasure is mine, I assure you."

"My daughter said you were in London, and here she is, right as usual." Baynard's hair was more gray than dark now, and his face showed the ravages of age more than Wrathell would have expected. He wondered if his own father was similarly aged. Baynard, however, was no mere country plebeian reaching for the right to be called a gentleman. His clothes were well tailored, and his walking stick was brightly polished mahogany and trimmed in gold. He'd done well for himself. But not well enough to see his daughter dressed in fashion? "Do you paint still?" Baynard asked. "Or have you given that up."

"I do. Some. Yes."

"Don't waste your talent, my boy. Come by my studio." He pointed left. "Not two doors from where we stand. Show me what you've done. I should be happy to see."

Wrathell searched his pockets. He had only cards from his days in Bombay, but even so there was nothing he could write with. Honora had not told him where he might call on them, and he very much wanted to re-establish his acquaintance with his former teacher.

Honora produced a pencil from her coat pocket.

"Thank you." He put his card against the side of a shelf and wrote on the back. "You may find me at Queen Anne Street."

"Number five."

"Yes, Miss Baynard."

"You are not far from our lodgings."

"Oh?"

"Papa's studio is here, but we are at Manchester Square."

He returned both pencil and his card to her and addressed her father. "You must dine with me soon."

"It would be an honor."

"Tomorrow. I am having a few guests over, nothing formal, and I should like it very well if you and your daughter came. About six, I should think."

Baynard replied without the slightest hesitation. "I'm afraid we are engaged."

"We are at the Morin Hotel," Honora said. "In the other Duke Street."

"A hotel?"

"Papa keeps a studio in London for the winter. He finishes as many portraits as will leave him months to paint whatever he likes."

He considered Baynard. "You take commissions, then?"

Baynard bowed. "Indeed, my lord. Your esteemed brother engaged me to paint his portrait."

"I did not know." Likely, the painting was with his father, along with the rest of his brother's possessions. "If it is at Marrable House, I regret to say I have not seen it."

"No, my lord. Alas, it remains unfinished."

His impression was that Baynard was sorry to have brought up a painful subject. What a tug at his heart, to learn there was a recent portrait of his brother. "Do you have it still?"

He looked to his daughter. "Honora?"

"At home."

Yet another lurch to his heart. "So close to Marrable Gate?"

"No sir," she replied. "We no longer live in Elderford. The portrait is in Bury St. Edmunds." Again her father looked to Honora. She spoke in a low voice and addressed him, not her father. "It is very nearly complete. We can have it brought to London." He gripped the brim of his hat, and Honora again read him perfectly. "Shall Papa finish it for you?"

"Is that possible?"

Baynard nodded. "Of course, dear boy. Of course."

Chapter Three

FREDERICK BAYNARD'S STUDIO was at the very top of a narrow building not far from the Duke Street Bookshop. Or was the dashed place called On the Shelf? The stairs to the studio narrowed with each landing. The last flight was bare wood leading to a corridor with four doors, two on each side. On the second door to the right someone had affixed a note card printed with the words *F. Baynard, Portraitist.* Underneath that, in beautiful script, was the word *Enter.*

Wrathell let himself into a small parlor that overlooked the street. No one was in the room, but the scent of turpentine permeated the air and there was a greatcoat draped over a chair. An Indian rug covered most of the floor. Someone had arranged a series of small paintings of fruit along the stone fireplace mantel. Of the art displayed on the walls most were still lifes and country scenes, but there was one lovely quite tasteful nude and three or four with naval themes. In short, an effective demonstration of the considerable breadth of Baynard's talent.

He was glad he'd not brought any of his own efforts. "Hullo?"

Baynard replied from the other side of the only other door. "A moment!"

Wrathell walked to the hearth. The paintings on display were magnificent. He was reminded of his time at Baynard's house, standing before a sheet of paper, pencil and charcoal in hand, wishing he were half as talented as his instructor.

Conversation from the other room was too soft for him to make out. Baynard had company. A model, perhaps? He continued his perusal of the parlor. The furnishings were spartan with but three chairs, a table, and a small writing desk tucked into a corner. A stack of books, a newspaper, and the remains of a meal, no doubt purchased from one of the nearby taverns, obscured most of the table. Several finished canvases were wrapped up for transportation. Unframed paintings leaned against two of the walls.

Baynard came in from the other room, wiping his hands on a cloth as he did. His eyebrows lifted in surprise. "My lord." He bowed. "I'm honored. Have you brought me a portfolio to look at?"

"Lord, no. I'd not dare show you my scribbles." He wanted to. He would have liked to have the courage. But he'd been without competent instruction for ten years while Baynard had made a name for himself with his art. "I have come to discuss commissioning a portrait from you." He stayed by the fire. "A work by Baynard, I've discovered, is much coveted." He looked past Baynard to the door he'd come through. He wanted to paint again. To draw from life. "I hope I have not called at an inconvenient time."

"No, no, not at all." He smiled with genuine warmth.

As a boy, Baynard had been a revelation to him. A patient man who instructed with praise that proved the validity of his criticisms. Between his brother and him they'd had a fair degree of native talent. George had caught on more quickly and had drawn with more instinct and a deep disregard for mastery of the basics. He, however, had applied himself and found that his hours spent sketching paid off in improvement and a love for art.

Baynard shoved the rag into his coat pocket and gestured at the table. "Won't you sit?"

"Thank you. But first, may I look?" He meant the paintings, both those on display and the ones propped against the wall.

"By all means." He gave a hearty grin. "Sample the wares, if you like. May I offer you tea?"

"Yes, please."

Baynard crossed to the other room. "Honora, my dear," he called. "Lord Wrathell is here. Bring tea, if you please."

Honora came to the door, a paintbrush in one hand. She did not have on gloves, as one would not if one were painting, yet her bare hands seemed unduly intimate. She curtseyed, solemn as ever. She wore a gown of soft gray with an apron much stained with paint, completely informal. "Good day, my lord."

"Miss Baynard. I am astonished to see you here."

She looked from her father to him. Her hair was in disarray, and there was a smear of gold paint across her forehead. Several curls had come loose and hid most of her left cheek. Without the scar so visible, she was almost painfully beautiful. What a waste, he thought, to have such beauty spoiled. She used the tip of a finger to pull the wayward hair behind her ear. "I do much of the detail work for the portraits."

"You make an able apprentice, I'm sure." His riposte gained him a ghost of a smile. Never let it be said he could not charm a woman when he put his mind to it. "Had I known you were here, I would have stopped at the confectioner's on the way."

"The jam tarts from Euphan's are excellent." This was a pronouncement, not a hint. She might as well have remarked the weather. The few times he'd spoken to her at Marrable Gate, she'd used a quotidian tone that made it impossible to ascertain the intent of her words. Perhaps because there never was one. She spoke when she had information to relay. "If you should happen to be at loose ends one day I recommend them to you."

"Perhaps I'll buy some on my way home."

"You would not regret it." She nodded. "I'll fetch tea, then."

"Thank you, my dear." Baynard neatened the table and discarded the remains of the morning meal. Wrathell, meanwhile, studied the paintings. One was an arrangement of lemons and pears on a wooden table. Another was of a vase of white roses. Between the two, he liked the roses better. The styles and brushwork were so different, they might have been done by two different artists. A third was a view of a street he did not recognize, somewhere in London, he thought.

When he'd finished examining the work on display to potential customers, he looked through the unwrapped paintings that made up one of the stacks propped against the walls. He tipped the front paintings forward to see those behind.

"You wish to commission a portrait?" Baynard asked.

The moment before he meant to glance at Baynard, the painting at the very back of the stack caught his eye. Honora's face gazed at him from the canvas, brilliant and alive. She was seated on an armchair, her face at three-quarters profile, dressed in red silk. Tiny yellow flowers crowned her head, and in one hand she held a white rose just past full bloom. Her other hand rested on the pages of a book open on her lap. Her focus was on something to her right. Her scar was exaggerated, as if the man who had painted her had seen nothing but the imperfection.

He could not look away. Baynard had perfectly captured his daughter's spirit in expression and emotion. Every detail of the painting, from the book to the stitching on her gown, was exactly to life. She might emerge from the painting, a petal of the rose falling to the ground at her feet. Despite her smile, Baynard had captured a hint of sadness that one did not see in the living woman. This version of Honora Baynard, in all her heartbreaking beauty, was filled with hidden sorrow.

Honora entered from the other room and set the tea things on the table. "Indian black," she said. "I hope that's satisfactory. If not, I am happy to send for something else."

"No, thank you." He searched her face for signs of that sorrow and found none. All this time, he'd thought of her as impervious to strong emotion. God knows she'd shed not a single tear after any of George's attacks, verbal or otherwise. "India made my fortune." He returned his attention to the portrait of Honora. The work haunted and unsettled him, yet he could not stop looking at it. He tore away his gaze to look at the artist who could put this on canvas and break his heart. "Magnificent, Baynard. Magnificent."

"Thank you."

"The still life with lemons?" Honora had joined him, but assumed, incorrectly because he'd been looking in Baynard's direction when he spoke, that Wrathell had meant one of the paintings on the opposite wall. "That is my favorite of his this year." Her voice was low and mild, but there was a richness to the way her words landed on the ear. Very inappropriately, he imagined what it would be like for a lover to speak to him like that, a soft, silky warm tone to keep his spirits uplifted.

She looked at the canvases he'd been going through. "Oh," she said. "No. Lord Leoline—" She regrouped. "Forgive me. I mean, Lord Wrathell. No. That is not a painting anyone was meant to see." She would have pushed the others to cover it, but he refused to be moved.

"Is it for sale?"

"No."

"Everything on those walls is for sale," Baynard replied. "Those"—he meant the paintings where he and Honora stood—"are not."

"If you wish to buy a painting, buy the still life with lemons." In a lower voice, she said, "That is mine, Lord Wrathell."

"I'll buy it from you."

"You misunderstand." She was resolute. "It is not for sale to anyone." She pushed his hand from the painting, and the others fell against it. "I have not burned that one yet."

His head instantly filled with an image of fire blackening the canvas and melting the paint. Sacrilege to say such a thing. "I beg your pardon?"

"That painting is one of mine." He saw, or thought he saw, a flash of sadness in her eyes. No. He must have imagined that.

"Your father said everything here is for sale."

"Everything of his, yes."

"Is not this his studio?"

She kept her voice low. "My lord. That is not his. It is mine."

Of course. "You father made you a gift of that magnificent work and you repay him by burning it? That cannot be. I will buy it of you."

"You misunderstand. That is a self-portrait."

He was momentarily confounded. Baynard could not have painted a self-portrait of his daughter. His brains loosened up. Good God. "You painted that?"

"I will burn it later today."

From the table, Baynard said, "You may have the lemons, my lord. Honora, wrap it for him, won't you?"

"Yes, Papa." To him, she said, "An excellent choice."

Wrathell crossed his arms. Where was the docile, agreeable woman from the bookshop? "I could not possibly accept it."

"Nonsense."

"I prefer the flowers." He pointed at the white roses.

She let out a breath. "The lemons are superior work."

He gave a flippant reply. "Why?" What did her defiance mean? "Because you painted the flowers as well?"

"What a question."

He stared at her, and she returned his look so implacably that the whole world felt turned upside down. "You did."

"That is absurd." Honora walked to the other side of the parlor, lifted the still life from the wall and took it into the other room. As she did, she said, "Your descendants will thank you for obtaining at least one painting they can bear to look at." She lifted a finger and pointed at the ceiling. "'Leoline, the fifth and most favorite of our predecessors. We bless him for a painting by Baynard, the master.'" She lowered her hand and looked at him over her shoulder. There was a wall of defiance there. "What better way to be recalled, my lord?"

"I can think of nothing." He followed her and stood, hands on either side of the doorway.

"You would do Papa a great favor to have a painting of his on display." Docile, obedient Honora was back.

"I'd rather have the flowers."

She cocked her head at him. "Your tea is getting cold."

"So it is." She'd endured a great deal from his brother and had never once broken. Not once. He was in no way fooled by her pleasant expression.

"Of all his pupils you were his favorite."

He laughed, but he was not about to let her pretend with him. "Others will say poor Wrathell went and got himself a Baynard. What a pity he took lemons when he might have had roses."

She set the canvas aside and fetched packing materials. He was ravished by her brisk manner with him. "They'll say you've more taste than they credited you with."

He laughed again. Twice in the space of a quarter of an hour, but not for any decent reason.

"Sit with Papa while I finish this. He wants to visit with you." This was a decided dismissal best obeyed since her father was in the other room.

"Very well." He returned to the paintings stacked against the wall and looked again at Honora's self-portrait. Beauty. Sorrow. That scar. Every other detail perfectly rendered yet the scar took up more space than warranted. Without looking at Baynard, he said softly, "Why has she never married?"

"My lord?"

He left the self-portrait against the wall, hidden behind the others, and joined Baynard at the table. "She's not married." Her scar was nothing compared to everything else, her wit, her intelligence. "Why? She's young yet, I understand that, but she's the daughter of a noted artist."

Baynard shook his head. "With a face like hers? She'd frighten her children." Baynard's amusement faded in the face of Wrathell's appalled silence. The other man picked up his spoon and ran a finger the length of the handle. "Do not think I laugh at her expense. Others have not always been kind to her. You saw that for yourself."

"They were boys. Young and foolish."

"I have observed, my lord, that children are far from the worst. True, they haven't learned the kind of lies adults tell, the ones that do more damage." He glanced over his shoulder to the other room. "The harm we do to those who are different is another case entirely. How am I to keep her safe from that?"

"I should think the connection with you would be advantageous. Particularly for another artist."

Baynard went still. "No one I trust to protect her."

"You have a bleaker view of humanity than I." He could not stop thinking of Honora as an artist's model. "A gentleman respects his wife and protects her for no other reason than that she is his wife."

"A woman marries her husband's family. How can I send her into such uncertainty as that? I saw what she endured as a child and what she endures when strangers see her. The stares and whispers. I do not wish that cruelty on anyone, and I would not wish it on her. Not again. And again and again. Cruelty upon cruelty. I would spare her that."

Further discussion ended because Honora returned with the wrapped painting. She set it against the wall by the door to the corridor. Wrathell brought the third chair around to where she came to stand at her father's right.

"Thank you, my lord."

"You are welcome."

She poured her own tea and added two lumps of sugar. They spoke of inconsequential subjects for several minutes, polite talk. The damnable cold, the prospect of more damnable cold. Whether Baynard and Honora had been to the panorama on display at Leicester Square. He'd been himself the previous week and had been hugely impressed. Baynard had been, but Honora had not, as she had been engaged that day. So she said. With perfect sincerity. He was certain she lied about that.

She put down her tea. "Have you and Lord Wrathell settled on terms for a portrait?"

"No." Baynard gestured at the walls. "Having seen my work, what do you think? I won't take offense if you had rather have some other fellow paint you."

"I should very much like one by you, sir. To match my brother's portrait."

One leg crossed over the other, Baynard tapped his fingers on the table. "The going rate for a portrait depends upon size and complexity. Five hundred to a thousand pounds." He flashed Wrathell a smile. "A certain duke, not your father, desired to be painted mounted upon a rearing stallion, on a canvas ten feet by fifteen. You may be sure that came at a higher price. I might charge a deal less for a beloved pet." He laughed again. "In my day, I've painted many a hound for the lord of the manor. A cat once. Several horses. Children come at a premium. I agree to portraits of children only when there is a nursemaid to manage them."

Honora put down her spoon. Only then did he understand the insult Baynard had dealt her. She managed her father's affairs, this was plain. But he had kept her away from children. "How large a portrait were you thinking of?" she asked.

"Not ten feet by fifteen, if that's what you were hoping. The same size as your portrait of my late brother. I should like to have both paintings by Christmas if possible." He took a breath. "I wish to make a gift of them to my father."

Honora quirked her eyebrows.

"Three weeks from now?" Baynard asked.

"Is it possible?"

Baynard lifted one shoulder. "A portrait of you as you are now, or something else?"

He wanted to amuse Honora and make her smile. "A Legionnaire, I should think. With an entire army."

Baynard straightened. "A Legionnaire, you say?"

"Papa. Lord Wrathell's remark was meant in jest."

He gazed steadily at her and took a sip of his tea. "I should like to hear you make a better joke."

She folded her hands on the table with feigned serenity. "I foresee no difficulty with having a finished painting for you by next Christmas. Don't you agree, Papa?"

"Next Christmas?" Wrathell suppressed a smile and managed outrage quite well.

She gazed at him with complete innocence. "There. You see? With no effort at all, I've made a better joke than you."

"Honora." Baynard's reproach ended the moment.

He relaxed on his chair. "I took no offense." He waved away the tension. Or hoped to. "Tell me, can a portrait be done before this Christmas, Baynard?"

"The portrait, yes, but the paint might not be entirely dry."

He knew this was so. The colors used and the weather must be taken into consideration. "Dry enough for me to make a gift of it, yes?"

Baynard turned to his daughter. "Honora?"

She frowned. "Two weeks to finish. A week to dry, if we are lucky with the weather. With caution, perhaps, but there are no guarantees. If we are also to finish your brother's portrait, that is less certain."

He did not bother appealing to Baynard. "I'll double your usual fee."

She pursed her lips. Infuriating woman. "As I recall, your brother's portrait lacked only the completed background. Laid in, Papa, without the finished details, is that not correct?"

"Ah," said Baynard. He and Honora exchanged a glance, but Wrathell had no idea what silent acknowledgment passed between the two. "If Honora says the work can be done, then yes."

How fascinating that Baynard deferred to Honora. She chewed on her lower lip.

"Your schedule can be cleared, Papa. Mrs. Rosen will be done by tomorrow, I expect. The day after at the latest. Mr. Kingsley can be put off until mid-January." She nodded. "Yes, my lord, I think we could meet your schedule. At triple the usual fee, of course."

"Of course."

"Your brother's portrait can almost certainly be completed in just a few days," she said. "Yours is another matter. You'd have to be here every day until Papa can work without you as a model."

"Here? I'll freeze to death."

"One suffers for great art, my lord."

"I've a better idea," he said. "Stay at Queen Anne Street for the duration. I've rooms that may be used as a studio." He looked at the two of them. "You may come and go as you please. Maintain the studio here, maintain your lodgings as you like, I will cover any reasonable expense."

Honora kept her hands folded on the table. "That is not necessary."

"It is. If you are at Queen Anne Street, we'll save a great deal of time. I shan't be inconvenienced by the cold or a walk up all those stairs." He assumed his lordliest air. "Nor by the journey here."

He'd won, for Baynard approved of the idea.

Chapter Four

THREE ROOMS INTO her investigation of Wrathell's residence, which took up nearly a quarter of the street, Honora concluded this was not a home. Granted he'd barely moved in. One must expect a degree of disorder in such a case. From the occasional bursts of noise and the whiff of paint in the air, she took it that the staff continued to open crates and arrange the contents elsewhere in the house. She'd encountered several rooms bare down to the floorboards and walls stripped to the plaster. Trunks and crates filled two more of the rooms she looked inside.

His staff was predominately English, but in her short time here, she'd seen three men with dark eyes and hair blacker than hers. Just such a man, with the distinctly un-British name of Niraj, served as butler. Like the others Lord Wrathell had brought with him from Bombay, Niraj dressed in a combination of English and foreign garb.

The furnished rooms were those most likely to be seen by visitors. That is, three parlors, a small and large dining room, and a music room. There was in all of them a distinct flavor of his time in Bombay. She could not shake the feeling that the rooms still mourned the previous owner. She found it odd that so little of the present Lord Wrathell's spirit infused those spaces, for he was nothing if not a commanding presence.

She lingered in a room in a state of transition. The walls were freshly painted in brilliant coral. Here, the furniture was not English and not yet arranged. A set of carved elephants had been lined up on the mantel, which was a dark wood carved with multiple squares, each decorated with a different design. Beside the mantel was a pink and yellow footstool. She was inspecting an equally remarkable table when someone called her name.

Lord Wrathell stood in the doorway, resplendent in a silver waistcoat and a dark blue coat. A lock of fair hair fell across his forehead. His warm smile did not deceive her. A razor-sharp wit lay behind that agreeable appearance.

She averted the left side of her face and curtseyed. "My lord."

"Have you and your father settled in?"

"Yes, thank you. I advise that we compare our calendars and arrive at a schedule for your sittings."

"Agreed." He brought one of the chairs to the hearth. "Do sit while we discuss this."

She sat so that he had the right side of her face, but Wrathell moved to the fireplace so that she had to turn again. He put a foot on the fender and an elbow on the mantel. She cleared her throat. "There is one matter of delicacy I wish to bring to your attention."

"Yes?" He picked up the smallest of the elephants, and she wondered what memories he had while he did that.

Best get this over with. "My father has a dear acquaintance whom he visits regularly."

"A dear acquaintance." His smile faded and then his expression shuttered.

She looked anywhere but at him. "He will wish to continue his visits."

He coughed once and replaced the small elephant at the end of the train of them. "I do not anticipate that will present any difficulties."

She interlaced her fingers and rested them on her lap. What a handsome man he was. "Given our time constraints, I hope you will agree his studio must be well lit in case it should be necessary for him to work past the time there is sufficient natural light."

"I'll see to it."

She ran through the list of engagements that could not be rearranged, but Wrathell lifted a hand. "If you please, do give this information to Niraj. He'll see to it they are relayed to my secretary.

"I will do so."

He was at his leisure here, but she was not half as relaxed as he. "I hope you know I am a reasonable man." He had the small elephant in his hands again, now smoothing the wood.

"He does not want to disappoint you, that's all I meant. He will be working long hours, I assure you." She could scarcely believe she was here. At No 5 Queen Anne Street, the London residence of Lord Wrathell. This was simply remarkable.

"I'll not ask either of you to go without sleep or"—a grin flashed on his mouth then vanished—"amusements."

She leaned forward, absolutely determined that he should not regret his asking them to stay here. "Do inform me if you entertain, my lord. I warn you, Papa will forget if you tell him. I'll see that we make ourselves scarce. There will be no difficulty there."

"You are my guests. I don't expect you to hide away in the attic." He gave her a doubtful look. "We dine at seven here. Did Niraj not tell you?"

"I have noted that in Papa's calendar."

"I feel we have not come to an understanding. If I entertain, I expect you and your father to attend. Provided you haven't other plans. If I failed to make that clear, I apologize."

"How kind of you." She, of course, would not attend any public function, and it was unlikely she'd come downstairs for any meal. "I hope you are available to sit from say, eight in the morning to eleven or twelve?"

"I'll see my schedule is clear."

She clasped her hands and stood. "Excellent." He did not stir from his place by the fire. She gave him an inquiring look and shooed away her thrill of admiration. Yes of course she admired him. How could she not? But he was Lord Wrathell.

"What of my brother's portrait?"

Of course. "We expect it to arrive within the week. I assure you the work can be completed without interfering with your sittings." He shivered once, and she, rather stupidly, said, "Are you cold, my lord?"

"Constantly." His discomfort cleared. "Tell me you find it as abominably cold as I do."

"There have been colder winters than this while you were away."

"I daresay."

She shifted her weight, but Wrathell showed no sign of wanting to dismiss her. She did not know what to say to the man Lord Leoline had become. He was confident, easy with himself, and unbearably handsome. She knew too much of him and his life to be at ease. He was not properly a stranger to her.

"I take small comfort in knowing that." Another of his easy grins appeared. "It is the present cold I must endure."

"I expect I am inured to our London winters." She had never known him. Not when he was a boy, and not now, however much she knew about his career. "Compared to you, that is. Here in England we have winter every year without fail. Does it really not snow in India?"

"Not in Bombay." He turned all the carved elephants on the mantel to face the opposite direction. "There is snow in the mountains, though."

"Have you been there?" She had read extensively about Hindustan and its mountainous regions. "To the mountains."

He nodded. "They're quite beautiful. Stark. Nothing like England. Or the Alps, even. I was cold there, but I don't recall it being like this." He exaggerated a shiver.

She could read another dozen geographies and never know the truth as he did. She had not thought of the weather during her reading, only of the geography as best she could imagine. This was the difficulty with living life in one's head. "There are coats, you know. And furs. You might wear two shirts. Have you tried that?"

"And ruin the line of my clothes?" He pretended to be aghast at the idea. "My dear girl, I should think not."

He had yet to look at her with any sign of distaste. He had defended her against his brother and his cronies, and she believed, wanted to believe, must believe, that he would do the same today no matter who she was or what she looked like. "Are you a Corinthian, a dandy, or a Macaroni?"

"Vain is all," he replied. He moved to the other side of the mantel. She shifted until the left side of her face was again out of his line of sight. "My valet found a tailor for me. I don't know if he's any good, but he delivered a greatcoat this afternoon that I hope will answer the purpose when I walk out."

"You might wear it inside."

"I suppose I might. You needn't do that."

"Wear a greatcoat? I haven't got one."

"Move about so I don't see your scar. You are hardly hideously deformed."

She stilled. She had taken a risk, she knew, in walking about the house without her veil at hand. "Others do not care to look at me. I accept that. Just as I accept that others behave as if my face exists for the sole purpose of horrifying or disconcerting them."

"Have I offended you?"

"No. Never. Why would you think that? You never did. You never could. It's I who offends others."

He frowned. "You are a peculiar thing, aren't you?"

He said this as if he had given the subject a great deal of thought. Like as not he had. "I must seem so to you."

His frown continued. "I don't know how to behave with you."

"I understand if you had rather not see me while I am here."

"I have offended you."

"I haven't much experience with conversation except with Papa, and so I think I am not very good at them. I hope you will make allowances for my awkwardness. As to the rest, I am happy to wear a veil if you prefer. I hadn't thought anyone would see me in this part of the house. I apologize."

"Now you offend me, Miss Baynard."

"I apologize again."

He arranged the elephants in a different order, glancing at her several times as he did. "May I ask a question? A serious one. Don't make a joke of it."

"Very well."

He looked at her sideways without any discomfort at his view of her face. She wasn't certain she liked him pretending he did not notice. "You do not owe me an answer."

"I await your question."

"Have you never met a man you hoped to marry?"

She laughed with relief. "I was expecting something more difficult to answer. No, never."

Wrathell's expression turned skeptical. Why? She'd answered truthfully. "I perceive my error. Allow me to restate the question. Has there ever been a man you wanted to marry?"

"I have no answer to that question."

"Why not?"

"Because." She lifted her hands, baffled. "Because it is an impossibility. As well ask me if I have ever wanted to have an undamaged face. The answer is yes, but the woman who can have that does not exist. She is not, and will never be me."

"Why?"

"If Papa had property, if he were richer, there might be someone willing to accept the penalty of a wife such as me in return for property and a fortune. But that is not reality. We do very well now. Especially since the Royal Academy accepted him. But not so well as to attract the attention of that sort of man."

"Honora." The sorrow with which he said her name tugged at her heart. She did not mean to make him sad.

"I do not to consider my life to be sad in the least. There are many people whose lives are not nearly as pleasant as mine." She smoothed her skirt, pressing hard on a bit of decorative cording that had loosened from the fabric. "I do not mind solitude. Often, I prefer it. People can be such wretches, you know."

"True."

He was thinking of his brother's cruelty to her. So was she. She could still feel rocks crashing into her, the sticks whipping against her arms. "They can also be kind. Most people are. They can mend their unkindness. It's just we notice unkindness more than kindness. As we notice a burning house more than a house that is not on fire."

He let out a breath and pushed away from the mantel. "I expect you have the right of it."

"I do." Her face was her face. Nothing could alter that.

"Tell me what you have done while you are in London."

She wondered if this interaction between them was what other people experienced. Did others talk back and forth like this?

"I should like recommendations for my winter amusement," he said.

She tapped her foot while she mentally ran through the advertisements she had seen in the various papers and broadsides Gilmore brought home. "There were several pantomimes week before last."

"Did you enjoy them?"

"Two were very well received by critics. One was thought abominable whilst the other was pronounced dull." Wrathell's eyebrows drew together, and she quickly went on. "Three farces were found excellent. There were several exhibitions of artworks. Papa declared them most enjoyable, particularly the panorama, but you already know that. Dr. Eddings presented a paper on fossils that was said to be quite edifying. There were lectures on the subjects of economy, zoology, planetaria, mathematical physics, and the benefits of coffee over tea. That last is absurd. Tea is clearly more beneficial to the constitution."

Wrathell held up a hand. "I am exhausted listening to you. You have attended all those events? You can't have."

Was he daft? What a question. She knew so much about his life, and nothing, really, about the man. What he liked, or did not like, what amused him or not. She had no way of knowing if he would prefer farce over tragedy. "I attended none of them. You asked about events of the sort you might find amusing whilst you are in London. I listed several for you, as I do not know your tastes."

"How did you know about them if you did not attend?"

"I read about them."

"I see." His smile was devastating. He shook the smallest of the elephants at her. "What have *you* done that you found amusing?"

"The subscription library at The Duke Street Bookshop is excellent and keeps me well entertained."

"Yes, where we met. What have you seen besides the bookshop and your father's studio? Have you been to Ackermann's or Regent Street? Any of the parks? The British Museum? The zoo?"

"Your list is as exhausting as mine."

"You continue to fail in an answer."

"I have not been to any of them."

"I thought you'd been in town for weeks."

"Since November, sir."

"In all that time, you've been to a bookshop?"

"And Euphan's."

"I shall take you and your father to the museum. After today's sitting."

She clasped her fingers together so hard it hurt. She trusted him. She believed his intentions were nothing but the best. "Papa will not agree."

Chapter Five

A T THE APPOINTED time the day after the Baynards' arrival at Queen Anne Street, Wrathell put on his uniform in preparation for his first sitting. The uniform fit well, though a bit snug in the shoulders. He looked quite dashing, he thought.

As he headed upstairs to the rooms transformed into a studio for Baynard, he fingered the mend in the upper right lapel of his jacket. He'd had his share of injuries, including a saber cut across the back of his thigh that had hurt like the devil but left almost no scar. The bullet wound was another matter. He'd nearly died from that. The surgeon had told him afterward that he hadn't expected Wrathell to survive. The man had then handed over the letter of condolence he'd meant to send to his father. He'd kept it as a reminder that his life could easily have ended that day.

He wasn't in the Navy, and this uniform had no power to transport him to the deck of a ship except in his imagination. Yet he'd not had his head so full of memories since his early days in Bombay.

Upstairs, Baynard greeted him with a smile and a bow. "Ah, young lordling. One hopes you are in fine fettle on this most excellent of days."

"Sir." This was how Baynard had greeted him every day they met at Marrable Gate or at Baynard's home in Elderford. "Were it not for this uniform, I would expect to sit down to my anatomy lessons."

He picked up several sheets of loose paper. "I've a few ideas of how to pose you. May I?"

"The same as my brother?"

"Similar, perhaps. A man in uniform must be dashing in addition to handsome." They spent some minutes working out a pose while Baynard took sketches and muttered to himself, quite lost in his thoughts. "Like so, my lord." He demonstrated. "If you could maintain that position, yes?"

It happened that standing without leave to move was not as simple as he'd imagined. The moment he took the pose, his nose itched. Then a strand of his hair tickled him, and he needn't stay frozen, but his fidgeting became an issue, and by all the angels in heaven, this was mind-numbingly dull. "Baynard."

"Mm."

"What do you say to a visit to the British Museum later today?"

Baynard replied without taking his eyes off his work. "Ask Honora after I've released you, my lord. She'll know if I am free."

"We can have luncheon after. There are several decent places to eat nearby."

"That would be agreeable."

They lapsed into silence for several minutes. Standing with nothing to do to occupy his mind was damned boring. His thoughts flitted from subject to subject. The pleasure of having Baynard and Honora with him. Whether he ought to repaint the third parlor in a different blue—no. Should he buy the property in Shropshire or the one in Dorset? The Dorset estate. His portrait in one of the parlors for the admiration of his future children who must learn that their father had once been a splendid young lieutenant. Except, of course, the portrait and its fate would be with his father. "I've just realized."

"Yes?"

"I'll need a second portrait."

"Oh?" Baynard scratched his cheek with a charcoal-covered finger and left a black smudge in its place.

"A civilian pose too. Same terms as this, naturally. To have here. Will you do it?"

Baynard chuckled. "I am happy to oblige you, my lord."

"You won't mind staying awhile longer, then?"

"We are obliged to return to Bury St. Edmunds before the New Year. I'll not have the use of my studio after January. Honora will know what may be done at what time."

"Excellent." He was bored again in five minutes. Eons later, the door opened and Honora came in. She did not have her veil. Was this defiance of her father? "Please say you're here to distract me."

She laughed at him. "I thought you'd hold up better than this. He's been awful, hasn't he, Papa?"

"Never."

"A perfect model, aren't I, Baynard?"

Honora curtseyed. "I shan't disturb you."

"Amuse me, Honora." Peculiar she might be, but he'd not been bored talking to her. "I demand it of you."

"My lord. Since you demand it of me."

"I beg of you."

She took a seat and placed three unbound volumes of various sizes on the table by her father. "Shall I read to you?"

"What have you brought?"

"A pamphlet." She held up a slim set of paper-bound sheets. Her father paid no attention to them.

"What is it?"

She read the front. "*The Zoological Society's Pheasant Expedition.*"

"What else have you got?"

"*A Synoptical Catalogue of British Birds.* By Thomas Forster."

"You are fixated on birds, Honora? I'd no idea."

She opened the book. "'Ordo one, Accipitres. Genus I. One. Falco Chrysaetos. Aquila Aurea.' He's put a question mark after that. I wonder why. 'The Golden Eagle.'"

"What else?"

"I'm sure you won't like it." She picked up the volume and dropped it as if bored. "Indeed, my lord, I hesitated to bring it with me."

"It can't possibly be as thrilling as *The Pheasant Expedition*, I concur completely. Nevertheless. I will be obliged in this."

"It is a novel." She spoke with such a conviction of disregard for the form that he almost believed her. "I've no idea how it got into the books I brought back from Duke Street. Most peculiar." She brought the third volume to the top. "The title is apropos. As soon as I saw it among my books, I thought of you."

"What is it?"

"*A Winter in London.* By Thomas Surr." With a sigh, she shut the cover. "I can tell you already what happens. It will be winter. In London. We've only to go outside to know all that will happen." She frowned. "What a shame to give away the plot in the title."

He wanted not to laugh, but she had mightily amused him. "Read, and we shall see if you have the right of it."

"If you think you won't be bored."

"If it begins with London in winter, you have leave to skip to a chapter with a different season."

Honora opened the book. "Oh. How very odd."

"What?"

"It's not London at all. This is shocking. Most shocking."

"Read out loud, Honora. Out loud." Thank God she had come here to amuse him. He would still be mad with boredom otherwise.

She maintained a delightfully somber expression. "It will not be improving of your character."

"I've faced similar perils and lived. Read on."

She did, in a voice of silk infused with smoke. Fifty minutes passed with him absorbed in the story of a shipwrecked orphan boy.

Baynard tapped the top of his easel with his pencil. "My lord?"

"Hmm?"

"I release you for the day."

"Already?"

"Yes."

He walked to the table where Honora was seated and took the empty chair. "I don't know that I've ever been so glad to sit in my life." He reached for the book, but Honora swept it out of his reach. "About the museum and luncheon. Honora, your father says I am to ask you if he is free this afternoon."

"He has no appointments until tonight when he is engaged to dine."

He kept a straight face. "With someone amusing, I hope."

"Yes."

"That is good news." Did she keep her father's entire calendar, personal and private, in her head? "The very best news. There are several excellent places we might eat once we're done at the museum. Have you a preference, Honora?"

Her eyebrows lifted. "I cannot know where you would prefer to have your meal. Papa has a fondness for German chefs. Is there an establishment such as that near the museum?"

Baynard stood behind her chair, hands gripping the top stretcher. "You must not expect Honora to accompany us."

The words were carelessly said, as if they contained no power to harm. Honora looked away.

"But I do." He understood the reason for her adroit deflections of him, no more her father's expectation that she would go nowhere and be seen by no one. The heartbreak was that Baynard meant well. He loved his daughter and wanted only the best for her, but keeping her out of sight like this? Prevented from most every opportunity to enjoy herself or make friends? "I say we make a day of it."

"In weather like this?"

"We'll have the use of my carriage," Wrathell said.

"Alas," Baynard said. "Honora has a great many obligations that prevent her from going out."

"A pity." Retreat was sometimes the better option. "Perhaps another time."

"Honora does not go out," Baynard said. "She finds it disagreeable."

He leaned back, unwilling to engage Baynard in this respect. "On the subject of one's social obligations, I will have guests to dinner on Thursday. To welcome Admiral Goldin to London."

Honora put her hand over her father's. "The significance, Papa, is more than just him inviting an admiral to dine. I presume, my lord, that he is in town on the matter of his possible appointment as Third Sea Lord."

"I cannot comment as to that. However, he is a close friend and advisor."

"What Lord Wrathell did not say, Papa, was that he served under Admiral Goldin, who was commander of the *Active* and later the *Miramount*."

"Yes. That's so. He's brought his wife and daughter to London with him. As you might imagine, he is anxious that they be amused while they are here."

Honora fell silent. Motionless and without expression. Wrathell did not understand how he could have upset her, but he feared he had.

"There can be no doubt the admiral is a great man." Baynard's reply was careful. "I am equally certain Miss Goldin is a delightful young lady."

"This will be her first time in London." Why was Honora so deathly silent? "I should like to introduce her to you, so that she meets at least one young lady her own age."

"Ah," Baynard said. "I understand now." He shook a finger at Wrathell. "The admiral is your colleague, friend, and advisor."

"Yes."

"You are a Marrable and now your father's heir. If I were Admiral Goldin, I too would bring my daughter to London."

"Papa."

"My dear boy. You forget that I have known you since before you joined the Navy. You are a man of parts. No one who knows you can doubt your excellence. What I mean to say is that no man of discernment, which the admiral surely is, could know you and not believe you would be a worthy husband for his daughter."

Wrathell looked away. Baynard was right. There was such an expectation between the admiral and him. Honora had guessed that sooner than her father.

Chapter Six

WRATHELL REGRETTED HIS decision to go to his club after sitting for Baynard, for not two minutes into his walk home a bone-numbing wind whipped snowflakes through the air. His lunch of overcooked and under-spiced mutton and vegetables was not sufficient reward for being out in this cold. Granted, his new greatcoat was a help, but twenty paces from the door his toes became lumps of ice. The ancient Greeks had missed the mark giving Hades torturous heat in his realm. Gods who wished to torment hapless mortals ought to trap them in an endless London winter.

He shoved his hands into his pockets and hunched over, moving as fast as was safe given the conditions. As he approached The Duke Street Bookshop, he thought with longing of the stove inside.

Too late he realized someone had just left the shop, and that he was moving too fast to prevent a collision. He bowled the fellow over. Oh God, not a man. A woman. She cried out as she was thrown toward an overloaded wagon heading down Duke Street. He fought for balance in the ice and slush, got hold of the woman's upper arm and shoved her away from the street. Off-balance, he slid on ice and slush and careened toward the shop window.

He braced himself for an impact that never came. Instead, someone gripped him by the upper arm and hauled him around, no easy task given he wasn't a small man. His hat flew off and glanced off the window with a sharp rap that rattled the glass.

"Here now," said a male voice. "Are you hurt, milord?"

Wrathell steadied himself and took stock. He had not crashed into the window. He had not fallen and broken his head. Miraculously, he was in the grip of Baynard's hulk of a footman. The fellow released him and stepped back.

"No, no, I'm not hurt." He looked in the direction he'd shoved the woman and did not see her. The wagon driver continued down the street. "Thank you."

"She'd have gone through the window if you hadn't put yourself in harm's way, milord." The servant—Gilman, that was his name—was ashen.

The young male clerk from the bookshop dashed out, no hat, no proper coat. He skidded to a stop. "Is aught well. Sir? Miss?"

Behind Gilman, Honora stood white as snow, a hand on her chest. Her veil hid her face so once again, he had no idea of her state. He could well imagine. A parcel lay in slush, slowly turning dark. The entire right side of her mantle was wet, and that could only have happened if he'd knocked her to the ground.

"Miss Baynard?" The clerk knew her name? Half a dozen of the ladies inside the shop peered out the windows, eyes wide. "Are you injured?"

Wrathell said, "Honora?" He damn well had the right to use her given name.

"I am unhurt." There was no emotion in her voice.

The clerk picked up Wrathell's hat, looked at it, and buffed it against his sleeve before he handed it over. "Nothing that can't be made right by a valet who knows his job."

Wrathell accepted the hat and put it on. "Thank you."

"Are you certain you're well, miss?"

"Yes."

"I thought we were about to lose the window and a customer." The fellow surveyed Wrathell, then Honora and Gilman. "I'll take myself back inside. Anyone who'd like a cup of tea to settle their nerves, please come in."

Wrathell took several deep breaths, because Gilman was correct. She might've been badly injured. "Are you all right, Honora?"

She lifted her veil and turned her head half an inch toward him. As if he gave a fig about her scars. She was as pale as Gilman, but to all appearances unperturbed. He knew better than to assume she'd come through without harm. He'd seen her with this same implacable calm after his brother and his odious band of youths who ought to have known better had pelted her with rocks and sticks.

Back then, he'd thought her ungrateful for his intervention, she was so cold and silent, and he'd walked away from her without another word. She'd run after him, calling out, "Lord Leoline! Please wait."

She'd thanked him gravely, with a curiously ungraceful curtsey.

He remembered that day as if it were yesterday. The blood trickling from her right temple to the side of her throat, welling from cuts opened on the backs of her hands.

"I apologize," he'd said. Back then, her scar had been an unsightly mass of twisted red, pink, and white. From the time he first saw her after her injury, she couldn't have been much older than ten or eleven—so thin and solemn—and what business had his brother tormenting her like that? Marshaling an attack on a child who could not help whatever had happened to her face. "On behalf of my brother. The others can be damned."

Her silence had changed and transmuted and when, in the face of that awful quiet, he'd walked away from her, her eyes and face had been imprinted on his soul. The second time he'd fought his brother over her, his brother had sneered and said, "Have you fallen in love with the ugly thing?"

By God, he *had* been put on this earth to protect her. His punch had broken his brother's nose.

Now, as on that day, her eyes fixed on him, wide and an impossibly dark blue. He'd never seen anyone with eyes like hers. "Again, you come to my rescue."

"Rescue? Hardly. I knocked you over."

She looked at the street and back.

"No gentleman allows a woman to come to harm." He forced a smile. "That will teach me to walk with my head in the clouds."

"Are *you* all right, my lord?"

"I am." He shook off his mood. "Thanks to your man Gilman here."

Her mouth twitched up at the corners, not a smile by any stretch, a mere acknowledgment of him before her features returned to unreadable gravity. She curtseyed, a belated motion, and he thought, but could not be sure, that she'd only now realized she ought to.

"Yes," she said. She wrapped her arms around her waist. "Brave, courageous Gilman. We commend you, Gilman." She glanced in the direction of the servant. "If you had not already earned my enduring appreciation and gratitude you would have them now."

"It was his lordship saved you from harm, miss."

"You fell," Wrathell said.

"I did not."

"Look at your gown there." He pointed, annoyed, anger building that she did not trust him with the truth of her condition. "You fell to the ground. I saw it. I heard. Gilman, go to Queen Anne Street and fetch a carriage to bring her home."

"My lord. You are overwrought. If you do, Gilman, I shall never speak to you again."

The wind came up again, and he shivered. Her dark, thick eyebrows rose. "Perhaps you ought to confirm that you have not been injured." She walked toward him with no sign of a limp. "Shall I have Gilman check you for injuries?" She meant for him to laugh, but he didn't. "Or shall I?"

That did him in. He shook his head. "Five years of sun and monsoons, and a few flakes of snow make me miserable."

She smiled, and it was ravishing, but the curve of her mouth vanished after mere seconds. Wind blew wisps of her dark hair around her forehead. "We stand at an impasse."

"Easily broken." He held out his arm. "We'll walk together and see who is injured and who is not. Gilman, be prepared to fetch the carriage for one or both of us."

"Milord."

She took his arm. "Is your new coat insufficient to a London season?"

"It's the rest of me that's cold now."

"Have you considered winter boots?"

He looked at his feet. "I like these. I had them made in Bombay. They're comfortable. And I'm setting a fashion. Three of the fellows at my club asked where I got them."

"Thicker stockings, then." A fleeting smile pulled at her mouth.

"My feet must fit in these, you know." Perhaps she had a point. His toes had gone numb again.

"Your poor, frozen feet bear an unreasonable burden for your pride."

He grinned. "My fashionable frozen feet."

"Gloves?"

He held up his hands. "The finest kid."

"Lovely. Sufficiently warm I trust."

He wriggled his fingers. "I daresay."

"Unmentionables of a warmer weave?"

"Un-what?" He put a hand to his heart. In the Navy, he'd developed a black humor that had stayed with him. Laugh while you can, he'd learned, at whatever you can. Or go mad. "This is not something I know." Wind barreled down the street, and he shivered once, then again, so frozen his words turned to ice in his throat.

She slowed, then stopped, obviously considering his attire. He spread his arms wide while she tapped her chin with a finger. "Haven't you a scarf?"

"No." Let her admire his person to her heart's content.

"At all, or not at the moment?"

He gave a sheepish shrug. So far, he saw no sign that she'd been harmed by her fall, but he knew her capacity for disguising injury. "Not at all."

"There is a shop not far from Papa's studio where we may remedy your appalling lack of winter attire. I can vouch for their goods."

"Lead on, Macduff."

She lowered her veil. He frowned, but this was her choice, was it not? If she wished to be veiled, it was no business of his. They headed to the corner and waited for a clear crossing. Their route took them past icy debris and gutters running with God only knew what. He detected no limp in her stride.

At the shop she'd mentioned, Gilman moved in to open the door for them. The servant, Wrathell noted, wore a thick knit scarf around his throat.

"Good day," she said to the clerk, who came to his feet when they entered. Gilman stayed by the door, dangling Honora's still-wet package from the bookshop.

"Good day to you, madam. Sir." The shopkeeper bowed to them both, but his attention was on Wrathell. His clothes might not be adequate for the season but tailors in India were as skilled as English ones. "How may I assist you?"

Honora patted his arm. "My companion is in need of a warm scarf. Several of them, actually. My father and I were here recently, and I quite admired them. You have them still, I hope."

"Indeed." He gestured in the direction of the items.

Wrathell walked to the fire at the other end of the shop and held out his hands. Heat soaked into the bits of him closest to the source. His toes tingled, then hurt as the heat penetrated his boots. He sighed at this evidence that he must retire his favorite boots in favor of footwear better suited to the climate.

Honora had gone to the display. "One white," she said. She handed the shopkeeper something he supposed was a scarf. "Wrathell, come here would you?"

The clerk's desultory manner came to an end, and Wrathell found himself the subject of a second assessing look. This reaction to his title was so new to him that he continued to be taken aback when it happened. He held his hands closer to the fire. "Can't you bring them here?"

She looked over her shoulder at him. No one was more serious than she, even in the matter of scarves. "No. I must confirm that this gray matches your eyes."

He approached, amused and flattered that she took the selection of a scarf so seriously. "Is it warm?" he asked the clerk. "For that is my chief requirement, that this thing be warm. I don't give a fig for the color."

"You will later," she said.

"Our very best woven silk, my lord. Kept close to your body you will not find a warmer material than this." He clasped his hands and rubbed them. "Put good English wool over that, and you will never suffer the slightest coldness of your neck or throat were there a blizzard." He picked up another scarf. "We carry only the very finest wool. Hand combed and spun, knitted by the most gifted women in Nottinghamshire. They work exclusively for me, my lord. There are no finer scarves anywhere in the kingdom."

"I'll take the one on top." He pointed. "A woolen one, too. That one there." He grinned at Honora. "We are done shopping."

In scathing tones he had never yet heard from her, she said, "We most certainly are not." The clerk had reached for the top scarf as directed, but Honora lifted her head. "My dear sir, you do him no favors by acceding to his uninformed whims."

"Whims?"

"Sir," she said to the clerk. "Consider this. Whom will he blame when at home he sees that the color does not suit him in the least?"

"A fair point, miss."

"Correctness is often excellent. He'll have one white, a blue, dark blue, please. Do come here, Wrathell."

When he had, she held a scarf to his cheek. He enjoyed the fuss.

"Ah," the clerk said. "A very close match for his eyes. What exquisite taste you have, miss."

Wrathell wound the fabric another time around his neck. "I don't care what it's made of, or what color it is, or whether it matches my eyes. I require only that it be warm."

"I guarantee you that, milord." The clerk bowed. "You are welcome to take this one with you. If for some reason you do not find it satisfactory return it at your leisure."

"This will do." Honora handed over a scarf of scarlet wool. "A matching number in wool. Burgundy and that striped one to start."

"I've only got one neck."

She was all crisp business. "One neck to be clad for morning calls, afternoon calls, luncheons, dinners, and formal engagements. You have here a start, my lord, but nothing like what you ought to have on hand. Ask your valet. He'll not gainsay me."

"My valet is Indian and as unfamiliar as I with dressing for a London winter."

That got her attention away from selecting him a scarf for every day of winter yet to come. "May I recommend that you buy him one or two as well? Perhaps for all your native staff. They too must suffer from the cold."

She was right. The servants he'd brought with him from Bombay were even less able to deal with winter than he was. He nodded to the clerk. "A selection of woolen scarves. A dozen should do."

The clerk beamed at him. "Shall I send them to Marrable House, my lord?"

"No." He set one of his new cards on the counter top so the bill could be sent to him for payment. All but one of the scarves were set aside for later delivery. Honora handed him the scarlet one, and he put it around his neck.

Outside the shop, still in the recess of the doorway, she examined him, veil lifted for the purpose. She adjusted the scarf. "That wasn't difficult at all now, was it?"

He wanted to sketch her. To capture in paint all the contradictions of her. Her beauty. Her sadness. The wit that lived in her eyes. "You've taken very good care of me, Honora."

"Someone must." She patted his chest.

He caught her hand in his and pointed up with the other. "Look."

"What?" But she saw what he did. The proprietor of the shop had not only hung a wreath on the door, he had suspended a sprig of mistletoe from the ceiling.

He brought her close, and before he could think the better of it, he kissed her. He kissed her until Gilman coughed discreetly.

Chapter Seven

⌘

Honora's bedroom window overlooked the back of the house. The sky above the mews was a dull pewter slice above roofs covered in a light dusting of frost and snow. She could not stop thinking of Wrathell's kiss. It had meant nothing to him and ought to have been the same for her. There had been mistletoe. He had kissed her as the season obliged. And so. Nothing. But it had been the most extraordinary experience of her life.

Today, with her father visiting his mistress and Wrathell out for the afternoon, she considered a walk to Cavendish Square or to her old haunts at Manchester Square, a route that would take her very near The Duke Street Bookshop. With luck, she would find a title within her means. No sooner thought than she moved to action. Her maid fetched her cloak and veil, and not ten minutes after, she was out with Gilman following a few paces behind.

Today, Charlie had the management of the store. When he took her coins in exchange for a magazine, he said, "No permanent harm from your smash-up with Lord Wrathell the other day, I hope?"

"Not at all." A rank lie, for she'd a wicked bruise where the back of her thigh had hit a corner of her book when she fell.

"I thought my heart would stop when I saw you two collide. He saved your life, miss. No mistake about it." He gave her a devastating grin. Would he smile at her like that if he had to look at her face? She rather thought he might. "He saved our window too so he's twice the usual hero."

"He is, sir."

"Ah. There's the look. What better time to fall in love than Christmastime?"

"I do not understand."

"Why, your heart and Lord Wrathell's as one, what else would I mean?"

"Me? In love?" Her stomach fell to her toes. "Whatever gave you that idea?"

"He's on his way to falling in love with you, make no mistake of it. I'm never wrong about such things."

"You are wrong about me. And him." Charlie had seen her face. He must know it was impossible.

He tied a bow in the string around her parcel. "I think I know the look of a man falling in love."

"What nonsense."

He handed her the package. "Happiest of reading to you, Miss Baynard."

"You deluded man."

"If I were a betting man I'd ask you to wager on it."

"Good day to you too."

On her way back to Queen Anne Street, she passed Euphan's and slowed to admire the display of goods that called to her of buttery sweets to melt in her mouth. Alas, she had but a half penny, and she was determined to save that toward several jam tarts for her birthday on Christmas Eve.

As she sighed over the display of tarts and cakes, from the corner of her eye she saw a gentleman striding toward her along the same walkway. A man of fashion bundled up against the cold and walking rather too fast. She moved closer to the windows to give him room to pass her by. He walked with admirable athleticism, and she'd just thought he seemed familiar when she realized why. It was Wrathell.

She waited for him to reach her and ignored her racing pulse. He would not kiss her again. He was not falling in love with her. She was not falling in love with him. Perhaps he'd cross the street before he saw her. But he did not. Perhaps he'd not notice her standing there by the shop. But he did.

"I thought that must be you. My dear Honora." He doffed his hat and bowed as if she were any of the fine ladies one might meet in London. The dark blue scarf was wrapped around his throat, and his boots were new. "Have you been somewhere thrilling?"

"My lord." She curtseyed. "All the way to the bookshop and back."

He glanced at Gilman. The footman held the magazine she'd bought. "I hope you bought something to read to me."

"Are you bored with *A Winter in London?*"

"Not in the least, but we'll soon finish it and then what?"

"*The Pheasant Expedition?*" She imagined for a moment she was a normal lady. Miss Goldin, perhaps, engaging in flirtatious banter with the handsomest man in London.

"Where else did you go besides the bookshop?"

"Nowhere."

"Nonsense. You came here." He looked around her to the door and the name painted on the glass. "Euphan's. The confectioner you mentioned, as I recall." He looked at her empty hands. "Not a jam tart in sight."

She turned her hands palms up and stared at them. "Alas, my lord, not a one."

Wrathell tucked her arm under his, and Gilman opened the door for them. They went in. The clerk greeted them with a cheerful smile. "Two jam tarts," Wrathell said. "Raspberry, if you please." Money changed hands and then the tarts. He gave one to her.

"Thank you." She savored the novelty of someone not her father purchasing anything on her behalf. Her tart smelled delicious.

Wrathell ate his in three bites and licked his lower lip. "I'm disappointed in you, Honora."

She froze, the tart still on her palm. "My lord?"

He laughed at her. "You should have told me they were so delicious."

"Very popular item," the clerk said. "Shall I box up a dozen for you to take home, milord?"

"Four more, please." More money changed hands, and Honora found herself with a second tart to join the first, this one still warm from the oven.

Her mouth watered in anticipation. Unfortunately, Euphan's wasn't a large shop and they'd installed mirrors on the walls so she could not safely lift her veil.

Wrathell leaned in, unexpectedly close. His voice warmed her ear. "Eat your tarts, darling girl."

"Oh happy, happy day." She breathed in the scent. "I cannot wait to get home."

"I adore a woman so easily pleased." He ate another himself and handed the last to Gilman. "Eat yours, Honora, and I'll buy us a dozen more."

She stared at her hand and then at her reflection in the mirrored wall. Why shouldn't she? If anyone saw her face and was offended, did that mean she hadn't the right to be seen? She put a hand to her veil, horribly aware of the clerk behind the counter and of Wrathell's regard of her, and of Gilman too.

"To hell with what anyone thinks," Wrathell said softly.

She lifted her veil. Out of habit, she turned her face to the left to keep that side of her face out of Wrathell's direct line of sight. She took a bite.

"Delicious, isn't it?"

"Mm." She ate her tart with full enjoyment at the taste and, undeniably, a degree of anxiety about standing in a shop in public, where anyone might see her. Nothing happened. No one objected or stared. She ate her second tart.

"A dozen more of those." He placed a coin on the counter. "And three more for us to take with us. Box up the others."

Wrathell kept a tart for himself and gave one to Gilman before handing him the box. "On your way, my good man," he told the servant. Wrathell held the door for her and let it close when she walked out. He stayed by the door, though. "Look at this," he said.

She came back to him. "What?"

"Up there." He pointed, grinning.

Mistletoe.

Wrathell continued to grin.

"No," she said. "Oh no."

"What luck. Here is your veil, out of the way." There was no time to think or object or even fall boneless into his arms. He kissed her again, and his lips were warm and soft.

"You taste of jam," she said when he drew back.

"So do you." He handed her another tart and ate his in two bites. As they walked toward Queen Anne Street, she ate another tart while anyone passing by might see her face. She felt bare. Exposed. Vulnerable. She was safe only when no one could see her scar. There were others on the street, and some of them stared. Did Wrathell not notice? She reached for her veil.

"Let them think what they like. You have tarts to eat."

"I do." They continued walking. She took a delicate bite, exaggerating the motion and chewing slowly and with great delight.

"We should have these for Christmas dinner, don't you think?" he asked.

"I'm saving to buy some for my birthday."

"Your birthday? When is your birthday? Is it soon?"

"The same day as yours, my lord."

"Is that so? We should have a joint celebration. With jam tarts for all."

She laughed. He'd not meant anything by kissing her again. He couldn't have. She'd never spent time with anyone who followed traditions like kissing under the mistletoe. A kiss or two under the mistletoe meant nothing. "That's the most splendid idea I've heard in all my life." She leaned against his arm, and for a time they walked in silence while she made her final tart last as long as possible. "You are staring at me," she said.

"I am."

Since he could not see her scar, that could not be the cause. "Why?"

"Curiosity, I suppose."

"About?"

"Whether you can finish that tart." Behind them, Gilman snorted. They kept walking. "I should hate for you to be uncomfortably full."

"You bought a dozen of them."

"Agreed." He continued to stare at the last of the tart in her hand.

"My lord." She stopped walking. "The heavens are surely weeping." She extended her hand. "Here."

"I couldn't possibly." His eyes told a different story, and he exaggerated his longing.

"You could," she replied. "You desire to. More to the point, you will be cross if you do not."

"You are entirely correct." Instead of taking the tart from her, he leaned in and ate it from her fingers. She wore gloves, of course, but it was such an intimate thing for him to do, she was both thrilled and taken aback. The flood of emotions shattered her peace of mind while he was entirely unaffected. "You are the very best fellow I know," he said. He licked his lower lip and nodded in Gilman's direction. "Those tarts won't survive the day, I promise you. What do you say we sit in the parlor and devour them all?"

"If we did that neither one of us would be able to eat our dinner."

"I do not follow you."

"Forgive me, I was speaking nonsense. Yes, of course we must eat all the tarts."

"I'm happy you understand that."

A gentleman walking the opposite direction lifted his hat as he passed them. He recoiled when he saw her, eyes wide in shock. He could not help but see her because she had turned to face Wrathell. Her chest clenched, and she reached for her veil.

Wrathell stopped her. "What shall I do?" he asked, no trace of a smile on his face. He shoved her veil over the back of her head. "Ignore the next fellow to gawk at you? I shall if that's what you want. Politely emphasize his error? I'll do that too. Shall I wish them all good day or tell them all to go to the devil? I'll break all their faces if you wish it."

"Not the devil." He was so close to her that when she lifted a hand, she touched him. "Nothing at all. Do nothing. It does not matter."

He gazed at her. Locked eyes with her. He stared at her mouth and she could not think of anything but the surge of tension through her that could served no purpose but to increase her misery. Gilman cleared his throat. Wrathell took a step back. He tugged on the lapels of his greatcoat. "The tarts, Gilman."

"Milord."

He fished out his penknife and cut the twine. "Let them all go to the devil. You and I will celebrate a winter in London."

"You cannot protect me from that."

"I can try."

"Brave Lord Leoline."

"It's you who is brave."

"No." She reached into the box and handed him a tart, then gave one to Gilman before taking one for herself. "I know how to live the life that belongs to me."

She lifted her tart to his mouth, and he took a bite. They finished the rest before they reached Queen Anne Street and arrived there to the happy news that the portrait of Wrathell's brother had been delivered while they were out. The portrait, Niraj informed them, had been taken straight to her room.

"Well, my lord, what do you think?" She bounced on her toes with excitement. "Do you wish to see it now, or wait until Papa and I have assessed its state of completion?"

"What do you think?"

She picked up her skirts and dashed up the stairs, leaving him behind. Halfway to the first landing, Wrathell was at her heels. "A turtle could move faster than you," he said, taking the stairs two at a time as he passed her.

"That's because you have those great long legs." She hurried after him. He would not beat her up the stairs. Absolutely not. She flew past him and was ahead by the first landing and was in the lead from a strategy of blocking him from passing her. A few steps from the second landing, she cried out, "Hah! You are the loser!"

Wrathell's boots clattered on the steps, and he leapt three stairs to the landing. "Ho, there, my little rabbit." He gripped the bannister on either side of him and leaned over. "Who is the loser?"

She was too out of breath to laugh. She reached for his coat to stop his dash down the corridor but missed. "Wretch!"

All in one movement, he came back to her, and then she was in his arms, and he was striding away with her amid their gales of laughter. He carried her to her room as if she weighed nothing. She gasped and huffed and pretended to beat his shoulders. "...not...your rabbit."

"You are my very own little hare."

"...too full...tarts."

His arms and chest were hard and solid, which she had not expected, but, then, she'd never been in a man's arms before. Through some feat of athleticism she did not understand, he opened her door without her having the slightest worry he might drop her. He strode inside, and she let go one arm to point. "There it is."

He adjusted his hold on her when she had just one arm around his shoulders, and that brought her into greater contact with him. The painting lay on the table, wrapped in brown paper and tied with thick twine.

He set her down, and she straightened her clothes and caught her breath while he made use of his penknife again to cut the twine. She edged in and helped him remove the paper and cotton batting. He fetched an andiron from the hearth to pry open the wood frame intended to keep the painting inside from damage.

"Let me see."

"Patience, my darling rabbit. Patience." He lifted it from the packing and took it to her desk to prop it up against the top cabinet. She stood beside him, transfixed by a work she'd not seen for over a year. Though her father hadn't known the details of the late Lord Wrathell's harassment of Honora, he'd known something was to be laid at his feet. And still he'd done magnificent work.

"Did my brother ever see this?"

"Papa never lets anyone see until he's done."

He ran a hand along the frame. "Why did he agree to do this?"

"The prestige of having it known he had a commission from a future duke." She touched the side of the canvas where she recognized her father's hand in detail and finish work he usually left to her. "You understand, my lord, that talent is a revenge all its own."

"Yes." He looked at her and back to the painting. "Even unfinished, this is a glorious revenge."

Wrathell's brother was seated at a desk but turned to face the observer. On top of the cubby holes and drawers that formed the top of the desk, her father had painted a stack of papers with the coat of arms of the marquessate on them. Beside that, an astrolabe, a compass, and a vase of chrysanthemums. She would have to finish the flowers and other details Papa had not, but there, in shadow and light, was an enamel bowl of twigs and rocks, finished, like the coat of arms, to the last brushstroke.

"There's more left to do than I remembered."

Wrathell kept a hand on the top of the canvas. "Will it bother you to do the work?"

She did not reply.

"Come now. Did you think I would not have deduced that you and not your father would finish this?"

"I don't suppose I thought you would. No one else has."

"After I'd seen your self-portrait?" He faced her. Once again, they stood too close. Too close when it meant nothing to him and everything to her. "You're as talented as your father."

"I can paint this out," she said.

"Don't."

Chapter Eight

"**M**Y LORD," BAYNARD said when he joined Wrathell in the crowded front parlor. "I count only seventeen for dinner."

He swung around to face the man. "No, we are eighteen."

"You have miscalculated. There are only seventeen. Or do you expect another arrival?"

Wrathell counted his guests and came to seventeen, himself included. At which point he feared he understood Baynard's conclusion. Sedately, he said, "When Honora comes down, we shall have the proper number."

"Honora?"

He maintained his outward good temper. "Is she ill?" That was possible. She'd been locked in her room all day, slaving away for the cause of his ridiculous idea of using George's portrait to mend relations with his father. She may well have worked herself into illness. If she had, he had major amends to make to her and her father.

"Not to my knowledge."

"Then she will be downstairs shortly." He suspected Baynard had other ideas about that. The man had the right to look after his daughter as he saw fit. He, on the other hand, had no right to the resentment seething through him. Except Honora was of age. She was of age, and did she not have the right to decide if she would remain hidden or if she wished to walk out with no veil? Or join a dinner party?

Privilege attached to being the younger son of a duke. The Navy had been proof of that. He was well used to the courtesies that came with being Lord Leoline Marrable. He was learning that being the heir to a dukedom was another thing entirely. He summoned his father's tone and manner. God knows he'd seen and heard it often enough in his youth. His father's words carried weight. His approval could make a man's career. His disapproval could destroy it. "She must come down, Baynard."

"She does not attend parties," Baynard said with chilling finality. "They are unpleasant for her. Imagine, my lord, what your guests will think."

"Mr. Baynard." His temper slipped, and that would not do. She'd come down for meals on other occasions when their schedules happened to intersect, but, now that he thought of it, there had never been more than the three of them, and once or twice only him and Honora. "I thought I'd made it clear you and your daughter were expected tonight."

"I fear not." Baynard shrugged regretfully.

"All my plans depend upon eighteen." He did not have to feign concern. He *had* made his invitations based on even numbers. "I cannot have seventeen to dinner."

"My lord—"

"Baynard." He pinched the bridge of his nose and stared at his feet. Even if he accepted Baynard's right to keep Honora upstairs, which he did not, seventeen was a social disaster. He met Baynard's gaze. "If Honora does not join us, before noon tomorrow my Aunt Carter, whom I love dearly and who adores me in return, will nevertheless tell everyone the numbers were uneven because the heir to Marrable Gate is incapable of counting."

Baynard's pained reaction told Wrathell he understood the problem very well. "My lord..."

He would have his way. He had only to insist on his privilege. "You have already been introduced, sir. Your retreat is not acceptable. The precedence—Lord, the precedence. Sir, I beg you, Honora must be here to make us eighteen." He could hear his father in his tone, and that shocked him. "Your daughter is intelligent and amusing, and I anticipate and require that my guests be charmed and entertained by her presence. This must be."

"Even if she could be persuaded to come downstairs, there is no time for her to dress for dinner."

He glanced at the clock on the mantel. Ten minutes until seven. "I will delay dinner, then."

Something of his father's iron will had penetrated the man's blasted stubbornness, for Baynard bowed. "If she is the least reluctant, my lord, I pray you do not press her."

"Her happiness is ever foremost in my mind."

He sent a footman with instructions to delay supper by thirty minutes and to have Miss Baynard's maid fetched if she were not already with her mistress. He would never force her to come down if she did not wish it. But neither could he countenance her languishing in isolation when she needn't. Besides, he wanted his guests to meet her and find her as delightful and amusing as he did.

He knocked on Honora's door, and she replied immediately. "Papa?"

He put his hand on the door lever, aware of an unwarranted entitlement to her attention and her obedience to his will. Could Baynard be right? "It's Wrathell. May I open the door? I must speak with you."

"It's open," she called out.

He went in and was for a moment stunned and astonished. Her hair was only loosely pinned, and though her lilac gown was in no way up to the task of a dinner party, the color suited her vastly. He was, for a reprehensible cascade of seconds, filled with lust. The thoughts in his head did not belong there in respect of Honora

Baynard. He did not know what to make of his desire. He was appalled and intrigued by it and uncomfortably aware that this was not the first time his thoughts had been improper.

She waved her brush at him in greeting.

He concentrated on the smear of green paint across her scarred cheek. "You've color on your face."

"Oh?" She swiped at her other cheek. Obviously, she had not believed herself expected downstairs. Why? How could she think he would slight her like that? He knew the blame for that lay at her father's feet. "Have I got it?"

Her frock fit close to her bosom. He wanted to kiss her again as he had done—twice—under the mistletoe. He wanted to strip her naked and spread her legs with him between them. He wanted to arrange her on a sofa of the same red as the scarf she'd bought him, with all that smooth pale skin for him to kiss and caress. He wanted to paint her when she was in the nude. God save him. She would never let him.

"There are seventeen people for dinner. Before much longer, they will be hungry and out of sorts, and I shall be blamed."

She touched her brush to the canvas. "If you go downstairs, there will be eighteen, no?"

"No." He touched his cheek at the same spot where hers was smeared with color. She did the same and made a wider streak. "Have I got it this time?"

"Worse, I'm afraid."

"Drat."

He pulled his handkerchief from his pocket and went to her. "Hold still." She closed her eyes while he wiped the paint from her cheek, tense and with no sign of a smile. He stopped. "Am I hurting you?"

"No."

He finished the job. "There."

She opened her eyes, and here they were. Here he was, staring at her bosom. The tops of her breasts were round, and he mentally filled in what must be below her bodice based on what he saw uncovered. He longed to know if he was right.

Honora fluttered her thick, dark lashes, but not to flirt. She was puzzled. She had no ability to see that men were terrible, lustful creatures, or that she had any appeal whatsoever. "My lord?"

He wanted to kiss her, but not like before. No light and friendly peck on the lips. Well, almost friendly. He wanted to open his mouth over hers and take, and take, and take whatever she would give him in return.

He heard a door open somewhere. Not behind him, an interior door. He pulled himself away, pushed her away, and was a decent distance from her when her maid appeared from what was Honora's bedroom. She halted when she saw him, eyes wide with astonishment.

"There are sixteen people downstairs," he said. Best to ignore that he'd been thinking of kissing her with an enthusiasm that led to indecencies such as a hand under skirts. "You see the problem. I know you do."

"Yes." Honora drew a slow breath. Thank God her maid remained behind her mistress. "But what has that to do with me?"

"There are but two solutions. Either they dine without us, or you dress and come down to dinner." Yes. Yes, let her come down to dinner so that he could cease thinking of her as a woman he wanted to take to bed.

She had recovered herself, but he knew from her smile that she did not see he was serious. "There is another solution."

"What?" He fiddled with one of his cuffs.

"You could send everyone home."

"Very well. There are three solutions, two of which are absurd." Wrathell gestured to the servant. There was nothing out of the ordinary about this. Not in the least. He refused to admit there was. "Dress your mistress for dinner as quickly as possible."

"I cannot," Honora said.

"Why not? I've asked that you dress, not grow wings and fly about the room."

"My lord."

He softened. "Are you ill?"

"No." He wanted to paint her like this, in a gown that showed off her bosom, or, better yet, no gown at all.

"It's not because you're working on that, is it?" He pointed at the easel. "I absolve you. It was mad of me to think either painting could be done in time."

She gestured with the paintbrush. "I shall be done in plenty of time for you to send your brother to Marrable Gate."

"Excellent. Then there is no difficulty at all." He looked at her maid. "Have her downstairs in twenty minutes. Less if you can manage it. That color suits her. If she has an evening gown in that or a similar color, she will make a very good impression."

"Wrathell."

He stepped closer and touched her cheek again, and never mind the damned maid. He wanted her naked and in his arms. Stripped of that gown, her hair loose, his fingers filled with those black tresses. "Are you ashamed? You should not be."

She shook her head, and he put out of his mind entirely the fact that he had ever kissed her.

"Does it pain you too much if someone stares or is rude?"

"Not much."

"This is you. This scar. This other cheek." He touched the scarred side of her face. Her trust in him was why she did not move, and he did not want to do anything to damage that. "When I look at you, I see Honora who has a scar and who amuses and entertains me. A woman who makes me laugh and see the best in everything." Her smile broke his heart in half. "What is your maid's name?"

"Marie."

Without looking away from her, he said, "Marie, have you found a gown for her?"

"Not a lilac one."

"Anything suitable for dinner will do."

"Anything?" Honora said.

"I don't trust that look, but I don't give a fig if you come downstairs in cobalt blue, burnt sienna, jet black, or naked as the day you were born."

Marie squeaked when he said the word *naked,* which only focused all their attention on the word. Honora looked away to hide her laugh from the scandalized maid.

"Come downstairs, Honora." He'd never needed to seduce a woman, but he wanted to seduce her. There. Admitted. He wanted her and could not have her. "In whatever color gown you have. I want you there." He brushed a finger across her cheek. "For me. Will you for me?"

"Wrathell," she whispered.

"Don't leave me to face the gossip tomorrow when all anyone can speak of is that Wrathell gave a dinner for seventeen. Whoever goes in alone will never forgive me. Not ever, and God forbid it's one of the ministers."

"Papa won't like it."

"Your father can hang himself." Her maid was here, and Honora did not show the slightest sign that she was aware of him as a man. If not for Marie, he would seduce her. This very moment. He would. He saw it happen, imagined it. Covering her, whispering in her ear as he slid into her for the first time.

He leaned in, and for a moment time suspended. He'd been about to kiss her on the mouth, and he could not do that.

Except, now that was all he could think about. Her mouth. And the fact that she possessed a bosom, and he had said the word *naked* to her in respect of proper attire.

Naked.

Chapter Nine

H ER BEST FROCK was a white muslin that bore little resemblance to the evening gowns she saw in ladies' magazines. It would have to do. Marie pushed the last pin into the curls at the back of Honora's head. "You look lovely, miss."

She stared to the side, unwilling and unable to look in the mirror. It wasn't true, of course. "It's kind of you to say so."

There was no frothy lace or train, no fancy bows such as a lady of the *ton* might wear to a dinner given by a future duke, but Marie had threaded her mother's pearls through her hair, and she had to admit they added an unexpected touch of elegance.

Marie handed over Honora's finest shawl, which, while not the lacy confection most ladies of fashion possessed, was a gauzy white netting that went well with her gown. She slid on her gloves, and there was no more to do. Nothing more that could be done. Her stomach clenched, in part because of the prospect of meeting Wrathell's guests, but mostly because her father was hurt by every startle or pitying look at her. With her father's outrage to manage, there was no space left for her. There was only the constant reminder that her father was disappointed in her.

In the corridor outside her room, she leaned against the wall and collected herself. Lord Wrathell had no idea what he'd asked of her. She was not defined by her scar, yet she was. Inside, she felt no different than anyone else, but every moment of her existence was encircled by other people's reactions to her appearance. If she were a man, the damage to her cheek might have been considered romantic. In a woman, it was tragic. As if she had no value but her degree of perfection.

A soldier or a sailor could afford an imperfection like hers. *Be a man about this,* she told herself. If Wrathell does not care, then neither would she. Courage was not the sole domain of men. Women could be brave too.

She went downstairs, repeating to herself that she was a brave woman. As a child, she had survived a severe injury, and later she had endured taunts and teasing and worse. She had been called names and stared at, hissed at, told to keep her face covered, and she had lived every day wondering if her father would have preferred she'd died than be damaged as she was.

Outside the parlor door, she smoothed her skirts, touched the pearls in her hair and adjusted her gloves. She had never in all her life attended a dinner party. Not once in twenty-three years. She had no experience of such things. What did one say? What did one do? She was terrified she would make a fool of herself. Her throat went dry as the desert.

At first, no one noticed when she came in. Then, a very pretty young woman saw her. The young woman smiled at her until she saw Honora's cheek. There was no point in attempting to hide the scar, after all. She cried out, "Oh! What's happened to her face?"

Everyone turned, and there was a moment of dire silence in which she wished it were possible to vanish from the earth. The older woman, likely the young woman's mother, whispered something that made the girl blush.

Papa emerged from the crowd across the room, and headed for her, eyes full of pity and anger. Her heart somersaulted in her chest. Her palms went cold and clammy. She could not stay here. Papa was right to have kept her away from everyone. Wrathell appeared behind her father, and in three long strides stood before her.

He took her hand and held tight. "Honora. Here you are."

She curtseyed to him, overcome by a ridiculous, hopeless admiration of him for treating her as if he believed there was nothing wrong with her. He did believe that. He did, and the knowledge made her heart and spirits lighten. "My lord."

He gestured to the footman at attention by the door and said, "Tell Niraj we are ready for dinner."

"Milord."

"You look lovely, Honora." He walked with her to the center of the room, the very center from which she could not escape without anyone noticing. "This is Miss Honora Baynard," he said to an extremely distinguished gentleman with silver hair. "Did I tell you she and her father once lived near Marrable Gate?"

"Delighted to make your acquaintance."

"Sir." Papa had swung around and followed Lord Wrathell. His pity would kill her. She felt it twisting her stomach into knots.

Wrathell lowered his voice, and that had the effect of making it appear he was whispering of private matters between them, when all he said was, "Let me introduce you to my Aunt Carter. My mother's sister. She's delightful and the only person I know who might read as much as you."

Mrs. Carter had Wrathell's easy smile. Her attention darted to Honora's scarred check and then away, and then it was done. His aunt did not refuse to meet her nor recoil in horror. She pressed Honora's hand. "I am astonished, Miss Baynard, that we never met the many times I visited Marrable Gate."

"I lived in Elderford." She took a long slow breath. She would be calm and serene. Untouched by stares or surreptitious glances. "But we did meet. Once. I am relieved you do not recall."

Mrs. Carter pursed her lips and studied her anew. "I am quite sure I would have remembered you."

She brushed a hand across her cheek. She had been injured, she had a scar, and neither of those things could be changed. The scar was a part of her. "It's not often children are introduced to grand ladies. But you saw me and told me no proper young lady ever ran at church."

"As indeed one must not. I hope you ceased immediately."

"Not entirely." She concentrated on Mrs. Carter, doing her best to block out her awareness of the others. She knew she was the subject of much curiosity. "I've never forgotten your advice and have often applied it in other situations." She glanced at Wrathell. His presence steadied her. "I only wish you'd given your nephew the same sage counsel."

The woman's smile was genuine. "I long to know what mischief that young man has been up to. Running where he ought not, you say?"

"Just the other day. Up the stairs here, if you can image that."

Wrathell threw an arm around Honora's shoulders and hugged her close. Mrs. Carter tapped his arm. "Dear boy. You'll spoil her charming coiffure."

He released her. "She was running too."

She curtseyed to Mrs. Carter. "I'll never run on the stairs again." She flashed a smile at Wrathell. "Unless he wants another race. Then I shall, and I don't care what anyone says but you."

"You and I will be great friends."

"I hope so. I would like that immensely." She sent another look in Wrathell's direction. "I hope that terrifies him."

"I shake with fright even now." He leaned away from his aunt and took Honora's hand. "Come meet the Goldins. I hope you like them as much as I do."

Her first test was over, and she had done well, she thought. Wrathell's aunt seemed to like her.

"I'm sure I shall."

As they walked to the Goldins, he spoke in a low voice. "Miss Goldin is very young. Twenty-two, I think her father said. She hasn't had a Season yet. This is her first time in London. She's a green girl, that's plain. A little spoiled, I think. Be kind to her. She needs a friend in Town. Someone with her head on straight."

The idea amused her no end. "I look forward to meeting her."

Miss Goldin was the young woman who had cried out when Honora came in. If one decided to call her beautiful, the compliment would not be far off the mark. She was tall and slender with hair the color of dark honey. When she looked at Wrathell, there were stars in her clear blue eyes.

The admiral and his wife were charming and exceedingly kind, and Miss Goldin was gracious when they were introduced. Miss Goldin's gaze constantly slid to Honora's face. It was obvious she was fascinated and repelled and, further, that she had been scolded by her mother. "Miss Baynard."

"I am delighted to make your acquaintance, Miss Goldin." She turned so that Miss Goldin could not see the left side of her face. "Admiral Goldin. What an honor to meet you." Captain, and then Commander, Goldin had featured largely in many of the battles she'd included in her notes on Wrathell's career. "I've read of your many exploits and adventures."

"Have you?" He looked pleased, and that eased some of her anxiety, even more when she saw his wife smile.

"You were at the Battle of Lissa."

"He was," Miss Goldin said with pride. "He commanded the *Active* then, the fastest ship in the Navy." Miss Goldin stood very straight, and Honora found it easy to attend to the conversation, for this was something she knew a great deal about and that interested her immensely. "Lord Wrathell served with my father from 1808 to 1811."

"I did know."

"He saved Papa's life."

Wrathell had moved to Miss Goldin's side, not so close as to be remarked upon, but not so far away that one did not see the possibility of a match. They were a striking couple.

"That he did," the admiral said. "He took a French bullet for me."

She'd painted scenes from the Battle of Lissa, constructed and imagined from her reading. She felt, wrongly of course, that she knew the facts quite well. Better than most anyone but those who had been there. "That occasion was his first commendation for bravery."

"We are grateful to Lord Wrathell for saving Papa's life." Miss Goldin was so earnest that Honora liked her much better than she'd expected to.

Wrathell was watching Miss Goldin with undeniable appreciation. "The amount of information in Miss Goldin's head is astonishing."

She did not want to watch him fall in love with Miss Goldin, but she feared that was what was happening. They were well suited. How could he resist a beautiful young woman who revered him? "I have questions for you, Admiral, if you do not mind my asking, about the engagement and the officers who interrogated Colonel Gifflenga. My documentation is incomplete. Perhaps after we've dined, you and your daughter would oblige me with more information. I would be grateful."

The admiral patted her shoulder. "We should be delighted, my dear."

She turned to Miss Goldin, determined to do her best by Wrathell's future wife. "I understand this is your first winter in London." She did not wish ever to find herself in dislike of Wrathell's duchess. Perhaps she would end her collection with a page about Wrathell's marriage.

"It is."

She could picture their wedding now. At St. George's of course. The Goldins, proud and happy for their daughter. Sailors in uniform and Wrathell in his very best clothes. His father the duke would attend. Whatever the state of relations between them now, they must reconcile before then. But did the duke understand anything of his only living son? She'd read once that Quenhaith refused to speak of his youngest son and that once, when asked about one of Wrathell's commendations, he'd replied, "This does not concern me. I disapprove entirely of his naval career."

How sad that Miss Goldin might well know more about Wrathell's bravery and qualities than his own father.

It occurred to her that she had documented Wrathell's career. What more fitting fate for her work than for her to send it to His Grace? She would. This very night, she would pack up those pages and send them all to Marrable Gate. If, after that, the duke was not moved to a reconciliation, why, then he was not a man she could admire.

She brought herself back to the present. "Tell me, Miss Goldin, are you enjoying your time in London?"

"I am, very much so." The young woman was doing her best not to stare at Honora's cheek.

Wrathell beamed at Miss Goldin, and she beamed back.

"What sights have particularly impressed you?"

"I have been shopping." She touched the skirt of her gown. "I never saw so many beautiful fabrics in all my life. When Mama saw how much I liked this color, she told Papa we must have a gown made up for me. And so it was done." She turned in a circle. "Does it not suit me wonderfully?"

"You are fortunate to have such excellent parents."

"Yes," she said with sincerity. "I am. Papa always says he loves me best when I am pretty."

"I hope he loves you when you are clever too."

"He loves me no matter what."

"You have a most excellent father." Oh, to have the unreserved love of one's father. "What else have you seen? The Tower of London? The gardens at Kew Park? The museum? The zoo?"

"I have been to the museum with Mama and Lord Wrathell. I never saw so many paintings in all my life."

"Did you like them?"

"The frames were very pretty." Her silvery laugh was delightful, and removed all question of whether she was a beauty. No child of Miss Goldin's could ever look at its mother's face and recoil. "Did you know, Miss Baynard, there is the most wonderful milliner just off Bond Street? You never saw so many hats in all your life. Have you been? All the ladies of fashion go there."

"I have not recently felt the need of a new hat."

Niraj appeared to call them to dinner and the subject of hats came to an end. Honora, as the lowest-ranking woman, walked in on the arm of the baronet who would have been the odd man out, but for her. Perhaps he was aware, for he complimented her with sincerity and told her he wished to one day own a painting by Baynard.

The meal went well. Everyone near her was kind and the conversation quite engaging. From her reading, she knew enough about the people and events that came up in discussion that she was not hopelessly at sea.

After dinner, she sat beside the admiral and asked him about the Battle of Lissa and other engagements of the recent war. He proved an obliging historian. At one point, the baronet joined them and then Lord Pilford, and how remarkable, she was at a dinner party for the first time in her life and making a good account of herself.

Much later, in the parlor after the last of the guests had departed and her father had excused himself to, she was quite sure, call on his mistress, she and Wrathell were alone but for servants clearing away dishes and goblets and putting away playing cards.

Wrathell poured himself a brandy. "Do you mind?"

"No." She leaned against the wall by the door, her head back.

He lifted his glass to her. "To women who make the numbers even." He took a sip. "Are you sorry you came downstairs?"

"No. I was happy to lend myself to the cause of even numbers."

He loosened his neckcloth. "Did you enjoy yourself? I hope you did."

"Yes."

"Chef outdid himself."

She rested a hand on her stomach. "I don't think I'll eat again for a week at least."

"You were a triumph. As I knew you would be." He wandered over to her and stood so close her pulse thumped. It meant nothing, of course. He touched the pearls in her hair. "Very pretty."

"Thank you." The last of the footmen left the room, without putting out the lights yet.

"If I could capture a moment tonight," he said, "it would be when you came in. I was with Pilford. He took notice, I promise you."

"He was polite to me."

"I would paint you standing in the doorway like that. Terrified but brave."

"I wasn't—"

"Terrified? You were."

"Brave. I wasn't brave. I was myself."

"I want a likeness of you one day. I shall paint you as you are, not as you think you are."

She laughed.

"God, Honora, I've wanted to do this all night," he said in a low voice.

"What? Have a drink? I do not blame you."

He put his brandy on a nearby table. "No. This." He slid his fingers into her hair. "So soft."

She was misunderstanding him, that's all. To lighten the mood, she looked up. "There isn't any mistletoe, my lord."

"It's not required for kissing. Did you think it was?"

She blinked several times, and her heart ran away with her. His eyes were half closed, watching her through his lashes, and her breath caught in her throat, and then he pushed away and took himself and his brandy to the other side of the room.

"Go to bed, Honora. I won't behave well if you don't."

Chapter Ten

IN BED HONORA stared at the canopy overhead. She'd not turned down the lamp yet because she meant to read when her ability to concentrate returned. At present, her head was filled with recollections of the way Wrathell had looked at her when there hadn't been any mistletoe. The way his fingers had threaded through her hair.

He hadn't kissed her. Couldn't have meant to kiss her. She knew that. Yet her body trembled from the possibility of that moment when she'd thought he might. She stared at the shadows again. In the dark, the green canopy looked gray. Someone had wound lengths of silk gauze, butter yellow and orange, around the upper posts. In daylight, those bright colors were cheerful.

Elsewhere in the house, a clock struck half past one. She wasn't the least tired. This was not an abnormal state for her. However, her usual remedy of reading did not answer the purpose. Her mind spun too fast to even think about opening a book. She'd been with people tonight. She had a friend, she hoped, in Lord Wrathell's Aunt Carter. She had exchanged witticisms with several gentlemen of *ton*. Others had been amused by her. She had even come away thinking it would not be impossible for her to like Miss Goldin.

She closed her eyes, but there was no hope of sleep. She pushed aside the covers, decided it was not too cold to go upstairs to her father's studio. Wrathell complained of the cold so the servants kept the fires higher than they might otherwise and banked them much later than usual, so she was never very cold even at night. She got out of bed and thrust her feet into her slippers. She would have a look at Wrathell's portrait and plan what she might do with the background when Papa turned it over to her.

When she reached the studio, she saw she was not the only one awake, for light gleamed from underneath the door. This meant that either Wrathell's portrait was going so well Papa could not resist doing additional work, or it was going so badly he was preparing a new canvas so he could start over. Both events had been known to happen.

She opened the door and went in. At first, all was as she'd expected. The drapery over the canvas had been removed, and someone stood before the painting. She was speaking before she realized it wasn't her father.

"Good evening, Papa. Shall I make you some tea—oh."

Wrathell looked around the side of the canvas.

"What are you doing here?" she asked.

He wore a banyan, unbelted and unfastened to reveal him in nothing but his trousers, braces, and shirt-sleeves. "Honora."

"You were told, my lord, that you are not to see the portrait until it is complete. That is a firm rule, and you have broken it."

He quirked his eyebrows, and in that moment, she was strongly reminded of his terrifying father. "My dear Honora." He'd never sounded so lordly before. "This is my house. Any rules here are mine." He winked at her. The rogue. "Allow me to point out that I am paying for this painting. A premium price, I might add. Why shouldn't I have a look?"

She walked farther in. He knew why. "Have you no shame?"

"None at all." He was all good nature, primed by the success of his party, and, she imagined, the fact that he had been much taken with Miss Goldin. "Would you resist the temptation?"

"Of course I would."

"Pshaw. Dissembler."

"I am not."

He made a dismissive gesture in her general direction. "You're as curious a woman as ever I met." He stood beside the easel, hands on his hips, attention moving between her and the canvas. "Why are you here, if not to see how my commission is proceeding?"

Honora walked to the table used for Wrathell's pose and put down her lamp. He had not come empty-handed, for on the table there with volume two of *A Winter in London* were his lamp and a glass a quarter full with what she suspected was more brandy. "I came to fetch my novel."

"You cannot mean *your* novel when it is ours." An angel from heaven would surely have such a smile. His happiness was contagious.

She picked up *A Winter in London* and held it up. "I will bring it back in the morning."

"You would read without me?" His expression smoothed out, his incandescent smile faded.

"I could not sleep, and it was deadly dull staring at the ceiling."

"You came here to steal a march on me. What perfidy is this?" He held out a hand. "Bring me that brandy, won't you?"

She handed him the glass, and he drank from it. "I confess the truth then. I suspected an intruder running amok in London stealing artwork in half-done condition."

"Darling Honora. You read too many novels."

"I speak absolute truth."

"You have no experience of life. If you had, you would be a better liar."

"I am an excellent liar. Having reason to believe this work was next on the list of masterpieces to be stolen, I raced upstairs to face the thief in combat to the death."

He picked up a piece of charcoal and clipped a fresh sheet of paper to the smaller easel beside the one that held her father's work in progress. "Brave girl, rushing here to rescue my painting."

She bent a knee.

"With what weapon did you mean to confront this desperate thief?"

"None but my face."

He looked at her, serious now, not even a trace of a smile. "No more of that, Honora. Not even Miss Goldin fainted at the sight of you."

"It was a near thing."

"You charmed my guests tonight," he said.

"I'm flattered you think so."

"I assure you it's an opinion now shared by fourteen others."

"Only fourteen? Why not seventeen?"

"I exclude you, myself, your father, and Miss Goldin." He returned to his sketching. "That is fourteen out of our eighteen. It's not a bad result."

She stared at his hand moving across the page. Suspicion crept over her. "What are you drawing?"

The soft sound of a pencil creating lines and shapes on the paper continued unabated. "Has your father ever painted you?"

She fussed with the book, lifted the cover half an inch, and let it close. "Have you not observed my skill at sitting motionless with a pleasant but intriguing expression?"

He looked up, curious. "He hasn't recently, I'll warrant."

"No." She pushed the book left, then right and left again.

He smudged an area of the paper with the edge of his smallest finger. "Hold still. I wonder why he hasn't."

The thought that he was sketching her filled her with dread. There was no need to memorialize her scar. "You don't want a likeness of me."

He looked at her through half-lowered lashes. "You've no idea what I want."

"To always be right?"

He laughed, more to himself though. "Touché." He picked up his brandy and took another sip. He made a face at it. "I think I've had enough of this." He returned the glass to the worktable. "What you mean is that you do not wish for me to take a likeness of you. Cease your squirming. I thought you said you could pose without moving."

"I can. When I am aware I am posing."

He huffed and glared at her. "Prove it, then." Her father had been so disappointed when Wrathell had joined the Navy. He'd had some hope of persuading him to dedicate himself to art rather than war. She watched him work and imagined her scar taking over the page. "Why wouldn't I want a likeness of you?" he asked.

"I should think that's obvious."

"Do you?" His gaze flicked to her and trapped her.

She gripped the edge of the table. "Obtuseness is not a trait one wishes to encounter in a gentleman."

"Stop moving." He pierced her through with another disapproving look. "Did you burn your self-portrait?"

"Yes."

He met her gaze straight on with no hint of a smile. "You owe me a portrait, then."

"I do not."

"I wanted to buy it of you."

Ridiculous. Absurdly flattering. Impossible. "Have you drawn much since you left Marrable Gate? Or was there no time for such things?"

"There are moments of leisure at sea." He stared at her as if she were a table or a chair. An artist's stare, seeking lines and shadows and the shapes they made. "I had more leisure for such activities while I was in Bombay."

"Did you paint?" He was drawing her, and it made her throat close off. He would see her scar with his artist's eye, and then he would see her as she was. At last. That was for the best.

"Pencil or ink in the main." He lifted the bit of charcoal he'd found. "And this. Some native materials. There were few opportunities to try my hand at oils. Not without an instructor. I never did find another teacher like your father." He stared at his paper and then at her. "You can't imagine how often I wished he'd come to Bombay."

"Papa would be so pleased to know that. Have you told him?"

"No."

"I should like to see what you've done."

He stopped drawing and stared at her for several long moments. His attention ensnared her and tied her stomach into a shivery knot. "If you let me sketch you, I'll show you."

She laughed. "You are sketching me now."

"I mean properly. Where we shan't be interrupted. Where I have my own materials instead of a stub of lead and charcoal."

"When do you mean, since this one is not sufficient for the purpose?"

His hand fell to his side. The quiet stretched between them. "Now."

"Right now?"

"Yes. This very moment." He knocked back the rest of his brandy and dropped the glass into the pocket of his banyan. He removed the paper from the easel. "Come along. Leave the book here." He headed for the table and took up his lamp. He gave her a glancing pat on the head. All was well between them, she decided. "Come along. While the brandy has given me the courage."

"Are you drunk?" He did not seem to be. She had little experience with drunken men.

"Not in the least, dear girl."

They headed downstairs, him in the front, holding his lamp high. At the landing, she followed him to the right. To the left would have led to her room and her father's. She increased her stride to keep up. "Is there another parlor or office this way?"

"No. Well, yes. I suppose there is." He stopped and opened a door for her.

She went inside and lifted her lamp. The decor was not at all familiar to her. The far wall had been painted bright orange, another brilliant yellow. None of the furniture had the familiar look of English goods. She recognized a portable desk on a table, but not the purpose of the elaborately carved box next to it. "Is this your room?"

"It is." He'd brought up more lamps while she'd been looking around.

"Wrathell." All was well. He did not think of her as the sort of woman whose reputation must be protected. This circumstance made her safe with him wherever they might be. Her gender made no difference to him.

"I keep my sketches in there." He meant a chest of drawers carved with tiny squares and triangles. He arranged his paper facedown on the table where she'd put her lamp.

"Am I to divine from this, my lord, that you do not wish for me to see your unfinished work?" Did she want to know how he saw her? Yes. Yes, because this giddy hope must not be allowed to blossom.

"You are."

"You mean to kill me with curiosity."

"It wouldn't be hard to do, you curious girl."

"I am not amused. Nor am I a girl either."

His smile changed. "No. No, you are not. At the moment, however, it is a help to me to think of you as too young." He opened one of the drawers and lifted out what she immediately recognized as an artist's portfolio, thick with paper. "Here we are."

This was a too wonderful distraction. She joined him. "You've not shown Papa? I know he'd like to see."

He stood for a moment with his hand on top of the thick portfolio. "I haven't shown anyone what's in here."

"Not even Miss Goldin?"

"No."

"Why not?"

"I would be obliged if you did not tell Miss Goldin you have seen these. If— when I show her, it will be because I am ready for her to see them. Most of them."

"Most?"

He untied the ribbon that held in the contents of the portfolio and made room for her beside him. "I might not marry her."

Without looking at him, because he did not mean it the way her hopes whispered to her, she rested a hand on his portfolio and said, "You might, though."

"I might."

"I think you ought to." She opened the cover.

The first was a very decent study of an anchor, drawn on a scrap of paper. There were several more like it. Studies. Exercises to keep his skills sharp. Obviously, he placed the papers so that the oldest would be on top.

"They're nothing like what your father does."

"I expect your work to be yours. Not his." She flipped through the sheets, carefully turning them over. Sketches of ships, the ocean, sailors, men fighting. Seabirds and fish, a crab. Several seashells. A harbor. "These are lovely. Oh, Wrathell, beyond lovely. They take my breath."

"Do you mean it?"

"I do, oh, I very much do." She continued to pore over his sketches and studies from his days in the Navy. Eventually, she came to work he'd done in Bombay. He was more ambitious here, with mixed results at times, but he began to succeed more and more often. She stopped at one scene of a city street. "Is it Bombay?"

"Yes."

"Then I am in Bombay, breathing the very air."

He pointed. "That fellow stood on the same corner every day selling curries and the most delicious dishes of rice you ever had in your life." He put his hand atop the page, preventing her from picking it up to see what was underneath. "Not that one. That's not—"

She shoved away his hand. "Wrathell."

A nude. A beautiful young native woman reclining on pillows, a length of silk in one hand. Her dark hair was down and falling about her shoulders. The longer she examined the page, the more certain she was of the emotion behind this particular work. "You were lovers."

When he answered, he spoke curtly. "Yes."

"She's very beautiful." She ran a finger along the edge of the paper. "You must miss her terribly."

"I couldn't bring her here. She wouldn't have come, and I couldn't have married her. Here or there. It's better this way."

She put a hand on his cheek, meeting his eyes. "I'm sorry for your broken heart."

"We knew it would not come to anything." He fell silent a moment. "It was harder to leave her than I thought. But easier too. I was relieved in a way. To get the break done with."

She returned to his portfolio. He'd done several drawings of the woman. "The female form is ever fascinating to men."

"As the male form is fascinating to women," he said.

"Is it?"

"I don't want to believe otherwise."

In the next one, his lover was standing with her back to a wall. Beside her was a window through which one could see the suggestion of a street at night. It would not do to linger on these heartbreaking depictions of his intimate life. She continued turning pages and came to work he'd done in color. Not images from life, but patterns bright and thick with color.

"I was copying, or trying to, some of the local art I'd seen."

"The designs are exquisite." She was glad to have their conversation move to happier subjects. Poor Wrathell, to have loved without hope. There was another of his former lover, in color. Her father had been right. Wrathell was gifted. "Lovely."

"Have you painted from the nude?" he asked.

She looked at him. "What a strange direction to take this conversation."

"Have you?"

"Of course not." She returned to the painting he'd done.

"I've never known a woman who was so vital even when she is not moving."

"You've captured her spirit."

"I've also never known a woman as unable as you to see a compliment when it's given."

"I don't know what you mean."

He smiled and relieved some of the tension between them. "I want to try." He touched her undamaged cheek. "To capture you in lines and color."

"Who would want to paint my face?" She touched her scar. He was talented enough to want experience with oils and more complicated compositions than what she saw here.

"I hardly think of your scar anymore." He paused. "Is that odd? I don't know if it is. I suspect so."

"It is."

He started to speak, then stopped, started again. "Why? Why is it odd? Because your father's made you ashamed to be seen when there's no reason for it?" He pressed both palms to the table and leaned toward her. "You are lovely. Breathtaking. You must see that when you look in the mirror."

"I never do if it can be helped."

"No one who comes to know you will care about your scar."

She shrugged. "They do."

"How would you know? You've hardly let anyone know you. He's kept you away from everyone."

"You've had too much to drink."

"I haven't. You look at yourself and see only that scar, as if you consist of nothing else. But I see you. You have that scar. What of it?"

"Miss Goldin found me horrible to look upon."

He frowned. "I apologize. It was not well done of her."

"As if you had anything to do with that."

He took the sketch she held and placed it on top of the others. "Let me sketch you from life."

She spread her hands apart. "Here I am, alive before your eyes."

"Alive, yes." He gazed at her. "Let me," he said. "Let me, and I'll show you the Honora Baynard you do not know exists."

"What do you mean?"

"I need to practice, don't I? Any artist who intends to make something of himself must paint from the nude." He plucked his incomplete sketch of her from the bottom of all the rest on the table.

"The light's not good."

"It's good enough."

"Wrathell, no. Someone might interrupt."

"In my private rooms? I think not. But I'll lock the door." She watched as he arranged the lamps to his liking. Her father painted nudes. Women most often, but he'd paid boxers to pose for him. She'd seen the studies.

"Here, I think," he said. He'd just pulled the sofa away from the fireplace. "Yes, this will do."

Chapter Eleven

H E FROWNED AT the sofa, aware of Honora, silent by the table, but caught up in his enthusiasm. "Closer to the fire." He gestured. "Lie down for a moment? Just so." She did, and he examined the shapes and colors and how they would translate to the page. She'd be a splendid model for him, a contrast of beauty and sorrow, a woman who had no notion of the light contained in her. "Good, good. Stand up, then."

In her matter-of-fact way, she said, "You can't be serious."

He stood, hands on his hips. "Do you think I can't?"

"I think you would be better served by a different model for your talents. Your considerable talents. Miss Goldin, for example."

"Miss Goldin. When it's you I want to sketch? You understand art. If I showed her the rudest sketch, she'd proclaim me a genius. You could tell me where I've gone wrong."

"I'll pose if you promise to show me."

"Done."

"Not in the nude." Ridiculous even saying the words.

"I don't see why you wouldn't. I'd let you sketch me from life."

"That's the most scandalous thing anyone has ever said to me."

"That's because you are a recluse." He fetched his supplies, paper, pens, pencil, gum eraser. Ink.

"So you mean to say gentlemen make a habit of speaking so too ladies?" She stood where he'd left her by the sofa. She'd removed her slippers and stockings and set them on the seat of a chair.

"I don't. But gentlemen say scandalous things to women all the time. Yes." He looked at her bare feet. "That's more interesting than your slippers." He thought of colors, the white, pinks, tans and browns of her body, the inky black of her hair. The blue of her eyes.

"Sitting or lying down?"

"Half of each?"

She laughed and sat on the sofa. "Like so?"

He turned his head and saw her in the position he'd wanted. On her left side. Her eyes were closed, but there was tension in her shoulders that would not do. He sat on the edge of the sofa and examined her. He pulled her braid over her shoulder and left it there. He saw lines and curves and shadows and light and how was he to capture all that on a sheet of paper? "Do you mind if your hair is down?"

Her eyes fluttered open. "I suppose not."

He untied the ribbon and dropped it into his pocket. He made quick work of unbraiding and loosening her plait and arranging it to his liking. Such thick, soft locks. Nearly to her waist. "Lean back."

"Like so?"

"Against the side there, as if you'd just opened your eyes. But turned, like so." He demonstrated what he meant. Her back against the arm of the sofa, her far leg bent, near leg straight, leaning slightly into the corner. A portion of her hair fell over the side of the sofa. "There. Don't move."

"I shan't." She let a beat pass. "Unlike you."

He tapped the end of her nose. "Your leg." He tapped the one he meant. "Bend your knee?"

She did.

With her hair down, she was another creature entirely. He knew he was in dangerous territory, for this was too intimate, too intimate for the sort of thoughts he had about her. He took a handful of her hair, then released it. He touched the top fastening of her night-robe.

Her eyes opened. "All right," she whispered.

"You don't mind?" He popped the hook. And another. "This. Around your hips."

"I don't..."

"We needn't. I needn't."

"I do not understand the way I feel. Peculiar. Curious." She smiled, tentative, uncertain.

He undid another fastening. "Do you like it?"

"Yes. I think so."

"You should leave." He rested his forehead against hers. "You ought to leave. It's best if you do."

"I don't want to."

"No?" he said softly. She shook her head, and he leaned down and kissed her, open-mouthed. Because he was mad. Lunatic. And then her night-robe was open, and he breathed once. Then again, and not normally after that. "This too?"

"Yes." She lifted her hips and then her arms, and he threw her chemise over a chair and studied her body.

"This is not safe for you." She was naked. Jesus. Honora was a spectacular nude. "I've been telling myself I won't take you to bed, but I think I will. I do want you." He put a hand on her thigh and stroked, nudged her thighs apart. "Like so. I'll draw you like so. And then perhaps I'll come to my senses."

She opened her eyes slowly. "Papa's mistress modeled for him."

"I will attempt to have more restraint with you than that, I hope." He retreated to his chair and his mind stopped teasing him with reprehensible thoughts about Honora and her nudity and the fact that she was quite beautiful. He put pencil to paper and began.

Two hours passed in silence with him thinking only of the image taking shape on his paper. At last, though, he lay down his pencil and charcoal. "I think that's enough for tonight."

She stirred. Slowly, like a cat stretching, and all he could think was that he wanted that body in his arms, her voice whispering to him, crying out, calling on him for release. All of which was impossible and ridiculous and improper. One didn't think of one's female acquaintances in disrespectful ways.

Still on the sofa, she bent for her night-robe, and he was hit hard with the realization that this was Honora, and she was naked, and her figure was uncommonly arousing, and he must not have disreputable thoughts about her.

Any shyness she might have experienced earlier had vanished. She had let that go in the first ten minutes of him drawing her. He had just enough wits to pick up her chemise and hand it to her.

"Thank you." He tapped the page.

"You promised you would show me." Her voice was smooth and cool.

"So I did."

He handed the sheet to her. He could not take her to bed. He wanted to. All his adult life he'd drawn a line between the women who were potential lovers and those who were not, and Honora stood before him having destroyed his understanding of the difference.

Her night-robe was in disarray, and both it and her chemise lay mostly on her stomach. Her hair fell black ink around her shoulders, and all he could think was she wasn't a woman who was one thing or another. She had lived in a portion of his heart for years. Ever since the day he'd stopped his brother tormenting her.

"This is very good." She moved the paper for better light. "You ought to do more like this."

He wanted her with a selfish ache. He wanted her. Honora. However wrong it was, he could not deny the longing. His desire. "Yes, that's so." He knew what was right and what was improper. He knew. "Honora."

She cocked her head, and there was so much there in her eyes and in the curve of her mouth that his heart came apart in his chest. He wasn't thinking straight, he knew that. He was absolutely unable to separate any of the emotions flooding through him. His respect of her, the fact that he'd always thought of her as his because he'd protected her from his brother and others who thought she was fair game for insults. Over a scar that had nothing to do with who she was, and everything to do with the woman she'd become. There was desire too, overwhelming. He was bloody randy from looking at her body for two hours.

He took his drawing of her and let it fall to the table. What made him think he could get out of this with his soul intact? He met her eyes. "Stay with me."

"Another drawing?"

"No." He went to the sofa, and stood there looking at her.

"What, then?" He heard the loneliness behind the curiosity. He saw it now, because he'd learned to see her, and his heart shattered anew. He did not understand this rending of himself when he'd already given over to his lust.

"You think the only reason I'd have you naked in my room is for art." He recognized the stillness of her now, he'd seen it so often, that iron control of hers. He sat on the edge of the sofa and watched the tremble of her breasts as she took a shallow breath. He drew one finger underneath the curve of her, then two fingers, more until he was holding her breast. She sucked in a breath. "I want you to tell me yes because you feel the same as I do. Baldly, Honora. Honestly. I don't want us slipping into this because our bodies seduce us. Tell me yes because you think you can't live otherwise. We'll face the rest."

He brought her into his arms. "Do you want to leave? Tell me if you do. It's all right. I'd never keep you here if you wanted to go."

Facing him now, straddling his lap, she took his head between her hands, and this was Honora. He slid his hands around her waist. He wouldn't love her anyway but this. Exactly as she was. "If I don't? What if I don't?"

He was mad with desire. She was soft, so soft, and her hair was loose, and her legs were slender and her breasts were round and her nipples were taut, she was everything he wanted when he was intimate with a woman. She gasped when he touched her there, a brush, then held her between thumb and forefinger, a flick across the top of her nipple. "If you don't leave, I will put you on your back and kiss every inch of you I can reach with my mouth. I'll make you spend, and when you've lost your mind, I will take you until you've lost your mind again."

"All that?" she murmured. "It sounds exhausting."

He rested his forehead on her shoulder and laughed softly. She wasn't like any other woman he'd met. Objectively, that was because he knew her better than any other woman. He cupped Honora's breast and then lowered his head to her. She was soft and warm, and he loved the gasp he heard when his mouth and tongue touched her.

He put her on her back, his fingers between her legs, urging her thighs apart while he kissed her until he was lost in her and in his arousal. Everything was new for her, kissing and, Lord—They started out with kisses that were a prelude to coitus, and he shed his banyan and his shirt and all he could see was the brilliance of her eyes and her body, perfect, exquisite, arching against him.

He watched while she came, him pushing his fingers into her, shuddering himself at the slick softness of her. He didn't give a damn about her virginity except that it meant she was new to this. He did not want to be a clod, but the danger was there with him fumbling at his trousers' buttons and pushing aside his clothes.

There was the act of getting between her thighs, which was beyond sublime, just the nudge and settling of hips, and him whispering to her that she was driving him mad, that he wanted her badly, and then he entered her. Soft, so soft and warm. He had no idea how he managed to wait until he knew he hadn't hurt her. "If you don't leave, I'll come to you like this." He pushed deeper inside her. "God, Honora, you feel good." She gave herself to the act without inhibition. She gave herself to him. He hoped it was him she thought of. There was some awkwardness soon solved, smoothed away, incoherent whispers, kisses, and him stroking into her and her moving with him, arms tight around him and then they were greedy, the both of them.

He withdrew in time, but it was a near thing.

Chapter Twelve

H E MADE THE room too small, the way he stood there, staring at her as if he were a dying man and the only thing that could save him was her. They were in the sitting room attached to her bedroom, because she'd finished the painting of his brother, and it was five days before Christmas. With two days travel at least to Marrable Gate, the portrait must be on its way immediately if it was to reach his father in time.

She had so few days left with him. Papa would be done with Wrathell's portrait by Christmas, and then they would return to Bury St. Edmunds, as they did every year. Her departure would mark a natural end to their affair. Christmas would be a bittersweet day for her, but a day she intended to enjoy as fully as possible.

"You've made this more than it was."

"It's not too late to paint that out." She meant the rocks, the taunt to George Marrable.

"Leave it."

"I think Papa knew your brother would not accept this."

From behind her, Wrathell rested his chin on her shoulder and wrapped his arms around her waist. "I'd say it's likely."

"That's why it's like this." She lifted a hand. "He's never done anything better." She considered George Marrable. She hadn't known she needed to tell her father he had apologized. "Yours might be as good."

"Not because he hates me, I hope."

She pressed her hands over his. "No. Because he loves you, and he'd never let your brother's portrait be better than yours."

"Flatter me. I adore it."

"Lieutenant Lord Leoline Marrable is so handsome it would be impossible to paint him badly."

"You don't mind if I bring up the fire, do you?" His voice was liquid silver. Wicked and warm.

"No. Please."

He did so, and then he sat on the chair by the table. He stretched out his legs and watched her from half-closed eyes. "The men who'll take him to Marrable Gate will be here in an hour or two."

"So soon?"

"Yes." He unbuttoned his coat to reveal a gold waistcoat and starched white linens. He was her lover, her beautiful, handsome, brave lover. "With this weather? I want to be sure it gets there even if they're delayed."

"Wise man."

"Sit, Honora, or I'll have to stand when I don't feel in the mood."

She let her shawl slide off her shoulders, and he followed the motion with his eyes. "Kiss me?"

He stared at the ceiling. "No mistletoe."

"Can you imagine that I have hung some? Right there." She pointed above her head. He stood with a physicality that made her heart turn over.

"Very well. I am imagining that I must kiss you or die trying. There."

"On the forehead?"

"Where else might I kiss you?" He put a finger under her chin. She turned her face away, but he brought it back to him and kissed her. Softly at first. His other hand found hers and their fingers intertwined. "Say yes," he whispered.

"Yes, yes. Of course yes." Their eyes met, and she had the right to touch him. Indeed, he hoped and expected she would. "When I am back in Bury St. Edmunds, I want to remember us like this. I want to know that during my winter in London, I did more than stay inside alone."

He walked them back to the sofa and they ended up sitting, but with him facing her, knees on either side of her thighs, hands on the back of the sofa. His beautiful eyes were on her face, and he gave her a smile so wicked she forgot to breathe. "What else? A visit to Rotten Row?"

"Yes."

He dropped a kiss on her mouth. "The museum?"

"That too."

"What memories of me, Honora?" He shrugged out of his jacket and let it fall to the floor. His fingers sped along the buttons of his waistcoat and the chain of his watch, setting all the fastenings aside. "I've lost count of how many times I've thought about this. Touching you. You melting in my arms."

She drew the stickpin from his neckcloth, and he took it from her. He put that in the pocket with his watch. She set a hand to his stomach while he turned and let his waistcoat drop to the floor to join his coat. Muscles flexed while he moved. He traced a finger down the side of her face.

"You amuse and fascinate me, Honora Baynard. But you have this tragedy about you, a resignation to your fate and a determination that you shall not be made unhappy by whatever may happen. I find that irresistible." He pushed away her hands and drew the linen from his neck.

"What does that mean?"

He shoved his braces off his arms and whipped his shirt over his head. His torso was perfection, muscles wherever she looked. She touched the scar near his right shoulder where he'd been shot. He didn't flinch when she passed a finger over the depression in his skin there. "I had supposed that you were not badly hurt. You were in action again so soon after."

He pushed back and stripped down without any reservation about the wisdom of them doing this in the middle of the day.

She devoured him with her eyes, and he laughed. "Before I leave London," she said, "I want to experience everything. All that is possible."

"Oh?" He put a hand over his erection and smiled, long and slow. "Will you give me your mouth?"

"You make that sound wicked. Is it?"

"Exceedingly." He sat beside her, then turned sideways, and lay back with one foot on the floor, the other hooked over the top of the sofa. His sex was beautiful, and yes, he had a body that went very well with his male parts.

He set about showing her what he wanted from her, and at one point, he pressed his head against the couch and set his trembling hands to her head. "You"— his words came unevenly—"are a devilishly quick study."

He moaned and arched toward her, and she swept her fingers over his lower belly. He was nothing but muscle and sinew, and that made her feel her own sex. She was aware of the response of her body, the need to touch him and hear him cry out, to elicit the responses from him she must learn and remember, and never forget.

"Honora." Her name was a reverent breath. "Honora. Harder, harder, God, yes."

She was more than happy to oblige him.

"You've killed me dead." He crossed an arm behind his head, and her heart constricted with regret that they must part in so short a time. She committed everything to memory. The scent of him, the taste, the silk of his hair. The perfection of her heart.

"I imagine you've been told countless times how lovely you are."

He grinned at her. "Never by you."

"I've just done."

"Once is not countless."

She stood. "You are a lovely man. The most beautiful I have ever seen."

"It's your turn to undress, my darling Honora." His voice was rough, but when he grinned at her, his beauty rocked through her. Of course a beautiful smile. He was constitutionally unable to do anything but be beautiful. But instead of helping her, he took her hand. "I want us in a bed this time."

"Very well."

"What?" he said. "You cannot look as if you are about to burst into tears and expect I won't demand to know what you're thinking."

"What's to become of us?" she asked.

He reared up on one elbow and held out a hand. "Come here. I want to kiss you once more before I navigate these waters."

"Meaning?"

"No one can tell the future."

"One can predict based on facts observed." She would not survive this, leaving him, never seeing him again.

"True." He drew her in and onto his lap and kissed her again, and she melted against him. "What is it?" he asked. He touched her face and stared into her eyes. "Why do you feel so far away?"

"I thought... I thought everything would last much longer. That time would not pass so quickly, and now—"

He said, "You want to know the future when I think I fear it more than you."

"What does that mean?"

He captured her hands with his and gave her brutal honesty. "Under the circumstances, if I told you what I wanted for the future, I would lose you."

"I would be your lover," she whispered. She kissed him on the mouth and reveled in her right to do that. "I would be your lover."

"Your father has spent too many years being careful of you and is too unwilling that you should not be hurt. You cannot be my lover, Honora. Not unless you stay here."

She pulled her hair away from her face. "I went to the zoo today."

"You did, my darling. And lived to tell the tale."

"I saw the lions, and I thought of you."

He put his mouth by her ear and softly did his best imitation of a roar. She giggled.

"I wanted to let them all free," she whispered. "Is that not awful of me?"

"No. I've felt the same, looking at them."

"I like Miss Goldin. And I believe she likes me. I think we shall be friends."

"I cannot marry her. You know that."

She lay quite still. "Why not?"

"There is no solid ground here." He sighed. "Because the thought of living without you is intolerable to me."

"What will happen to us?"

"Honora, I am convinced there will never be a time I can tell you this without fear that I will lose everything." He touched her cheek, her scarred one, and for once she did not evade the touch. "I love you. I have been falling in love with you from the moment we met again."

"Don't kill me like this."

"Do me the honor, please, of becoming my wife. Then I can tell you something about our future that you will like."

"Wrathell. Your father will never allow it."

"I am twenty-eight years old. He cannot tell me whom to marry. He can't disapprove of me more than he does, so I hardly see the problem. Listen to me. I don't require an answer of you. It is enough, for now, that you understand the state of my heart. You make me laugh. I am happy when you are near. I have always, always, from that day at Marrable Gate forward, had a hole in me where you were not."

"You want to reconcile with your father. Not drive him away forever. You can't have a wife like me."

"You give me little hope that I might."

"I won't cost you your father. I can't. What am I to do now that you've said all that?"

He shrugged. "Know that it is safe for you to love me."

"It isn't," she said. "It isn't at all." She didn't want to leave him, but she saw no future for them but to part. "How can it be safe to love you when you have already broken my heart?"

He stood, and she touched him, caressed him. Kissed him.

"How many times shall I make you come?" he asked.

"Until we lose count."

Chapter Thirteen

H ONORA SPENT THE week before Christmas working in a room she begged the servants to arrange for her without telling Wrathell. She explained her absences by telling Wrathell that she was working on his portrait, and that was so. But she worked as long as she could on her own project. Hours and hours, it seemed to her. Twice she carefully scraped off paint and started over.

There was no possible way for the paint to be safely dry before Wrathell's birthday and hers, but her portrait only needed to be completed. Her hours here set her mind free to wrestle with everything that troubled her. She had not yet been able to tell Wrathell that she loved him. The words refused to come past her lips, and she did not understand why they stopped between her heart and her lips.

She poured all her feelings into the image on the canvas instead.

The trouble became clear to her as she worked. If she did nothing, nothing would change, and right now, Wrathell was here. He believed he had tender feelings for her and if only that never changed, why, she would never lose him.

She would. She knew she would. Her father would take her away. She would lose her courage. She was so horribly afraid that if she took the happiness he was offering, she'd lose everything. What she had of him now was better than nothing at all.

On the twenty-fourth, Wrathell asked if she would walk with him to the panorama at Leicester Square. She agreed because the new Honora emerging as her old life sloughed away accepted that she would be stared at. That fact did not change what Wrathell loved about her. She was a woman who painted, and read, and who had a scarred face, and who managed in the world just fine. She was a woman who had far more than she had ever dreamed of for her life.

The panorama of Rome was spectacular, and Wrathell, who had been to that city, declared the paintings put him in mind of the Italian spring when he'd visited the city. She stayed close to him as they walked along the canvas that stretched for several feet, immersed in Rome. They made a second circuit and then, in silent agreement, headed toward Queen Anne Street. He engineered a detour to Euphan's, though, and bought all their jam tarts, with all but one of the boxes to be delivered to Queen Anne Street as soon as possible.

He kissed her cheek before he accepted the single box. "Happy birthday, Honora."

"Thank you."

When they were once again on their way home he leaned toward her and whispered, "Let's lie in bed and make love and eat tarts."

"What a wicked man you are."

"That's settled, then."

"Yes. It is." She tucked her arm in his. "This is the first time in six years that Papa and I will not have Christmas dinner at the Morin Hotel."

"I suppose I should ask Chef to pick up a goose for our dinner. What do you think?"

She jabbed him in the ribs, and he pretended to be injured. "What would we have besides goose, you goose?"

He straightened. "Roast beef?"

"For Christmas dinner?"

Their conversation continued in a similar light vein until they were home. Her father came down the stairs as they were handing over their coats and hats. Initially, she braced herself for his objection to her having gone out, but none came. Her heart turned to lead in her chest when she came down the last step and saw his face. "Wrathell's portrait is done," she said.

"It is." He held his arms open, and she went to him. "On time, by Jove."

"Congratulations, Papa." She hugged him close and fought the tears welling up. He'd worked fiendishly hard these several days to complete the portrait, and she told herself to be glad for him. Except in the back of her mind, she was thinking that now there was no reason for them to stay in London and the world she'd been so careful not to disturb began to crumble under the weight of her inaction.

"We'll have a celebration tonight," Wrathell said. Papa released her to shake his proffered hand. "Your daughter's birthday and mine, and now this." To Niraj he said, "Bring a bottle of champagne to the parlor."

They gathered upstairs, where Wrathell himself poured the champagne Niraj brought. The first glass went to her father, who slumped gratefully on one of the chairs by the fire. He served the second to her. Her father made no objection to that either.

She said, very carefully, "Thank you, my lord."

"A toast." Wrathell raised his glass in her father's direction. "To your triumph, sir."

"Hear, hear." Honora raised her glass to her father and sipped. "A triumph indeed." She toasted Wrathell too. "Many happy returns, my lord."

He nodded. "To you as well, my darling Honora."

Thank God, Papa had not noticed Wrathell's endearment. Her father raised his glass. "To you both."

From downstairs, she heard the faint sound of the door knocker. Curious, she went to the window and looked down to the street. A carriage and four horses were stopped in the street. A coachman bundled up in a heavy coat held the reins. Her pulse sped up, and she faced the others. "Wrathell."

"Yes?"

She took a breath, but by then Niraj had returned with the news. "My lord." He bowed. "Your esteemed father is calling. Are you at home?"

The room fell silent.

"Show him up."

Papa put down his champagne. "We'll leave you."

"That is not necessary. You are my guests."

"Honora," her father said. "You must not allow him to see—"

The remnants of Wrathell's good cheer vanished in an instant. "You will stay, Honora."

Papa leaned forward, not at all deterred by Wrathell's icy words. "Then she must fetch her veil."

"No, Baynard. She must do no such thing."

"His Grace was quite specific in his—"

"In my house, sir, no guest will be treated in such a vile and disrespectful manner."

She stood as frozen as the frost on the windows. Her father turned and placed himself between Honora and the door.

Niraj returned and stepped just inside the parlor door. "His Grace, the Duke of Quenhaith."

He'd changed little from her memories. He was a tall man whose blond hair was graying now, but she saw the resemblance between Wrathell and his father more clearly than ever. The duke glanced around the room. His eyebrows arched when he saw her, but he said nothing. His attention fixed on Wrathell. "Leoline."

"Father." Wrathell nodded. "You are acquainted with Mr. Baynard and his daughter."

The duke bowed. "Mr. Baynard. A pleasure."

Papa gave a formal bow. "Your Grace."

Quenhaith continued into the parlor until he stood directly in front of her. She dreaded words that could only drive a further wedge between him and Wrathell.

"Have care, Father," Wrathell said softly. "I mean to marry her."

Honora's breath stopped. Her father whirled to Wrathell, but a sharp gesture cut off the objection she was certain he meant to make.

Quenhaith hesitated, then extended a hand to her. "Miss Baynard."

Heart racing, she placed her fingers on his palm and sank into a curtsey. "Your Grace." She straightened, but he did not release her hand. "May I tell you in person, Your Grace, how sorry I was to hear of your son's passing?"

"Thank you." The pain of Quenhaith's answer tugged at her. How could it not? He'd lost a beloved son. "It was... a tragedy."

She pressed his hand, and his gaze softened.

"I presume, Miss Baynard, that you and your father are in some measure responsible for the remarkable portrait my son had delivered to Marrable Gate."

She nodded to him. "It was your son's fervent wish that the portrait be completed and sent to you, yes."

The duke addressed her father. "My heartfelt thanks, Mr. Baynard. You are a true artist."

"Thank you, Your Grace."

At last, he went to his son. "Leoline." The two were silent for several torturous seconds. "Wrathell."

"Quenhaith."

"Thank you." The duke's voice broke. "For that magnificent gift. You have—" He struggled for composure. "Leoline. It is Christmas when we ought to forgive those who have hurt us." He put a hand on Wrathell's shoulder. "Will you forgive me?"

He let out a breath. "Words said in anger."

"Badly said. Pompous. I wish us to end our estrangement, Leo, if you will forgive me for my stubbornness. I have wished it for years. Long before I received Miss Baynard's gift. I was too stubborn. Too stubborn."

"What gift?" Wrathell looked past his father to her.

She swallowed hard. "I hope you are not angry with me, Your Grace."

The duke replied to Honora more than to his son. "She sent me an illustrated collection of your naval career. Not that I was entirely unaware." He brushed a hand over his head. "There was much there I had not heard. I did not sleep for two days, Miss Baynard. Two days reading that extraordinary paean to my son." He returned his attention to Wrathell.

"Honora, what is he talking about?"

She swallowed against the lump in her throat. "I assembled a record of your life. From the papers."

"The illustrations bring the battles to life," Quenhaith said. "It is quite... remarkable."

Wrathell held her gaze.

"You were kind to me at Elderford," she said. "I was grateful for all that you did and more than a little in love with you. Even then."

"Are you more in love with me now?"

Her heart overflowed. "But for you, I would believe everyone is disgusted by me. So yes. Yes, I am more in love with you than ever."

"Honora—" Her father took a step toward her. "Never say that you believe you must hide from others. I never meant—"

"Papa, you meant well. I know you did. You didn't want me hurt."

Her father took her hand, unable to speak for long moments. He cupped the side of her face. "My darling Honora, beloved daughter."

She pressed her hand over his. "I mean to marry Wrathell," she said. "Will you object to that?"

He glanced at Wrathell. "That young puppy?" He humphed. "The fellow hasn't seen fit to speak with me on the matter."

"If you've a moment later this afternoon, sir," Wrathell said, "I should like a word."

"More than one, I hope."

"As many as it takes." He touched his father's arm. "You are at Marrable House, I presume."

The duke nodded.

"Will you come for Christmas dinner? We would be honored if you did."

"I should be delighted."

"Then why leave? Stay here, sir. If only for the night. You are welcome here."

"Thank you."

"There is another portrait for you to see."

Later, after the duke had settled into hastily prepared rooms and her father had retired to his rooms, Honora found Wrathell in his quarters. He stood when she rapped at the side of his door. He held out a hand. "Darling."

"You're not angry with me, I hope."

He shook his head. "I only wish I knew what you sent him."

"Perhaps he'll show you one day when next you visit Marrable Gate."

He gripped her hand and brought her in for a kiss. "Your father has kindly granted me permission to marry you. When shall we wed?"

"Whenever you like." She kissed him on the mouth, shaking with joy. Overcome with it. Shedding tears from happiness.

"Before the New Year." He held her close.

"So soon?"

"I do not wish to wait. Honora, not when it's possible we should not wait. Besides, your father and mine are in town. What better time than immediately?"

"Dearest love," she said. The words felt strange and foreign, but his face when she said the words erased all doubt. "I have a third portrait for you to see."

"Have you now?"

She took him to the room his servants had cleared for her and, taking her nerves in hand, uncovered the painting she'd been working on. "I'm sorry I hadn't a larger canvas. As it was, I had to take one from Papa's Duke Street studio."

Wrathell put an arm around her waist and brought her close. "My love."

"You said I owed you another self-portrait, and here it is. My gift to you for your birthday."

"I have no words for this." He put an arm around her waist. "None that do this justice."

"Most I did from memory. I studied your sketches when I had the chance. As you can see, I took liberties with the lighting and the color."

"It's perfect. Beyond that."

"I can paint over my scar."

He swung her around so that she faced him. He kissed her once on the lips, hard and fast. "Never. Not ever. Paint another from the right side, if you like. But this one is mine."

She put her arms around him. "You, Wrathell." She hugged him tight. "You could paint me like that, if you wanted to."

"We'll begin tomorrow, my love. On the happiest Christmas Day of my life."

A Prince in Her Stocking

BY
Shana Galen

Acknowledgements

Thank you to Susan Knight and the Shananigans for their help with the title of this novella.

And thanks to Grace, Carolyn, and Miranda for all your suggestions and inspiration.

Chapter One

H E WAS BEING followed. Lucien hadn't seen them, hadn't heard them. Still, he couldn't shake the feeling someone watched him.

Perhaps he was delusional. God knew he came by it honestly, as his mother saw plots and assassins behind every door. The moral of every bedtime story had been not to trust anyone, not to be fooled. The sweet baker wanted to slit his throat, the smiling maid waited for an opportunity to smother him in his sleep.

His father had called it all rubbish, much to his mother's dismay. The king had called it rubbish until the night the *reavlutionnaire* attacked and slaughtered the entire royal family.

In the end, his mother's suspicion hadn't saved her.

It might not save him either, but Lucien couldn't help looking over his shoulder one last time as he stepped inside the bookstore in St. James's. The heat reached out tentative fingers and stroked his frozen face as soon as he entered. He'd quickly learned December in London was colorless, cold, and compassionless. No one had the time or inclination to spare even a second glance at a poor man out in the sleet with only a threadbare coat for protection against the damp and cold.

His face stung as it began to thaw, and he unwound his scarf, exposing his face to the shopgirl, although he suspected she already knew it was he. He came here almost every morning right after the bookstore opened, partly because he wanted out of the cold and partly because he was still searching.

"Good morning, Mr. Glen," the pretty blond shopgirl said in greeting.

It wasn't his name, but when he told people his name was Prince Lucien Charles Louis de Glynaven, they didn't believe him. Mr. Glen seemed easier.

"Good morning, Miss Merriweather. How are you today?"

"Very well, and yourself?"

He was cold and hungry and so tired he could sleep a week. "Just fine. Thank you for asking." He unfastened the top button of his greatcoat, although he didn't intend to remove it. The store was warm, but old books were dusty. He took pains to keep his clothing clean and presentable. He could not afford to soil his coat or shirt, as they were the last vestiges of respectability he had.

"May I help you find anything in particular, Mr. Glen?" Miss Merriweather asked. She already knew the answer. They performed this play nearly every day.

"Just browsing, Miss Merriweather."

The bell above the door tinkled, and a woman of middling years entered On the Shelf, which was the name of the little bookstore in Duke Street. Lucien took the opportunity to slip away, walking along the rows and rows of shelves along three walls of the store until he found the location where he'd left off the day before. The shop was as familiar to him as the lines on his hands by now. It had become an old friend to him, the smell of paper and ink and leather bindings almost as comforting as the smells of the palace in which he'd grown up.

Lucien had no trouble finding the shelf where he'd paused his search the evening before, which was not far from the counter where Miss Merriweather spent most of her time. He took solace in the fact that he was now several shelves deep in his search. He had made progress. Last night he'd ceased searching when he reached the bottom of the shelf, of course. His back had ached by the end of the day, and he'd left the lower shelves for the morning. Unfortunately, he'd spent the last of the money he'd earned tutoring students in Glennish, which meant he'd spent the night in a doorway of an abandoned shop, rather than in his usual spot in a cheap boarding house where men slept twelve to a room on straw pallets infested with lice and other vermin it was too dark to see.

As a consequence, his back felt no better than it had the evening before. He leaned against the shelf behind him and closed his eyes. How much longer could he go on this way? He'd fled the revolution more than seven months before and had been all but living on the streets of London for the last six and searching the bookshop whenever he did not have tutoring work for more than four months. He was hungry, cold, and tired. He didn't want to give up hope, but at some point he must accept that he might never find the goddamn papers. He might never reclaim his title or the money so carefully put away for just this eventuality. He might die on the streets of London, and no one would give a damn.

To the world, he was already dead.

"What is that man doing?" he heard a woman ask Miss Merriweather. "Is he sleeping?"

"Oh, he's harmless enough. I think he comes in to stay out of the cold," Miss Merriweather answered. As he was the only man in the shop—for some reason, the bookshop seemed to always attract more women than men—he assumed the ladies were speaking of him. He wished he had a few coins so he might buy a book today. He tried to do that when he could in order to maintain the illusion of actually patronizing the bookshop.

"Miss Merriweather!" the first lady admonished. "Half of London will be loitering in your shop if you continue to allow this. I must insist you send him on his way."

Lucien drew in a breath and held it. He might be weary of the search, but he was not ready to be forced to abandon it or the little shop he had begun to think of as home.

"Lady Lincoln, I assure you the man is no trouble. Please do not allow him to concern you. Now, just the volume of Fordyce's Sermons today?"

Lady Lincoln sniffed. "Your mother will hear of this. See if she does not."

When the bell tinkled again, signaling her retreat, Lucien blew out the breath and crouched. He pulled the first volume of a book of poetry from the shelf, opened it, and turned every single page. He liked to think of this as his "no page left unturned" method. He knew it was highly unlikely the papers he sought had found their way into a book of English poetry—mediocre poetry, he decided after scanning a page or so—but all other methods of obtaining the books and documents had failed. He had no other choices, no other options, and so he did the only thing he knew. He searched.

"Will she really tell your mother?" a voice he recognized as the young Miss Hooper, the auburn-haired friend of Miss Merriweather, drifted across the shelves. She'd lowered her voice, but the store was almost empty and quiet, and he knew every sound by now. Lucien paused in his perusal of a poem about a lovelorn shepherd to listen.

"She has nothing else to occupy her time, so I imagine she will."

"Will your mother force him out?" Miss Hooper asked.

"I don't know. Why? Don't tell me you've developed a tendre for him."

Lucien could almost hear the blush rise to Miss Hooper's cheeks. "Of course not, but I do feel sorry for him. Imagine. The poor man thinks he is a prince."

Lucien laid the volume of poetry on the shelf and moved closer. He did not want Miss Hooper's pity—Miss Merriweather's either, unless it served to keep him from being evicted from the shop. Strange to be the object of pity after so many years of being reviled for his privilege.

"I am well aware of his delusions." That was Miss Merriweather's voice. "You forget I was here the morning he stormed in and demanded we hand over the shipment of Glennish books we bought at auction. I had no notion which books or which auction. The man was quite mad with desperation, so I showed him the only books we had on Glynaven."

"But he didn't want them," Miss Hooper said. She knew the story and could have probably told it herself at that point. "And he's come every week since?"

"Yes, and he even apologized for his rude behavior that first day."

"Did he? I am not surprised. He has a very kind look about him."

Miss Merriweather gave a bark of a laugh. "I beg to differ. He has no such thing. He has the look of a gypsy—all that dark hair and golden skin."

"But his eyes," Miss Hooper said with a sigh.

Lucien rolled his oft-mentioned eyes. In Glynaven, poetry worse than the volume he'd just perused had been written about his leonine eyes. They were brown—a golden brown, yes—but brown. He might think it ludicrous, but he was not above using those eyes to persuade the Merriweathers to allow him to continue his frequent browsing.

At this point, he was not above anything. Oh, how the mighty—and haughty—had fallen.

He turned, intent on returning to the shelf of mediocre poetry, and almost rammed into a petite blond woman, who circled her arms frantically for balance. Acting on instinct, he reached out and caught her shoulders, hauling her back to her feet. Lucien realized immediately he wasn't quite as gentle as he might have been. The force of his action sent the woman careening toward him, and he was forced again to right her.

He held her shoulders, ensuring she was finally stable.

"I beg your pardon," he said. "I didn't see you there."

She had the fair complexion typical of the English, and a pink flush crept over her cheeks when he spoke. "It is my fault," she said in a voice little more than a whisper. "Please forgive me."

She wore spectacles, and her eyes behind the lenses appeared quite large and blue. Those were the sort of eyes one should honor with bad poetry. They were the blue of the Mediterranean Sea.

"Excuse me," she whispered, looking down so he had a view of the top of her head of golden hair. She'd pulled it tightly back and secured it at her nape with a black comb.

"If you would release me, sir?"

Lucien released her as though she were poison and stepped away. "I apologize. I didn't realize—"

"No apology necessary. Excuse me." She moved toward a small round table of books in the center of the shop, her black skirts swishing as she moved.

Lucien returned to his shelf of poetry only to find someone else had taken his place—a woman with a bonnet trimmed in yellow flowers and a black net veil over her hair. He could not see her face. He turned to occupy himself with the novels until such time as the lady moved on, but the shelf of novels was also occupied by a tall well-dressed gentleman and a woman in a dark green redingote. He thought he recognized the woman as the shopgirl from Markham's Print Gallery, which was situated just next door. She often watched the bookshop when Miss Merriweather was away on an errand, and she'd always been kind to him.

The shop was damnably crowded now that the holidays approached. Lucien took a book from a shelf he'd already searched and looked through it in order to appear to be shopping. He wondered about the woman he'd bumped into earlier. She must have been a widow to be dressed in such severe black without any adornment. Was she one of the many women who frequented the shop, or was this her first visit? He did not recall having seen her before, not that he paid much attention to the shop's patrons. He was engrossed in searching the books. He continued his search, ignoring the slight headache from lack of food and drink. Lucien withdrew another book, examined every page, then replaced the volume. Before he withdrew the next, he glanced behind him, hoping he'd see the Englishwoman in black again.

CASSANDRA HURRIED HOME through the cold, wet streets of London. The day had barely begun, but the sky was as gray as twilight. Worse yet, fog stole in and began to blanket the streets, making everything even grayer and darker.

"Watch your step, my lady," Riggersby, her footman, called over his shoulder. He walked slightly in front of her to lead her through the dense fog. Usually, he walked behind her, but today she needed his help navigating the way back to the town house. "Almost there, my lady." His tone was full of censure, and he had every right to be cross with her.

Riggersby and Vidal, the butler, had both suggested she take the coach to the shops, but she hadn't wanted to go to the trouble. At least that's what she had told them. The truth was, that even after nearly three years as Viscountess Ashbrooke, Cass did not feel comfortable ordering grooms from their warm quarters solely for her pleasure. And she certainly did not want the poor horses out in this foul weather. Riggersby would have taken issue with that opinion—not ostensibly, of course. But she would have read the thoughts on his face: *Not want the poor horses in the foul weather? What of the poor footman?*

She longed to return home and sip a cup of hot tea by the fire. She was almost completely frozen, inside and out. The only part of her that retained any degree of warmth was her shoulders, where *he* had touched her.

A prince had touched her!

Ridiculous notion, she knew. The man was no more a prince than she was a fairy. She'd overheard the shopgirl and her friend speaking of him. Clearly, they did not believe him a prince. Equally clearly, he did believe himself one.

Which made him quite mad. Weren't all the handsome ones mad, though? She'd seen portraits of Byron, and he was quite handsome and, many argued, quite mad.

A man moved aside to allow her to pass and lifted his hat to her. Cass wondered if she knew him, but she could not pause to study him, else she would lose Riggersby. She hurried on, happy to huddle in her pelisse and muff, her head down to keep her face out of the worst of the wind.

Of course the man in the bookshop had not been a prince, though she could certainly picture him in that role. He had all that dark hair and olive skin paired with a face that would have made a sculptor weep. No sculptor would have been able to capture the eyes, though. That color was so terribly unusual and so absolutely breathtaking. She'd seen him in the aisle and moved into it because she wanted a closer look at the "prince," but when he'd caught her and she'd looked into those eyes, she hadn't been able to speak or even breathe.

He must think her an absolute ninny, if he thought of her at all, which she doubted very much. In the meantime, she could still hear his voice, slightly accented when he spoke, and feel his strong hands burn through her dress.

Her ugly dress. Widow's black because her husband had died fourteen months before. She should be ashamed of herself for thinking of another man—*lusting* after another man—as Euphemia, her late husband's sister, would have said. And Cass was ashamed.

Mostly.

"Here we are, my lady," Riggersby said, indicating the steps leading to the front door. He allowed her to climb them first, then rapped for her. The door opened, and Vidal blinked at her with his large owlish eyes.

"You have returned, my lady. Miss Ashbrooke has been worried."

"Oh?" Cass handed Vidal her muff. "Riggersby was with me."

"Is that Cass?" a feminine voice called.

"It is I, Effie. I'm returned and quite well."

Effie moved as quickly as a woman with two canes might, then stopped short when she spotted Cassandra. "Why, you are frozen through! Do come sit by the fire." It was not so much a request as an order, and Cassandra complied because she was quite cold and desperately wanted the fire.

And because she always did whatever Euphemia told her. Cass did what everyone told her. She was meek and malleable and all but mute in company. As a child, it rarely, if ever, occurred to her to object to her parents' dictates, even when they dictated whom she might marry.

That was how she, a merchant's daughter with no title or connections, ended up a viscountess. That was also how she'd found herself married to a man forty years her senior, who had been more like a grandfather than a husband to her.

Euphemia was almost sixty herself now, and when Norman had passed away, she had slid into his place, eager to order Cass about as she saw fit. Although only two years shy of thirty, Cass was not allowed to express a single original idea. No idea was worthwhile unless it was Effie's idea first. Cass had wanted to dress in half-mourning a year after Norman's death. Effie insisted on full mourning indefinitely. Cass had wanted to acquire a cat or a dog, some sort of pet to keep her company. Effie claimed animals were far too dirty to keep inside. Cass had asked the cook to make more-flavorful meals. Effie had objected, saying anything stronger than bland potatoes and boiled beef bothered her stomach.

The few friends Cass had made among the wives of other peers when Norman had taken her out had long since abandoned her. When they came to call, Effie was so unpleasant, they did not return. Cass never went out in Society anymore, and so she saw no one and did nothing of interest.

Some days she wished she had died when Norman had.

But not today. Today she had been touched by a madman who thought he was a prince—that was certainly more exciting than anything else that had happened in the past two years.

Cass followed Effie into the small parlor where they often took tea in the morning. It was not a particularly cheerful room. It had been designed to allow the sunlight to warm and brighten the space, but Effie had decorated it with heavy brocade drapes that were closed unless Cass was in the parlor alone. The furniture was old and worn, upholstered in a faded olive green fabric. Cass would have preferred something lighter and airier, but though she was the lady of the house and should have been allowed to decorate the parlor as she desired, Effie had shown so much resistance to any change in the parlor or the entire house, Cass had not dared.

Now Effie rang for tea and ordered a maid to stoke the fire and bring her a blanket for her lap and a shawl for her shoulders. Very soon, Cass was no longer frozen. Indeed, she was far too warm.

"Girl!" Effie said to the maid. "I am still cold. I told you to stoke the fire."

"Yes, miss."

Effie scoffed. "It is so hard to find good help these days," she said to Cass, who wiped her forehead with her handkerchief. She could not be cross at Effie for being cold. She was so thin and bony, much like her brother had been, whereas Cass was much shorter and rounder. Her hips, touted as perfect for childbearing, had been one of the qualities that recommended her to the viscount, who'd needed an heir. Her hips and her father's money.

Alas, she had not borne him an heir, but her hips were still ample.

"Did you find the thread I wanted?" Effie asked.

"Yes, I did. I found the thread and the fabric. I think you will be able to remake the hat nicely."

"Good." The tea arrived, and Effie prepared it for both of them. Although Cass had said time and again that she preferred it black or with only a dash of milk, Effie made both teas with copious amounts of milk and sugar. Cass found it nearly undrinkable.

"And where else did you go?" Effie asked, eyes narrowed over her teacup.

Cass thought about lying, but Effie would only ask Riggersby, and then she would be found out. "I went to the bookshop."

"Which one?"

"On the Shelf," Cass said quietly.

"Eh? Speak up! None of your mumbling."

"On the Shelf."

"Why ever would you go *there*? It's the haunt of spinsters."

Cass wanted to point out that she *was*, for all intents and purposes, a spinster and so was Effie, but she knew better.

"I wanted a book," she said simply.

"A book?" Effie leaned back and blew out an exasperated breath. "We have books here."

She'd read all the interesting books, and those that remained were dry texts on botany or mapmaking. But what did Effie care, as she never read? That had been the one interest Cass and Norman had shared.

"Well?" Effie demanded.

Cass blinked at her.

Effie sat up in exasperation. "What book did you buy?"

"I..." Cass closed her mouth. "I didn't buy one. I...forgot."

It was the truth. Seeing the prince had made her forget everything, and then she'd been so embarrassed by her clumsiness, she'd just wanted to escape. She couldn't reveal any of that to Effie.

Effie stared at her with a look of disgust. "Well, I suppose my brother didn't marry you for your mind."

꧁❀꧂

Chapter Two

S HE WAS IN the bookshop again. She'd come twice in the past ten days, and
although they hadn't spoken, he'd seen her come in and known when she
departed. Now he looked for her daily. He had a simple life, and it was a small matter
to add one more task to his routine—wake, buy a bun or an apple for breakfast if he
had the coin, if he had no students he'd go to the bookshop, search the stacks, look
for the woman, buy soup or broth if he had coin, find a place to sleep.

These days he did not have enough coin for food and lodging. Most of his students were in the country for the winter. Now that it was cold, he usually chose
lodging. He'd always preferred clean, well-tailored clothing, and even as a boy he
hadn't liked to be dirty. Of course, he enjoyed playing as any boy might, but he never
argued about the bath he had to take as an inevitable result of tromping through
mud. Now baths were a luxury he couldn't dream of, but he found he could manage
well enough with water, soap, and a clean cloth.

As for food, he was always hungry. Often, he met his students in coffeehouses.
Those sessions were torturous because he could smell the delicious stews bubbling in
the kitchen but could not partake. Some of his students preferred to meet at their
lodgings, and they usually offered refreshment. Lucien was grateful for their
generosity. He had not lowered himself to stealing. He was still too proud to join the
ranks of common thieves.

The bookshop was crowded this morning. The sleet and freezing temperatures
had given the city a brief reprieve, and all of London seemed to want to brave the
chilly weather for the chance at feeling the sun on their skin. Lucien had also realized
Christmas was near. A smattering of laurel, rosemary, hawthorn, and bay had sprung
up outside homes and shops, and he'd overheard people speaking of their plans for
the holiday. Of course, families wanted to be together for Christmas. Lucien tried
not to think too often about family, and the subject of family Christmases was one
forever banned from his mind. If he thought of all he'd lost, he might decide not to
go on, and he had no choice but to go on.

Something in the air around him changed, and he looked up from the book
whose pages he'd been turning. *She* had stepped near the shelf where he stood and
appeared to be studying the volumes at the other end quite intently. She probably

had not seen him at this end, and even if she had, she would not remember their first meeting.

He looked back at his book, but as he did so, he thought he saw the flick of her gaze in his direction before she resumed staring at the volumes on the shelf in front of her.

Lucien's heart hammered rapidly. He could not have said why. He was no whelp, inexperienced with women and shy. When he'd been a prince, he'd had to fight the women off. That was not a problem in London, where most probably saw him as little better than a beggar. If women looked at him at all, it was with pity in their eyes.

But Lucien did not think it was pity he'd seen in that brief glance.

He finished the book he was searching, replaced it, and withdrew another. As he did so, he cut his eyes to the petite blond woman again. He did not know her name, but he had heard the shopgirl call her *my lady*. She was obviously a woman of some consequence and, judging from the black crêpe and broad hem of the gowns she wore every time he saw her, a recent widow. He pretended to peruse the first page of the volume he held, but his attention remained on the lady.

She was no great beauty. He had seen great beauties in his life, more than he could count. She was not tall and regal with a slender, willowy form. She was no taller than his youngest sisters, but she was no girl. Her widow's weeds could not hide the lush curves of her body, accented as they were by her small waist.

Her hair was a lovely golden color, though he had never favored blondes. They always looked too pale and lifeless for his taste. Of course, they were not usually blessed with such lovely blue eyes. Those were the widow's best feature, even hidden behind the spectacles. He'd caught a glimpse or two of them, and they reminded him of happier days under warm, sultry skies.

Best not to turn his attention to memories. He could not dwell on the past or all that he'd lost. Instead, he would concentrate on securing his future. He spent the next quarter hour engrossed in his work, though he was constantly aware of her presence just a few feet away. Gradually, she moved along the shelves until she was only two or so arms' lengths away. Lucien knew it was folly to hope that she might wish to become acquainted, but his heart raced nonetheless. How he craved conversation with another, *real* conversation, not pleasant greetings or discussions on verb conjugation.

She didn't look at him again. Her gaze remained steadfastly fixed on the books on the shelf before her. Lucien might have spoken to her, but he did not want the shopgirl ejecting him for disturbing the lady patrons. So he did not speak, though he was excruciatingly aware how long they had been in the same aisle and every single movement she made.

Her hands were small and her gestures graceful. When she read, she tended to cock her head to the left as though pondering the words. And now that they were closer, he thought he'd caught her scent. He knew the smells of the bookstore, of the wood polish and smoke from Mr. Merriweather's pipe, which meant the light, floral scent must be hers.

Unless he imagined the scent, which he did not think an impossibility. It had been so long since he'd been in close quarters with any woman who might have the means to purchase fragrances or bathe frequently, he might have misjudged.

The scent grew stronger, and Lucien had to restrain the urge to inhale deeper. He also forced his head to remain bent, his attention on the history text he held open. He wanted, desperately, to look at her, and because he wanted it so deeply, he would not give in. Everything he'd had, everything he'd wanted, had been taken from him. Desire was dangerous, and he would not give in.

Thud.

Lucien's head snapped up when the book hit the floor. For a moment, he thought he'd knocked a book from the shelf.

"Oh dear. Pray, excuse me," the lady said. Her hands were empty. Before she could bend to retrieve it, Lucien had scooped it up. He held it out to her, his eyes touching on the title: *Agriculture in the Roman Empire.*

"It is no trouble."

She took the book, and Lucien wondered if he only imagined that she had dropped the book on purpose.

"You have a lovely accent," she said.

He tightened his mouth to keep it from curving into a smile. He had not been mistaken. She *had* wanted to speak to him. Probably too shy to approach him directly, she'd engineered this meeting. The flush in her cheeks testified to her shyness, but she was not so meek as to allow this opportunity to pass by.

"I might say the same to you," Lucien said.

Her brow furrowed, which had the effect of wrinkling her small nose. "I don't understand."

"Your British accent is lovely." He smiled. "You see, to me, it is you who has the accent."

She stared at him for a little longer than was proper before finally lowering her eyes. "English is not your native language."

"It is not, no." He knew she wanted more, wanted him to answer with detail, but then the conversation might end too soon.

"What is your native language?" she asked.

Oh, he liked her. The boldness of her question made her delicate skin turn from pink to red, but she was brave enough to pose it anyway. He wondered if her nipples were as pale pink as her lips and if they flushed red when she was aroused. The thought was wildly inappropriate and absolutely lecherous, but he was a prince, not a saint.

"Glennish," he finally answered. "Though I speak English, French, Gaelic, and a fair bit of Italian."

"Oh." She looked down at the book she now clutched tightly to her breast. Lucien feared he'd said too much.

Finally, her eyes fastened on his face again through spectacles that were just slightly askew on her nose. "I fear I am terribly ignorant. What is Glennish?"

"It is the language—"

The lad who was often in the shop shelving books and assisting customers passed by, then doubled back after he saw Lucien and the lady in conversation. As her back was to the lad, the lady did not see him, but Lucien saw and interpreted the lad's glower perfectly. Lucien was allowed to warm himself in the store and peruse the volumes all he liked, but he was not to accost the patrons.

Lucien looked back at the lady before him. As much as he wished to continue to speak with her, he could not risk it. "Excuse me," he said. Placing the volume back on the shelf and noting where he had left off, Lucien made a quick bow and walked away. He strode all the way to the door of the shop and out onto the sunny street.

The weak light warmed him, and the breeze invigorated him. Or perhaps it was the attention from the lady. For a moment, he felt human again, not one of the countless masses populating London.

He would always remember her for that kindness, one she couldn't possibly realize she'd bestowed.

He did have one regret. He did not even know her name.

CASS STARED AT the book in her hand, some dusty volume about Rome, and sighed. What had she done wrong? Why had he left so abruptly? Oh, she was such a ninny to think that a man like him would want to speak to her. He was all tawny skin and broad shoulders, and those sensuous eyes. She'd never used a word like *sensuous* before, but she could not think how else to describe his eyes. When he looked at her, she felt warm all over.

And when he'd smiled...

Lord, she'd thought her legs would fail her. He was the most handsome man she'd ever met, and the first man she had ever wanted so much that she'd dared to approach him. Now she'd had her brief interlude with him, but it was not nearly enough. She wanted more.

She couldn't have more—not because Society forbade it. She was a widow, and Society would look the other way if she chose to take a lover.

The very thought of such wanton behavior made her blush with shame.

But, of course, Effie would not allow such a thing, and Cass did not have the freedom to engage in such a liaison without Effie knowing. Freedom such as that would require her to stand up to Effie, to cause conflict. Cass could think of nothing she disliked more than conflict and discord.

She sighed, feeling despondent despite the pleasant mood she'd been in when she awoke this morning and knew it was another day when she could make an excuse to go to the bookshop. If she went too often, Effie would chastise her. She turned, intending to find a novel to purchase so she would not return home empty-handed, as she had the first time she'd met the mysterious man.

"My lady?" a man said from behind her.

Cass glanced over her shoulder.

"I am sorry to trouble you. I could not help but notice Mr. Glen was speaking to you."

So that was his name. *Mr. Glen.* It was not a particularly foreign name, which made him all the more mysterious.

"Yes," she said, forcing the volume of her voice beyond a whisper. "I dropped a book, and he was kind enough to retrieve it for me."

"I see. I worried he was troubling you."

Now Mr. Glen's abrupt departure made perfect sense. By engaging him in conversation, she'd jeopardized his place here. If he truly came every day, as she'd heard the shopgirl remark, perhaps he had nowhere else to go. And he did appear to be looking through each and every book for...something. He'd left rather than risk being asked to leave for accosting her.

How awful that she'd placed him in that position, when it was she who'd accosted him.

"Thank you for your concern, but he was not troubling me at all," Cass assured him, perhaps a bit too forcefully. "He was very proper and polite," she added.

The clerk nodded slowly, as though he saw right through her to her real motive for speaking with Mr. Glen. "Very well, then. Is there anything I can help you find?"

"Oh yes. I want something exciting. Perhaps *Frankenstein* or *Mandeville*?"

The clerk gave her a wan smile. "Of course."

Walking home, Riggersby behind her with her packages, Cass tried to devise a plan to speak with Mr. Glen again. The only location where she knew she could find him was the bookshop, and yet, if she attempted to converse with him there, she was doomed to failure. He would most likely leave as abruptly as he had today. But what if she could arrange a chance meeting with him outside the bookshop? She had to assume he spent all day inside the bookshop, which meant if she arrived when the shop was closing, he would be leaving. She could ask him to escort her home.

Except she had Riggersby to escort her. Cass looked over her shoulder. She had to find a way to escape Riggersby.

Throughout dinner and Effie's tedious droning on and on about every single ache in her bones, Cass considered. One might have said she schemed, but she had never schemed in her life. She was merely trying to arrange to speak with a friend.

Not that Mr. Glen could be considered a friend... yet.

"Cass, are you listening?" Effie asked, staring at her across the gleaming wood table. Although it was only the two of them, Effie still insisted they dress for dinner and indulge in at least four courses. Effie had very little appetite, so most of the food went back to the kitchens.

Cass did not think the servants minded.

"Of course," she lied. "I was thinking we might ask Allen to make you a tonic. It might relieve some of the discomfort."

Effie nodded approvingly. Her maid was known to use brandy liberally in her tonics, and Effie loved any excuse for her brandy. "That is an excellent suggestion."

Cass smiled. It was so rare that Effie gave her any sort of compliment that she almost felt guilty for not having truly listened to all of the woman's complaints. She would listen diligently tomorrow.

Effie was eager for her tonic and retired early, which meant Cass could also escape to her room. She still resided in the viscountess's room—Effie had not been able to justify taking that for herself—and it adjoined the viscount's room. The master's room was empty now, all of the furnishings draped in Holland covers. It would likely never be occupied again, considering Norman had had no heir, and his will stipulated that in the event there was not an heir, the house was Cass's until she either died or remarried.

Not that she would ever remarry. What man would want to marry her?

Content to wait until Allen had finished with Effie, Cass curled up on the bed and opened *Frankenstein*. She didn't see the words, though. Instead, she tried to remember what it had felt like to have Norman in the bed, lying beside her. She tried to remember a time when she hadn't been alone.

Norman had not visited her bedchamber often, but he'd come often enough that no one could accuse him or her of not having done his duty for the title. But he grew ill only six months into the marriage, and then he was mostly confined to his bed.

She'd spent all day and many nights nursing him, reading to him, talking with him. She hadn't loved him, but she'd had an affection for him. He had been a kind man who had treated her well. She suspected that in his estimation she had been like a loyal dog. One allowed it inside, allowed it to rest by the fire, and fed it scraps from the table. One felt affection for it, patted its head, but when it finally passed away, one went on with one's life and acquired another pet.

She'd slept with Norman, spent his last moments with him, held his hand through the worst of the pain before he'd passed into unconsciousness, but she'd never really known him. They'd both enjoyed reading books, but as to his other passions, he'd never divulged them, nor had he asked about hers. Or perhaps he had, but she had none to speak of.

Now he was gone, and she would sleep in this bed alone for the rest of her life. She'd never know true passion or what it meant to be in love.

The very thought depressed her—and made her all the more determined that her plan to spend an hour with Mr. Glen did not fail.

Chapter Three

S HE'D WAITED FOR him outside.

Lucien knew what time the bookshop closed, and although he did not have a watch, he knew the closing routine. He did not like to be asked to leave and made certain he was always out of the shop before such a request became necessary.

He trudged out, disheartened that his search had been as fruitless today as every other day, but buoyed by the knowledge that it had not started to rain while he'd been inside. Perhaps he could sleep outside tonight and use the little coin he had to fill his belly.

"Mr. Glen?"

He turned at the tentative voice, half certain he had imagined it. She stood beside the shop window, her bright hair the only relief from the darkness of her widow's weeds.

He covered his surprise with a bow. "Good evening, Miss—Lady—I'm sorry. You have me at a disadvantage."

"My fault entirely," she said with a look over her shoulder. "We have not been formally introduced. I am Lady Ashbrooke."

"A pleasure to make your acquaintance," he said. "I'm afraid the bookshop is closing." He nodded to the door he'd exited. He could hear locks rattling as they were put in place.

"The bookshop?" She seemed to wake from a dream then. If he'd been the arrogant man he once was, he would have attributed her distraction to himself. But here, in his tattered clothing and unkempt hair, he could not fathom why she would speak to him, much less find herself flustered after staring at him.

"Will you walk with me, Mr. Glen?" Another furtive look over her shoulder. Was she looking for someone, or was she fearful someone might be looking for her?

"Of course." He could not allow her to walk about London unprotected. He offered his arm. She took it and all but pulled him away from the bookshop in the opposite direction of the way he'd wanted to go. But of course she was for Mayfair, while he would have ventured west and into the city's rookeries.

"You must think me terribly forward." This was said with her head bowed and her cheeks flushed pink.

"I worry you do not have a footman to chaperone you."

Another look over her shoulder. "Yes. I seem to have lost Riggersby. Perhaps you might escort me home."

"I..." He couldn't refuse to assist a lady in need, but he did not wish to walk all the way into the heart of Mayfair. It would take hours to find a place to sleep, and he did not like walking in the rookeries after dark.

She opened her pelisse and produced a small package wrapped in brown paper. "I just bought these currant buns, but now I find I am not very hungry. Would you like them?"

Lucien's mouth watered at the very thought of currant buns. He'd take her to the ends of the earth for one bite. "I cannot possibly eat your food," he said, his voice strained with the effort it took to refuse.

She looked up at him, her eyes very blue behind her spectacles. "Oh, then I suppose I could give them to a beggar—"

He snatched the package from her hands. "I don't want them to go to waste." Good God, he was only human, after all. He struggled not to rip the paper open as they walked, but he could smell the yeast rising from the package and feel the warmth from the bread. These were freshly baked. His head felt light with anticipation. As they were on Piccadilly now, he did not have the luxury of distraction lest she be jostled or both of them become victims of pickpockets.

"Why don't we stop at Green Park so you might enjoy them while they are still warm?" she suggested.

He liked that suggestion very much, especially as they had almost reached the park. "I wouldn't want your family to worry."

"Oh, I'm not expected home yet."

Interesting. "Won't your family worry when the footman returns home without you?"

She sighed and turned to him. "Mr. Glen, may I make a confession?"

He raised a brow. The woman grew more interesting by the minute. "Of course." He gestured toward Green Park, now visible down the length of Piccadilly. "No one should have to confess all in the melee of Piccadilly. We shall find a park bench."

They strolled along the street until they reached the park, stopping when they found an unoccupied bench. Though it was not raining, the clouds hid the sun, and the park was all but empty. He allowed her to sit and took a standing position beside her to better see the park and any ruffians who might approach.

"Will you sit?" she asked.

"I prefer to stand."

"Will you at least eat the currant buns before they grow cold?"

That he would do. "Would you like one?"

"No. I'm not at all hungry."

He could barely remember what it was like not to be hungry. Lucien struggled to take small, civilized bites of the buns. Still, he finished the first far too quickly. There were three in all, and he vowed to savor the last of the three.

"I suppose I should confess and be done."

Her voice was small and whispery, and he glanced away from the two remaining buns and at her face. It was as red as the falcon on the blue flag of Glynaven. "I promise to be a very lenient priest. The world needs more of them."

"Are you Catholic, then?" she asked.

"Only on the Continent." He rested a foot on the bench and leaned an elbow on his knee. "What is troubling you, my child?"

She smiled at his mock-serious tone. "I'm afraid I did not actually lose my footman."

"I am shocked." He did not even blink.

"I actually sent him on an errand so I might have the chance to meet you." It hardly seemed possible, but her face reddened further, and she looked down at her lap.

"Appalling," he said in a monotone. He had not been wrong in assuming she'd sought him out. Perhaps he did not look as bad as he thought. That illusion lasted only as long as it took him to look down at his scuffed boot.

"It is, isn't it? It's just that I heard Miss Merriweather talking about you, and she said you were a prince. I suppose I was intrigued."

"I can hardly blame you."

She glanced up at him, probably trying to determine if he was in jest. With her face flushed pink and her eyes so large, she looked quite pretty. "You must think me very silly."

"Not at all. Does that mean you believe what Miss Merriweather said?"

"I don't know what to believe."

A breeze blew, ruffling his hair. "Oh, come now, Lady Ashbrooke. That is a very diplomatic reply. What happened to the forward young woman I met earlier?"

"She's gone back into her shell."

That, he could believe. Lady Ashbrooke did not strike him as a woman who took many risks, which made it all the more surprising that she'd approached him. She must be terribly curious. Why not reward her?

Why not satisfy his own curiosity in turn?

"I will tell you the truth about who I am if you promise to return the favor."

Her pretty eyes widened. "You want to know about me?"

"Of course. If I tell you something about me, you must tell me something of yourself. That is only fair, after all."

"I suppose."

"Do not fret, my lady. I will not seek out all your dark secrets." Her lips curled in amusement at that remark. "I will give you leave to ask me three questions, and in turn, you give me the same privilege." This was not a new game to him. He'd played it often at the royal court.

Lady Ashbrooke took her time to consider. The woman was no fool.

"Very well," she finally agreed. "How do we begin?"

He really should have been thinking of where he would sleep tonight. Instead, he rewarded himself with another bite of currant bun. "You ask me a question, and I must answer truthfully."

"But you also have three questions."

He smiled. She was definitely no fool. "Ladies first."

She looked down at her hands again, considering her question. Lucien was disappointed to find his second currant bun gone and even more disappointed to realize he missed seeing her face. When she looked up again, her cheeks were once again pink. "My first question is, are you really a prince?"

He should have known she would ask that, and he was bound by honor to answer truthfully. "I am. I am Prince Lucien Charles Louis de Glynaven." He gave a little bow, which was more theatrics than courtesy, and was rewarded by her smile.

"Glynaven? I looked it up after you mentioned the language. It's a small country on the Continent. Was there recently a revolution?"

"There was. My father was overthrown as king, and I barely escaped with my life. And that is your second question. My turn."

"What?" She stood abruptly. "I didn't ask a question!"

"You asked if there was a revolution in Glynaven."

"That was a clarification, not a question."

He gave her his best princely stare, but she did not back down. "I'll allow it. This time." He held up a finger. "But from now on, clarifications also count as questions."

"Fine." She sat back on the bench with a huff.

His fingers itched for him to eat the last currant bun, but he wanted to savor it and thus denied himself. Instead of eating, he pondered his first question. Should he ask her if she was a widow? Yes, but how best to ask it?

"Who waits for you at home?"

"I live with my late husband's sister. She will certainly worry if Riggersby returns without me." She twisted a finger of her gloves. "But I am willing to risk the repercussions."

English was not his first language, but that didn't make her statement any less telling. She was a widow, and she didn't like her husband's sister. If the woman frequently imposed *repercussions* on Lady Ashbrooke, he could hardly fault the woman for wanting a brief respite.

Finally, he knew one more fact. She was willing to risk the annoyance, or perhaps even anger, of her family to spend time with him.

He couldn't allow that.

"Lady Ashbrooke, you have no idea how pleased I am to make your acquaintance. It's been weeks since I've had a civilized conversation with another person and months since I have not had to pretend I am only mere Mr. Glen. But there is a reason I choose to eschew my title. You're not safe in my company."

She looked up at him, her eyes wide. "Are you in danger?"

He ran a hand through his hair, which had grown thick and almost to his collar during his months in England. "I don't know. I have every reason to believe I am the last surviving member of the royal family, and I am the heir. If the *reavlutionnaire* realized they didn't kill me, they would stop at nothing to complete the task. I've stayed away from my friends in London, not wanting to endanger them and because I assume that if the *reavlutionnaire* tracked me here, those are the people and residences they will watch."

"But then where are you living?"

He'd scanned the park as he spoke, but now he looked back at her. "That is your last question."

She pressed her lips together. "I know."

"At present, I have no home. I spend my days at the bookshop and my nights wherever I can find a bed."

"Don't you have any funds? Any resources?"

He lifted a hand. "It's my turn to ask questions."

She sighed with obvious frustration. She'd fallen into a very common trap—that of asking all of her questions in rapid succession.

"How long were you married to the viscount?"

"Sixteen months," she answered. "He's been gone over a year now."

He had one question remaining. "You still wear your widow's weeds, though the requisite year has passed. You must have loved him very much."

She looked away, and for a moment he thought he had upset her. But when she looked back, her expression was firm and serious. "The truth, Your Highness?"

He lifted a hand. "Too dangerous to refer to me as such. Mr. Glen will do."

She looked as though she might protest, but then she sighed. "The truth is, Mr. Glen, that I didn't love him at all."

SHE'D SHOCKED HIM by her last statement. How could she have done otherwise? What sort of woman was she to admit she hadn't even loved her own husband? Her *dead* husband. She was supposed to honor him and his memory. She felt like a traitor.

The feeling only intensified when, immediately following her declaration, the prince suggested he walk her home. He'd asked his three questions, and she'd asked hers, and now their acquaintance was at an end. Cass wanted to weep as they entered the quiet streets of Mayfair, and the Ashbrooke town house grew ever nearer.

She'd thought meeting with him would assuage her curiosity and her desire for adventure, but talking with him had only fueled her desire to know more about him.

Initially, she'd been motivated by lust. What woman would not have been? The man was dangerously handsome. But the more he'd spoken, the more she'd detected a sadness in him, and a desperation.

The sadness she understood. He'd lost his entire family. What must it be like to be the lone survivor of an entire line? Did he feel guilty that he'd survived when everyone else had perished? She might have asked, if she'd still had questions.

But first she would have asked about the desperation.

She saw the town house just a few yards away and slowed. "We had best part here, Mr. Glen. I do thank you for your escort."

"The pleasure was all mine." He bowed with practiced elegance.

She should walk away now, return home, and make her excuses to Effie. Even the thought made her chest tighten as though a vise had once again been locked into place.

"Will I see you again?" she asked, and then wished she had shut her mouth. How absolutely pathetic she must have sounded. How clinging and desperate.

"That would not be wise," he answered. "Not that I have ever been wise in the past." He tipped his hat. "I will watch until you go inside. Good evening, my lady."

She stared a moment too long and then mumbled her own good-bye. She practically walked on air the remainder of the distance to the town house. What did he mean he had not been wise in the past? Did that mean he wanted to see her again? If there was even a small chance of speaking with him again, walking with him again, she wanted to take it.

Vidal opened the door, and Cass's good mood dissipated. Vidal's expression was severe. "Miss Ashbrooke has taken ill with worry for you."

"Where is she?" Cass handed him her bonnet and gloves.

"In her rooms."

"I'll go immediately." Cass started up the stairs, knowing thoughts of her next meeting with the prince would have to wait.

She gave in to the impulse to see the prince again two days later. Effie was still cross with her for making her worry when Riggersby had returned home without her. Cass had apologized profusely but had not given an explanation for how she and the footman had come to be separated. She did not want to lie, and so, despite Effie's demands and angry outbursts, Cass kept silent. It felt strangely empowering to defy Effie even in that small way.

Riggersby, of course, made no demands, but he had become a hawk. She knew she wouldn't escape his notice so easily again. Cass did the only thing she knew would guarantee seeing the prince again—she went to the bookshop.

She found him one shelf over from where she had seen him last. He was on one of the lower ladder rungs, a volume in one hand. His fingers were blurs as he flipped the pages. He didn't seem to be reading, though his attention was fixed on each and every page. Finally, he closed the book and replaced it on the shelf. She would have needed to be two rungs higher on the ladder to reach that shelf, but he accessed it easily.

As though sensing her gaze on him, he turned her way. His beautiful golden brown eyes warmed but did not seem surprised. At his look, she felt rather warm herself, and she loosened the scarf at her neck.

"Lady Ashbrooke." He nodded. "How good to see you again. Am I in your way?" He spoke formally—as he should, considering they hardly knew each other—but she still had the sense he did so for the benefit of anyone listening.

"Not at all. I saw you browsing and thought I would say hello." Dear Lord. Now she had nothing else to say, and he was still looking at her with those eyes that made her face heat until she thought she might explode. "Uh, hello," she said with a wan smile.

"Hello." His voice was deep and velvet soft, and was it her imagination, or had his gaze dipped to take in her body? It must have been her imagination. Men did not look at her in that way.

She could think of nothing else to say, and when an uncomfortable silence descended, she cleared her throat, hoping he would fill it.

He didn't.

"I should be going."

"Good day to you."

She turned to walk away and simply could not do it. *Stop being a ninny, Cass!* She clenched her hands into fists and turned back. "Unless I can be of some assistance?"

His look was veiled and impossible to read. It was probably some sort of technique all the royals were required to master so they might better negotiate treaties or whatnot. She was behaving in a most abominably forward manner, but he was a man. If he did not want her company, he could tell her easily enough.

She bit her tongue, praying he would not be too unkind.

"I'd like that," he said.

"Of course. I'm so sorry to trouble—"

He was smiling at her. He hadn't dismissed her at all. He'd invited her to help him. Her heart thumped so hard she could not manage to take a breath. Perhaps she hadn't heard him correctly.

"Did you say you would like my help?"

He nodded. "Very much, but I don't want to keep you if you have another engagement."

She shook her head violently. "No. I don't! I have nothing else to do. I'll help you in any way I can. I'll do whatever you ask." Now her cheeks heated for quite another reason.

His gaze seemed to darken, and she feared he would comment on the double meaning of the remark she'd just made. Part of her *hoped* he'd take the double meaning, though she hadn't meant it that way.

Instead, he reached for the next book on the top shelf and handed it to her. He was far too much the gentleman to remark on her ill-advised choice of words.

"It would make my search go faster if you looked through this book."

She longed to ask what he searched for, but this was neither the time nor the place for questions, not to mention she'd used all of hers already.

"What do I do?"

He moved beside her and opened the book. His hand brushed hers as he did so, and she became aware of the warmth of his body and the scent of sandalwood. She swallowed and forced herself to breathe slowly lest she begin to pant.

"I want you to turn every single page and examine it." He spoke softly, his voice low enough that only she could hear. She held the book with both hands now, and his arm slid against hers as he pointed to the open page. "I'm looking for any loose pages or papers slipped inside." He indicated the shelves nearby, most of them filled with unbound books.

"I see." Her voice was but a breathless whisper. "Just the bound books?"

"No. All of them. To be certain." He turned the page, the action bringing his bicep briefly in contact with her breast. Heat surged through her, and she couldn't help but gasp at the shock of sensation. Surely he hadn't even noticed. He had on a coat and she a dress with several layers under it. He couldn't have known he touched her where no man but a husband should.

"If you find anything, show me," he said, withdrawing. He pulled his hand back, and this time he did not touch her. Her face was likely as red as a tomato, and she did not dare to look at him.

"I can do that."

"Thank you."

From the corner of her eye, she saw him take down another volume. She had also noted the kissing bough someone had hung from the ceiling. Evergreens and mistletoe seemed to stare down at her, daring her to kiss the man she desired. Cass swallowed and looked away. At the window, a gentleman who looked every bit the Corinthian stood and pretended to read a novel, while watching the street. The romantic in her liked to think he was watching for the woman he loved. With a sigh and a refusal to spare the kissing bough another glance, she went back to her employment, working beside the prince in silence for at least a quarter of an hour. She turned every single page and scanned it carefully, but her thoughts were not on her task. Her thoughts were on the prince, and they had drifted into forbidden territory.

In her mind the two of them stood in the library of a royal palace. She was dressed as a princess in silks and satins, the likes of which she had worn only during the most choice events of her brief Season. She reached up to remove a book from a bookshelf, and her arms glittered with jewels. She'd barely opened the book when the prince put his arms around her tiny waist. This was only a daydream, so of course she had a tiny waist and such perfect vision that she didn't require her spectacles.

He murmured something seductive in her ear, and she shivered with anticipation. Finally, his mouth lowered to graze her bare shoulder. At the same time, the hand on her waist inched higher to cup her breast. He kneaded it expertly, causing the nipple to harden to an aching point. His mouth continued to worship the skin of her neck, and his other hand slid to the juncture of her thighs.

"Lady Ashbrooke?"

Cass opened her eyes, momentarily disoriented to realize she was not in the palace library but inside On the Shelf.

"Are you well?"

The prince watched her with concern in his narrowed eyes.

"Perfectly. Why?" She realized she'd closed the book and, wanting something to occupy her hands, replaced it on the shelf.

"You were standing quite still with your eyes closed and one hand pressed to your abdomen. Your breathing had grown rather rapid—"

Cass felt her cheeks heat in mortification. "Did you have a library in the palace at Glynaven?"

His brows rose slightly, an indication she'd surprised him with her question. She'd surprised herself.

"Are we playing three questions again, Lady Ashbrooke?"

"Yes." It might not be wise to play the game with him again, but neither had it been wise to approach him today. Besides, she was past the point of acting wisely. She had the rest of her long, lonely life to behave wisely.

He gave her a slow smile, which should have made her question what he would ask her in return. Instead, she rather hoped it would be something scandalous. At that thought, she peered about them. They were the only patrons in On the Shelf at the moment and at the back of the shop, away from the clerks and the doorway. Business was slow today, and Cass heard only the shopgirl humming to herself as she dusted the volumes in the window.

The prince leaned one shoulder against the shelf, tucking the book he held under his arm. "We had a magnificent library."

"What was it like?" she asked, leaning close because he spoke softly so the shopgirl would not hear.

"That's two questions."

She nodded, not caring.

"The chamber was domed, and the cupola was painted by famed Renaissance artists from Glynaven—mythical images of satyrs and wood nymphs and enchanted forests. In the daytime, the library shone with light from the tall windows spaced throughout. If the lawn was not lit with lanterns at night, one could see all the stars from those windows. I used to sit for hours on the red velvet chaise longues and read. Of course, my younger sisters thought it most diverting to sneak up to the second level, squeeze behind a pillar, and spy on me. They must have been exceedingly desperate for entertainment to find watching me read of any interest."

Cass smiled, imagining the girls tiptoeing and giggling as their older brother pretended not to notice them. She'd never had any siblings and had often been so lonely that a chance to spy on an older brother would have been welcomed.

"And now it's my turn," the prince said. "What is your name—your Christian name?"

Cass smothered a smile. He did care about her. He would not have wondered such a question if she didn't hold any interest for him. "My name is Cassandra, but everyone calls me Cass."

He nodded slowly. "Cassandra, the cursed princess of Troy."

Cass ducked her head. "I do not think my parents are great readers. I believe they just liked the name. And I have no great gift of prophecy, though I imagine if I did, no one would believe me either." Fortunately, her head was bowed, and she did not have to look at him when she spoke. She feared she'd revealed too much.

"I have another question," he said quietly, so quietly she had to lean closer to hear his voice. She again caught the scent of sandalwood and took a shaky breath.

"I suppose it's only fair. I asked two in a row." She glanced up at him, saw his lion's gaze on her, and darted her eyes back to the worn boards beneath her feet.

"What were you daydreaming about?"

She froze. The object of the game was honesty, and she could not reveal the subject of her fantasy. She began to shake her head.

"Tell me, Cassandra." The sound of her name on his tongue made her breath catch.

"I cannot," she whispered. "It is too"—*mortifying*—"personal."

"I answered your questions, and remember, you have another yet to ask. You can ask me anything you want, and I'll answer."

His voice was so seductive and so low that it rumbled through her, bringing warm spirals of pleasure with it. She could not tell him what she'd been thinking, and she also knew she didn't have the willpower to deny him anything.

Chapter Four

H E'D PUSHED HER too far. He could see by the way she drew away from him and how she wouldn't meet his eye. He'd asked too much of her too soon, and she wouldn't reveal her daydream. Curse his impatience! And curse his need to know as much about her as he could. There was no point in it. It was not as though he could marry her, or even become her lover. Even speaking with her now was dangerous for her if they were observed.

If the assassins who had murdered his family were in London, and he had to assume they had pursued him, then the best way to protect her was to walk away.

Now.

"I shouldn't tell you this," she said as he found the strength to bid her adieu.

Those words silenced his tongue. It was always the forbidden that made him want more. "But you will."

He moved closer to her because he liked being close to her and because her voice was but a mere whisper.

Her head was lowered, and she wore a black bonnet on her golden crown of hair, but just past the brim he could see her scarlet cheeks.

"I was imaging you and me in a royal library."

Ah, that was why she'd asked about the library at Glynaven Palace.

"Tell me what we were doing in the library, Cassandra." It was a statement, not a question. Even if he'd asked a third question, he did not think she would notice. But he could not risk losing his third question, because he had already decided what it would be.

"You had your arms around me."

He could barely hear her.

"I embraced you."

"From behind, and you'd lowered your mouth to… kiss me. Here." She touched her collarbone, and Lucien had the mad urge to strip away her clothing and kiss that collarbone right then and there.

"This was a fantasy."

Her blue eyes flicked to his face and back down.

"I like it so far. I believe if I had come across a beautiful woman like you in the library, I would have certainly kissed your neck and your shoulder. Tell me what else I did."

"You touched..." She pressed a hand to her abdomen and lifted it so it skimmed over her breast.

His cock hardened at the gesture, and he had to swallow before he could speak again. "There's more."

She shook her head, fiercely this time. "I've said enough. It's my turn to ask a question."

He wanted to know all of her fantasy, but he was not so mad with desire as to think this the time and place. Of course, this was the only time they might have and the bookshop the only place.

"Ask me, then," he said.

The bell above the shop door jangled, and Cassandra jumped. He heard a man's voice greet the shopgirl and then a woman's.

Cassandra cleared her throat and reached for another book on the shelf. He should do the same, pretend to browse lest they be observed conversing.

But he didn't reach for another book. He wanted Cassandra alone, wanted to continue this conversation.

"Come with me." He took the book from her hand, replaced it on the shelf, then grasped her wrist. He knew every exit from the bookshop. He'd found them all the first time he'd come. He always knew every exit from any building where he spent time. Now he pulled her toward a rear door with a bar over it to keep it secured from the inside. At one time the door might have been used for deliveries, but Lucien's investigations had uncovered a back room with a larger door where carts might be more easily divested of their contents. He reached the barred door, glanced about to make certain no one watched, and slipped the bar from its mooring. He'd had to release Cassandra to do so, as the bar was quite heavy and not easily moved after long years of neglect. When the door was open, he indicated she should step out first, and then he followed, closing it behind him.

They stepped into a shadowed lane that ran behind the shops in Duke Street. At one point it might have housed mews, but now they were quite alone. The day was gray and cold, and either the first drops of rain or wet snowflakes dusted his cheeks.

"Why did you bring me here?" she asked, her cheeks still pink from her earlier embarrassment. The color made her look fresh and pretty despite the solemn black of her clothing.

"Is that your question?"

"No, but I think you must know what it is already, else you would not have brought me out here so we wouldn't be overheard."

If that was what she wanted to believe, he would not argue. "You want to know what I'm searching for."

She nodded, leaning her back against the door behind them.

"That is a dangerous question, Cassandra. Suffice it to say I'm searching for proof of my identity, and I have reason to believe it's hidden in one of the books in this shop."

"What reason?"

"That is four questions. It's my turn."

Her gaze met his expectantly, her blue eyes magnified behind the spectacles. Slowly, he lifted his hands and removed them from her face. She blinked at him, her eyes still amazingly large and lovely even without the lenses. He dropped the spectacles into his pocket.

"What are you doing?" she asked. "Without my spectacles, I won't be able to see any distance and make it home."

"Right now, all you need to see is me. Right here. In front of you. May I kiss you, Cassandra?"

She took a sharp breath. "Is that your question?"

He made a sound of acknowledgment, not daring to touch her until she gave her assent.

"Yes," she whispered.

He felt as nervous as a youth kissing a girl for the first time. For a moment, he did not know where to put his hands or how to begin. Then he leaned one hand against the door and placed the other on her cheek. Her skin was cold but soft. His fingers brushed against her silky hair, and his thumb rested on her flesh. Lovely Cassandra, as fair as he was dark. His bronze skin seemed a blot against her pale flesh.

He brushed his thumb over the curve of her cheek, then bent until his lips were a mere fraction from hers. She lifted her chin, anticipating his kiss, angling her head so their noses would not bump. He brushed his lips over hers, his flesh meeting hers with a mere whisper. Still, he felt the jolt zing through him and knew that one brief caress would never be enough. He brushed his lips over hers again, then pulled back enough to see her face. Her eyes were closed and her pink lips parted. He watched as the hand he rested on the door clenched with the effort it took not to crush her against him.

A snowflake landed on his lips, the cold a tonic against the heat generated from the kiss. Lucien could resist her no longer. He fisted his hand in her hair and dragged her body against his, lowering his mouth to hers.

But just as he would sink into the sweetness of her lips, he heard the sound of horses' hooves on the packed dirt of the narrow lane where they stood. He moved instinctively to place his body so he might shield her from view. When the cart finally passed, he handed her the spectacles. "Why don't we walk for a few minutes?"

He would have rather kissed her again, which was why he thought it best to walk. He could not kiss her if he had to focus on putting one foot in front of the other.

She followed him down the lane and then out onto Duke Street, not far from where her footman waited in front of the bookshop. "Riggersby is waiting to see me home," she said, "else I would ask you."

"It probably isn't wise, at any rate." He moved away from the bookshop as he talked, not intending to take her far but wanting some distance from the shop. "I haven't felt watched the past day or so, but I've felt eyes on me before. I believe the *reavlutionnaire* have tracked me here. I'm running out of time."

"Time for what?"

"Time to find the papers I need, the papers that are my only hope of salvation. My mother was not the trusting sort. She was French, and she watched with horror as the revolution swept through her country. Had she not been married to my father and safe in Glynaven, she knew she would have been one of the first on the guillotine. In fact, almost her entire family was murdered during the first weeks of the revolution."

"I'm so sorry. I've read a little about it. My late husband enjoyed histories, and I read to him after he grew too ill to read for himself. It was a gruesome thing, what happened in France."

She was such an innocent. What could a book show her of the realities of the massacre and bloodshed that accompanied revolution?

"The fate of her family meant she never truly trusted the people of Glynaven. She saw the signs of revolution long before my father. He turned a blind eye to the growing unrest, while she prepared. That preparation might yet save me."

"How?"

It had begun snowing harder now, and those still out shopping were hurrying to finish and retreat indoors. Lucien could hardly blame them. The lack of people made the two of them far too conspicuous. He could see her footman shuffling from foot to foot in front of the bookshop. The man would spot them in a moment.

"Some other time, Cassandra. Meet me—"

Prickles ran up and down his back, as though an unseen hand raked him with sharp nails. He spun around, searching for the source of the danger. That boy huddled in the doorway? That couple with their arms linked? That young clerk pulling his hat down to keep the wet snow off his nose?

He wasn't safe here. He'd endangered Cassandra. "Walk to your footman now," he ordered her. "Don't look back at me. Don't acknowledge me."

"But—"

He gave her a small shove, then doffed his hat as though he'd accidentally bumped into her. "Don't question me. Just go."

Her face paled, and she took a step back, then awkwardly turned and arrowed for her footman. Lucien watched her until the servant noticed her and moved to intercept his mistress, and then he pulled his collar up and walked the other way.

He hadn't walked far before he knew they were following. He didn't know how many, and he didn't know when they'd fallen in behind him, but he knew they were there. Lucien prayed they hadn't seen him with Cassandra Ashbrooke, or if they had, they'd seen nothing more than a man bumping into a woman.

The snow fell more heavily, the heavy clouds hanging low in the sky and turning the afternoon as dark as evening. Lucien had threaded his way toward Piccadilly, knowing the street was busy enough that he might be able to lose his pursuers, but only the poorest or most stalwart were still about in weather that had all the makings of a storm. Lucien pushed against the wind, ignoring the bite of it, until his legs felt weak from the exertion and from hunger.

He chanced a look over his shoulder and wished he had not. He counted three men, too many for him to handle on his own without a weapon of any kind. They had hats and coats, but the quick look he'd managed told him they were most likely Glennish. They had features typical of south Glynaven, where the rebellion had begun and flourished—height, dark hair and dark eyes, and the sun-touched skin so typical of the coast.

He couldn't be certain, but he thought he recognized at least one of the men. If they caught him, they would kill him.

The snow blew more thickly now, and Lucien used it to his advantage. He headed into the wind, even though it depleted his strength. Finally, when he'd gained a small lead, he cut across Piccadilly, darting dangerously close to the few conveyances still on the street. He ran past buildings shuttered tight against the cold and snow, then crossed Piccadilly again, turning down a side street. A broken wheelbarrow sat askew in the middle of the lane, and Lucien crouched behind it. It was barely large enough to hide his broad shoulders, but he slouched down so his head almost touched the dirt and brought his knees up to his chest.

He could only hope the rapidly falling snow would obscure his footprints. Even so, with the limited visibility, if the assassins passed the lane without venturing inside, they would see no sign of him.

Lucien had no way of knowing whether the men had seen him zigzag across Piccadilly and no way to judge the passing of time. He lay for what seemed hours on the cold, hard ground, watching as a light dusting of snow covered his threadbare coat. He shivered, and his empty belly protested its lack of food. The snow-laden clouds had blocked out the dreary winter sun, bringing an early evening. If he closed his eyes now, he would probably be dead by morning.

No one but the refuse collectors would mind, and they might even benefit from the few coins in his pocket and his boots, which had no holes yet. His family was dead, and his people already thought him dead. Only Cassandra Ashbrooke knew who he really was, believed he was the man he claimed to be. Would she mourn him?

Lucien closed his eyes and pictured her face turned up to his, waiting for his kiss. He blew out an annoyed breath and opened his eyes again, forcing himself to sit. He didn't want to die. He wanted to kiss her again, *really* kiss her this time. He wanted to test the weight of her hair with his hands, divest her of those ugly mourning dresses, and hear her laugh.

And he wanted to find those *bluidy* books his mother had sent. All of his searching couldn't be for naught.

Ignoring the ache in his stiff shoulders, Lucien peered around the wheelbarrow. Piccadilly looked all but empty, the passersby merely dark shadows in the gathering gloom of nightfall. Time to find food and shelter for the night.

❧

EFFIE HAD TRIED to prevent Cass from going out that morning. She'd claimed it was too cold and the snow hid ice that made walking treacherous. But Cass would not be deterred. She wore her warmest dress and pelisse, even though the outer garment was not black. Lucien had been out in the snow all night. Cass could hardly justify staying warm and safe when he had no option but to freeze.

That was if he'd made it through the night. She'd been terrified when he'd ordered her to walk away from him. She knew he'd been trying to protect her from whoever hunted him. She wished she could protect him too.

She'd thought about it all night and had come to a conclusion.

A conclusion Effie would not like. At all.

Riggersby didn't complain when they stepped outside that morning. The snow still fell, and Cass had to negotiate a few of the larger drifts. Despite her efforts, her feet were wet and cold by the time she reached the bookshop, which had been open two hours by then. It was no little effort to escape Effie. She couldn't ask Riggersby to stand outside with the weather so foul, so she settled him inside and went straight back to the shelf where she and Lucien had been searching the day before.

The shopgirl gave her a knowing smile when she passed by, but Cass just pushed her nose in the air and walked faster.

She turned into the aisle and halted. Lucien wasn't there.

Her heart dived into her belly, and she reached a shaking hand for the nearest shelf. *Lucien.* They'd caught him. They'd killed him. Now she'd never know what it was he sought in these books. She'd never help him claim his true identity.

She'd never kiss him again.

Was it wrong that losing the chance to kiss him again hurt most of all? She was a selfish, selfish creature. For the first time in... well, in her entire life, she'd felt alive. Since she'd met Lucien, she'd risen in the morning with a smile, with hope, with a sense of purpose.

Foolish to believe she might be in love. She did not even know the man, not really. But she respected him, admired him, esteemed him. He was tenacious, kind, an unfailing gentleman.

Or at least he had been.

Were not respect, admiration, and esteem the beginnings of love?

And now her chance had been torn away. She would never know if she could love a man, never know if one might come to love her. She would never know passion. Without him, her life would go on as it had before—long, meaningless days filled with tedious niceties.

"Lady Ashbrooke?"

She turned, and just as quickly as her heart had sunk like a stone, it rose like a bubble. "You are alive!" she gasped, forgetting to lower her voice.

He glanced toward the door and motioned for her to follow him into a shadow farther back in the shop.

"Oh, I see. You've started the next shelf," she said. "That's fast work."

He paused midway down the aisle and faced her. "I have to work fast. I don't know how much time I have left."

"Was it assassins yesterday?" she whispered, because he had been whispering.

"Yes. I lost them in the snow and the crush of Piccadilly, but I might not be so lucky next time. If they track me to the bookshop, I'll have to abandon my search."

"Then we must search quickly," Cass said, pulling down the nearest book and opening the cover.

"No." The prince put his hand on the book and closed it. "There is no *we*, my lady. It's too dangerous for you to be seen with me. I must insist you go home and keep as far away from me as possible."

"You insist?"

"Yes. This is good-bye." Like the royalty he was, he took her gloved hand, bent, and brushed his lips over the back. Then he stepped away and nodded a dismissal.

Cass didn't move. She wanted to move. Everything in her urged her to move. She'd always done as she'd been told. She never argued or disobeyed or remotely considered the idea of defiance. But her chin had risen stubbornly, seemingly of its own accord, and her hands had landed on her hips.

"I don't think so." She shook her head. "No. This is not good-bye."

The prince's golden eyes narrowed, much like an angry lion's. "I say it is, and I bid you *adieu*." He moved away from her.

"I don't accept." Cass raised her voice, causing him to retrace his steps.

"Shh!"

"I am not one of your subjects, Your Highness. I am a subject of King George, and as such, you have no authority over me. You need help, and I'm not abandoning you in your hour of need."

The prince gave a rather undignified bark of laughter. "Well said, but I'm afraid you are more of a distraction than a help." He leaned close, so close his breath caressed her cheek. "When you are near, I can't seem to stop imagining kissing you."

Cass was momentarily speechless. No man had ever said such a thing to her. She was relatively certain no man had ever thought such a thing about her. Oh, she was most definitely not leaving now.

"Be that as it may," she stammered, wishing with her whole heart that she did not blush so easily, "I can help you, and not simply by looking through books."

He raised a brow.

"Now, hear me out," she began.

"Never a good beginning."

He was probably correct, but it was too late to go back now. "The men who are after you don't know you and I are... friends. I propose you stay at my town house until the threat has passed."

He huffed out a breath, but she ignored him.

"You have nowhere else to go—I know you don't, so do not pretend otherwise—and the weather is not fit for man or beast. If the snow continues like this, half the city will be under a foot of white. We have beds, coal, and plenty of food and drink. I couldn't forgive myself if I didn't offer you the most basic of English hospitality."

More to the point, she couldn't forgive herself if she allowed him to walk out of her life without a fight.

"What you suggest is impossible," he said, the words spilling out as soon as she'd taken a breath. "My presence alone would endanger you, your servants, and your friends. I will not put you in jeopardy."

The words had barely escaped his lips when the sound of crashing glass made them both cringe and drop to the floor. The prince pulled Cass under him, using his body to protect her as more glass shattered.

Chapter Five

~~~~~~

THEY'D FOUND HIM. He didn't have to assess the situation, or even see the shattered glass, to know this was the moment he'd feared. And his worst fear—that he had put Cassandra Ashbrooke in danger—was also realized. She lay under him, her small body trembling with fear.

Around them, the sounds of chaos erupted—a woman screamed, a man cursed, and something crashed to the ground—but in this back area of the bookshop, it was only him sheltering her, her warm body under his, her sweet feminine scent making him long to bury his nose in her hair.

"My lady!" Booted footsteps neared, and Lucien reluctantly sat on his haunches. The footman he recognized as the one always with Cassandra appeared before them. He spotted his mistress lying on the floor, and his ruddy face went pale. "Lady Ashbrooke! Are you hurt?"

Cassandra sat up and lifted a hand to her collar, a gesture that made Lucien smile. His mother always lectured his sisters when they appeared rumpled or disheveled before her. *A true lady is always straight and neat.*

Lucien had thought true ladies must never have much fun if they always had to worry about mussing their hair or muddying their dresses. He rather liked a rumpled lady, but being older now, he could also appreciate more refinement and elegance. Cassandra Ashbrooke had both in abundance.

"I'm quite well, Riggersby," Cassandra told her man. She struggled to her feet, her legs tangled in her skirts, and Lucien offered a hand. The footman gave him a dark look and shouldered himself between the two.

"A ruffian has thrown rocks through the shop window," Riggersby told his mistress. "I must see you home immediately."

But Cassandra was having none of that. "Is anyone hurt? Has the Watch been summoned?"

Riggersby gaped at her. "I couldn't say, my lady. I only know I must see you safely home."

"I'll hardly tuck tail and run if someone needs me," she said, and pushed past him toward the front of the shop. Lucien followed, but the footman blocked his path.

"And just where the devil do you think you're going?"

Lucien nodded toward where Cassandra had just disappeared. "To see if Lady Ashbrooke needs any assistance."

"She's my responsibility. You can go to the devil."

Lucien had had enough of pesky interlopers—be they footmen or assassins—bullying him. He shoved the man against a shelf and glared down at him. "She is my responsibility too, and you'd best take care not to stand in my way."

He shoved away from the servant and stalked after Cassandra. He hadn't anticipated speaking the words he had, but neither did he wish to retract them. She was his responsibility, whether he wanted the duty or not.

Cassandra stood beside the shopgirl, who was crying, and seemed on the verge of hysterics. Cassandra patted her shoulder, and both women stared at the wreckage that had once been the window. As the footman had said, two large rocks sat on the floor, having been thrown through the glass. The cold air and snow had already begun to penetrate.

"I d-don't understand," the shopgirl sobbed. "Who would do such a thing? And to think we almost lost that window, but Lord Wrathell caught the lady. And now it's broken!"

Cassandra glanced at him, and he gave her a slight nod. He couldn't know for certain, but if it hadn't been the Glennish assassins, he would have been very surprised.

"What can we do for you, Miss Merriweather?" Lucien asked. "Shall we send Lady Ashbrooke's footman to fetch your parents?"

The muffled sound behind him attested to the servant's displeasure at the suggestion.

"Oh, would you?" The pretty shopgirl looked from Cassandra to Lucien with teary eyes. "Charlie tore out of here after the rogues."

"Of course." Cassandra turned back to her man. "Miss Merriweather will give you the directions. Go and fetch her parents directly."

"But, my lady, I must see you home."

"I'll do that," Lucien volunteered.

"But—"

"Riggersby!" Cassandra seemed to have found her voice. Lucien liked a woman who stood strong in a crisis. "Do not argue. If Miss Ashbrooke takes you to task later, I will claim full responsibility."

Riggersby glowered at Lucien. "Yes, my lady."

While Miss Merriweather instructed Riggersby, Lucien took Cassandra's arm. "I think it would be better if we leave now, before they have a chance to come back."

She looked up at him, her eyes even wider than usual behind her spectacles. "Do you think they will?"

"No, but I don't like to tarry."

They took their leave and stepped out into the cold. The bitter wind and snow weren't quite as much of a shock as they might have been, considering how quickly the temperature in the bookshop had dropped after the window was broken. Still, Lucien shoved one hand in his pocket, his other being free and icy so that Lady Ashbrooke might hold his arm. Like the other people out and about, they walked quickly with their heads down.

"When we reach the house, you will come in and warm yourself," Cassandra said.

Lucien made a sound of protest.

"You will," she argued. "I cannot possibly send any man out in this weather, and if there is danger, I am most certainly already in it."

Lucien did not mention that she'd sent her footman out in the snow, but he could not argue her other point. If the assassins had tracked him to the bookshop, they might very well have seen him with Lady Ashbrooke. And that meant she wasn't safe, even in his absence. Was it merely the desire to be warm and fed that convinced him she was actually safer with him present? If the assassins did attack her home, he could defend her. He was already on guard for any possible attack. Would her household staff be so alert?

"Very well."

She glanced up at him quickly. "Then you will come inside?"

"I will."

"And you will stay?"

She didn't add *the night*, but it was implied. "I will. I'll protect you until I can make a plan to leave London, and when I go, I'll lure the assassins with me." He would never find what he sought now. He would have to give up his hope of any sort of future beyond merely eking by. But Cassandra was worth the sacrifice. She was worth that and much more.

"Is that wise? Leaving London? What about the bookshop and the papers you seek?"

"There's nothing for it," he said, not allowing the despair to sink in. There would be time to wallow in self-pity later. "If I want to stay alive, I must flee." Run like a coward in the night. Good God, but he hated himself sometimes.

She looked as though she might say more, but the wind kicked up just then, and they both had to focus their attention on making their way to Mayfair. Lucien tried to look behind him, tried to make certain they were not followed, but it was an impossible task. The snow fell too quickly.

Finally, they arrived. The door to the town house was opened by a very English-looking butler. "My lady, Miss Ashbrooke was worried." The butler spoke to Cassandra, but his gaze was locked firmly on Lucien.

Behind the servant, a curved staircase led to the upper floors. The banister was swathed with Christmas greenery. Shiny red apples and hellebore added splashes of color. The scent was sweet and fresh as a meadow.

"I'll speak to her directly, Vidal." Cassandra gestured to Lucien. "This is my friend..." Here she paused and seemed to consider how to introduce him.

"Mr. Glen," he said, bowing. "Lucien Glen."

The butler looked down his nose at him. "I see. And where is Riggersby?"

"There was an incident at the bookshop," Cassandra explained, unfastening her pelisse and handing it to Vidal. "I sent Riggersby to fetch Mr. and Mrs. Merriweather as Miss Merriweather was there alone."

"What sort of incident?" a shrill voice interrupted.

Lucien's attention snapped to the top of the stairs, where a thin woman with a rather yellow pallor stood, clutching her throat.

"Some ruffians threw a stone and broke the shop window," Cassandra explained, sounding very calm and composed. One might never have guessed that she'd been trembling beneath him when the glass had shattered.

"Oh, dear me!" The woman, clutching the stair rail, took several steps toward them. "You are not to return there. You must stay home."

"I will not set foot outside again today, Effie," Cassandra told her. "And I've invited Mr. Glen to stay with us as well."

"What?" That exclamation came in unison from the Effie woman and the butler.

Cassandra seemed unconcerned by their astonishment. "Mr. Glen is a friend, and he is in need of shelter for a few days. I've offered my home."

"A *few days*!" Effie sputtered. Lucien could only assume the butler was too shocked to speak. "You cannot allow a man to stay here for an hour, much less a few days."

"Perhaps I should wait in the parlor," Lucien said.

"That's not necessary." Cass placed a hand on his arm. "I have offered my home, Effie, and I will not change my mind now. There's nothing scandalous in it. You are here to chaperone, and it is not as though I am an unmarried miss. I am a widow."

"Exactly!" Effie pointed a bony finger at her, and Lucien could have sworn Cassandra shrank back slightly. "You dishonor my brother's memory, bringing your lover here!"

"My lover? He is not my lover, and even if he were, this is *my* house. It was left to me by Norman. I may have any guest here I choose, and you can be certain that were Norman still alive, he would certainly offer the same hospitality I do to a friend in need."

"How can you—"

Cassandra held up a hand. "That is all I shall say on the matter. It is decided. Vidal, have the maids prepare a room for Mr. Glen, and then inform Cook we will have three for dinner. Tell her I want her to serve the best she has. No bland dishes tonight. I want wine and flavor and dessert."

Lucien's belly rumbled at the thought. The butler, obviously reminded of who his true employer was, scurried away to do the viscountess's bidding.

"Well!" Effie huffed. "If that is the way it is, then you will have to do without me. I shall not eat at your table. In fact, as soon as the snow has passed, I will remove myself from *your* house."

Cassandra sighed, as though she'd expected this response. "There's no call for that, Effie. I promised Norman I would take care of you, and there will always be a place for you here."

"My dear brother would be shocked were he here now."

"He is not here now," Cassandra said. "He has been dead for over a year."

Effie gasped.

"My period of mourning is over." As if to illustrate that point, she ripped off the black bonnet she wore. "I will never disrespect Norman's memory, but neither will I hide in my room, waiting for my time to die. If you choose to leave, that is your decision. If you choose to stay, know this: There will be changes."

Effie all but fled in horror, and Lucien clapped quietly. "Brava! That was well done. What do you do for an encore?"

She gave him a shaky smile, and he realized just how much the confrontation had cost her. "Cassandra, do sit." He steered her toward a small, stiff-backed chair against a wall. "Why are you shaking? You were brilliant."

"I feel as though I will be sick." She tried to lower her head into her lap, but he caught her chin.

"No, you won't. I don't know your late husband's sister, but I venture to guess that dressing down was well deserved and well past due."

"I should not have spoken to her thus!" she protested.

"You're right." He crouched beside her. "You should have told her off with much more colorful language."

Cassandra laughed lightly. "That is not what I meant, and you know it."

"No. What I know is that you are beautiful and strong and brave."

She gave him a look of incomprehension. "I'm none of those things."

"You are all of them and more."

Behind them, the butler cleared his throat. "Mr. Glen, if you would follow me, I will show you to your room."

"Thank you," Lucien said without taking his eyes from her.

"Will you tell me what you were looking for in the bookshop?" she asked, her voice so low only he could hear. "Over dinner? Will you finally tell me?"

He nodded. "I'll tell you every detail."

SEVERAL HOURS LATER, he had bathed, slept, eaten a small meal of bread and cheese, and dressed in clean clothing, which he suspected had belonged to the late Viscount Ashbrooke. They smelled of tobacco and mothballs. They were a bit small for him—the viscount had been shorter and thinner—but they were clean, and if he did not move his arms too much, the tight coat would not bother him.

When the butler summoned him to dinner, Lucien followed the man to the dining room, where he found Cassandra already waiting. "My apologies." He bowed. "I have kept you waiting."

When she didn't speak, he looked up. She stared at him as though he were a stranger. He looked down and immediately realized she must be shocked to see him in her dead husband's clothing.

"I do apologize. I found the clothes laid out after my bath. Should I change back?"

"No! It's not the clothes. I mean, it is strange to see you in his clothing, but that is not it." Her words bubbled up, sounding as though she'd had to force them through a tight throat.

"Then what is wrong?"

"Nothing. It's only... you are so impossibly handsome."

He felt the slow smile on his lips.

"I am certain you must have heard that a thousand times, and I suppose I did know you were handsome." Her cheeks were flaming red now. "But seeing you dressed properly, with your hair washed and your stubble shaved, it's rather a shock."

"A pleasant shock, I hope." He stepped closer, far more pleased by her compliment than he ought to have been. Of course he'd heard such flattery a thousand times—she was correct—but he had never thought of it as much more than flattery. He could see in Cassandra's eyes that she meant it, and he could also see the effect on her. She was doubting herself now.

"I—Lord, I have behaved like an idiot. If you will excuse me."

"I will not." He took her hand before she could escape. "You can't possibly be thinking of forcing me to endure Miss Ashbrooke's company alone."

Her hand trembled in his. She wasn't wearing gloves, and her skin was very soft and very pale. "Effie has chosen to dine in her room."

"Good. Then we shall have the evening to ourselves."

"But—"

"Cassandra, I want to dine with you. You really do not see yourself, do you?"

"Of course I do."

"Then you don't see what I see." He drew her closer and would have taken her into his arms if he hadn't known the footmen were on the other side of the door, waiting for them to take their seats so they might serve the first course. "I look at you and see a beautiful woman. That rose-colored gown is the perfect shade for your skin, the neckline just modest enough but teasing me with a hint of what lies beneath."

It did not seem possible, but her cheeks reddened further.

"And I don't think I've told you how much I love the color of your hair. It's like spun silk. And your eyes—"

"They're behind spectacles!"

"That takes nothing away from their blueness or your beauty. You cannot possibly think of denying me the sight of you at dinner tonight. If you do, you will also force me to break my promise."

"What promise?"

"I vowed to tell you my story."

"Oh." She looked at the table then, and he knew she would stay. Her interest in his tale was much more incentive than any compliment he might give her. He would have to remember that.

He moved his plate to the seat close to hers, so they would not be at opposite ends of the table, then she rang the bell and the first course arrived. Lucien could not speak for the first three courses. He was so completely focused on the food. It was not until the fourth course was set on the table that he'd eaten enough to realize he'd been utterly silent for the past three-quarters of an hour.

But when he looked at Cassandra, she was smiling at him.

"I have been an intolerable bore," he said. "Forgive me."

"There is nothing to forgive. I knew you were hungry that day I brought you currant buns. You must have extraordinary willpower to have eaten them so slowly."

"One does try to remain civilized."

"Oh, some days I do wish we could send civility to the devil."

"And what would you do? If we sent civility to the devil?"

A flush crept up her cheeks.

He grinned. "Ah, we shall come back to that later. First, I believe I owe you a tale. I must earn my keep."

"You do not need to sing for your supper."

"I would have told you even if you hadn't fed me. As I told you before, my mother was a suspicious woman. She had been born in France, and though the people of Glynaven loved her—or at least they seemed to—she never saw them as fully *her* people. Not the way my father, the king, did." He paused as the fourth course was taken away and the fifth presented.

"Perhaps that was why she heard the first strains of discord before any of the rest of us. She saw the unrest brewing and knew the inevitable result. My father shook his head at what he called her silly ideas, and my siblings and I followed his lead. I suppose I knew more of the situation than the other children, being that I am the eldest and the heir. I knew about the accusations the Parliament made against my father. They claimed he stole money from the treasury and imprisoned innocents with secret letters."

"Was any of that true?" she asked, bringing him back from the stone chambers of Glynaven Palace and into the cozy dining room in London.

"I suppose every accusation has a kernel of truth at the center. My parents were the king and queen. They lived lavishly, and they had enemies. But my father was not a cruel man or an unjust one. I believe he would have listened to the dissent if the leaders had come to him. Instead, they chose to attack his private guard. Such an attack angered my father, and he instituted curfews and curbed other privileges that sent many to prison for seemingly small infractions."

Cassandra poured him more wine, and he realized he'd drunk all of his and his throat still felt dry. "My mother warned him of the dangers, but he didn't listen. He saw the uprising as a trifle stirred up by a few malcontents. I don't think any of us, save the queen, realized how persuasive the *reavlutionnaire* were and how easily convinced the people were to follow their cause.

"One night, not long before the massacre, my mother called me to her private chamber. She showed me a stack of old books. Most were Glennish, but a few were English and French. As I watched, she opened one of the volumes and ripped out several pages. Then she secured an envelope with money and papers inside. One of the papers had the name of a bank and an account number. In that account, she had secreted hundreds of thousands of English pounds so that, in the event of an uprising, the royal family could flee to London and live there until peace could be restored in Glynaven."

"So that is why you look through all the books. She didn't tell you where she was sending it?"

"Her most trusted adviser took custody of the shipment of books, and he set sail for England only a day or so before the palace fell. My mother thought it wise to hide the money and papers in a book, because though the adviser might be searched and his personal artifacts rifled, she did not think the sailors would take much interest in a pile of old books."

Cassandra leaned forward. "She is an amazingly intelligent woman."

He nodded and sipped his wine again. "She was. She died in the massacre. All of them did."

Her hand was warm when it covered his. "I'm sorry. I'm certain you must miss them, especially at Christmas."

She did not know the truth of her statement. While some in London festooned shops and wished everyone happy now that Christmas was nearing, most Londoners took little notice of the upcoming holiday. In Glynaven, Christmas had always been the biggest celebration of the year with a week of merriment preceding it. He and his family decorated, sang songs, put on plays, and made each other gifts. The family also followed the German tradition of a Christmas tree.

Lucien glanced at the bowl of cloved oranges that stood in the center of the table. "I do miss them, but your greenery reminds me of happier times."

She tightened her hand on his. "Effie tells me it is bad luck to bring the evergreens, holly, and ivy inside before Christmas Eve, but I like to enjoy it. We'll have a Yule log and an extravagant dinner on Christmas. The servants will play snapdragon and sing carols at the top of their voices. You must stay and celebrate with us. It's only two days away."

"Thank you." She was unfailingly welcoming and kind. He did not know if he would still be in London, still be alive in two days, but at least he did not face the prospect of a cold Christmas alone.

She tried to release his hand, but he held firm. She couldn't eat with only one hand, but he suspected she was no longer hungry for food. He was not. He wanted her touch.

She took a breath. "How did you escape the massacre?"

"I was not in the palace when the *reavlutionnaire* attacked. I had been out with friends and heard the palace was sacked. I rushed to the palace, but it was too late. The grounds outside swarmed with bloodthirsty men and women. I was recognized instantly and chased through the streets of the capital. I finally made for the quay and swam to a British ship anchored in the harbor. The sailors pulled me on board and set sail at the next tide for home. They feared the violence in the city might spill over, and the captain was wise to sail immediately. I later heard many of the ships who tarried were burned or plundered when the *reavlutionnaire* tired of looting the palace and the city."

Her hand gripped his again. He glanced down at it, but her attention was riveted on his face. She must have forgotten he'd claimed her hand.

"What happened to the adviser?" she asked. "Did he sell the books to On the Shelf?"

"No. I found his rented flat, but he was no longer there. The current occupants sent me away, claiming they had never heard of the man. I hired an investigator. I did not know how precious the few coins I had with me then would be. I squandered them and hired the best, who found out that Absolon was murdered in a house-breaking."

"You don't believe that."

He smiled without humor. She did not miss anything. "No. I knew the assassins had found him and staged the murder to look like a theft. They'd probably been looking for valuables, but they did not know where to look or even if he had any with him. They took personal items, like his pocket watch and the silver candle-sticks, but the books were untouched."

"Lucien." The word was a breath on her lips.

He stilled, then lifted her hand to his mouth. "Say that again."

"Say what?" Her cheeks were pink.

"My name. I believe that is the first time you have said my name."

She ducked her head. "Lucien."

He wanted to kiss her, wanted so desperately to pull her close. Instead, he would finish his story. There was not much left now. "The investigator told me the books and all of Absolon's belongings were sold to pay the rent still owed. I used the last of my meager resources to pay the investigator to track down the buyer of the box of Glennish books. There had been an auction, and the auctioneer had clearly noted the books went to The Duke Street Bookshop. From there it was an easy task to go to

Duke Street and find the shop. The name of the shop had been painted over, but it was full of books. The Merriweathers tell me they have no record of buying any books from the auction, but they must have. Else, where would the books have gone?"

She lifted her wine and drank. "But why would they lie to you?"

"I do not know. People lie. They kill. They loot and pillage. Perhaps it is human nature."

"Perhaps, but suppose I go back with you tomorrow and we speak to the Merriweathers together? They might give us more information if I am with you and inquire."

Lucien had little hope that any more information would be forthcoming, but as a viscountess and a patron of their shop, the proprietors would be anxious to please her.

"You would do that for me?"

"Of course." She lifted her free hand to her pink cheek. "Shall we retire to the drawing room? Or would you rather be left alone to your port and cigars?" She smiled, and dimples appeared in her cheeks.

"I'd rather stay with you," he said honestly.

She led him to the drawing room, which did not look to have been refurbished in the last fifty years. The upholstery reminded him of that favored by his grandmother in her chambers. Everything was of good quality and very well maintained, but he knew instantly the style was not Cassandra's. She would not have chosen the dark burgundy velvet drapes or the dour gold paper-hangings on the walls. He had not seen her private chambers, but he suspected they were light and airy and cheerful.

He sat on one couch, and she took the one opposite, both of them with a glass of untouched wine in their hands. Lucien looked up at the portrait of the old man above the fireplace. He could imagine that man wearing the clothing he now wore. "Your husband?" he asked, nodding to the painting.

"Yes. That was painted a few years before we married."

He studied her face as she looked at the portrait. There was no trace of sadness in her eyes, no softness either.

"And you never loved him?" Lucien asked, perfectly aware the question was impertinent whether he was in England or Glynaven.

She cut her gaze to him. "Not in the way you mean. He was like a father."

"Or a grandfather, I imagine."

She glanced down. "It was a good match. My parents are wealthy merchants, and this was their plan to gain a title. Unfortunately, I never conceived, so the line ended with Viscount Ashbrooke. I fear I've been quite a disappointment to everyone."

"You?" Lucien rose and took the place beside her. She moved over to make room for him, though he had purposely sat close. "Did he even come to your bed?"

She made a sound of shock, but he did not believe she felt it. "I cannot possibly answer that question."

"Why? Don't play that I've shocked you, else I'll believe you are still an innocent."

"He came to my bed," she whispered, staring determinedly at her small white hands, clutched in her lap.

"And was there passion?"

"There was duty."

"I see." He moved closer to her, heard her inhale sharply. "Have you ever wondered what it might be like if there was passion?"

She swallowed, her gaze never rising to meet his. "Yes."

"Would you allow me to show you?"

Now she looked up at him sharply. In the candlelight, her eyes were luminous and so dark blue. "You are a prince. Why would you want me?"

"What man would not want you? I want you, unequivocally. The question, Cassandra, is, do you want me?"

Chapter Six

W AS THE MAN daft? Of course she wanted him. She was in love with him. Initially, she'd fallen in love with his golden eyes, his handsome face, his thick dark hair. But now she saw the man inside the godlike trappings, and she loved that man.

"Would you think me a lascivious wanton if I said yes?"

His mouth curved in a suppressed grin. "No. I would think myself the luckiest man in the world. Shall I come to your room when the servants are abed?"

She shook her head. Her room was too near Effie's. "I will come to yours."

He reached up and stroked her cheek. She had the urge to lean into his touch, like a kitten craving attention. "If you change your mind and do not come to me, I will understand."

Oh, foolish man. To think she would change her mind. "I won't."

He withdrew his hand, but she could still feel the heat of his touch.

And now she was eager to go to her chambers. The sooner she retired, the sooner he would touch her again—touch her all over.

She made a show of yawning. "Mr. Glen, I find myself suddenly quite weary. Will you forgive me if I retire early?"

"There is nothing to forgive. I will retire as well." He winked at her, and she summoned the footman to light them to their chambers. Allen helped her undress and prepare for bed. When Cass dismissed the lady's maid for the night, she dug into her wardrobe until she found a pretty nightgown her mother had bought as part of her wedding trousseau. She'd never worn it, fearing the small pink bows and light filmy material made her look too young. Now she slipped off her plain woolen nightgown and donned the much thinner one. She covered it with a robe, lest she freeze, and sat by the fire, brushing her hair. It gave her hands something to do while she waited for the house to quiet. Finally, when the bracket clock on her bedside table read midnight, she blew out her candles and crept into the hallway.

Lucien's room was on the other side of the town house, and she had to pass Effie's room to reach it. She tiptoed, her feet bare and freezing, avoiding the boards that creaked. She half expected Effie would throw open her door and scream, "Harlot!" at her, but her door remained firmly closed.

Finally, Cass stood outside Lucien's room. She wondered if he'd fallen asleep and if she should knock or simply go inside. She lifted her hand, but the door opened before she could rap.

Lucien stood in the opening, his shirt untucked and open about his throat. His hair was mussed and his feet bare. He took her arm and pulled her inside his room, closing the door and locking it once she was inside. Now that they stood facing each other, she found it impossible to look away from him. His skin was burnished gold in the low firelight, his eyes like a predator's on the hunt.

But she did not feel hunted. His appreciative gaze swept over her, and she felt like the most beautiful princess in the world.

"You came," he said simply.

"I couldn't stay away." Her voice sounded strange, low and throaty.

"May I kiss you?"

He was such a gentleman. She loved that about him, but she would never survive this first time if he insisted on gaining her approval at every turn. "Are you always so polite when you take a woman to your bed?"

"There is no correct answer for that dangerous inquiry," he said, raising a brow. "But I would never force myself on a woman."

"I am here of my own volition." She stepped toward him, winding her arms around his shoulders, moving quickly before she could think too much about what she did. "I want what you want."

She kissed him. She'd never been so bold, but then again, she had never wanted a man in the way she wanted Lucien. Her lips touched his, and she felt as though her entire body lit with heat and desire. His mouth moved tentatively over hers at first, matching her slow and deliberate explorations, but soon he kissed her deeper. His hands fisted in her hair, and he took her mouth with a ferocity that made her breath catch.

Her body throbbed with need when his tongue delved inside her lips, stroking her tongue and teasing her gently, then more insistently. He possessed her, until all she knew was Lucien. Her hands were on him, under his shirt, fingers trailing the hard muscles of his back and the flat planes of his abdomen. His hands must have touched her too, because she felt the cool air on her arms when he slid her robe off her shoulders.

He made a strangled sound, and she opened her eyes.

He said something in a language she did not understand, and then he repeated, "Where the devil did you get that?"

"It was part of my trousseau, and I've never worn it. Is it too scandalous? Shall I take it off?"

"Oh, I want you to take it off." He lifted a hand to run the backs of his knuckles over the slope of her breast, almost visible under the transparent material. "But not yet."

He kissed her then. He kissed her lips, her jaw, her shoulder, her breasts. He lifted her and carried her to the bed, then began again, kissing every single inch of her.

She thought she would blush with mortification when his mouth found her slick core, but she enjoyed what he did far too much to feel embarrassed. She was naked beneath him, flushed with pleasure, when he pulled his shirt over his head and tossed it on the floor.

She caught her breath. Lucien had his hands on the fall of his trousers, but he paused. "Shall I slow down?"

She shook her head. "No. It's just... I've never seen... you are like one of the statues in the British Museum." She lifted a hand and ran it down his sleek torso.

"And you are a Botticelli." His gaze touched her body, and she knew he meant it. She felt no embarrassment with him and no fear. She knew what was coming, and she wanted it. She wanted him.

He stood and removed his trousers, and she made no effort to look away from his erection. It was as beautiful as the rest of him. When he climbed back into the bed, he was warm and solid against her. She wrapped her legs around him and offered her mouth. He took it with his own, kissing her and stroking her body with his hands until she was whimpering with need. Only when she thought she could take no more, did he slide into her, filling her so completely that she gasped at the fierceness of the pleasure rippling through her.

"Not yet," he whispered, moving inside her with slow, tantalizing strokes. He took her hands and clasped them on either side of her head. His eyes locked with hers, and in his gaze she saw desire and pleasure and a need that matched her own.

Finally, his jaw clenched, and he growled low. "Now."

He thrust into her, and she came apart in his arms.

LUCIEN HAD NEVER been known for moderation. When he enjoyed a pastime, like riding or drinking or fencing, he gave it all of his time and attention. He enjoyed Cassandra in his bed. She was such a mixture of innocence and experience, such an apt pupil and a tender instructor.

He did not want to give her over to sleep, but when her eyes finally closed on a sigh of pleasure, he knew she needed rest. He lay beside her, watching her in the flickering firelight, wondering if this night was all they would ever have.

He had always known he would have to marry one day. He was the heir to the Glennish throne, after all. When he'd turned five and twenty, his father had told him to "stop dallying and choose a bride."

Lucien would have been happy to oblige, but he couldn't seem to find the right woman. He'd courted foreign princesses, duchesses from his own land, and even peasant women. He'd considered women who were friends, including his sisters' closest friends. But no woman had captured his interest. No woman until now.

Cassandra was everything he wanted in a woman, in a wife. Ironic that he should find her when he no longer needed a wife, when the throne was no longer his to claim.

Not only did he not need a queen, he could not justify marrying her when he had nothing to offer her. He had no name, no money, and his meager earnings gained from tutoring would not feed a cat, much less a family. It was wrong to want her, and yet he could not seem to put the feelings aside.

That did not mean he had not protected her from the consequences of their joining. After she'd climaxed, he'd pulled out and spilled his seed on the bed. He did not want to saddle her with a royal bastard, especially one hunted by assassins.

After their lovemaking, he did not sleep, though his body wept with joy at the comfort of the bed. Instead, he held her in his arms, and when it was close to morning, he woke her with a kiss. "Your staff will arise soon. You should return to your chamber."

She kissed him back, her sweet lips so tender against his. "I don't want to leave you."

"Then stay, and we shall shock them all."

She smiled. "How I would love to see the look on Effie's face. But I don't want anything to detain us since we are to go to the bookshop this morning. Effie's lectures can be rather lengthy."

"Then I shall see you again at breakfast."

She kissed him again and was gone.

A footman brought him fresh clothing and clean water to shave and wash, and when they set out in the carriage for Duke Street, he felt almost like himself again.

The snow had finally stopped, but all of London sparkled under a cover of clean white. The horses' bells jingled, reminding him of sleigh rides back home.

At the thought, a pang of sorrow rose in his chest, and at the same time Cassandra put a hand on his arm. She seemed to know when he needed her touch.

"We will find the book" she said, as though she had no doubt in her mind. "Tomorrow is Christmas. I believe we are due a miracle."

He did not believe in miracles, not until he had met her. The coach stopped before On the Shelf, and the coachman opened the carriage door.

"The sign says closed, my lady. That board there is covering the front window."

"Knock anyway, John Coachman. Tell them Lady Ashbrooke must see them."

The coachman shrugged and did as he was told. He banged for several minutes before the door finally opened and a dusty, silver-haired Mr. Merriweather stood in the doorway.

The coachman pointed to the carriage, and Lucien alighted, assisting Cassandra down after.

"Oh, not you again," Merriweather said, frowning at Lucien. "The shop is closed today. We're making repairs, and it's Christmas Eve. A man has a right to spend Christmas Eve with his family."

"I agree with you, Mr. Merriweather," Cassandra said, "but I wonder if you might speak with us for just a few moments. I would be so grateful."

Merriweather was not about to turn away the gratitude of a viscountess. "Of course, my lady. My wife just made tea. Would you like some?"

The three of them sat down to tea in the small office behind the counter. Lucien had had glimpses of the office before, but this was the first time he'd been inside. It was small but tidy, everything in its place. It smelled of tobacco, and indeed Merriweather's pipe rested on the desk. Lucien had rather hoped the office might be wild and unkempt. Then he could believe that an auction slip could be lost. But this was not the sort of room where anything would be lost.

"As you know, Mr. Glen is searching for some rather rare books," Cassandra told Merriweather after they'd sipped tea and talked of the weather. Apparently, it had not snowed in London for years.

"He's in here almost every day. I know that much."

Lucien opened his mouth to say that if the Merriweathers would just tell him where they'd put the books they'd bought at auction, he would gladly leave and not return. He would have been happy never to set foot in another bookshop for the rest of his life.

Cassandra spoke first. "A good friend of his died recently, and the man had borrowed several books belonging to Mr. Glen. All of the man's belongings were auctioned, including the books. Mr. Glen would like the volumes returned. They are not valuable, but they have sentimental meaning to Mr. Glen." She smiled at him. "We will of course pay for the books. And for your trouble, I am willing to give you double what you paid at auction."

"No!" Lucien would not take her money, not that he had his own, but he would work out some sort of trade with the shop owner. In fact, he didn't even need the book, just the papers inside.

"You may pay me back, Mr. Glen," Cassandra said firmly.

"I would, of course, but I would prefer to work out a trade with Mr. Merriweather. I don't want charity."

Merriweather held up a hand, silencing them before the discussion could continue. "I'm afraid you are arguing over nothing, Lady Ashbrooke. I do not have the books you speak of. I rarely buy any books at auction. I much prefer to have the latest novels on hand, rather than invest in any more dusty tomes." He indicated the shop and the shelves of unbound books, their pages between boards until they were purchased and bound by the new owner.

Lucien had probably looked through every single bound and unbound book in the store. If Merriweather did not have any stock in reserve, the books Lucien's mother had sent were not here. He might as well just accept that they were gone forever.

Cassandra's smile faltered. "I see. And there can be no mistake."

"No, my lady." Merriweather straightened officiously. "None."

Lucien rose. No point in sitting here sipping tea. His world had ended. He did not know what he would do now, but he wouldn't spend another minute in the *bluidy* bookshop.

Cassandra rose too, and Merriweather showed them back into the shop and to the door. She and Merriweather were still chatting amiably, but to Lucien they sounded incredibly distant. The crumbling sound of the rest of his life falling to ruins deafened him.

"I'm terribly... window," Cassandra said.

"Catch... culprits," Merriweather answered.

Lucien closed his eyes and attempted to concentrate. He should listen to news of the assassins.

"This isn't the first time the shop has been vandalized, after all."

"Really?" Cassandra asked. "Was it the same window?"

"No. It was the sign. Some fool thought it would be jolly good fun to paint over the name of the shop, owing to the number of more seasoned ladies who patronize us. Turned out we all rather liked the new name and kept On the Shelf."

Lucien stilled, the roaring in his ears subsiding. "What was the name before?"

"What's that?" Merriweather asked.

Lucien clenched his fists to keep from grasping the owner by the lapels and shoving him against the door.

"What. Was. The. Original. Name?"

"Oh, The Duke Street Bookshop. Not very clever, eh? There's another shop with the same name on the Duke Street near the northeast corner of Grosvenor Square."

"Oh my God." Cassandra's gaze met his, and it was only the blue of her eyes that kept his world from spinning. "Yes, of course. There is another Duke Street. It runs from Grosvenor Square, crosses Oxford Street, and ends at Manchester Square. I forgot all about it. I haven't been to the bookshop there in some years."

Lucien's limbs were paralyzed. Another Duke Street. Another bookshop.

"That's the shop that must have bought the auctioned books," Cassandra said.

Merriweather considered. "It's possible. Certainly possible."

Cassandra gripped Merriweather's hand, shaking it vigorously. "Thank you." She turned to Lucien. "Let's go. Now."

"Best hurry," Merriweather advised. "It's Christmas Eve. Most shops will close a bit early."

"Of course." She all but dragged Lucien out of the shop and into the coach. She gave the coachman the direction and turned to Lucien. "This is it. I know we will find the books now."

For the first time in weeks, he had the same hope. Overwhelmed with sudden joy, he pulled her into his arms and kissed her. "Thank you. I owe you everything."

She blushed, whether from the compliment or his kiss, he did not know. "It is I who owe you everything. You've given me so much more than I ever could have expected." Before he could ask what she meant, she pointed out various landmarks to him. They were heading back toward her town house until they turned onto what she said was the other Duke Street. Finally, the coach stopped in front of the shop.

It was larger than On the Shelf and better maintained. Lucien supposed the patrons were wealthier and expected as much. As soon as they entered, Cassandra approached the shopgirl and gave her the same story about Lucien's friend and the auctioned books. Again, she offered to pay double the auction price, which Lucien would have never allowed, but the young woman, who had dark hair in a braid on top of her head, waved a hand in dismissal. "If we have them, you're welcome to them. Never want to take another's property, and it's Christmas Eve, after all."

"Where would they be?" Cassandra asked.

She furrowed a brow and tucked a pencil in the coil on her head. "You said they were books in French and Glennish?"

"That's correct," Lucien said, finding his voice once again.

She smiled at him. "Oh, then you want to look on that last shelf to the left. We keep the foreign books there. We have quite a few Frenchies come in, we do."

"Thank you."

With single-minded purpose, Lucien set off in the direction the shopgirl indicated. His fear now was that the books his mother had sent had been purchased. What if he'd come this far for naught? Finding the books wasn't simply a matter of papers and money any longer. They were the last and only reminders of his mother, his family. He needed to touch those books, touch the papers she'd caressed and so lovingly set aside for her family.

He stood before the shelves and stared at the rows of books. Where to begin? The shop would close soon. He had no time to waste debating. Lucien felt a warm hand clasp his. Cassandra was beside him, smiling up at him. He couldn't help but smile back at her. Her small gesture of support meant more to him than he could possibly express in words.

"I'll start on this side, and you start on that," she suggested.

He nodded his agreement. With trembling hands, he skimmed his fingers over the titles of the old books. Italian titles, German titles, Portuguese...

"Lucien."

His attention snapped to Cassandra, kneeling on the floor, her skirts spread around her.

"I've found the books in Glennish."

He dropped to his knees beside her. He pulled the first book off the shelf, the familiar language like coming home as he read the title. *A Natural History of Glynaven.*

He stared at the cover, wondering if this was one of the books his mother had sent. Was this one she had touched?

"Shall I?" Cassandra asked, holding a hand out.

"Please."

She opened it, shuffling through the pages. Before she finished, he knew it was not one of them.

"Oy! We're closing soon!" the shopgirl called.

"Damn it all to hell," Lucien muttered. Why did it seem as though everything, even time, was against him?

"Which one next?" Cassandra asked, her voice as level and calm as ever.

Lucien looked at the other Glennish titles on the shelf. It might be one of them or none of them. His mother might very well have hidden the papers in one of the French books or one in English. Good God, he would never find it if it was one of the English books.

Think, Lucien! Think. He'd been standing in her private chamber in the palace when his mother secreted the papers. He could remember the scent of candle wax and roses. He could hear the ripping sound when she'd torn the pages out of the book. If only he'd paid attention to the book, known what it looked like. He was running out of time. He willed the book to be there, scanned the titles, then paused.

A Collection of Poems for Children.

"There," he said, reaching for the volume wedged in the corner. A volume with gold lettering and a tattered cover.

"Is that it?" Cassandra asked when he didn't open it right away.

He stared at the book, his hands shaking so badly he feared he'd drop the book. Of course she would have chosen this book. It had been a favorite of the royal children, and his mother had read it to them before bed when they'd been younger.

Lucien met Cassandra's gaze, and her hands slid over his trembling ones. "Open it," she whispered.

How would he have done this without her?

He opened the book. The first page was familiar to him, not only the title but the scribbles his sister Vivi had made one afternoon when she'd found a pen and ink.

He stared at those scribbles, at the evidence of his past life. In the last few months, he'd almost feared he'd dreamed he'd once been a prince, once been the heir to the throne of Glynaven.

He turned several pages, his hands moving more quickly and surely now. He knew who he was, and he knew what he would find in the center of the book. Still, when he reached the space made by the extracted pages, he felt a shock rush through him. He must have jerked, because the papers fell out, Cassandra reaching to catch them before they could land on the floor.

She beamed up at him, her smile so large he had to smile back. "We found them!" she squealed.

He dropped the book and opened the first yellowed paper. It was a letter of introduction for the family, including himself. It had been written in his mother's hand, and he ran a fingertip over his name.

"There is the name of a bank here and an account number. At least I think that is what it is. I cannot read Glennish."

"That is exactly what it is. The Bank of England," he said. He'd known it would be the Old Lady of Threadneedle Street, but his efforts to access the bank accounts of the royal family had been in vain without any papers or the account numbers.

"Oh, and here is a five-pound note. Goodness. If anyone else had found this, he would have thought himself the luckiest man alive."

He took her hand. "I am the luckiest man alive because I have you."

"Me? I didn't do anything."

"You never doubted me," he said, bringing her hand to his lips. "You never once doubted me. That faith means more to me than gold."

"Shall we go to the bank?" she asked, her gaze lowering as though she was embarrassed. "We should hurry if we want to arrive before they close for the holiday."

He'd forgotten time was not on his side. He'd forgotten the assassins were still searching for him. The sooner he went to the bank and distanced himself from Cassandra, the safer she would be. Every minute spent with her put her in danger.

At one time this foray to the bank would have been all that mattered to him. He would have run all the way there. Now he did not want to rise, did not want to begin the trip.

He knew every minute closer to the bank was one last minute spent with Cassandra.

Chapter Seven

THEY'D RACED TO the bank for naught. If Cassandra could have beaten the bank manager with a birch, she would have done so. Now that they were back in the carriage and returning to her town house—the book, papers, and money clutched in Lucien's hands—she could admit he had reined in his temper far better than she.

"I do apologize for my outburst," she said. "I'm certain Mr. Sutton has no idea what came over me. I have known him for years and never so much as raised my voice."

His mouth twitched as though he wanted to smile but would not allow himself to do so. "You have nothing to apologize for," he said again. "In fact, you were quite magnificent."

She was about to deny it, when he crossed the carriage and pulled her into his arms. She loved being in his arms. They were strong and so very warm. When she was in his embrace, nothing else mattered. Not Effie's disapproval when they returned home, not the ridiculous bank manager who would not see them on Christmas Eve, not the fact that Lucien was leaving her.

He hadn't said as much, but she knew it. He'd said good-bye with his eyes a thousand times. He worried for her safety. He worried he asked too much of her. He was not good at accepting charity from others. He did not want to impose on her.

If he'd have but listened, she would have told him it was no imposition. She would have told him she never wanted him to leave. Unfortunately, his sense of honor would force him to keep her safe from the assassins targeting him. It was honor that would force him to leave. He didn't love her, else he would not have been able to go away.

She loved him. Completely. And she was a weak, desperate woman. So desperate, in fact, that she did the one thing she'd been telling herself she must not do.

"Stay with me tonight."

He drew back. "Cassandra, it's not safe for me to be near you."

"I don't care about safe. Lucien, it's Christmas Eve. You cannot spend it alone."

But of course he could. He had money now. He would find a room in a hotel and sleep in comfort. The unspoken words were hers.

Don't leave me alone.

Another solitary Christmas, listening to the servants' games and wishing she had someone to kiss under the mistletoe.

She turned to look out the windows at the dusky evening quickly falling. The last rays of sunlight made the melting snow sparkle.

"Cassandra." His tone was placating, asking for understanding.

For once she would not accommodate. She would not be placated. She would ask for what she wanted, and she would have it too. "Stay with me," she said, looking at him again. "Come to my bed. Make love to me this one last night. Surely even assassins do not work on Christmas."

He gave a small bark of laughter, then gathered her into his embrace. "How will I ever leave you? Yes, fair Cassandra, I'll stay with you tonight."

The simple words made the rest of the long evening bearable—Effie's hysterics, the awkward Christmas Eve dinner afterward, the stilted singing of carols when the Yule log was brought inside. Cass had been relieved to retire as early as Effie and leave the servants to their revelry. Lucien had retired before either of them, and she lay in her large bed for an hour before he finally tapped on her door and slid inside. Cass had gone to him the night before for fear Effie would know she was with the prince, but Cass no longer cared about Effie's opinion. Effie's behavior then had been nothing short of embarrassing. Cass no longer felt she owed her late husband's sister anything but the most common courtesy.

She sat. "I thought perhaps you'd fallen asleep."

He wore no coat, and he drew his shirt over his head as he approached the bed. "The thought of you kept me wide awake."

Cassandra swallowed at the sight of him as he stalked across the room, his broad shoulders tapering into a lean waist and slim hips encased in tight breeches. Lord but she did love to look at him. He had to be leaner than before he'd fled Glynaven. He must be nothing short of a god when in top form.

He watched her watch him as he raised a hand to the fall of the breeches. "It took me a moment to find your room. I fear I almost disturbed Miss Ashbrooke's peace."

Cass giggled at the idea. Effie would have perished from merely the thought of a man touching her.

The bed sagged under Lucien's weight as he sat to remove his boots. They were his own and quite tightly fitted. He had to struggle for a moment before he finally shed them. Then he stood again, but Cass caught his hand before he reached for his breeches.

He raised a brow. "Too presumptuous of me?"

How could the man possibly think she—any woman, really—would not want him in her bed? "Not at all. I want to do it myself."

She bit her lip to stem the rising flush. She had promised herself she would ask for what she wanted, and damn the mortification. He'd looked so beautiful last night, rising proudly from the juncture of his muscled thighs.

"I am at your disposal, my lady," he said, all graciousness.

She sat up, and the sheets fell down about her waist. Lucien drew in a sharp breath at her nudity. "I see I was not being presumptuous at all."

"I thought this might save us time."

"In a hurry, are we?"

"Just eager."

He made a low sound of agreement in his throat. "Then touch me."

She'd seen his hands shake at the bookshop this morning, and now her hands shook as she took hold of the fall of his breeches. She felt like a virgin as she unfastened them and slid the clothing down over his hips, freeing his hard member.

He was aroused, by her. He wanted her. She could see it in the way he clenched his hands to give her time to touch him, the way his eyes devoured her body, the way he groaned when she stroked his manhood.

"You will be my undoing," he said finally, after she'd explored every hard inch of him, cupping the soft underside and even running her tongue along the shiny tip. "I want to touch you. Let me make you ready, and then I promise I'll allow you to have your way with me."

His words, though partly in jest, sent a shiver of excitement through her. His gaze slid to her suddenly hard nipples. "Oh, you like that idea, I see. Far be it from me to deny you anything at Christmas."

He touched her then, his large hands cupping her face so he could kiss her as deeply and thoroughly as he wanted. And then those hands were on her breasts, giving them the aching relief they needed but stroking a stronger need in her too. Finally, after forays to her belly, her legs, her buttocks, he cupped her between her legs, touching her in the place that throbbed for him.

"Yes," she moaned, letting her head fall back and shamelessly rocking her body against his skilled fingers. He'd been kneeling before her, but now he skated his hands up and took her by the waist. He pulled her onto his lap, situating her so his erection brushed the tingling spot where his fingers had been.

"Put your arms around me," he ordered. She wrapped her arms about his shoulders, clasping her hands behind his head and feeling the tips of her breasts brush against his solid chest.

He kissed her, shifting her so her legs parted farther.

"Take me inside you," he murmured, nipping at her jaw. "Give yourself the pleasure your body is yearning for."

She was yearning. Everything in her reached and groped for that elusive pleasure. All she need do was rise up and tilt forward. His tip slid inside her, and she gasped at the beauty of it, of the feel of him inside her. She lowered herself, feeling him stretch her, fill her, claim her.

Her body moved without her telling it to. Her hips circled and thrust, and every single groan he made gratified her. His hands on her back tightened until the pressure of his fingers was all that anchored her.

"Lucien," she gasped when she could not contain the spiraling feelings building in her any longer.

"You are beautiful, Cassandra. So beautiful."

Her body unraveled then. Strand by delicate strand, tendrils of pleasure flowed through her until she practically sobbed with the exquisite torture of it.

Afterward, she was so boneless she slumped against him, and he rolled her onto her side, his arms coming around her to press her to his chest. She buried her face in the scent of him—the scent of both of them mingled together.

"I love you," she whispered. She shouldn't have said it, but she couldn't let him go without saying it.

"Yes," he said, and stroked her hair. "Yes."

HE WAS NOT a rake, but he knew very well how to play the part. Christmas morning he played it well. He rose long before Cassandra, trying very hard not to admire the way the first glimmerings of pale morning light washed the soft slopes of her back and hips.

He dressed in silence and crept out of her room, not to his own chamber, but downstairs, where the only servant about—a weary maid—glanced at him quickly before looking back at the fireplace she was lighting.

He put a finger to his lips and crossed to the front door. He unlocked it silently and paused before pulling it open. He should have left a note. Bloody hell, the woman had told him she loved him.

He loved her too—God, how he loved her—but he could not afford to love anyone or anything at the moment. If he loved her, he would leave her. Yes, it would mean giving up the hope of finding the articles he could only access with the papers his mother had left him, but those mattered nothing when he thought of the danger to Cassandra. Perhaps one day he could come back to her. One day, when assassins were no longer a threat, he could knock on her door again. She might welcome him back. She might still love him.

If she ever forgave him this treachery.

He opened the door and stood in it, dumbfounded. A coach with a ducal crest sat in front of the town house. Lucien watched the footman jump down and make for the door, indicating the conveyance had only just arrived. The door opened before the footman could reach it, and a well-dressed, fair-haired man stepped out. He waved the footman away and held out a hand. A gloved hand gripped it from inside the curtained coach, and then a woman with a hat that covered her face emerged. Cassandra had not said anything about guests, most especially not a duke. He wavered, torn between going back and leaving as planned.

And then the woman looked up, and his world flipped upside down.

She seemed equally shocked, staring at him in silence, almost as though she had seen a ghost. He knew the feeling. He'd thought she was dead. He'd already mourned her, and now to see her standing there, very much alive, was both confusing and an extraordinary relief.

"Lucien!"

He didn't so much hear the word as he saw her mouth move. The man looked at him with interest, and Lucien had a moment to wonder who the devil he was and why he thought he had the right to touch her.

And then she was rushing toward him, and he didn't think anymore. He met her in the middle of the walk, racing to embrace her and twirl her in his arms.

She laughed and kissed both of his cheeks, repeatedly. On a laugh, she said, "I thought you were dead."

"I thought *you* were dead." His eyes stung with what felt suspiciously like tears. He had honestly never thought he would see her again, would never see anyone from his past life again.

"I cannot believe it is you. Let me look at you." She cupped his face and looked long and hard into his eyes. When she had seen whatever she searched for, she hugged him again. Hard. "My poor darling. What you have suffered. I can only imagine."

Behind her, the man, presumably the duke, approached. As though she sensed his presence, she turned. "Nathan, I have forgotten my manners completely."

"It's quite understandable."

Nathan? Lucien narrowed his eyes. Exactly who was this man?

"Prince Lucien Charles Louis de Glynaven, this is my husband, Nathan Cauley, Duke of Wyndover."

"Your husband?" Lucien stared hard at the man.

The duke bowed. "It's a pleasure to make your acquaintance. Your sister did not sleep at all last night, I'm afraid. We received a letter from the manager of the Bank of England that you were alive. He thought you were an impostor."

"I know this is terribly early, but I couldn't wait another moment." She glanced at the house behind him. "Mr. Sutton mentioned you were with Lady Ashbrooke, but how is it you have come to reside in her home?"

"How is it you are married?"

She laughed again, a sound so familiar to him, he wanted to hug her again. Vivi was alive.

"I see we have much to discuss. Might we go inside, where it is warmer? Or must you be away?"

"I..." What to say? That he was sneaking away like some sort of thief? "There are assassins in London," he said finally.

The duke lifted a finger, and his outriders jumped down. "Watch the house," he commanded. "Keep the horses moving. I don't want the carriage spotted outside."

The four outriders spread out along the front of the house, while the coachman urged the horses to walk.

Well, they were safe enough, but Lucien could hardly invite guests into Cassandra's home. "Very good," he said. "Now there is just the matter of Lady Ashbrooke."

"And what matter might that be?" said a voice from behind.

It was her, of course. She'd probably heard the horses and the voices. The entire house probably had. He turned. "Happy Christmas."

"Is it?" Her blue eyes were wary. She'd dressed in haste, her lavender gown wrinkled and her feet bare. Her hair fell in golden waves down about her shoulders.

"It is," Vivi said, flashing the smile she always gave when she wanted to charm someone. "This morning I have the best Christmas present I could ever hope for. My brother is alive."

She looked at Lucien, who gave her a nod. "Princess Vivienne Aubine Calanthe de Glynaven, this is Lady Ashbrooke. Lady Ashbrooke, my sister and her husband, His Grace, the Duke of Wyndover."

He wasn't certain if he'd done all the introductions correctly. He couldn't remember the exact protocol the English used.

Cassandra curtseyed. "Please, come in out of the cold and wet." She indicated the few piles of slush that were all that remained of the recent snows.

Lucien had expected Cassandra to be less than hospitable. After all, she'd awakened Christmas morning to find her lover had fled and unexpected guests at her door. Not to mention, she was short-staffed since she had given some of the staff the day off. It was also no secret that her late husband's sister was silently protesting Lucien's arrival by keeping to her room.

But she made the best of it, going to the kitchens herself to ask for tea and scones and listening attentively to Vivi's story. She'd been in the palace during the massacre and had escaped by hiding in the secret room. He did not ask her for the details of what she had seen and heard. He would ask her later, when they were both stronger and ready to confront that horrible time again. Their father's trusted adviser, Masson, had helped her to safety in England before assassins had killed him. She and Wyndover had confronted three other assassins at his estate in Nottinghamshire. That explained why Wyndover traveled with additional guards.

After Lucien had also told his story, Cassandra, who had been quietly attentive, cleared her throat. "Princess, do you mind if I ask how you knew to find Lu—your brother here?"

Vivi withdrew the letter the bank manager had sent, whereupon Lucien showed his sister and the duke the papers he and Cassandra had found at the bookshop.

"But this is remarkable!" Vivi said. "We must see what is in that account."

"Unfortunately, the bank is not open today. It's Christmas," Cassandra pointed out.

Vivi looked at the duke. He gave a sigh. "Give me a moment. May I borrow pen and paper?" he asked.

Cassandra directed him to the small desk in the corner of the parlor where they sat. Vivi followed him, watching over his shoulder as, presumably, he summoned the bank manager to the bank with the sorts of promises and threats only a duke can make.

"Would you ever have told me good-bye?" Cassandra hissed at Lucien when the duke was fully engaged in his task.

Lucien passed a hand over his eyes. "I should have left a note."

"Saying what?" she asked under her breath. "Thank you and Happy Christmas?"

"No." He rose from the chair where he was seated and joined her on the couch. "I would have said, I am sorry to have endangered your life. I was weak and foolish. I'll leave now before I do you any further harm."

She stared at him. "You are an idiot."

Lucien blew out a breath. He had expected gratitude or, at the very least, understanding. "For trying to keep you safe?"

"No. For not understanding that you mean more to me than my own safety. That I understood the cost long before now and made the choice to help you anyway. I told you I love you, Lucien. Doesn't that mean anything?"

"Yes." It did. It meant everything. He loved her too. That was why he had to leave her. "That is exactly why I had to go," he began.

She looked stricken, but before he could explain further, Wyndover stood. "I'll send this directly. The bank manager will meet us with all haste, I assure you."

Lucien wished he could have seen the missive, but the duke carried it to the door, where presumably he handed it to one of his men to deliver.

Vivi lifted her reticule. "Shall we go? I think it's past time we saw what Mama has sent us from the grave."

Chapter Eight

❧

I F CASS HAD not wanted to hit Lucien, hard, she would have enjoyed the duke's carriage. It was delightfully luxurious with velvet squabs, brocade draperies, lovely brass lamps, and a silk interior. The footman gave them all warm bricks wrapped in cloth and cozy blankets. Cass thought the conveyance warmer and better appointed than her town house.

The men sat across from her and the princess, which made hitting Lucien more difficult. Unfortunately, it also made it easier to see his face. His beautiful eyes were filled with regret and apology. Apology for what? For leaving her or not loving her? She had said she loved him, and the words had driven him away. He was an honorable man. She had always known that. If he couldn't love her, he would rather leave her than stay and give her false hope.

Perhaps she should have stayed home and allowed him to leave with his sister. That would have saved both of them the awkwardness of a good-bye. But she hadn't been able to do it. She was a foolish, weak woman. She did not want to let him go yet. When he left, her life would return to the way it had been.

No, she would not go back to wearing widow's weeds. In fact, it had felt wonderful to dress in this lavender gown, though it was desperately in need of pressing. No, she wouldn't go back to bowing and cringing when Effie spoke, or trying to make herself invisible so she would not trouble anyone else.

But she would go back to a life devoid of passion. Her clothing might not be drab, but her life would lose all its color when Lucien was gone. She would rather be dead than suffer that fate.

She heard a loud explosion, and one of the horses screamed and reared. Vivienne cried out, and then everything was a blur of velvet and gold as the carriage tilted to the side before righting itself again. Cass pressed her hands to her ears to drown out the screeching sound before she realized it was she making the awful noise.

She clamped a hand over her mouth, holding in her screams. Her chest hurt from the way her heart slammed against it. Wyndover scrambled to draw his pistol as Lucien parted the curtains. Cass wanted to order him to close the curtains, to hide, but she couldn't seem to utter any sounds other than screams. Beside her, the princess reached under the seat and withdrew a bow and arrows.

Cass half expected to wake at any moment, but when she heard another explosion and a man's anguished cry, she knew this was no dream.

"*Le reavlutionnaire!*" Lucien shouted right before he pulled her and the princess to the ground. The window of the coach shattered, and Cass couldn't hold back her cry.

More deafening sounds erupted. Cass looked up to see the duke lowering his pistol from the broken window. "Missed. Damn it!"

"Stay down," Lucien ordered her.

Another pistol ball slammed into the coach, and Wyndover knelt beside her, adding powder and shot to his pistol. Meanwhile, the princess had withdrawn an arrow and nocked it against her bowstring.

"Careful, love," Wyndover cautioned.

"Always." Then she was up, and quick as a cat, she fired the arrow and ducked down again. Another explosion, this one rocking the coach again, and then Wyndover was up, firing through the window.

The duke flattened himself, but there was no return fire.

"I think I hit one." The princess sounded hopeful.

"*You* hit?" Her husband scowled at her. "Perhaps it was my pistol ball."

"Darling, you know I never miss."

Cass tentatively raised her head. Lucien's body shielded her from harm, but he rose slightly to allow her to look up.

"Stay down," he told her again. "They might be waiting for us to step out."

"Good point." Wyndover withdrew his powder bag again. "One of us will have to go out and assess the damage. I fear my coachman is dead."

"I'll go," his wife offered.

Lucien uttered a word Cass did not know. "No, you will not. I'll go."

The princess looked at him as though he'd grown horns. "You don't even have a weapon."

"I—"

The door upon which Cass's shoulder rested flew open, and she nearly spilled out into an assassin's arms. Wyndover and the princess, who had been expecting another attack from the opposite side where the first shots had been fired, were unprepared. Cass screamed, right before she was yanked out by her hair. She would have fallen to the ground, but Lucien caught her arm.

For a moment, a dreadful and painful tug-of-war ensued, and then one of the princess's arrows whizzed by, hitting the man holding her in the shoulder. He dropped her, and Lucien lost his hold. Cass tumbled to the ground. Her shoulder gave a violent scream of pain, but she managed to ignore it long enough to look about. Two more assassins headed for her. The first, a very large man, looked more angry than injured by the arrow in his shoulder. He ripped it out and growled at her.

With a swipe, he reached for her hair again, but Cass rolled away and under the carriage. She saw a blur of movement, and the assassin landed on his back beside the carriage, Lucien on top of him.

More shots rang out, and Cass was not certain if they came from Wyndover or the remaining assassins. Her gaze was riveted on Lucien, who fought the huge assassin valiantly but was losing ground. The assassin gave a heave, and Lucien flew off him, flipping onto his back. He lay stunned for a moment.

Behind him, another assassin came around the front of the carriage, his pistol in his hands.

"Lucien! Behind you!" Cass yelled.

Lucien rolled just in time, and the pistol ball hit the ground where he had been a moment before. He grabbed the man's ankles and brought him down, but now the other, injured assassin had gained his feet. He lumbered toward Lucien, hauled him up by the neck, and lifted him off the ground.

"No!" Cass screamed. "He's choking him!"

Another arrow whizzed from the coach, but it hit the third assassin, preventing him from joining his comrades attacking the prince.

"Shoot him!" the princess cried.

"I can't get a shot! Bloody hell!"

Lucien's body looked like that of a rag doll in the large assassin's bloody hands. Lucien clawed and fought, his movements erratic. Any shot the duke fired at the assassin might also hit Lucien.

Lucien didn't have time to wait until the assassin moved into the line of fire. Cass was not about to allow him to die on Christmas Day, there in the middle of London. She had no weapon, but that didn't seem to matter. She crawled out from under the coach and rushed toward the assassin holding Lucien. With a shriek, she jumped onto his back.

"Lady Ashbrooke! No!" the duchess called.

It was too late. She couldn't turn back now.

The assassin tried to shake her off. She slid down his back, but before she could fall off, she wrapped her arms around his neck and squeezed. He staggered, releasing Lucien.

The other assassin promptly swung at the prince, and Cass only knew the blow landed because she heard the thud. The assassin shook her violently, but she locked her hands and closed her eyes. Wetness dribbled over her wrists, and she realized it was the blood from the arrow wound.

More thuds. Another pistol shot. A man—or was it a woman?—yelped. Cass screeched too, squeezing with everything she had. The assassin stumbled to his knees. She felt the arrow whoosh past her and heard the thunk as it made contact.

And then Lucien was calling her name. "Cassandra! Let go. I have him. Let go. Cassandra!"

She let go, sliding to the ground.

Lucien raised a boot and kicked the assassin, and he fell beside her. His eyes met hers briefly before they rolled back and closed.

For a long moment, all she heard was her own panting breaths. And then she was in Lucien's arms, her face pressed against his chest. She heard the solid beat of his heart, and nothing else mattered.

❧❀❧

"LEANNAN. MY LOVE." Lucien cradled Cassandra. "What the devil were you thinking?"

He'd almost lost her. Twice. He knew his sister was absolutely—what was the English word? Daft?—but she was skilled with a bow and arrow and could defend herself. Cassandra had no such skills, which made her efforts to save him that much more meaningful.

She'd risked her life for him.

And he had been ready to leave her because he had no kingdom. What did such things matter? He'd wanted to keep her safe, but the assassins had found them anyway. Together they'd defeated the enemy.

He looked up from where his cheek was pressed against her hair, assessing the bodies strewn around them. Five men lay dead or wounded. Vivienne had an arrow pointed at one, and her duke trained a pistol on another. The two beside him were not moving, and the last looked dead or dying from his wounds.

"He was choking you," Cassandra said. "I had to do something."

Lucien realized she was answering his question.

"You risked your life." That was more than obvious, but he still couldn't quite believe it.

"So did you," she said, her tone full of accusation. She looked up at him. At some point, her spectacles had fallen off, and her blue eyes looked so naked and vulnerable without them. "I couldn't let him kill you. I told you. I love you."

"Leannan. Don't you know by now that I love you too? I couldn't live with myself if anything happened to you. I was afraid of this"—he waved a hand—"I was afraid I'd lose you."

"The risk is worth the gain," she said.

"You are a wise woman, Lady Ashbrooke, and you were right."

"About?"

"I am an idiot."

She laughed, a tear falling on one pink cheek. "Yes, you are."

"Will you have me anyway?"

She blinked, looking at him long and hard. "Do you mean..."

"Will you be my princess? You'd be a princess of a lost kingdom, but that's all I have to offer."

"If I have you, Lucien, that's all I need."

NOTHING COULD RUIN Christmas night for Cass. Not Effie's declaration that her brother's will stipulated she was to have the town house if Cass remarried. Not the throbbing pain in her arms from gripping that assassin so tightly. Not the hours of questioning they'd endured from Bow Street, who had taken the assassins into custody.

Lucien had his papers and the contents of the vault his mother had entrusted to the bank. The bank manager had tried to protest, tried to insinuate Lucien was an impostor, but the duke had said something to the man in low tones, and he hadn't uttered another word after that.

Now she and Lucien sat in her bedroom with the contents of the vault laid on the bed before them. A large purse held thousands in pounds, and there were other accounts as well. Lucien had access to all of them and was a very rich man. Perhaps not as rich as he would have been if he'd been king of Glynaven, but rich nonetheless.

Several miniatures had also been included, paintings of all his brothers and sisters and his mother and father. Lucien had looked at them for a long time before putting them down. "I will share these with Vivienne," he'd said solemnly.

Other treasures abounded, including jewels and priceless heirlooms. Lucien had barely glanced at them, but Cassandra was a bit awestruck at the amount of glitter on her coverlet.

"This is the last of it," Lucien said, indicating a small wooden box with an intricately carved pattern of ivy on the sides and top.

"What do you think is inside?"

"I have no idea."

He opened it, unclasping the latch quietly and raising the lid. He stared down at it for a moment, then smiled.

Cass did not have the patience to wait. "Well?"

"Bits of lace from her coronation dress and her favorite jeweled combs. I will give those to Vivienne. And then there is this smaller box. This is for you."

He held it up, a small box covered in green satin with gold braid.

"For me? I didn't know your mother."

"But she knew one day I would find you." He removed the top of the box, and inside shone a ring with a large oval emerald set in gold, the gem surrounded by glittering diamonds.

"Oh." That was all she could think to say.

"Come here," Lucien said quietly.

She was already right beside him, but she moved close enough to where he sat on the bed so her knees brushed his.

He lifted her hand and slid the ring on her finger. He stared at it for a long time, then looked up at her. "It fits perfectly."

She tilted the ring so it caught the light. It was impossibly beautiful. "I can't take this. You should give it to Vivienne."

Lucien made a shushing sound. "She will say it should go to my wife. You are my bride-to-be, are you not?"

She nodded. "Yes."

"Then it goes to you, Princess Cassandra. Happy Christmas."

Happy Christmas. The very happiest." She lifted her aching arms and wrapped them around him, kissing him with peace and joy and, most of all, love.

The Appeal of Christmas

BY
GRACE BURROWES

To those who find the holidays trying

Chapter One

GERVAISE STONELEIGH HAD no patience with seasonal good cheer or holiday folderol, but when he crossed the threshold of his favorite commercial establishment, a small and reliable miracle befell him nonetheless.

After days of ignoring Snee's whistled renditions of Handel, and weeks of enduring rapturous descriptions of Mrs. Snee's plum pudding, Gervaise needed the company of the most trustworthy ally ever to grace a tired barrister's winter evenings—a good book.

On the Shelf bookshop, as it was locally known, was tucked not far from Piccadilly, and thus lay partway between Gervaise's home in Mayfair and the Inns of Court. The mere sight of the shop's unprepossessing exterior, even swagged in holiday greenery, was enough to lift his spirits.

"Good evening, Mr. Stoneleigh," Annabelle Merriweather said as Gervaise stomped snow from his boots and unwrapped the scarf from his neck. "Haven't seen you in a while, sir. Mama wondered if you'd gone to visit relations for the holidays."

Annabelle was a pleasant young woman who knew her books. Nonetheless, her reference to visiting family rankled.

"I am expected to call on my sister and her offspring at some point before the New Year," Gervaise said. "I'll thank you not to mention such unpleasantness when there are books to be enjoyed."

For the very scent of books, the soothing, vanilla-and-wisdom fragrance of them, effected Gervaise's personal miracle. When he was at this shop and surrounded by books, all the misery of his profession, all the tedium of dealing with his family, and even the squabbles of feuding solicitors faded to nothing.

Here was peace on earth. Here was comfort and learning, wit and sense. No holiday hypocrisy intruded into the literary world, no housemaids were transported for the crime of being too pretty when the lady of the house was in a spiteful mood, no peers were allowed to dodge their creditors by virtue of titled privilege.

In books, Gervaise found beautiful language, profound thoughts, and the occasional sardonic witticism that put all the world's foibles in a more bearable light.

"Would you be looking for a Christmas gift for Miss Hooper?" Annabelle asked, coming around the counter, several books in her hands.

Gervaise mentally reminded himself of the date—he avoided even thinking of Christmas—and found much of December had sneaked past his notice, obscured by criminal trials and whistling law clerks.

"Hazel Hooper knows better than to expect seasonal displays of sentiment from me," he said. "Nonetheless, if you know of something she'd particularly enjoy, then please say on."

Annabelle marched up to a ladder mounted on rails that ran around three sides of the shop. She tucked the books against one hip, and would have climbed the ladder one-handed had Gervaise not plucked the volumes from her grasp.

"Move aside, Miss Merriweather. If you think I'll let you risk your neck on this contraption, you are much mistaken."

Annabelle was pretty, in a harried, unpresuming way. Hazel had pointed out Annabelle's attractiveness to Gervaise in the middle of an argument about vanity or some other philosophical point. Hazel was not one to concede defeat simply because she happened to be in error.

Annabelle stepped back far enough to allow Gervaise onto the ladder.

"Horace goes on the top shelf, with Virgil and Plato. Mrs. Wollstonecraft is on the next shelf down with the heretics and rabble-rousers."

Hazel had developed the shop's shelving system when she'd been unable to find a volume of Sheridan two years ago. She'd spent days re-organizing the inventory with Annabelle and Mrs. Merriweather, while Mr. Merriweather—a sensible soul, with a grumbling disrespect for the Regent—had fled to the corner pub.

"What about Rochester?" Gervaise asked, for the poet could be lewd, tender, or both together in the same verse, and the shop had apparently got hold of a new collection.

One Gervaise did not own. Yet.

The poetical earl never disappointed, and he'd had no patience with seasonal hypocrisy either.

"Rochester tends to show up anywhere he pleases," Annabelle said, returning to the counter. "Put him with the philosophers, and by this time tomorrow, he'll have made his way down to the herbals and botanical texts."

Hazel did not care for Rochester, referring to him as an embittered court jester. Gervaise opened the volume nonetheless, for he prided himself on his library of poetry. A folded page slipped from between the leaves of verse and fluttered to the shop floor as gently as a dove alighting.

Annabelle was busy rifling the cabinets behind the counter, so Gervaise tucked Rochester between other learned rascals long dead, climbed down the ladder, and picked up the paper.

"I'll be right back," Annabelle said. "Make yourself at home, Mr. Stoneleigh."

Gervaise barely heard her, for the folded paper contained writing, a woman's flowing, graceful script, unless he missed his guess. He took the paper to the reading room at the back of the shop where Mrs. Huntsberry usually dozed by the hour.

Hazel claimed Mrs. Huntsberry could barely see, but frequented the shop to save on coal in the colder weather.

"I'll always know you," the letter writer had penned, "not by your handsome good looks. To other's eyes, your appearance will mature from dashing to distinguished, though to me, you are already distinguished, and you will always be dashing. I'll know you not by your nimble wit, and not even by your tender kisses, though your wit saves lives, and your kisses will ever bring me joy.

"I'll know you not for your fierce championing of the less fortunate, though I love you for that, too. I'll know you by your heart, by the passion and honor with which you love, by the honesty and kindness with which you greet all in your ambit, regardless of station, regardless of how weary or frustrated you might—."

The shop's doorbell tinkled as a gust of cold air riffled the paper in Gervaise's hand.

"Mr. Stoneleigh, hello."

Hazel Hooper stood near the door, snow dusting the hood of her cape, her hems damp. The cape was brown, her scarf was an incongruous red, and her gloves—

"I despair of you, Hazel Hooper," Gervaise said, folding up the letter and tucking it into an inner pocket. "You are abroad on a winter evening without benefit of proper gloves. What would your papa say?"

"Papa wouldn't have noticed if I'd worn chain mail and a tiara. Have you seen Annabelle?"

Gervaise was a competent barrister, and as such he relied on a mind well suited to analytical thinking. Hazel's response tweaked the tail of his instincts rather than his intellect, however. He'd known her forever, since he'd been a mere youth, learning the law under her father's tutelage.

"Annabelle has stepped into the back room. She said she'd be right back. What's amiss Hazel?"

For even Hazel, who cared nothing for convention, would not normally have come out of doors without gloves or a muff on a winter night.

"Nothing's amiss." Hazel plucked off her spectacles, for predictably, the warmth of the shop had caused them to fog.

Gervaise took the eyeglasses from her, produced a handkerchief and wiped each lens clean.

"Something is wrong," he retorted, returning the spectacles to their owner. "You haven't yet reminded me to find Christmas tokens for Peter and Daisy."

Gervaise didn't particularly enjoy his sister's company, but his niece and nephew were interesting little people, and he was their only uncle. Christmas was an inexcusable lot of bother, but an uncle's responsibilities were not to be shirked, not even his Yuletide responsibilities.

"I bought them each a book last week," Hazel said. "I've been meaning to send the books over to you."

Hazel threw herself into Yuletide nonsense with all the determination and sincerity of a veteran criminal begging the court for mercy prior to transportation. She decorated, she baked, she gave tokens to the servants and sprinkled half days around like biscuit crumbs cast onto the walkway for the birds. She exhausted herself on Boxing Day, and observed every absurd New Year's tradition ever to inflict itself on British society.

Watching the snow melt on the fringes of her worn scarf, Gervaise realized that he'd.... missed her. Missed her sharp wit, interesting chess, and liberal politics.

"Are you standing there in hopes I'll take pity on you, sir?" Hazel asked.

She had finally focused on Gervaise, and let go of whatever errand had sent her pelting through the cold to On the Shelf.

Hazel had blue eyes and auburn hair, a combination that had unsettled Gervaise until he'd realized auburn hair generally went with green or brown eyes. Hazel turned those blue eyes on him now, and more than their color, their clarity of focus struck him. She had an earnest quality, a directness that disconcerted as it endeared. She was like a child or an elderly woman, both blunt and kind, artless and insightful.

"What do you mean, take pity on me, Miss Hooper? If you've already procured books for Daisy and Peter, what pity is there left to take?"

With one bare, reddened finger, Hazel pointed upward, to the darkened rafters crossing the shop's ceiling.

Gervaise tipped his head back. Immediately above him hung a bunch of wilting mistletoe, pale green leaves and white berries dangling over his head like a noose.

HAZEL HAD BECOME accustomed to Gervaise hiding for the month of December. He hid in his work, in his library, in his legal tomes. Last year, he'd gone clear to Yorkshire in an attempt to ignore the holidays, and quite possibly, Hazel herself.

In January, he'd showed up in her parlor, muttering darkly about old friends with new wives, about amorous rabbits and the price of coal, though Gervaise Stoneleigh, foremost barrister in the realm, could afford to heat half of London.

Hazel suspected he *did* provide heat for many a poor household, and hope as well.

A year ago, Hazel had at least had a note from him. "Off to Yorkshire on a case. Please look in on Mallachan if you have time. G."

Not *Sincerely*, G. Not *Best wishes*, G. Most assuredly not *Love*, G.

He stood beneath the mistletoe, so good-looking that even after ten years of close acquaintance, Hazel still wanted to shield her eyes at the sight of him. Dark hair, darker eyes, and features cast in the mold of a righteous angel. Aquiline nose well suited to peering down, sharp facial bones such as a fasting saint would be proud of, enough height to intimidate criminals and judges alike, though Gervaise often considered criminals and judges of a piece.

Gervaise also had enough height that Hazel herself, whom he referred to as under-tall, could not have kissed him on the cheek without his cooperation.

He took a step to the left. "I will never understand why every modicum of sense must go begging at Christmas along with the drunken carolers. Kissing beneath a sprig of poisonous shrubbery must be the most ridiculous tradition of all."

"You're growing worse," Hazel said, marching up to him. "You've always been ill-natured around the holidays, but mistletoe's provenance goes back to Norse legend and beyond. The goddess Frigga declared that all who stand beneath the mistletoe are safe from harm, though they might be kissed. Are you really so uncomfortable over a few kisses, Gervaise?"

He'd kissed Hazel on any number of occasions, maddeningly harmless pecks on the cheek or the brow. She did not have time to bait him now, but somebody needed to tease or bully him out of his holiday megrims, and for years, that somebody had been Hazel.

He drew himself up, as if preparing to deliver one of his closing arguments. Hazel frequently observed him in court, and his rhetoric could bring tears to the eyes of hanging judges, and inspire accused felons to hope.

"I make no objection to kisses," Gervaise said. "In the right company, I might even venture an interest in kisses. This annual farce of feasting and imbibing to excess, of proclaiming goodwill to all, while ignoring the child starving on the church steps, that I cannot abide."

Hazel climbed one step up the ladder, so she was eye-to-eye with the pride of the Middle Temple.

"No sermons, Gervaise. Please, not in front of the books. I need to find Annabelle, and you apparently need to find a book."

He always needed to find a book, though Hazel had her own theories about what Gervaise Stoneleigh was truly in search of when he spent hours with Virgil and Seneca.

"Arguing again, you two?" Mrs. Merriweather asked, as she parted the curtain separating the bookshop from the family's office and makeshift parlor. "Bad form with the holidays upon us, if you ask me. My, that snow hasn't let up in the least, has it?"

"No, it has not," Gervaise said, reaching past Hazel to take down a slim volume. "The naughty earl will come with me, and he and I will walk the naughty Miss Hooper home. This will allow me a greater opportunity to scold her for not wearing gloves, and she can explain more Norse mythology to me."

So oblivious was Gervaise Stoneleigh to Hazel's person, so indifferent, that when he reached over her head to fetch down his book of verse—Gervaise was partial to the rascally Earl of Rochester—Hazel was fleetingly pressed between Gervaise's chest and the shelf that held morality pamphlets and sermons.

Gervaise's scent was both familiar and marvelous, as if Hazel stood in the middle of a pine forest, downwind from a honeysuckle hedge, with lavender blooming somewhere nearby.

Then the heat, scent and masculine contour of him were gone, and Mrs. Merriweather was cyphering under her breath as she wrote up the sale of the book of poems.

Even from the back, Gervaise was attractive. Broad shoulders, erect posture, Bond Street tailoring finished to perfection, dark hair a tad longer than was strictly tidy. Hazel might have fallen in love with those looks, though her pride would not allow it.

Handsome looks could disguise a mercenary heart.

If she were to fall in love with a man—and approximately ten minutes after meeting Gervaise, she'd done exactly that—then she had pride enough not to fall in love with something so shallow as his appearance.

"Take these," Gervaise said, shoving his gloves at her when she'd abandoned the ladder. "I can't have your death from a lung fever on my conscience. Mallachan would glower at me for the next age, and shed on my best waistcoat in judgment."

Mallachan shed on anything and everything he was pleased to shed on.

"Keep your gloves," Hazel retorted, tucking her hands into her pockets. "I'm not a delicate flower, and we don't have far to go."

Gervaise tried staring down his nose at her, which was entertaining, and then he held the door open, and allowed Hazel to sweep out of the shop before him.

"I have never met a creature as stubborn as you," he said, falling in step beside her. "You realize you are at risk for becoming eccentric?"

"I passed eccentric by the time I was twenty. How was court?" The question was guaranteed to keep Gervaise fuming and recollecting and strategizing for most of the distance to Hazel's door. Gervaise, unlike some barristers, took his work seriously, and chose his clients based on merit rather than ability to pay. This had the paradoxical result of creating demand for his services among the most wealthy, and he'd even been asked to consult on trials held in the House of Lords.

For Gervaise Stoneleigh would not represent a party unless he was reasonably sure the party was innocent. Charges were occasionally withdrawn, simply because Gervaise took the case.

Gervaise worked relentlessly on such cases, amassing evidence, preparing arguments, and interrogating witnesses 'round the clock. He toiled with the same zeal if his client was a Haymarket streetwalker or a widowed countess.

"You did not purchase a book," he said when they were two streets from Hazel's door. "Did you think to buy me a book for Christmas, and then change your plans when you found me at the shop? I've told you not to buy me gifts. Every year, I remind you that I have no patience with—"

"Hush," Hazel said, linking arms with him, though that meant her right hand was exposed to the chilly air. "I've bought you nothing for Christmas. You've no holiday spirit, and don't deserve any gifts. I'll get a little something for Mallachan, and there's nothing you can say to that."

"Suppose not," Gervaise replied, his gloved fingers resting over Hazel's knuckles. His steps slowed, now that he'd summarized the day's legal battles for her. He really ought to be a judge, though he was too good a barrister to succumb to that temptation. "How are you getting on, Hazel?"

He wasn't asking about the decorating, which had been done within twenty-four hours of making the Christmas pudding, nor was he inquiring generally about Hazel's health, which was reliably sound.

"I manage," Hazel said. "I still miss him, though. You?"

"I recall your papa fondly, of course. Have you ever considered traveling at the holidays?"

"And miss the pleasure of watching you grouch your way to the New Year?" She'd spoken a little too brightly, for Gervaise studied her by the light of a street lamp.

The snow was coming down at the softly relentless pace that muffled sound, and meant significant accumulation was likely. Hazel's memories of Gervaise were like the snowfall, gossamer soft taken individually, a significant weight considered as a whole. Deceptively attractive too, when viewed from behind a cozy parlor window, but nasty cold to slog through alone on a winter night.

"Your Papa was most inconsiderate, dying at Yuletide," Gervaise said, taking off his scarf. He shook it, then grasped both of Hazel's hands, and wrapped the scarf around them like a warm, soft muff. "I left you alone last year. I'm sorry for that, but it couldn't be helped."

"You needn't look after me," Hazel said, though Gervaise was a caretaker in a barrister's robes.

He took her by the arm, and led her in the direction of her home. "You look after me, so you'll have to bear with my fumbling attempt at reciprocity. Friends do that, you know."

Friends. Never had such a benign word left Hazel feeling so hopeless. "Does my *friend* feel up to a game of chess tonight? We can play in the library, which bears not even a wreath in the window to remark the season."

"You'll beat me," Gervaise said. "I'm not at my best after the day I've had. You've yet to tell me what sent you to the bookshop, Hazel. I'm a barrister, and getting answers to my questions is my stock in trade."

"You're my friend. Respecting a lady's privacy is a good friend's stock in trade, so I suggest you be about it."

Gervaise was the most intelligent person Hazel knew, smarter even than Papa had been, for Gervaise was quick like a lawyer and shrewd like a successful criminal, too. He'd known something more pressing than finding yet another Christmas gift had sent her out into a snowstorm after dark.

But he was her friend—drat and blast him—and thus he escorted Hazel the rest of the way to her door in silence.

GERVAISE WALKED ALONG beside Hazel, the snow turning a dirty city clean as if by magic, while the letter he'd found glowed in his awareness like a candle in a window.

To me, you are already distinguished, you will always be dashing...

What sort of fellow earned sentiments like that?

What sort of lady put them on paper and conveyed them in writing to her swain?

Hazel slipped a bit in the snow. Gervaise righted her and they resumed walking. A thought intruded on his musings about the letter.

Did Hazel want to reminisce about her papa? How did one invite such recitations, without demanding them? The longer Gervaise pondered that conundrum, the more the silence between him and Hazel rankled.

She'd asked him about court. Hazel always asked him about court, and Gervaise had obliged, at length, for Hazel had keen insights into legal strategy that Gervaise's clerks lacked. Then he'd asked her about her errand at the bookshop, and she'd slammed the conversational door in his face.

Hazel slipped again, this time stumbling into Gervaise.

"You aren't usually so unsteady," he said, righting her once more. She was a tidy bundle of female, even wearing a winter cloak.

"I can usually keep up with you," she retorted, sliding her hands free of the scarf Gervaise had wrapped about them, "but the snow slows me down, and I'd prefer to have my hands at my sides in uncertain footing. You needn't accompany me the rest of the way, Gervaise."

Keep up with him?

Hazel was smiling at him earnestly, holding his scarf out like a flag to be passed in a relay race.

"Tell me to slow down, Hazel." For Gervaise had marched along, sparing no thought for the woman who'd so often walked at his side.

"You'd soon resume arguing your case," she said, folding up the scarf, "and nothing would do then but a bayonet charge upon the evils of incompetent judges, and even if I asked you to slow down, we'd soon be racing along once more. You are an invigorating escort, Gervaise."

Hazel was panting a little, her breath coming in frosty puffs.

Gervaise longed to get home and study his unsigned letter, but the thought of Hazel nearly falling into the snow because of his inconsideration demanded that he make reparation.

"I find myself in need of a chess game, after all," he said, resuming their walk at a more decorous pace. "I trust you'll indulge me?"

"One game," Hazel said, as they turned onto her street. "When should I bring over Mallachan's token?"

Was she trying to get rid of him? The notion was unsettling, for if Gervaise enjoyed a reliable welcome anywhere, it was at Hazel's door. That door bore a fragrant wreath of pine, and the entrance hall was adorned with beribboned candles and bows affixed to the first floor balustrade.

"You haven't put the wreaths in the windows yet," Gervaise observed as Driech, the Hooper butler, took his overcoat. "Greetings, Driech. How is the gout?"

Driech hadn't been young when Gervaise had first made his acquaintance more than a decade ago, and while the butler's eyebrows grew bushier with the passing years, his reply to Gervaise's question was unchanged.

"The gout is tolerable, sir, thank you for asking."

Hazel draped Gervaise's scarf on a hook. "Sandwiches in the library, if you please, Dreich, and syllabub a half hour thereafter. Mr. Stoneleigh is in want of a chess lesson."

"Of course, ma'am." Dreich bowed, maybe a little more slowly than usual.

Ten years from now, Dreich would be very old indeed. Who would wait by Hazel's door then? Who would ensure the fire in her library was always lit on a cold evening?

Hazel had anticipated the privileges of spinsterhood, tending to her ailing father for more than two years, observing strict mourning for him, and then, when the time for half-mourning came, sending her widowed aunt packing.

Gervaise had wanted to object. A woman Hazel's age should not live alone, regardless that she was comfortably fixed and surrounded by loyal servants. Hazel had thrown herself into charitable projects, dressed as if she were a dowager, and like her father before her, had ignored convention while never once transgressing against propriety.

"Come along," Hazel said, while Gervaise tried to recall when, exactly, he'd begun allowing himself long evenings in Hazel's company, as if they were two old relics, decades of informality between them.

"I know my way to the library," Gervaise said, "but now who's in a hurry?"

"I am. I'll trounce you, see that you eat enough to get you home, and then have the rest of my evening to myself. I have gifts to wrap."

Hazel wrapped her tokens in pretty cloth, and the recipients were usually as pleased to have a length of lovely fabric as to have the gift itself.

Gervaise held the door for her, though he had nearly to dive for the door latch, so intent was Hazel on her destination.

"Have you wrapped Mallachan's gift yet?" What sort of gift would Hazel get for a cat, anyway?

"I have not," she replied, lighting a taper at the fireplace, and passing it to Gervaise. He lit the sconces, while Hazel, in a routine they'd settled into years ago, used a second spill to light candles on the card table and end tables.

"Whose turn is it to open?" Gervaise asked, as a knock sounded at the door.

"Yours. Come in."

Dreich tottered in, an enormous tea tray in his hands. "Cook was worried about you ma'am, the hour had grown so late."

Dreich had worried, in other words. Did Hazel know her staff fretted over her? And what had been so important that she'd braved the nasty weather to go to the bookshop?

Those thoughts plagued Gervaise throughout the chess game, and doubtless contributed to his defeat, though he'd given Hazel enough of a challenge to appease good form. She'd learned chess from her father, and brought a ferocity to her play that Gervaise saved for his courtroom appearances.

"Shall I send a footman with you?" Hazel asked, escorting Gervaise to the front door. "The weather is beastly, and half the street lamps have likely gone out."

Their back gates opened onto the same alley. Gervaise could find his way between their houses blindfolded in a howling storm.

"I'll manage, my dear. My thanks for a pleasant game."

The foyer was shadowed, Hazel having sent Driech off to bed directly after he'd delivered the syllabubs. A branch of candles glowed against the frosted window as Hazel held Gervaise's coat for him.

He didn't want to leave her. The notion was peculiar and unsettling. The oncoming holidays, charging at Gervaise like a complicated case of premeditated homicide, already had him unsettled enough.

"Next time," Hazel said, passing Gervais his gloves, "you'll trounce me. You weren't concentrating."

He'd been thinking of his letter, and of how Hazel's red hair and blue eyes had at some point become a very attractive combination, to him at least. They suited her, as this house full of holiday decorations and aging retainers did not.

"I miss him, too," Gervaise said, though he'd planned to wish Hazel a simple goodnight. "Nobody could argue me into a taking the way Phineas Hooper could, nobody could find the weaknesses in my cases as he did. I owe him much, and still feel his loss."

"He was proud of you," Hazel replied, taking Gervaise's scarf down from its hook. "He told me often you were his pride and joy."

Hazel looped the scarf around Gervaise's neck and tossed one end over his shoulder. They were alone, parting at the end of an evening as they had countless times before. The foyer was all dancing shadows as the chill breeze from the snowy night found its way to the candles on the windowsill.

"Then the infallible Phineas Hooper blundered in at least one regard," Gervaise said. "He placed the bleatings of a mere fledgling barrister over the accomplishments of a daughter as devoted, as she was kind, as she was quick."

Hazel's expression underwent a change, from the confident, pleasant young woman—she was still young, by God—whom Gervaise had known for years, to a lady fleetingly bewildered.

He and Hazel did not flatter each other, something Gervaise treasured about her, but when had that come to mean they could not offer each other sincere compliments?

"Thank you, Gervaise. You've given me a Christmas token despite all intention to the contrary."

He hadn't given her enough. Gervaise endured that realization, as he recalled Hazel nearly falling twice, in a silent effort to keep up with him on the way home.

Hazel listening attentively as he maundered on about theft and attempted arson.

Hazel wanting privacy, then graciously agreeing to a game of chess, when Gervaise had abruptly changed his mind.

He had not distinguished himself with her of late, and dashing out the door would not serve. Hazel was wearing a paisley silk shawl, and that could not be much protection against the chill of the foyer.

He drew her into his embrace, and again, he had a sense he'd bewildered his friend. "You must promise me something, Hazel Hooper."

Her arms slid about his waist, tentatively, her grasp loose. "What?"

"When you miss your papa, you must speak to me of him. My memories of Phineas are uniformly cheering, and if you'd like to share them with me, I'm happy to listen."

A great sigh went out of the small woman in Gervaise's arms. She braced her forehead against his chest, as if marshalling her patience.

"I don't want your belated condolences, Gervaise. I had your sympathy and appreciated it when Papa died. I'm simply tired, and a bit anxious about all that remains to do between now and the new year."

He could feel the tension in her, because he'd presumed to offer affection, when at some point, they'd apparently agreed that affection wasn't to be part of their friendship.

Just as they'd agreed that Hazel was to listen to him prose on endlessly about his frustrations and woes, while he was never to have Hazel's confidences in return.

They were to walk at the pace he established.

They were to play chess when he was in need of a game.

The barrister in him railed against such unfairness, and thus he sought a means of apologizing without further embarrassing Hazel, for she was anything but comfortable in his arms.

These thoughts passed through Gervaise's mind in the time it took the candles to waver, and the shadows on the ceiling to dance. In the light cast by the flames, Gervaise's gaze fell on the mistletoe hanging from the unlit chandelier above.

"You want a happy Christmas," Gervaise said, "and I have placed us squarely beneath the mistletoe, my dear. I suppose that means you must endure a kiss of seasonal good cheer from me."

He bent his head and kissed her. Hazel was apparently so surprised at his overture, that she raised her gaze to his, and thus when he was bending, she was raising, and what might have been a kiss on the cheek turned into a soft, unexpected meeting—and even a bit of clinging—of lips.

Chapter Two

NOBODY HAD WRITTEN an herbal about kissing, about the varieties, descriptions and expected habitats of different kisses, about what they needed to thrive and propagate.

Hazel stirred her morning tea, out of charity with the world as a result of this egregious literary oversight. Books were humankind's means of ensuring no wisdom became extinct due to inexact recollection, faulty hearing, or want of use. Books safeguarded every literate person from ever being entirely without resources or companionship.

Kissing was either a topic of obvious dimensions or one that defied accurate description. Hazel hoped the latter, for she'd grown weary of those many instances when the obvious eluded her.

Gervaise Stoneleigh's kisses were magic, even the kiss he'd bestowed the previous evening as an olive branch for his holiday preoccupation. The touch of his lips to Hazel's had been warm, intimate, gentle, and daring all at once. He'd pressed his mouth to hers lingeringly, not a quick, fraternal buss, but a benediction and an apology with a hint of mischief thrown in.

Mischief on his part, utter shock on Hazel's.

"A note has come for you, miss," Mrs. Figginwhistle said, depositing a folded, sealed epistle beside Hazel's plate.

"Thank you, Figgy," Hazel murmured, though she doubted her housekeeper heard her. Figgy's hearing had become increasingly selective over the years, and she'd somewhere along the way also lost sight of small courtesies, such as knocking on closed doors, or addressing her employer in anything but the imperative voice.

"You'll not keep up your strength if that's all you take to break your fast," Figgy said, jabbing at the fire and spilling ashes onto the hearth. "Up until all hours with Mr. Stoneleigh, out in the elements after dark. What would your dear papa think?"

Increasingly, Hazel did not care what Papa would think. Papa had likely never kissed anybody save Hazel's mama, whom she barely recalled.

"Annabelle's note was urgent," Hazel said. "If she found a first edition of Blackstone's *Commentaries*, then a short walk in brisk weather was little to ask." Every bookshop in London knew Hazel was mad for a copy of her own.

"Miss Annabelle is flighty," Figgy said, giving the fire another jab. "That note is from Mr. Stoneleigh."

Figgy's eyesight remained quite keen.

"I'll read it when I've finished my eggs," Hazel said, lest a certain housekeeper take it upon herself to peer over Hazel's shoulder. "Then I'll be down to work on the baskets, Figgy. Warn Cook her domain will be invaded by the lady of the house, and if Uilleam is free, I'll require his assistance."

"That boy, another flighty one. Why you must provide employment to every urchin in Mayfair is a conundrum for the Almighty."

"Uilleam is one young fellow and he works hard." Uilleam also worked quickly, unlike the rest of Hazel's staff. If she needed to send a reply to Gervaise's note, Uilleam would see it done with cheerful dispatch. "I'd appreciate your delivering my warning to Cook now, Figgy. She will want the time to fuss and dither and tidy up."

To put the bottle of cooking sherry out of sight, for the contents evaporated at an astonishing rate during the colder months.

"Oh, aye," Figgy said, trundling at last toward the door. "Christmastide leaves the kitchen in an uproar. Your eggs will get cold if you don't eat them, my girl."

"Figgy, the poker."

The housekeeper peered at the length of iron in her hand, then crossed the room to replace the poker on the hearth stand before making a final, harrumphing exit.

Hazel pushed her plate away, and not because her eggs had been delivered cold to the table.

Gervaise's kisses had been warm, like a beam of sunshine pouring through a window on a winter morning—all of the day's light, heat and cheer with the cold and wind distilled away. Hazel wanted to curl up like a cat in that benevolent beam, and soak in the pleasure of the kiss.

She was loathe to read his note, half-fearing he'd hared off for the north again, just when they'd taken the first, tentative step away from the meandering path of comfortable friendship and toward a closer association.

Though of course, that progression might have occurred only in Hazel's heart, for she had no way to interpret what a single kiss had meant to Gervaise.

She slit open his note, before her fears could whip themselves into dread.

My dear, I am in want of a Christmas token for my sister. Perhaps you'll join me on an expedition to the shops to remedy this lack? G.

Hazel stared at the note, searching the words, the penmanship, the spaces between the words for any significance… and finding none.

"I should publish a taxonomy of a lady's worst disappointments," she informed her unpalatable eggs. "The disappointment of one's dearest friend leaving for the north at Yuletide will rank near the top, though Gervaise is ever diligent about his cases."

She loved that about him. He was not merely a barrister, he was his client's legal champion. He used his connections with Polite Society to find positions in service for those teetering toward destitution. His servants were taught how to read, and expected to pass along their education to siblings and friends.

Gervaise knew every charity in London, which organizations were dedicated to worthy causes, and which were merely salve for the consciences of wealthy patrons.

"Gervaise cannot abide hypocrisy," Hazel muttered, tucking the note into a pocket. "I could not abide it if he dodged off to Yorkshire again."

She was talking to herself, which sparked both a determined indifference—Papa had talked to himself and been considered brilliant—along with a niggling fear that eccentricity's gentle hold on Hazel's household was becoming more like the parasitic twining of the mistletoe about the oak tree.

Gervaise's note required an affirmative reply, so Hazel took a final sip of cold tea and rose.

As she made her way to the library, she realized that her list of disappointments had undergone a rearrangement. She'd been prepared to endure the holidays alone, for Gervaise usually hid in his offices or his library for the duration, ignoring the entire season.

She was hurt when he did that, but knew he had his reasons. Hazel could not endure it, however, if Gervaise intended to ignore last night's kiss.

FRIENDS KISSED EACH other all the time.

Gervaise hadn't many friends, but he'd had a succession of clerks over the years, and knew from their behavior that kissing a friend was of no moment. Gervaise had in fact kissed Hazel occasionally—on the cheek, usually, and thus when he kissed her in greeting in the lemony sunshine of his morning room, it ought not to have brought familiar words to mind.

Your kisses will ever bring me joy.

"You were up late," Hazel said, scowling at him. "This is not well done of you, Gervaise. Your clients need you to be at your sharpest, and if we're to make a round of the shops, the day will be long."

He'd been up late reading and re-reading the love letter bequeathed by old Rochester, until he'd nearly memorized the words.

"Something is different about you," Gervaise said, circling Hazel's person. "You're out of sorts."

Had kissing her done that? If she scolded him for taking liberties, he'd be mostly relieved, for scolds and bickering figured comfortably in their friendship.

While mistletoe... hadn't figured at all, until last night. A small part of him had the temerity to wonder why.

"I'm out of patience with you, Gervaise. You will ruin your eyes, reading until all hours, and you already know English law better than any judge."

She stood as righteously straight, like an innocent defendant awaiting sentence in the dock, while Gervaise circumambulated her person.

"That's a new dress," he said, as pleased with his insight as if he'd spotted a telling inconsistency in the testimony of a lying witness. "That is a very fetching new dress. The plum shade becomes you exceedingly. I suggest you wear more of it in future."

Hazel twitched at the trailing end of Gervaise's cravat. "Thank you, I think. Shall we be off? Figgy says the snow will resume this afternoon, and finding something for your sister is never a brief or pleasant undertaking."

Kissing Hazel had been both brief and pleasant—also unnerving. She was apparently unnerved now, for Gervaise's compliment had put her to the blush.

A very becoming blush it was, too.

"Figgy's prognostications are invariably wrong," Gervaise said, "despite her equally unvarying certainty of their correctness. Have you any idea what I ought to buy for my sister?"

Hazel enjoyed solving problems, and Gervaise's question kept her predictably occupied as they made their way in the direction of Piccadilly.

"Why haven't you taken my arm, Hazel?" Gervaise asked when at least seventeen possible tokens for Gervaise's dear, dithery sister had been discussed.

"Why aren't you churning forth like a cavalry regiment in sight of the enemy, Gervaise?"

He didn't want to see her land in the snow, that's why. "Because I slept badly, and am not on my best mettle. If Judge Timsworth doesn't retire soon, I will have to change professions."

Timsworth slept through half his cases, and between his extended naps sentenced every prisoner to transportation. Gervaise nearly hated him, but dealing with Timsworth taught a lawyer to prepare for an appeal, and to carry a heavy law book into every courtroom. Gervaise would knock that book to the floor as loudly and as often as necessary to keep the eyes of justice open.

"I did not sleep well either," Hazel said as they rounded the corner onto Duke Street. "You kissed me last night, Gervaise."

Rather than allow Hazel to pelt off on that interesting observation, Gervaise linked arms with her.

"We kissed each other, my dear. A quaint Norse tradition." Very fond of their heat sources, those old Vikings. Who knew?

"I enjoyed that kiss." Hazel fired the admission at Gervaise like a hard-packed snowball.

"As did I." In an odd, unexpected way, Hazel's kiss, full of surprise and curiosity, had brought Gervaise joy—also a little worry.

"I also did *not* enjoy it."

"Inconsistency isn't like you, Hazel." Gervaise depended on her consistency, on her reliably remaining Hazel as he knew her.

"Nor is it like you, Gervaise. If you enjoyed the kiss, then why did you end it so quickly and scamper off into the storm? I must be honest, for we are friends, and I can tell you that the brevity of your kiss was not enjoyable at all. If we kiss in future, I should like more kissing and less scampering off. And I do want more of your kisses, provided you're willing to improve their duration."

Hazel marched on, right into the bookshop, while Gervaise came to a halt in the chilly air, for once at a loss for words.

IN HAZEL'S OPINION, On the Shelf indulged in a legal form of larceny. One walked in, expecting to purchase a book, to warm up in the reading room, or browse away an agreeable half hour among the shelves, but one was soon robbed of one's self-restraint.

The bluestockings of Mayfair were a stalwart regiment, and they invariably went down to defeat at On the Shelf.

A half-hour became an hour, the purchase of one book turned into three, and browsing turned into a lively discussion with the other patrons regarding a book's merits. Annabelle would bring out the tea tray, and a prosaic day went entirely to pot, whiled away at the bookshop.

Hazel had avoided the reading room's siren call recently, but today she had occasion to linger, for Gervaise loved this place. He and Mr. Merriweather debated politics, his smile for Mrs. Huntsberry was genuine, and his pleasure in good literature nearly matched Hazel's.

Though Hazel had another reason for visiting the shop twice in twenty-four hours.

"Excuse me, Mrs. Merriweather. Is Annabelle on the premises?" Hazel asked when Mrs. Huntsberry had engaged Gervaise in a lively defense of the Regent's artistic excesses.

Between the nearest set of shelves, Mr. Glen, a near-daily patron who looked to be of foreign extraction, leafed through a book's pages one by one. He did that rather a lot, but seemed an otherwise agreeable fellow.

"Annabelle is making deliveries with Charles, dear," Mrs. Merriweather said, reshelving three copies of a book purporting to describe the deeds of a band of Scottish highwaywomen. "She'll be sorry she missed you. Have you a message for her?"

Well, no. Hazel was responding to Annabelle's summons from the previous evening.

"Just a holiday greeting, Mrs. Merriweather."

Mrs. Merriweather remained one step up on the ladder. She was a tall woman to begin with, and the step ladder gave her an even greater advantage of height over Hazel.

"Annabelle worries about you," Mrs. Merriweather said, withdrawing a small, red leather volume from among the highwaywomen. "I worry about you. Losing your papa and your mama at this time of year, and you little more than an infant when your mama was called to her reward. I had a word or two with the Almighty over that, I can tell you."

"I beg your pardon?" Why must Mrs. Merriweather bring up this ancient history now of all times, and what book had captured Gervaise's attention? He presented the tome to Mrs. Huntsberry, and stood over her, pointing to something on a page.

Mrs. Merriweather leaned against the ladder's frame, her gaze distant. "You had only the one Christmas as a family, before your mama died the next winter. I wasn't sure your dear papa would recover, but we kept him supplied with books, the courts kept him supplied with cases, and he had you."

A queer feeling come over Hazel, chilly, despite the shop's warmth. "My mama died at Christmas?"

"She'd barely been ill a week," Mrs. Merriweather said, descending from the ladder. "The influenza was awful that year, and she took a turn for the worse. We buried her on Christmas Eve. Your papa couldn't bear to eat the Christmas pudding, for she'd made it and you'd been the youngest to give it a stir."

Gervaise patted Mrs. Huntsberry's shoulder and pressed the book into her hands. He looked up, smiling, just as Hazel might have looked away, but she was too late.

He was across the shop in a half dozen strides. "My dear, you are upset."

Well, yes. That queer feeling, so alien to Hazel's existence, surely qualified as upset. "My own mother..." She took Gervaise's outstretched hand. "Papa said he never cared for Christmas pudding."

Gervaise's arm came around her shoulders. "Mrs. Merriweather, might we avail ourselves of the back parlor?"

She led the way behind the curtain, into the cluttered, dimly lit space that bridged domestic and commercial parts of the building.

"How thoughtless of me," Mrs. Merriweather said. "How could your papa not have...? I'm sorry, Hazel. Shall I bring tea?"

Tea would not stop the tears welling in Hazel's eyes. Papa had never said anything, all those years Hazel had madly decorated every window of the house, all the evenings she'd whiled away in his company planning Christmas dinner while he'd prepared for trials, all the times she'd teased him about what holiday token she ought to buy him.

He'd been sad, and she'd simply been trying to cheer him. Why had he never, ever said a word?

"Thank you, Mrs. Merriweather, but we'll not be taking tea," Gervaise said, settling Hazel on the sofa and coming down beside her. "A bit of privacy is all Miss Hooper needs."

He was wrong. Hazel needed her friend beside her right now more than anything else. "I never knew my mama. I wish I'd known her, and how awful for Papa."

Gervaise's arm around Hazel's shoulders was a comfort, though against what particular grief, Hazel could not say. She'd been raised without a mother, that hadn't changed, but she'd been raised with a father determined not to let his own grief overshadow Hazel's holidays, too.

"Did Papa hate the holidays?" she asked.

"I find no evidence to support such a verdict," Gervaise said, tucking a lock of Hazel's hair behind her ear. "To the contrary, he loved you. I lost my mother while we were still in India. the time of year—late September—is no more imbued with grief than any other."

He'd never spoken of this before, but then, he'd never sat with his arm around Hazel, snuggled up in a dim parlor before either.

"If the time of year doesn't bring to mind your grief, Gervaise, what does?"

He took Hazel's hand, his grip warm. "Let's see... The scent of a good curry, oddly enough, particularly if there's saffron in the fragrance. Sunlight on a placid ocean, for my father sent us children home shortly after Mama's death. I began to read voraciously during that sea voyage, and I've never stopped. We were only allowed on deck when the weather was fair, so all my memories of the ocean are calm and sunny."

His calm, sunny memories would also be sad, as a small boy sent away from his only surviving parent would have been sad.

Devastated, more like.

"Papa never said much about Mama," Hazel murmured. "He carried her miniature with him everywhere." Hazel had that miniature now, but she didn't dare take it about with her. Thieves were everywhere, and she had no other portrait of her mother.

"He mentioned her to me from time to time," Gervaise said.

For the next half hour, he recounted what he knew of the courtship of Phineas Hooper and Nanette Dingle, which description included a ladder against a window, declaimed sonnets, and Hazel arriving less than the requisite nine months after the vows had been spoken.

"Compare the dates of the wedding and of your birth as they're recorded in your family Bible," Gervaise said. "Phineas vowed he'd never dissemble about such an obvious testament to true love."

"My papa was a dashing Romeo. I've owned that Bible for nearly ten years, and I never even thought to look. How lovely."

And how lovely to pass the time cuddled with Gervaise, unwrapping pieces of Hazel's own past that she'd never come across before. Pieces of Gervaise's past, too.

"He was an impecunious young barrister with a hard struggle ahead of him," Gervaise said. "Though how any barrister could be regarded as dashing eludes me. We're a prosy lot, much given to appointment books, reading, and gratuitous argument."

Hazel stroked her thumb over Gervais's knuckles. "Is that how you see yourself?"

The moment transformed, like a shift in the wind beyond a house's walls will yet affect how the candles flicker and the curtains flutter. Past griefs merited further study in solitude, the present moment was for sharing.

"I accurately describe a barrister's disposition," Gervaise said. "Our profession is a constructive use of men prone to combativeness and pomposity. I'm no different."

The shop bell tinkled beyond the curtain, and somebody coughed over the shuffle of booted feet. Mrs. Huntsberry, most probably. Possibly Mr. Glen, or maybe the quiet widowed viscountess who lived several streets over. Voices murmured, life went on.

"You're more than combativeness, pomposity, and punctuality, Gervaise."

"I'm rapidly on my way to becoming distinguished." He brushed a kiss over Hazel's fingers, as a distinguished fellow might have. "There's no hope for a man's derring-do once he's become distinguished. No decrying sonnets from among the roses, no eloquent toasts to a lady's eyes, no impassioned declarations—"

Hazel kissed him. *To me, you are already distinguished and you will always be dashing.*

She didn't dare offer him that impassioned declaration, but she could give him a kiss worthy of her regard for him. She was tempted to press her lips to his and then hare off to join a band of highwaywomen in Scotland, but she'd chastised Gervaise for the brevity of his kisses, and so she lingered.

He tasted of peppermint tooth powder, and his scent up close was damp wool and exotic shaving soap—a hint of sweetness amid woodsy spices with lavender notes.

Sunlight on a calm sea made him miss his mother. Hazel hugged that admission to her heart while she drew Gervaise closer.

And he... accommodated her, his arm around her shoulders becoming an embrace. Sitting on the sofa, she was not too short—and he was not too tall—and Hazel could trace his features with her bare fingers. His cheeks were freshly shaved, the clean angle of his jaw an exact fit against Hazel's palm.

His eyebrows were soft beneath the pad of her thumb—she'd wondered—and his hair was thick and dampened with melted snowflakes.

Hazel parted her lips, and got the first curious tentative, sensation of Gervais's tongue limning her bottom lip when the shop bell tinkled again.

Gervaise rested his forehead against hers. "Shall I apologize?"

"I think not," Hazel replied, nor would *she* apologize for a lovely, lovely kiss. "The duration of your kisses is improving. Improvement should be rewarded."

He drew back, his smile not one Hazel had seen before. A little puzzled, a little pleased. More than little kissable.

Annabelle's voice drifted through the curtain, greeting Mrs. Huntsberry and asking after her cat. Charlie said something to Mrs. Merriweather, who laughed in response.

Life went on, but in the space of a kiss, *how* life went on could change. Hazel brushed Gervaise's hair back—somebody had disarranged it—and traced her finger along his lips.

"Have you found a book for your sister?"

Gervaise sat back, and that was prudent of him. If he'd kept his arm around Hazel's shoulders, or his hand in hers, no telling what feats of endurance Hazel's next kiss might accomplish.

"I doubt I will. Lavinia isn't bookish, and giving her a gift that I myself would enjoy is hardly well done of me. You would like a book, I'm sure, but with her... I hardly know her well enough to do more than offer her a seasonal token."

Was this part of Gervaise's objection to the holidays? His only surviving sibling was a stranger to him?

"When you came home from India, what happened then?" Hazel asked.

"I went to public school, she went to...some other colonel's wife, until my father came home. I wrote to her, but we were too young to truly correspond. We saw little of each other once we left India, but we'd been thick as thieves before that."

His expression said he was only now recalling those bandit days of early childhood.

"Let's find her something reminiscent of India then," Hazel suggested. "Something lovely and colorful, and worth cherishing."

The shop next door occasionally carried prints of wildlife and landscapes from India.

"Excellent suggestion," Gervaise said, rising and offering Hazel his hand, though such courtesy was new between them.

"Don't apologize for that kiss," Hazel said, getting to her feet. "You may treat it as an aberration if you wish, pretend it didn't happen, or regard it as a Christmas token, but if you apologize for my overture as if it somehow became your transgression, I will be hurt, Gervaise. I enjoy kissing you very much. I'm not ashamed of that."

Hazel left the parlor before she could hear any argument from her favorite barrister, and bumped smack into Annabelle.

"There you are," Annabelle said, her smile forced. "Let me show you the newest installment of the *Adventures of an Intrepid Lady*, Hazel. They're right over here and we've only a few copies left."

Hazel knew exactly where the installments of the *Adventures* were shelved, because they occupied the only corner of the shop she herself never frequented. The Lady's adventures mostly consisted of getting herself into stupid predicaments, and relying upon the good offices of handsome, clever, male strangers to get her out of them.

"They are chronicles of foolishness rather than adventures," Hazel said, for she and Annabelle had this argument regularly, and Annabelle's eyes were pleading with Hazel to accommodate some subterfuge. "What grown woman yields to a compulsion to investigate a cave, for heaven's sake? Caves are home to bats, particularly by day, and they're dark, and none too fragrant. And what cave just happens to draw the notice of a fellow enamored of antiquities, I ask you? As if English hillsides provide such lures regularly."

They'd reached the back shelves, so Hazel lowered her voice. "Annabelle, what's wrong? You look like you've lost the proceeds of the last month's sales."

"Worse than that," Annabelle said. "Mama caught me studying the letter you'd written, and I set it aside to avoid her notice. Hazel, I can't find it. The most beautiful love letter ever penned by the hand of woman, and it's gone missing somewhere in the shop."

Mrs. Merriweather's voice rose above the bustle of the shop's custom. "She's with Annabelle among the serial publications, Mr. Stoneleigh. Shall I add anything to your tally?"

"You *lost* my letter, Annabelle?"

Annabelle nodded, worrying a fingernail. "I was trying to memorize it, for your example was inspiring indeed, Hazel."

That's all Hazel's letter had been, an example.

Annabelle was sweet on Charlie, the shop clerk who'd joined the staff that summer. He was a hard worker and a lover of beautiful prose, but shy. Hazel had suggested Annabelle embark on an epistolary wooing, and Annabelle had asked for an example of a love letter.

The exercise had been both sad and delightful. The sentiments had flowed from Hazel's pen, a torrent of amatory eloquence, all the frustrated longings in her finding their way to the page. The man who inspired her flights would never read those words though, for Gervaise Stoneleigh might indulge a friend in a few kisses, but Hazel would never risk burdening him with her most passionate outpourings.

"Maybe Charlie found it?" That would be the best outcome, and Christmas was the season of miracles.

"Charlie treats me the same as he always has, not as if he suspects me of sending him a gorgeous love letter. What if Papa finds it, or Mrs. Huntsberry?"

Mrs. Huntsberry loved to read racy passages from the *Adventures* aloud, and her stentorian baritone could be heard halfway to Hyde Park.

"Oh, no," Hazel moaned, gaze slewing about to the books stacked shelf upon shelf to the ceiling. "Annabelle, you probably stuffed it into a book. You're always stashing papers between the pages of a book. We must find that letter before another patron comes upon it."

The shop had an eclectic clientele that included everybody from neighboring shopkeepers, to the occasional literary duke, to Hazel's own pastor, and a steady stream of book-addicted spinsters.

"I'll find it," Annabelle said, "if I have to stay up all night going through every volume on every shelf—but I might have tossed it in the rubbish, you know. Might have twisted it into a taper."

"And you might not," Hazel said. "If I can come back tonight, I will, but start without me if you have the time."

A tattoo of booted heels on the plank floor behind Hazel was joined by a whiff of spices.

"My dears, you are conspiring," Gervaise said. "I'm a man of the law, and I know a conspiracy when I overhear one. Miss Merriweather, you may not kidnap Miss Hooper for some nefarious biscuit-baking scheme until at least tomorrow. She has agreed to spend the day shopping with me. You will have to wait your turn."

Annabelle tidied the remaining three copies of *The Adventures*. "The shop is far too busy during the holiday season to allow me time to bake biscuits, and Hazel is very quick reshelving misplaced merchandise. We're not too proud to refuse her help when it's offered."

"Neither am I," Gervaise said, placing Hazel's hand on his arm. "Miss Hooper has offered to assist me in the hunt for a gift for my sister. When that miracle has been wrought, you two may bake all the biscuits you please. I prefer mine with vanilla and lavender."

Hazel let him tow her to the front of the shop, because his air was that of man who would not be thwarted. Did he think Hazel would prefer an afternoon in the bookshop to an afternoon with him?

Well, she wouldn't. Not ever. To establish that point beyond doubt, when they reached the street, Hazel unwound herself from Gervaise's arm, and took his hand in hers. She was being bold, but holding hands with a man was nothing remarkable, not when the way was slippery and holiday cheer was in the air.

That Gervaise merely gave Hazel a puzzled smile, and kept her hand in his, though—that was remarkable indeed.

Chapter Three

HOLDING HANDS WITH Hazel was oddly comfortable, and amid the shoppers thronging the snowy city lanes, not that unusual. One wouldn't want a lady to lose her footing, after all.

And yet, a part of Gervaise had apparently lost his footing, or his wits, because even while holding Hazel's hand, he searched the face of each woman they passed, wondering: *Did you write that letter?*

Was that passionate declaration from the hand of a mature lady, one with children in the nursery, a steady fellow at her side whom she alone saw as a knight in shining armor? If so, Gervaise envied that fellow his wife's devotion.

Perhaps the authoress of Gervaise's pre-occupation was an unmarried woman, writing to the man she'd set her cap for, ensnaring that lucky swain with her boldness and passion.

"Maybe we should go back to the print shop," Hazel said, before they were halfway to the corner of Duke Street. "We might find a brass letter opener or a print of an elephant there."

"I hadn't thought of that." Gervaise had been too busy daydreaming and holding Hazel's hand. Not well done of him, to escort one lady while wondering about another. "We can come back to the print shop any time, if other avenues are fruitless. I doubt my sister enjoys a wide correspondence."

Hazel shook free of Gervaise's grasp and rearranged her scarf. "What about a spice box?"

"She probably already has one."

"Silk pajama pants."

Gervaise tossed a coin to a crossing sweeper shivering in shop doorway. "A brother would never gift his sister with something so personal."

"A monkey."

Monkeys abounded in India. "I'll never find one for sale at a decent price in London, and my brother-in-law would kill me."

"Your niece and nephew would canonize you."

Gervaise leaned closer, as if aiming his best courtroom glower at a recalcitrant witness. "To be canonized is worse than to be distinguished. You plot my ruin, minx."

Hazel's smile turned... wistful? "You're arguing with a lady, Gervaise, and in the very street."

He grabbed her hand and tucked it about his arm. "I'm enjoying myself, and so are you."

Hazel allowed that truth to end the dispute, and wandered with him up one street and down the other. They stopped at Gunter's for an ice, and agreed that loyalty to On the Shelf meant Hatchards would not have their custom.

A pattern developed, though, one that did not flatter Gervaise.

At the silversmith's, Gervaise was reminded of the engraved standish Hazel had given him five years ago. She'd sent over her token on Boxing Day, and Gervaise hadn't called on her until after the new year.

At the stationer's, he was reminded that his favorite penknife, the one that took the best edge, had also been a Christmas gift from Hazel.

As had his warmest pair of quilted slippers, his favorite cravat pin, his most treasured books. When Phineas had died, the old barrister's entire estate had been bequeathed to Hazel, and she'd insisted on the law books all going to Gervaise.

What had he given Hazel in return? A few chess games? An occasional escort to the theatre?

Gervaise's letter writer, the woman of articulate passion and endless devotion, would have been ashamed of him. *I'll know you... by the honesty and kindness with which you greet all in your ambit...*

"Let's try in here," Hazel said, pulling Gervaise into yet another shop, this one all but deserted.

The scent hit Gervaise first, both floral and spicy, redolent of burning sun, brilliant flowers, and somehow, reminiscent of even the incessant noise of an Indian bazaar. That complex fragrance, more than any image or melody, evoked a happy childhood on foreign shores.

And yet, the shop was quiet, the little turbaned fellow behind the counter welcoming them with only a smile and a bow over folded hands.

Out of old habit, Gervaise returned the gesture.

"Good sir," Hazel said, "we need a gift to remind a lady of her early years in India. A token such as a brother might give a sister, a dearly loved sister."

The fellow still said nothing, but came out from behind the counter, and gestured to silk scarves in colors as rich and varied as the jewels of Solomon's treasure. Gervaise drew a blue, green, red, and gold scarf from among those displayed, the cool, whispery texture of the silk conjuring memory upon memory.

That sensation, of silk on silk, was from his boyhood, from the last time he could recall being truly happy. Had he heard his sister laugh even once in all the years since? Had *he* laughed?

"This will do nicely," Gervaise said, passing the scarf to shopkeeper. The old fellow's eyes were kind and knowing, also slightly reproachful.

Gervaise had *not* heard his sister laugh in more than twenty years. "Have you a shawl to match?" he asked.

"Oh, yes!" Hazel said, clapping gloved hands. "A silk shawl makes a lady feel so special, and they're surprisingly warm, and yet as light as moonbeams. Well done, Gervaise."

The proprietor produced not a matching shawl, but one in the same blue as the scarf with a similar paisley pattern. The combination was lovely, but the purchase underscored that Gervaise had been sadly remiss regarding presents for Hazel.

He'd sent Hazel sweets that a French client had had delivered to Gervaise's office after a successful verdict had come down. Hardly an act of generosity.

He'd made sure the solicitors dealing with Phineas's estate had done so efficiently and at a reasonable cost. Not exactly fierce championing of the downtrodden there.

"You're quiet," Hazel said, as the shop owner wrapped Gervaise's purchases. In the dim light of the shop, amid the shining brass and gleaming silk, her auburn hair shone with fiery highlights. She'd worn a scarf rather than a bonnet, a soft green lambswool that Gervaise might have given her a few years ago—except he hadn't.

She'd bought it for herself, of course.

"I'm impressed," Gervaise said, something else he should have told her more often. "I've dragged you all over London, not for the first time, and we've found a gift for my sister that's better than perfect. Your energy for the quest has been unflagging."

Gervaise was pre-occupied in addition to impressed, or still pre-occupied. Sometime during the busy, chilly, day, he'd stopped looking into the faces of the ladies passing him on the street. He'd stopped wondering: *Are you my letter writer?*

Being a barrister who liked neat syllogisms and decisive verdicts, he wished he might someday meet that woman, but his interest in her letter had shifted.

As Hazel had patiently suggested one gift after another, and accompanied Gervaise to one shop after another, he'd begun studying the men he passed on the street. Dignified old fellows with bushy whiskers, spry shop boys darting along with their deliveries, well dressed aristocrats, coal men, jarvies, everything in between.

Who among them was worthy of the sentiments in Gervaise's unsigned letter? Who among them saved lives with his wit, treated everybody he met with unflinching dignity, championed the downtrodden, and offered his lady tender kisses all the while?

The man who deserved to receive such a letter had become as interesting to Gervaise as the woman who'd written it.

Gervaise offered the shop owner the traditional bow of parting and made arrangements for the package to be delivered to his house the next morning.

"For once Mrs. Higginwhistle appears to have been right," Hazel said, peering out the shop window.

"And at the worst possible time," Gervaise muttered, leading Hazel from the shop into a steady snowfall. This time of year, the sun set early, and the streets were rapidly emptying as the light faded. "Come, my dear, and I'll see you directly home."

Gervaise was mindful to match his steps to Hazel's, for she had to be tired. He certainly was, and the day had given him much to consider as well. Nonetheless, it took him the entire distance to Hazel's door to formulate and pose the question he ought to have asked on any number of previous occasions.

"You have indulged me all day," he said, holding the front door for Hazel rather than waiting for Driech to totter forth from the house's depths. "Our mission has been successful. I have the best possible present for my sister. Indulge me yet further, and give me an honest answer to a sincere question."

Hazel paused in the act of shaking melting snow flakes from her scarf in the dimly lit foyer. "You're making an opening argument. Just get on with it, Gervaise."

She'd be truthful with him, for Hazel, like Gervaise's letter writer, was a woman of unwavering honesty and passionate conviction. How odd that two women who'd never meet, should share such virtues.

"Do you need anything?" Gervaise took Hazel's scarf from her, shook it thoroughly, and hung it on a hook. "That's not what I meant to ask. What I meant to ask is, what would you like as a Christmas token?"

"A Christmas token? From *you?*"

If Hazel laughed at him, he'd deserve it. Gervaise drew off her right glove then her left, shook both, and laid them on the sideboard.

"The Christmas token is a quaint custom," he said, "and one in which I've been remiss. In my distaste for holiday hypocrisy, I have neglected an opportunity to demonstrate my regard for you. Hence, the, um, question."

He was making a hash of this, like a newly admitted member of the bar, stumbling around with cross-examination of a hostile witness.

"The question, Gervaise?"

"We're friends," he said, drawing her cloak from her shoulders. "Friends exchange tokens at the holidays. I have been remiss. What would you like as your holiday gift from me? Ask me for anything. I've years of neglect to make up for."

Hazel took his hat from his head, which made no sense when Gervaise intended to step around to his own house, where a roaring fire and toddy would keep him company while he tried to make sense of the day.

And make sense of the eagerness with which he awaited Hazel's answer to his question.

She ran her palm up his scarf, a gray lambs wool she'd given him two years earlier. Her touch, even though layers of clothes, commanded his entire attention.

Almost.

Gervaise's mind spared enough focus to light on one other thought: Somewhere in Hazel's chilly, shadowy, foyer was a fat sheaf of mistletoe. Would she want another kiss from him? He was willing to share one with her, despite having no idea where these kisses were leading, or how he felt about their possible destinations.

"You want to know what you can give me as a holiday token?" Hazel asked, smoothing her hand over his chest again. "I don't need anything Gervaise."

In other words, she was a woman of independent means.

"It's unlike you to dodge, Hazel. We're friends, close friends, and I have years of foolishness to atone for."

"You're not foolish, you're zealous about your work."

Gervaise trapped her hand in his. "Hazel, I not only owe you, I *want* to give you something nobody else could give you. Not a beautiful chess set, not a first edition of Blackstone, not even silk pajamas."

Her brows rose. "Those would be excellent gifts."

Purchased with any old handful of coins, and that wasn't good enough for Hazel Hooper.

Gervaise kissed her on the mouth, strictly in an effort to assure her of his sincerity. "I want to give you the sorts of gifts only close friends would entrust to each other. You are dear to me, you know. Very dear."

He'd never told her that before, another oversight remedied. Perhaps there was hope for him.

Hazel leaned forward, rested her forehead against his greatcoat, and muttered something.

As a natural impulse intended to improve his hearing, Gervaise put his arms around her. She had to be cold in the foyer, for Gervaise could see his own breath.

"I beg your pardon, Hazel?"

"I said, what I truly, truly want, and could ask nobody else to give me, a gift worth years and years of close friendship, is an evening of passion. Will you give me that Gervaise? For you are the only person of whom I can imagine making such a request."

"ESTELLA MERRIWEATHER, YOU are wearing a smile that suggests you've been naughty."

Not all husbands could read their wives' smiles as accurately as Magnus Merriweather did. His looks had changed little from when Estella had married him nearly thirty years ago. His hair was mostly silver, but his smile was the same, and his love for his family as dependable as ever.

"You were right," Estella said, fishing pins from her hair. Her hair had silvered as well, particularly around her face. The bottom of her braid was still a chestnut brown, but in a few years, she'd look like the grandmother she hoped to be.

"I am right so often," Magnus said, cleaning his pipe. "You must be more specific, my love."

"Mr. Stoneleigh purchased the Rochester as you predicted he would, and Hazel's letter was tucked inside it."

Magnus tapped his pipe against his palm. "Ah, but has our favorite barrister chanced upon that letter? He buys every volume of Rochester we shelve, true enough. He's a busy man, though, and might not have time to immediately appreciate his purchase."

"He was appreciating Hazel at a great rate in our very parlor," Estella said. "Without benefit of mistletoe, I might add."

"About time. You have such pretty hair, Mrs. Merriweather."

"I have such a wonderful husband. I hope we hear of an engagement by the New Year."

Magnus set his pipe on the mantle and came to stand behind his wife. He took the brush from her, arranged her hair in three thick skeins, and started to work on a single braid.

"I cannot help but think," he said, "when Phin asked us to look after those two, he meant for us to do more than watch Hazel and her barrister worship each other from afar year after year. What have you done with your ribbon, Mrs. Merriweather?"

Estella passed him a plain white length of silk. "What shall we do about Annabelle and Charlie, Magnus? I can't divine any reason for Annabelle to have a love letter written by Hazel, unless Annabelle hoped to benefit from Hazel's example."

Or perhaps to benefit from the example of Hazel's exquisite penmanship.

"I have benefitted from Hazel's example," Magnus said, tying a bow on the end of Estella's braid. "Do you know how much I admire you, Mrs. Merriweather? How I treasure your patience with the customers? How I adore your talent with the ledgers, your knowledge regarding what inventory we should stock, and what titles will only gather dust? You are a genius, and the greatest gift life could have bestowed on me."

"Magnus, stop that right now. The boy has no prospects." Though Annabelle's plans for Charlie were clear enough, at least to Estella.

"He's not a boy," Magnus said, kissing the top of Estella's head. "He's a young man who somehow came by an excellent education, he works hard, even Mrs. Huntsberry likes him, and Annabelle won't be able to run this shop by herself when we're too old to scamper up and down that ladder."

Estella rose and tucked herself into her husband's embrace. "A thriving bookshop is an extravagant dowry, when the suitor brings nothing to the union."

"I will tell you what a wise young lady told me, almost thirty years ago, Estella Merriweather: Love is the only dowry any couple needs. Without it, all the wealth in the world means nothing. With it, all the challenges in life can be endured. The young lady was right."

"Magnus Merriweather, you are a romantic."

"Guilty as charged, Mrs. Merriweather. Now let's hope Hazel and her barrister don't bungle our little holiday gift to them."

"A gift of meddling," Estella muttered, joining Magnus in the bed.

"Meddling can be a very great gift," Magnus replied, blowing out the last candle on the night table. "I rather treasure the times you meddle with me."

"Still, Magnus?"

"Always, my love. Always."

ALL DAY LONG, as Gervaise had tossed coins to street urchins, tipped his hat to dowagers and shop girls alike, and searched for the right gift for his silly sister, Hazel had fallen more deeply in love.

Charm, he might lack, but good-heartedness, he had in even greater abundance than his handsome looks.

Watching Gervaise bow politely to the silent old man in the last shop, Hazel had been seized with a desperation. For once, she wanted her wishes to come true, wanted her dreams to count. For once, she wanted to be not sensible, dependable, self-sufficient Hazel, but a woman who was desired and cherished and treasured.

Gervaise hadn't even taken off his hat when he'd seen Hazel to her door. He'd had no intention of staying, not for chess, not for anything. Then he'd asked his preposterous question, and kissed her again. A nothing of a kiss, a nighty-night kiss. Hazel had kissed Mallachan with as much warmth.

Bah. She slipped from Gervaise's embrace. "Don't stare at me as if I've professed a preference for the *Code Napoleon*, Gervaise. You've a brilliant mind, you're of age and not under holy orders. My question was simple. Will you give me the gift of a few hours of passion?"

Hazel's motives were not so simple, but she'd worry about that later.

"The dilemma you put before me is complicated," Gervaise replied, clasping his hands behind his back. "I respect you above all other women, Hazel. If I capitulate to your request outside the bonds of matrimony, many would say I'm ruining you."

For a brilliant man, Gervaise could be an utter blockhead. The conundrum he posed might have been addressed by a simple proffer of marriage. Hazel's pride would not allow her to point that out.

"This discussion ought not to take place in a frigid entryway," Hazel said, unwrapping Gervaise's scarf from about his neck. "It shouldn't have to take place at all, in fact. You offered me any gift of my choosing, I named a simple exchange between consenting adults who are well disposed toward each other—dear friends, you said—and you're parsing the niceties. You can say no, Gervaise. I won't run howling into the storm."

But I'll want to.

"The snowfall is light," he replied, his tone distracted.

He was thinking through a strategy in other words, even as he stood motionless in Hazel's dark foyer. Outside, the streetlamp created a small circle of light, while snow fell in a shower of diamonds against the darkness. So pretty, and so cold.

"If you don't want me, then be honest," Hazel said holding his scarf out to him. "I'll not ask again."

Hazel thought he was reaching for the scarf, and for an instant, all the loneliness in her teetered above an abyss of despair. She'd see Gervaise at services, run into him at the bookshop, pass him on the street, and they'd be correct with each other, even friendly.

But they'd no longer be friends.

"You think I don't want you?" he asked, snatching the scarf and tossing it on the sideboard. "Well, what else are you to think? I spend ten years without ever once telling you how pretty your hair is by candlelight and in sunshine and every kind of light in between. I've never told you how much your willingness to listen to my legal maunderings has contributed to my success in the courtroom. I've never—this will be complicated Hazel, but I thrive on the complicated and delicate."

Still, he made no move to touch her.

"You'll grant my Christmas wish, then, Gervaise?"

"You'll have passion, but I won't ruin you, Hazel."

His words sounded like a yes, but felt like a no. "I don't understand."

"Do you trust me, Hazel?"

"Absolutely." No man claimed more integrity, more trustworthiness, or more steadfastness than Gervaise Stoneleigh.

"Then we shall contrive. Ring for tea, madam, and something to eat because you'll need your strength."

A MAN WHO wanted to be worthy of passionate letters and undying devotion had to use his wits when a lady tangled him in competing demands of honor. Gervaise would not ruin Hazel, but neither would he disappoint her. He owed her this boon, and more interestingly, he *wanted* to give it to her.

Her company was very dear, her mind a pure delight, her hair beautiful, her kisses intriguing, and her hands when he grasped them in his—freezing.

Gervaise might have asked for that hand in marriage, but Hazel had not yet signaled a receptiveness to such an overture.

"Your private sitting room will do," Grevaise said, shrugging out of his great coat. "Though you must promise me something, Hazel."

A shiver passed over her. "Promise you what?"

Gervaise wrapped his great coat over her shoulders. "Promise me the simple courtesy of honesty, Hazel. One can wish for something, then realize the wish was ill-advised. I am your dear friend, and nothing that happens in the next hours will change that."

She drew his coat close about her. "If you say so."

Gervaise relished the challenge of convincing a skeptical jury. Before he could remind Hazel of that salient fact, Driech came creaking up the stairs.

"My lady, very glad to see you're out of the elements. Mr. Stoneleigh, good evening."

"Good evening, Driech. Miss Hooper will need sustenance with the tea tray, and we'll be in her private parlor."

"Soup will do," Hazel said, "with bread and butter, and a pot of gunpowder, please. And if you'd send Uilleam across the way to let Mr. Stoneleigh's household know he'll be dining here, I'd appreciate it. They needn't wait up for him."

"Very good," Dreich said, bowing carefully. He went back down the stairs, his progress stately, at best.

The meal was a fine idea, for Gervaise's best legal performances benefitted from forethought, and nothing less than his credentials as Hazel's dearest friend were on trial, possibly even his entire future.

Hazel's parlor was chilly, suggesting the staff hadn't bestirred themselves all day. Her sleeping quarters would be colder than a Frost Fair.

"Somebody had best light the fire in your bedroom," Gervaise said as they waited for the dinner trays. "You will have company under the covers, true, but you'll want the sheets warm before I relieve you of your nightgown."

Hazel looked intrigued. "One doesn't wear clothing?"

"I prefer not to, but you must do as you please."

She was quiet throughout their meal, perhaps because the footman and maid were building up the fire in the bedroom next door—and taking rather a long time about it, too.

"What else do I need to know?" Hazel asked when the trays had been cleared away.

Gervaise took the last sip of his tea and stood, because he wasn't about to discuss the agenda for the next hours as if they planned another day's shopping.

"You need only trust me, Hazel, and trust yourself. This evening is about pleasure, not about strategy, verdicts, or clever cross-examination. Not about pretty speeches or good manners. We indulge each other, we share intimate pleasure. We do not sit in the jury box, assessing counsel's command of the law, or the demeanor of the witnesses."

Hazel rose, and when Gervaise had hoped she might lead the way to her bedroom, she instead wrapped her arms around him.

"I didn't think you'd comply with my wish, Gervaise, and I don't know where this will leave us, but I'm very glad you didn't deny me."

She fit in his embrace, something he'd never allowed himself to notice before. A gentleman didn't focus on soft breasts, a lovely shape, the flare of feminine hips.

A man, though, an honest man, could not deny those pleasures.

"We'll contrive Hazel," Gervaise assured her, cupping her jaw against his palm. He offered her a kiss for courage—his own as well as hers—because briskly marching into the bedroom as if his next case had been called by the bailiff wouldn't serve.

This was Hazel, whose courage and boldness had created an opportunity for their friendship to become something greater. He kissed her gently, refusing to plunder what ought to be savored, and the hesitance in Hazel's touch as she wrapped her arms around him suggested he'd chosen the right path.

"We have all night," Gervaise said, nuzzling Hazel's temple. "One lingers over these pleasures, much as one might linger over composing a letter to a dear friend."

Hazel hitched closer. "Or over a love letter?"

Gervaise had never written a love letter. A merciful Deity would allow him to address that oversight.

He cradled Hazel's jaw between his palms, and penned her a tender epistle, dropping slow, teasing kisses over her brow, her cheeks, her jaw. He'd seen her features countless times, but learning their contours with his lips was an adventure in patience rewarded.

A great sigh went out of Hazel. "I suspected you'd be good at this."

"For you, I want to be brilliant, my dear. Won't you please take me to bed?"

Chapter Four

NEVER HAD HAZEL taken so long to consume a simple dinner of soup and buttered bread. Between one spoonful of rich, hot broth and the next, her emotions had swung about, like the boom of a sail boat coming through the eye of the wind.

She wanted to study Gervaise, to memorize his appearance, and savor the anticipation of what they were about to do—a secret dream, and a desperate gamble.

She wanted to gobble him whole, drag him onto the bed, and leap upon him.

His comment about wearing no clothing slowed her down. So did the presence of Millie and Tom in the next room, making more of a racket than a fire. Tom was too deaf to eavesdrop, but old Millie was Mrs. Higginwhistle's creature entirely.

After four eternities, the maid and footman took the trays away, and Hazel was left with the prospect of a wish about to come true.

When she would have torn herself from Gervaise's embrace, and appropriated the use of the privacy screen in the bedroom—Gervaise would know if one lit candles on such an occasion or not—she instead remained secured to the one fixed attribute in the entire undertaking—Gervaise himself.

"The bedroom will be cold," Hazel said, the lace of Gervaise's cravat tickling her cheek.

"Are your feet cold?"

"No." Not in any sense. Gervaise desired her. He held her closely enough to make that fact reassuringly obvious.

"Then lead on, Hazel."

The mixed feelings, of wanting to savor and to charge headlong, of hope and doubt, assailed Hazel again, but she preceded Gervaise into the bedroom anyway. She was accustomed to her quarters being chilly—a warmer run over the sheets helped a great deal—but she'd never before been embarrassed by her staff's habitual parsimony.

"Do you prefer your quarters this cold?" Gervaise asked, closing and locking the sitting room door.

"Not especially, but I don't like to pester Millie or Tom for extra coal. In the morning, I fetch the bucket from the library across the corridor, or use up what's left in the parlor. How do we do this?"

"It's not complicated," Gervaise replied. "We take off our clothes, jump into the bed, make each other scream and moan with pleasure, have a nice nap, then repeat the screaming and moaning part until we can't move."

"You're serious."

"I'm teasing, and you're worried. You needn't be. Would you prefer the candles out?"

"I want them blazing when you undress, I want them snuffed before I remove a single stitch."

Gervaise picked up an unlit candelabra from Hazel's desk and lit seven more candles from the ones on the mantel.

And to think she'd called him a blockhead.

"Perhaps you'd like to use your toothpowder and remove the pins from your hair?" Gervaise suggested. "I'll deal with the warmer."

Behind the privacy screen, Hazel stumbled through the motions of preparing for bed, but the very fact of having another person in her bedroom during that routine—filling a warmer with coals, flipping back the covers, adding coal to the fire—was audible proof that her world was about to change. Her very dear friend was about to become her lover, and she, his.

She emerged from the privacy screen, her nightgown and bathrobe covering her from neck to slippers. Gervaise had built up the fire, though the immediate result was more light than warmth.

"You're welcome to use my toothbrush," Hazel said, though perhaps such sharing was too personal.

"Thank you. The covers should be cozy for the next two minutes. I'll join you shortly."

Thus was Hazel given relative solitude to climb into the bed, and dither over whether to take off her nightgown or leave it on.

Gervaise emerged from the privacy screen, his coat off, his cuffs undone, his cravat draped about his neck. The change was... intriguing. He was no longer the fashionable barrister, but had become the male beast in his prime, his dishabille hinting at the healthy animal beneath the civilized attire.

Hazel drew her knees up and prepared to gawk. When had Gervaise's walk acquired the quality of a prowl, when had his hands become fascinating?

He used those hands to undo his waistcoat, which he draped over the back of the chair at Hazel's desk. In one lithe movement, his shirt went next, right over his head. Hazel wanted him to hurry with the rest of it, and she wanted him to stand right before the fire, and give her a moment to absorb the look of him shirtless.

"You fence," she said, as firelight played over lean, sculpted muscle.

"And I ride in the morning if the weather is fine. I also walk half the breadth of London most days, because I need the time to think. Lawyering can be sedentary, which invites all manner of ills."

How was it that Gervaise, a beautiful man when dressed, became even more attractive when unclothed? He sat to pull off his boots, or perhaps to give Hazel time to admire him. Jealousy tried to steal a march on anticipation, for Gervaise was striking, while Hazel was... Hazel.

"What can that frown possibly portend?" he asked, rising and setting his boots away from the fire. "If you're having doubts—?"

"Stop that. Stop taunting me to give up the only boon I've asked of you in years, Gervaise."

The look he gave her was unreadable, even with the candles blazing.

He started on the buttons of his falls. "Has it occurred to you, Hazel, I might fear to disappoint you? I might worry that I'll fail you in some particular known to men of wider experience with idle pleasures?"

"You have *no* experience of idle pleasure," Hazel said. "You work nearly all the time. If you escort some baroness or widowed countess to the theatre, it's because one of the solicitors has asked it of you. You seldom take even a half day, and you only travel if a case requires it of you."

She'd surprised him. He was backlit by the fire, dark hair falling over his brow, one side of his breeches undone. The picture he made was decadent, magnetic, and yet still her Gervaise.

Had those countesses and baronesses seen him thus? Hazel pitied them if they had, because Gervaise had allowed them only a passing glimpse of his undone self, and then gone back to his criminals and cronies. He'd never discussed cases with those women, never let them win a chess match because they were in low spirits.

"Why are you smiling?" Gervaise asked, getting to work on the second set of buttons. "You all but label me a drudge, and then smile like a surprise witness for the crown."

He peeled out of his breeches, and with stunning and entirely male casualness, strolled over to Hazel's desk and made a tidy pile of breeches, shirt, stockings and cravat.

"You said no matter what happened tonight, we'd remain friends, Gervaise. You need a friend. You need somebody to scold you for working too hard, to drag you about shopping for holiday gifts, to listen to you prattle on about your clients. I am not beautiful in any conventional sense. I'm short, I have red hair, I have freckles. But I am your friend."

That recitation settled something for Hazel. She could not compete with the statuesque blonds who occasionally accompanied Gervaise on social outings. She had no title, she had no great fortune, but she had his best interests at heart, and always would.

She loved him, and very soon would make love with him.

Provided she could recall how to breathe.

"Shall I join you in the bed, Hazel?" he asked, as calmly as if he were inquiring whether Hazel would like a second cup of tea.

Hazel silently gave thanks for the extra candles Gervaise had lit. He waited by the fire's warmth, a glorious exponent of the fit adult male. Broad shoulders tapered to a trim waist, dark hair trailed down from his chest, narrowing as it went south, and then...

"You've wilted," Hazel said, though maybe that was a good thing. Even in his un-wilted state, Gervaise was impressive. Hazel had studied enough statues to know that much.

"You daft woman, I'm standing in the freezing air, mentally reciting the Riot Act to my wayward inclinations in order that you not be disconcerted by the effects of any animal spirits on my breeding organs."

"You're speaking like a barrister," Hazel said, though his spluttering reassured her. That handsome, naked, breathtaking creature across the room was very much her Gervaise. "Please blow out the candles and come to bed, sir."

He blew out the candles, and when he joined Hazel under the covers—he was rather a lot of bedfellow, compared to Hazel's cat—some of her confidence melted away.

Gervaise turned on his side, his hair an inky contrast to the pale linens. "I have come to bed, as you bid me."

Hazel expected him to recommence kissing her, but he lounged less than two feet away, studying Hazel as if she were an arrangement of chess pieces.

"Now what, Gervaise?"

"Now, I think you must have your wicked way with me."

HAZEL WAS SO pretty—and so nervous. Gervaise wanted to sweep aside her worries with passionate kisses and wicked pleasures, but a litigator's instincts held him back.

"*I* must have my wicked way with *you*? I haven't a wicked way," Hazel groused. "I have only Greek statues, an inconvenient curiosity, and the conviction that if I do not share this experience with you now, then I'll never have another opportunity to learn what—"

She smacked her pillow, fluffed the covers, heaved about some, then lay on her side facing him.

"To learn what, Hazel?" Her braid was trapped under her pillow. Gervaise tugged it free and brushed the end across his lips. "You know how my kisses taste. You know what I look like without benefit of clothing. You know that I wilt, and I un-wilt, and that you have such knowledge both shocks me and pleases me."

"Pleases you?"

Gervaise tickled Hazel's chin with her braid. "My Hazel is fearless. She easily grasps the intricacies of the law of evidence, she observes the proprieties without allowing them to tyrannize her. Even intimate biology doesn't daunt her. She's a creature of kindness and commonsense."

Also a sensitive soul. Why hadn't Gervaise seen this about her sooner?

More flopping about ensued on Hazel's side of the bed. "Commonsense and kindness are the virtues of dowagers."

"They are the qualities of the best judges," Gervaise said. "Cuddle with me, Hazel."

"How does one—Gervaise!"

He tucked her close, so they were spooned together, lover-fashion. Hazel fit the curve of his body wonderfully, a tidy, warm, feminine bundle of wonders and shyness that bore a faint fragrance of cinnamon.

Gervaise kissed her shoulder. "You remind me of Christmas biscuits."

"That makes me shiver. Do it again."

Hazel giving orders was Hazel finding her confidence. "Like this?" Gervaise bit her gently, then soothed her with more kisses.

"Like... you bit me."

"You're welcome to bite me back, or kiss me, or explain to me exactly how you'd prefer to be pleasured."

The notion intrigued her, apparently, for Gervaise felt the change in her breathing, the shift in her focus.

"You're aroused," she said, wiggling against the proof of her conclusion. "Kissing me got you un-wilted."

Thinking about kissing her had done that. "Kissing you, nibbling on you, tasting you, *touching you.*" Gervaise ran his hand over the curve of her hip, around the contour of her derriere, up past the nip of her waist. She was all of a smooth, sweet, lusciousness, like fine brandy savored late on a cold, dark night.

A few more minutes of that and Hazel shifted to her back. "This is my night of passion. You don't get to do all the touching, or all the nibbling."

Gervaise certainly hoped not. "I will bear up manfully under any nibbling you care to bestow on me." Manfully, and unwilting-ly.

She cupped his cheek against her warm palm. "You can't disappoint me, you know. Your nimble wit and tender kisses might impress some women, but for me, just to be with you like this is a wish come true."

Nimble wit, tender kisses... the words rang some distant bell, but the phrases were commonplace, and Gervaise did not want to *discuss* tender kisses, he wanted to share them with Hazel. He brushed her hair back from her brow, and in the interests of preserving his sanity, assayed a chaste kiss to Hazel's lips.

She had other ideas, opening her mouth beneath his, and foraging with her tongue while she sank her fingers into Gervaise's hair and held him still for her explorations. His delicate overture turned into her plundering of his self-restraint, then she left off pulling his hair long enough to grab his hand and place it over her breast.

Hazel kept her hand over his, though Gervaise made no mistake about her demand. Through the soft cotton of her nightgown, he gently shaped her breast. She was nicely endowed, and if her reaction was any indication, exquisitely sensitive.

The kissing ceased as Gervaise explored all the pleasures a man's hands, mouth, and inventiveness could visit upon a woman's breasts. Hazel wiggled, she squirmed, she arched her back.

She gave him another order. "Get this dratted nightgown off me, Gervaise."

He complied, tossing the nightgown to the foot of the bed, and then Hazel was twined against him, naked, warm, delectable and... busy.

She traced the length of his shaft in a loose grip, up and down, up and down. "You're hot, and... quite blooming."

Gervaise endured several more moments of bliss wrapped in torment. "If you keep that up, I will blossom entirely, and that isn't what I had planned."

She stopped, but didn't turn loose of him. "You said we weren't to bother with schedules and agendas."

"I say a lot of things, most of it ridiculous. On your back, Hazel, please. I'd like to take up where we left off."

Minus the nightgown, that was a fraught undertaking, for Hazel without clothing was a compelling argument against pleasure delayed. Gervaise managed to distract her with kisses and caresses while petting his way south past curves and hollows and smooth, warm flesh to...

"What are you doing?" Hazel said.

"I'm pleasuring you. This is the part where you trust me, Hazel."

Her expression in the dim firelight was disgruntled. Her braid was the worse for their exertions, and her mouth managed to look both well-kissed and displeased.

Gervaise closed his eyes and willed his hand to remain still.

"I have trusted you since the day I met you," Hazel said, brushing his hair back from his brow. "I will trust you until the day I die."

That single touch, so familiar, and in such an unforeseen context, reminded Gervaise that this was not an hour of pleasure substituted for the last act of some Drury Lane production, nor was Hazel a bored baroness who'd singled him out as her passing entertainment.

Everything he'd known about Hazel had been both stood on its head and confirmed since they'd climbed under the covers. Everything he'd felt for her, too.

He had taken her for granted, and she deserved better.

Gervaise kissed her, gently, fleetingly. "Now comes the passionate part, Hazel. The part with the screaming and moaning. I'll make you like it, or expire trying."

Hazel, however, was not a moaner. As Gervaise teased and petted and mapped Hazel's intimate treasures, she sighed, she rocked into his touch, she kissed his shoulder.

"This is most… most odd," she muttered.

Odd was not a harbinger of success. Gervaise slowed his caresses. "You don't like it?"

"How could one possibly like…? If you stop I shall kill you."

Ah, well, then. Gervaise nudged Hazel's knees apart, so she was open to him, and to the pleasure he'd bring her. Pride required a man to satisfy his partner before seeing to his own gratification. With Hazel, pride had no place in Gervaise's heart.

The impulse to give to her, to take nothing for himself, to enjoy *her* pleasure and wonder, made him diabolically patient. Hazel's feet moved restlessly, she twisted Gervaise's hair in her grip, then wrapped her fingers around his wrist.

"Gervaise, what is all this in aid—?"

She was struggling to think, while he was struggling to purely and completely give her what she wanted. Gervaise took one rosy nipple in his mouth, and slowed his hand, firming the pressure of his fingers.

Based on the quality of her sighs, Hazel's Christmas dream came true, for long, lovely moments. By the time pleasure eased its grip on her, she was riding Gervaise's thigh, her tongue was in his mouth, and her naked heat was plastered along every inch of him.

Gervaise held her, tightly enough to feel her heart beating against his chest, then more loosely, to allow the lady a chance to catch her wind. Her breathing became even, while Gervaise mentally listed exceptions to the rule against admitting hearsay into evidence.

"I am undone," Hazel whispered. "I am so utterly, entirely, completely… I'll not ridicule your dear Rochester ever again, Gervaise. This was why you mentioned napping for half the night, isn't it? One can't think, one can only float. I can't imagine what must come next."

Part of Gervaise was floating quite buoyantly, which was just too bad.

"You will have to imagine it," Gervaise said, kissing her nose. "Friends don't ruin friends, Hazel, especially not dear friends. Under oath, you could still call yourself chaste."

She rubbed her cheek against his chest. "I'm not under oath, I'm under the covers, you daft man. I know the biology, and I know what we did cannot result in conception. I've also made a study of the midwife's—"

The Almighty had dealt the male gender a severe blow by endowing women with intimate resilience. Hazel would be a fiend once she hit her stride in bed.

"Hazel, hush. I've granted you the boon you sought, given you pleasure. I'll give you as much pleasure as you like, and share with you any intimacy short of ruining you. Honor forbids me to cross that line, much as I might long to."

Hazel patted his cheek. "You're making this up. No judge ever pronounced that the law of the land forbids friends from becoming lovers in the truest sense. In the morning, I will be wroth with you, but now… now I cannot be angry. I can barely be coherent, in fact. Do you truly long to become my lover?"

"Passionately." At the start of the day, Gervaise would have said the law was his sole passion.

At the start of the day, he'd been an ass.

"I'll have a short nap, now," Hazel said, turning to her side, and nestling her derriere against Gervaise's honorable intentions. "You should rest as well. If you can."

Of course, he could not. Between rioting emotions, Hazel putting him through his paces again, and a hopeless tendency to speculate on hypotheticals and evidence, Gervaise slept not at all. An hour before dawn, while Hazel dreamed on, he rose, dressed, and took himself home through the cold, snowy darkness.

She'd said she'd be wroth with him in the morning, but at least she would not be ruined.

Chapter Five

~⟐~

"HE COULDN'T EVEN bother to stay for a cup of tea!" Hazel fumed, belting her dressing gown snugly. "Couldn't kiss me good-bye, couldn't let me tie his cravat."

Hazel's cat, a fat, long-haired gray hearth fixture named Caspar, squinted at her from the chair before the fire.

"The tea tray won't be up for an hour," Hazel informed the beast. "By which time, I will be in the first genuine taking of my life, or I will have expired from frustration."

The previous night, she'd expired from pleasure. Gervaise had hinted that a lady could be kissed in places too intimate to contemplate, and Hazel had dreamed of such goings on... She'd started a new list of dreams, in fact, one that included becoming thoroughly ruined, courtesy of her favorite barrister.

Except, said barrister had fled the scene.

"The staff would never breathe a word," she muttered, picking up the cat and occupying the warm spot he'd created in the chair. Caspar was a substantial soul, and an indiscriminate purr-er.

Hazel hugged him, though he was a poor substitute for Gervaise. "I'm angry, but part of me is also purring, you know. I had no, idea, Caspar. Not the first inkling. If I ever do find Gervaise a copy of Blackstone, I will wallop him with it."

Caspar kneaded Hazel's thigh through her robe and nightgown, surely a sign that his opinion concurred with hers.

Outside, feeble winter light filled a cloudy sky, a few hardy souls cut paths through new snow, and winter went on as planned. Inside Hazel's heart, nothing was the same.

"Everything is different," she said, petting the cat. "My body is new to me, my emotions... I'm smug, and worried... and why did Gervaise leave, Cat? No note, no farewell embrace, no parting kiss."

Hazel's spirits sank, for Gervaise had also assured her nothing about their situation would change as a result of last night's intimacy.

Nothing would change? *Nothing?*

"I lack the requisite *savoir faire* to pretend all is unchanged." While Gervaise could apparently get up, dress, and take himself across the alley without a backward glance. Hazel was halfway through a note to Annabelle offering to come to the shop and look for the missing letter when Caspar hopped onto the desk and sat, his tail wrapped around his paws.

"What? When the tea tray comes, you'll have your dish of—"

Something about the cat's expression admonished Hazel to be quiet, to think.

"I assume Gervaise let you in here," she said, petting the cat. "Something is different, though. You're right."

Hazel inventoried her room. Bed tidily made to save Millie the bother. Everything in its place, every single—

"My room is *warm*," Hazel said. "For the first time in ages, I woke on a winter morning to a warm room, and Gervaise managed to build up the fire without making a sound."

Caspar licked at a paw and began his ablutions. A warm bedroom in the morning was such a luxury, such a comfort. So thoughtful, when Gervaise might have slipped away and saved himself the bother.

"Perhaps I won't wallop my friend after all. But I will miss him until next we meet. I'll miss him a very great deal."

"I MISS HER," Gervaise informed Mallachan. The damned cat sat smug and cozy on the half of the newspaper Gervaise hadn't yet read. "Not two hours apart, and I miss her. I want to pen her a sentimental note, but that folly is doomed. Try as I might, the lady would receive a Motion to Join Parties Beneath Blankets."

Gervaise occasionally missed a night of sleep when preparing for a major case. Fatigue had never made him daft before.

"I'll find my lady a present, a real Christmas token, or perhaps—" By the time Gervaise could walk the distance to the jeweler's shops on Ludgate Hill, those shops ought to be open. Best friends might not ruin each other, but no law on earth prevented those friends from marrying each other.

Gervaise set out, intent on procuring a ring, but detoured into this shop and that, for a ring was not special. A ring was... expected, unimaginative, the done thing. He wasted so much time dithering over teapots and standishes that his errand among the jewelers consumed all of his remaining free time, and he was nearly late to his chambers.

"Good morning, Snee," Gervaise said, stomping snow from his boots. "You're here early."

"I'm always here early, and you're often here earlier, sir," Snee said, putting a kettle on the parlor stove in the clerk's chambers. "The Yule season sees many a crime committed. I know we're busy."

Gervaise consulted his watch. Was Hazel awake yet? He should have left her a note. Nothing so ambitious as a love letter, but *something*.

"I'm not to be disturbed," Gervaise said, shrugging out of his coat. "This is for you." He shoved a parcel at Snee, who looked as if the Virgin Mary's donkey had wandered into the law offices. "This is for Mrs. Snee," Gervaise said, withdrawing another package from his coat pocket. "Small tokens of my regard for hard work, et cetera."

"Thank you, Mr. Stoneleigh, and dare I wish you a Happy Christmas?"

"You may so dare. Is there enough water in that pot to spare me a cup?"

Snee was a placid soul, sharper by far than his bushy white brows and genial blue eyes might suggest. He kept the junior clerks sorted out, was on good terms with the other head clerks in the various law offices, and had been with Gervaise since his first case.

"As many cups of tea as you like, sir. Perhaps you'd care for a biscuit or two? Mrs. Snee made them just yesterday."

Gervaise never ate at his desk. Crumbs on the pleadings or a smear of butter or jam on correspondence was inexcusably unprofessional.

"Perhaps just one. I seem to have neglected to break my fast."

Snee smiled, looking vaguely like Mallachan. "Just one or two, then. I'll bring your tea directly, sir."

Gervaise spent most of the morning munching biscuits and swilling tea, all to no avail. He hadn't found Hazel a ring, he hadn't kissed her good-bye, and when it came to writing a love letter, he was utterly worthless.

He gave up at midday, and recommenced patrolling the shops, determined to find Hazel a Christmas token that would reflect all the tenderness, respect, liking, and affection Gervaise had for her.

And the desire, too.

"I'VE LOOKED EVERYWHERE," Annabelle said. "Your letter simply isn't here. Where does Catullus go, philosophers or poetry?"

"Antiquities," Hazel said, using the bookshelves to pull the shop's wheeled ladder two feet to the left. "The letter has to be somewhere, Annabelle. Are you sure Charlie doesn't have it?"

Annabelle's expression went from thoughtful to hopeful. "He might after all, and he's too much of a gentleman to ask me if I wrote it. He might have it tucked into his breast pocket at this very moment."

Hazel said nothing, to that bouncer. Charlie was a gentleman to his tall, handsome bones, but he'd seen enough of Annabelle's execrable penmanship to know the letter could not be hers.

"Where does a pamphlet on how to tie various knots in gentleman's neck cloth go?" Annabelle asked.

"Domestic arts."

They'd been at this for most of the day, while Mrs. Merriweather took care of customers. Searching the premises for Hazel's letter had proceeded under the guise of re-shelving mis-placed inventory. One by one, Hazel and Annabelle had taken out each volume and leafed through the pages. After hours of searching, they'd come across a number of books in the wrong places, but their efforts had revealed only three bookmarks lurking between a shopful of bound pages.

"Mr. Glen might have found it," Hazel said, for he was in the habit of leafing through books, page by page, as if the grip of an odd compulsion.

"If he finds something, he always tells Mama or me," Annabelle said. "We've instructed him to simply ignore any bookmarks he comes across."

So Mr. Glen hadn't found the words Hazel had poured onto the paper in an attempt to describe her feelings for Gervaise.

Where on earth could that letter have got off to?

"Are you two looking for something?" Mrs. Merriweather asked as the afternoon nudged up against the evening.

"We're bringing order to chaos," Annabelle replied. "I'm always surprised at how many books migrate on their own to the most unlikely locations. Somebody should waken Mrs. Huntsberry."

"Where has this day gone?" Mrs. Merriweather said. "One doesn't like to wake her too soon. The poor dear doubtless goes home to a cold hearth."

Hazel put a final volume of poetry back on the fifth shelf, and perched on the top step of the ladder. The day had left her with a gratifying sense of having helped put the shop to rights, but also frustrated with… Gervaise.

"Mrs. Huntsberry won't go home to a cold hearth tonight," Hazel said. "I had my coal man bring her a load this afternoon. I've wondered if she ought not to move in with me."

Mrs. Merriweather left off tidying a stack of receipts. "You'd hire a companion now? A bit late for that, unless you're feeling lonely. Of course, a young lady has other means to combat loneliness, though."

Hazel *was* lonely, also anxious to see Gervaise again, and dreading the sight of him at the same time. She could never be ashamed of the intimacies they'd shared, but he'd left without a word, and now…

"Our Hazel likes her independence," Mr. Merriweather said, emerging from the back parlor. "I've never seen such a lot of females for treasuring their independence."

He gave Annabelle a particular look, then snatched up the largest of the delivery packages sitting on the counter and headed out the door.

"What was that about?" Hazel asked.

"Never mind him," Mrs. Merriweather said, putting her receipts on a shelf behind the counter. "Annabelle, somebody has eaten the last of the biscuits. If you could fetch more from upstairs, you'd save me a trip. Hazel, would you be good enough to walk Mrs. Huntsberry home?"

"Of course." Mrs. Huntsberry lived two streets over from Hazel, but seeing the old woman to her door would provide an excuse to walk past Gervaise's house.

Mrs. Merriweather disappeared into the reading room, just as the doorbell tinkled yet again.

Hazel's heart sped up, and a gust of cold air hit her in the face. "Gervaise, welcome."

"Hello, Hazel." His expression—surprised and wary—confirmed that he was not pleased to see her.

Awkwardness, chilly and damp, wrapped around Hazel's heart. No smile, no kiss of welcome, not even a—

Gervaise came marching toward the ladder. "Madam, this contraption is not safe. Merriweather must have been in his cups when he built it. The last thing you need when you're intent on your Boxing Day rounds is a turned ankle, though it would serve you right."

He scooped her off the ladder, took one look around the shop, pressed a kiss to her mouth, and set her on her feet.

GERVAISE CONCLUDED THAT Hazel hadn't been exactly glad to see him, but neither had she recoiled from his kiss. She had thoroughly ruined his last, desperate attempt to find her a worthy Christmas token, however.

"Will you walk Mrs. Huntsberry home with me?" Hazel asked.

Gervaise had walked Wilma Huntsberry home on any number of occasions. Walking her to her doorstep in the snow would take until Twelfth Night, though at least Hazel would be with them.

"I'll gladly accompany you," Gervaise said. "I do hope you remembered to wear your gloves, Hazel Hooper. The weather is dreadful, and—"

She kissed him, and he could feel her smile against his lips. Charlie, a canny fellow with a fondness for poetry, was busily pretending to read the last copy of the *Adventures of a Lady*. Boxing Day would include a substantial basket for Charlie, if Gervaise had to bake the biscuits himself.

"You needn't scold me," Hazel whispered. "I've missed you too."

Well. The day's frustrations receded, as Gervaise leaned nearer to the woman who'd haunted his every moment, waking and dreaming.

"You looked so delectable snuggled beneath your blankets, I didn't want to wake you. I hope Caspar's company was welcome?"

Now Charlie was dusting the shelves, though Gervaise knew Mrs. Merriweather tended to that chore first thing every morning.

"Caspar's company was a consolation."

This exchange took place beneath the mistletoe, and for a mad moment, Gervaise was tempted to propose right then and there. On the Shelf was the stronghold of spinsters and bluestockings from all walks of life, though, and a litigator learned not to ask of a witness in open court any question counsel did not already know the answer to.

"Come along, Miss Hooper," Mrs. Huntsberry said, emerging from the reading room. "The mess in the streets grows treacherous when the temperatures drop. Mr. Stoneleigh, you'll escort us."

"But of course."

They toddled along, with Mrs. Huntsberry prattling all the while about her sister's gooseberry tart recipe, and Hazel making the appropriate exclamations and encouragements, as Gervaise's toes turned to ice. He'd left his law office early, and tramped the length and breadth of London looking for a proper Christmas gift for Hazel.

And he'd failed to find anything worthy of his sentiments, or of her.

"Thank you very kindly," Mrs. Huntsberry said as they reached her doorstep. "Happy Christmas to you both. If you'll take the advice of an old woman, find some mistletoe and keep each other warm. In my day, we didn't dither about for years, being coy and stupid."

She bustled off, leaving Gervaise feeling equally blessed and chastised. "Her advice strikes me as sound, but I haven't any mistletoe at my house."

Hazel took him by the arm and started off in the direction of her abode. "I have plenty, Gervaise, and I intend to stand beneath every bit of it, without my clothes if needs must."

SOMETHING ABOUT GERVAISE had changed in the past few days. His hair was less than perfectly tidy. His scarf was tied at an odd angle. He looked... delectably disheveled. His smile was different too, not the slightly bored, amused expression of affection, but something warmer and more personal.

"Haring about unclad this time of year could result in an ague, my dear," he said, matching his steps to Hazel's.

The lamplighter tipped his hat, Gervaise tossed him a coin, and—if Hazel's ears did not deceive her—a muttered, "Happy Christmas to you, too."

"I don't intend to hare about," Hazel said. "I intend to plaster myself to you, whom I know to be a reliable source of heat when unclothed. I have questions for you, Gervaise."

Do you love me? She couldn't bear to hear him stumble through some polite equivocation. Men and women were different, according to every female member of Hazel's staff. Men could be physically intimate without engaging their finer feelings, though would friends—?

Gervaise tugged Hazel into the door of a shop shut up for the night and kissed her.

"What was that for?"

He pointed upward, to a small sheaf of mistletoe, not a berry left, twisting in a cold breeze. "I'm getting warm, Hazel. I'll have you know I combed all of London in search of a token for you."

That confession warmed Hazel more than a fleeting kiss could. "You don't believe in Christmas tokens, and you'd best kiss me some more. I'm taking a chill."

"I'd best get you home," Gervaise said, resuming their progress. "I can't feel my toes, and I don't want to be within sight of Mrs. Huntsberry's door when she realizes I had a load of coal delivered to her cellar earlier today."

"That was very sweet of you, Gervaise."

"So sweet, I will expect you and your army of geriatric retainers to dispose of the resulting basket of gooseberry tarts I'm sure to receive. I don't care for gooseberries."

"I know."

"I care for you."

"You don't sound very happy about that."

"What I am, is very cold, and I suspect I've ruined my boots, too. Take me inside Hazel, and tell me some more about this foolish penchant you've developed for disrobing. I fear the ailment is contagious, for I'm suffering the same symptoms."

HOPE GLOWED IN Gervaise's heart, an emotion well suited to the Yuletide season.

"You want to dash about naked?" Hazel asked, as they climbed the steps to her front porch. "I'm trying to picture that."

Gervaise opened the door. "Who said anything about dashing? I'm more inclined to cuddle under nice warm blankets, my arms about my dearest Hazel. If you offer me a game of chess, Hazel, I will be crushed."

Hazel must have perceived that he was in earnest, for she drew him inside and unwrapped his scarf from his neck.

"No chess, but Gervaise, we must talk."

"A fine notion, for I have a few sentiments I'd like to impart to you, and—"

"Good evening, madam, Mr. Stoneleigh," Driech said. "Shall I tell Cook to prepare two trays?"

"Yes," Hazel said, at the same time Gervaise barked, "No."

"You're not staying?" Hazel asked.

"I'm not... I'm not hungry." Except he was famished from tromping all over Town. He was equally famished for Hazel's company. "A tea tray will do."

"Tea with all the trimmings, Driech. We'll be in my sitting room."

Driech tottered away, and Gervaise undid the frogs of Hazel's cloak and took it from her shoulders. She removed his coat, the ritual familiar but this time also fraught. Gervaise had nuzzled his way across those shoulders, beheld the pale hue of Hazel's nape, and kissed curve of her neck.

He knew the feel of her fingers fisted in his hair, the taste of her sighs, the music of her pleasure.

"Let's go upstairs," Hazel said, leading the way. She spared the mistletoe not so much as a glance.

Gervaise plucked down the entire bunch, tucked it in his pocket, and followed the lady to her chambers.

HAZEL WAS DETERMINED to say her piece to Gervaise before the tea tray arrived. He was not himself, though he wasn't acting as if he regretted the previous night's intimacies. He closed the door, and for once, the fire was roaring merrily in Hazel's sitting room. She kissed him, not for courage, but for... sustenance.

"I regret what happened last night," she said, stepping back.

He withdrew something from his coat pocket. "You do? Am I to throw this into the fire?"

Mistletoe dangled from his hand, the greenery the worse for having hung in the chilly foyer for several days.

"I love you, Gervaise Stoneleigh. I had hoped not to make a fool of myself, but then there was last night, and all day, I've been thinking."

He put a cool finger to his lips. "Hazel, stop."

"No," she said, pushing his finger aside. "I asked you for a night of passion, and you only half-obliged. I regret that. The pleasure was wonderful, but that you'd withhold from me what I truly asked for, that was... not wonderful."

Hazel braced herself for a lecture on gentlemanly honor, ruination, dear friends, and excessive sentiments. Being Gervaise, he might add a codicil on gooseberry tarts when all she wanted was to relieve him of his clothes and finish what they'd started the previous night.

Gervaise set the mistletoe on the mantel, where it looked forlorn and fragile. "I agree, Hazel. The pleasure was wonderful, and yet, we denied ourselves—I denied us—the ultimate joy. If you offer such intimacies to me again, and I hope you do, then you should at least have my proposal of marriage to consider first."

Hazel sank onto the sofa. "If you're feeling guilty, Gervaise, then—"

"I am feeling frustrated, Hazel Hooper, and tongue-tied, and very, very much in love."

He stood close enough to where Hazel sat that she could lean her cheek against his thigh. The wool of his trousers was expensively soft, but bore a hint of coal-smoke, as if he'd spent considerable time out of doors. He was solid muscle, and simply touching him was reassuring.

"Hazel, say something."

"You are never tongue-tied, Gervaise. I don't want false declarations brought on by remorse. Last night was wonderful, but it wasn't enough. I want—"

He came down on his knees beside her and wrapped his arms around her. "I hope you want passion and friendship, rousing arguments and quiet games of chess. I hope you want children, and I hope, I very sincerely hope, you want me."

Hazel drew back to study him. "Get up. You can't possibly be comfortable kneeling like that."

He remained right where he was. "I'm uncomfortable, you're right. I know the law, I know the motions to file, the objections to raise. I know how to argue before a jury or interrogate a witness. That's not enough, Hazel, and I want to be enough for you."

"You were impressive last night, Gervaise."

"I was caught unprepared, Hazel, and rather than give you what you asked for, I fussed about as if the rules of evidence can affect what's in a woman's heart. I love you. I have loved you forever, but the words to name my sentiments have eluded me. Hazel Hooper, I searched all day for a proper Christmas token to give you. The only item I found that seemed remotely appropriate for a woman I hold so dear is my own heart, but you stole it ages ago. Will you marry me?"

Hazel's throat developed an ache, but Gervaise's arms were around her, secure and real. "You hate to shop, Gervaise. You dislike Christmas."

"I dislike not knowing what to purchase for those I care about. I dislike enduring Christmas alone. I dislike how the cold makes those already wretched so much more miserable. I see that now. I love you."

Tears threatened, also laughter, because Gervaise did not know how to dissemble, and in his eyes were promises of all the holiday treats Hazel could imagine. Shelves and shelves of happily ever afters, bales and bundles of mistletoe, warm winter mornings and spring, summer, and autumn mornings too.

"You will make me cry, you beast. Of course, I'll marry you."

Oh, his kiss was everything. Sweet, naughty, tender, wild, comforting... Hazel didn't even stop kissing him when he scooped her into his arms and carried her into the bedroom.

Gervaise's lovemaking had the same passion as his courtroom advocacy. His opening argument was to undress Hazel, slowly, methodically, and every time she admonished him to greater haste, he silenced her objections with kisses both lazy and ravenous.

Hazel had her turn, undressing him as if he were her most anticipated Christmas gift—which he most assuredly was and always would be. He was to be her husband, hers to love, scold, tease, and love some more for all the rest of their days.

When they were naked in each other's arms, Hazel gloried in the moment, in the scent and texture of her lover's skin, in the rhythm of his breathing. Gervaise's fingers were busy with her hair, scattering pins on the floor, unraveling her braid.

"You will leave me a fright," she muttered against his throat.

"I'll leave you well loved, when I must leave you at all. We've years of catching up to do, Hazel."

She led him to the bed, lest he get to regretting and philosophizing and *wilting*.

"Not catching up," she said, flipping the covers back. "Years of... being us, Gervaise. We are not rash people, though we are passionate. I have loved you since the day you argued Papa into submission over the Irish question, and I still believe your views will eventually prevail. Had we leapt at one another then, we might have....'"

"Missed?" he suggested, climbing onto the bed and holding out his arms. "Failed to appreciate one another's many fine qualities? I suppose you're right—you often are. Also delectable."

Hazel learned just how relentless Gervaise could be as he explored with hands and lips the touches she liked best—on her breasts, especially, but he did not neglect the subtler pleasures of nape, back, fingers, knees, toes and everywhere in between. His lovemaking, like his courtroom endeavors, was thorough and well organized.

Until Hazel posed a few questions of her own: Would he enjoy being kissed *there*? Kissed and stroked at the same time? Was that a groan of pleasure or longing or both? Had he always been ticklish about the elbows?

By the time Hazel was on her back beneath Gervaise, the covers had been thrown back, the fire had died down, and two of the candles had guttered.

"If you do not oblige me now, Mr. Stoneleigh, I will—oh, that is *lovely*." A sense of completion and wishes coming true filled her as Gervaise joined them. A sense of wonder, too, and overwhelming tenderness for the man in her arms.

This was Christmas, this was joy abounding, love and hope, all the good things for which no words would suffice.

Gervaise apparently savored the moment too, and every argument, question, and objection Hazel might have lodged became one sighing appeal.

"Don't you ever stop, Gervaise. Not *ever*."

"I'm not too—?" His voice had acquired an odd rasp.

"I hear the angels sing in every particle of my soul," Hazel said, catching his rhythm. "Am I allowed to move like this?"

"If I asked you to hold still, would you be able to?"

"Not for an instant."

"A happy Christmas to all, then," Gervaise said, shifting up, and turning lovely to sublime. He was a fiend, teasing Hazel past reason, then showering pleasure upon her until she was limp and panting in his arms.

"You'll be sore in the morning," Gervaise said, kissing her brow. "I ought to be more of a gentleman."

"You ought to be more of husband. When can we be married, Gervaise? I know you have cases, and there's really no rush, but—"

"Cease fretting. We'll give each other vows for Christmas. A special license—"

Hazel sank her hands into his hair and kissed him to silence. "How I do love you, Mr. Stoneleigh. Vows for Christmas, the best possible gift."

She didn't let him hold forth about his own sentiments, because Gervaise would need his rest if he was to bear up under all the holiday expectations Hazel had of him.

Yuletide expectations. Marital expectations. Honeymoon expectations.

His satisfaction on this first occasion of marital intimacies was tender and easy, and Hazel let him get away with that. They would both be sore tomorrow, but they would also be happy.

And—happy, happy Christmas!—they would be married.

GERVAISE HELD HIS prospective wife as her breathing gradually slowed, then slowed further.

"Are you falling asleep on me, Miss Hooper?" She wouldn't be Miss Hooper much longer—delightful thought.

"Napping. I'm told it's required, like repairing to neutral corners between rounds of erotic debate. I love you, Gervaise, though I warn you, I intend to be a very demanding wife."

"You are so forthright, so bold and articulate." Gervaise's letter writer came to mind, the lady he'd never meet, though he suspected she and Hazel would get along famously. "I envy you the ferocity with which you express your sentiments."

She raised up enough to peer at him by the last of the firelight. "How can you say that? Your advocacy saves innocent lives. Your closing arguments are the envy of the bar."

They were to be married, and more significantly, Gervaise trusted Hazel as he'd never trusted another.

"I tried to write you a love letter, my dear. I could not put together two sentences without sounding lawyerly."

Hazel nuzzled his chest, which tickled his heart—and other places. "I would have treasured one sentence."

"I love you."

"A fine choice of sentence."

He loved her, and he wanted to share everything in his heart with her. This generosity of spirit was new, and Gervaise was plagued by the notion that if he did not act on it at that very moment, when his courage was newfound and at full tide, the habit might not put down roots and flourish.

"I saw a letter recently," he said, gathering Hazel close, "or part of a letter, written by a woman to the man she clearly loved. At first I wanted to know the woman who would put those sentiments on paper, bold, passionate, and so very smitten. Then I realized that I wanted to *be* the sort of man who deserved to receive such a letter. He's very fortunate, whoever he is."

"I'm very fortunate," Hazel said, kissing Gervaise's nose. "For Christmas, I've been given the hand in marriage of a man whom my heart will recognize when I'm old, blind, and deaf. I'll always know you, Gervaise, not by your handsome good looks. To other's eyes, your appearance will mature from dashing to distinguished, though to me, you are already distinguished, and you will always be dashing."

A curious sensation danced along Gervaise's spine. "Hazel?"

"Hush. I've wanted to convey these sentiments to you forever. I've rehearsed them, in fact, and edited them and refined them. When I'm stooped and gray, I'll know you not by your nimble wit, or even by your tender kisses,"—she kissed his brow—"though your wit saves lives, and your kisses will ever bring me joy."

Hazel had given Gervaise a new future for his Christmas token, also a new word: *Joy*. The curious sensation illuminating Gervaise from within was joy, so profound that even that lovely, ebullient word did not accurately describe his sentiments.

"Everything about you brings delights me, Hazel, and I'll know you too, by your heart, by the passion and honor with which you love, by the honesty and kindness with which you greet all in your ambit, regardless of station, regardless of how—"

"That's my letter," Hazel said, sitting up. "You found my letter. I wrote it to you, but hadn't the nerve to deliver it, and somehow—oh, Gervaise. We've had our own Christmas miracle."

"Rochester had your letter, though how he got his naughty hands on it, I suppose we'll never know. It's a beautiful letter, Hazel."

She snuggled back down against him. "You inspire me, Gervaise. Every word of that letter is true, and inspired by your example."

How he loved her. "The letter inspired me."

"Then I will write you many such letters, but for now, do you suppose you could muster a different sort of inspiration, just once more?"

"With some cooperation from my beloved, of course."

Hazel was feeling very cooperative, and though a deal of napping was required— and the special license—Mr. and Mrs. Stoneleigh did, in fact have a very, very, *very* fine Christmas.

All year long, every year.

From the Authors

You may enjoy our last year's Christmas anthology **Christmas in the Duke's Arms** (where you will meet Gervaise Stoneleigh from Grace's The Appeal of Christmas) and—if you wish it were summer—**Dancing in the Duke's Arms**, which includes the story of Princess Vivienne, sister of Shana's Prince Lucien from A Prince in Her Stocking.

There's nothing like an anthology at Christmas: shorter stories filled with love and holiday joy to keep you sane when you're too busy for much reading. We are happy to recommend books from these wonderful historical authors.

All I Want for Christmas is a Duke by Vivienne Lorret, Valerie Bowman, Tiffany Clare, and Ashlyn Macnamara.

What Happens Under the Mistletoe by Sabrina Jeffries, Karen Hawkins, Candace Camp, and Meredith Duran.

A Gentleman for All Seasons by Shana Galen, Vanessa Kelly, Kate Noble, and Theresa Romain.

Wishing all of you a wonderful holiday and happiness all year round.
Grace, Shana, Carolyn, and Miranda

About the Authors

ABOUT MIRANDA NEVILLE

Miranda Neville grew up in England, loving the books of Georgette Heyer and other Regency romances. Her historical romances include the Burgundy Club series, about Regency book collectors, and The Wild Quartet. She lives in Vermont with her daughter, her cat, and a ridiculously large collection of Christmas tree ornaments. Miranda loves to hear from readers and can be reached through her website, Facebook, or Twitter. To hear about future releases, sign up for her newsletter.

Eagle-eyed readers of The Rake Who Loved Christmas may have noticed the brief appearance of Tarquin Compton. The bibliophile dandy and his friend Sebastian Iverley appear in the Burgundy Club series and are the heroes of, respectively, *The Amorous Education of Celia Seaton* and *The Dangerous Viscount*.

ABOUT CAROLYN JEWEL

Carolyn Jewel was born on a moonless night. That darkness was seared into her soul and she became an award-winning and USA Today bestselling author of historical and paranormal romance. She has a very dusty car and a Master's degree in English that proves useful at the oddest times. An avid fan of fine chocolate, finer heroines, Bollywood films, and heroism in all forms, she has two cats and two dogs. Also a son. One of the cats is his.

Newsletter
Sign up for Carolyn's **newsletter** (http://cjewel.me/nl34WS) so you never miss a new book and get exclusive, subscriber-only content.

Visit Carolyn on the web at:
carolynjewel.com | **twitter.com/cjewel** |
facebook.com/carolynjewelauthor | **goodreads.com/cjewel**

ABOUT SHANA GALEN

Shana Galen is the bestselling author of passionate Regency romps, including the RT Reviewers' Choice The Making of a Gentleman. Kirkus says of her books, "The road to happily-ever-after is intense, conflicted, suspenseful and fun," and RT Bookreviews calls her books "lighthearted yet poignant, humorous yet touching." She taught English at the middle and high school level off and on for eleven years. Most of those years were spent working in Houston's inner city. Now she writes full time. She's happily married and has a daughter who is most definitely a romance heroine in the making.

ABOUT GRACE BURROWES

To the loveliest readers in the world (MINE),

I hope you enjoyed Gervaise and Hazel's holiday tale, for I certainly had great fun writing it!

You'll spot a slightly younger version of Gervaise in December's release, **Axel— The Jaded Gentlemen, Book III**, which finishes up my Jaded Gentlemen trilogy. This season also sees the release of another story very near to my heart, **Daniel's True Desire** (November 4, 2015), the middle book in my True Gentlemen series. Daniel Banks has to be one of the most deserving, dear, *stubborn*, heroes I've written, also the very best toad catcher. (Fortunately, Lady Kirsten Haddonfield has a soft spot for brave catchers of the ever-elusive schoolroom toad.)

If you'd like to keep up with all of my releases, you can **sign up for my newsletter** (graceburrowes.com/contact.php). I only publish when I have news, and I will never sell my mailing list, ever.

If you're interested in joining me and a small group of readers and writers on a tour in Scotland (September 2016), there's more information about **Scotland with Grace** on the **graceburrowes.com** website.

Happy reading!
Grace Burrowes

Made in the USA
Lexington, KY
14 July 2016